THE 24TH LETTER

Monica R. Sholar

Published by Eden Life Publishing, Canton, MI 48187
Copyright © Monica R. Sholar, 2014

ISBN 978-0-9842913-2-8

www.monicasholar.com

PUBLISHER'S NOTE

To my family, I love you. I hope to make you proud.

Acknowledgments

JD, thank you for listening to God when He told you to encourage me as a writer. I can't thank you enough for pushing me. To my literary glam squad, Sharon Greenblatt, Lauren Avetta, Sandi Franka, SuVon Treece, Andrea Gelmini and Tereasa Shepherd, thank you for helping me to be better at my craft. To my love, Steven Anderson, thank you for listening to my ramblings when no one else would. Most of all, thank you to my Lord God.

Table of Contents

Prologue

It was Walker Thompson's first day as a paramedic; the scene in front of him confirmed he was in over his head. The rookie EMT ran nervously alongside a gurney down the hallway of Beaumante Hospital. With him, several nurses and another EMT worked to keep the gunshot victim alive. Walker figured the woman was a bigwig in town, because the police secured the trauma ward around her.

An older woman garbed in a black robe had been brought in just minutes before her. Walker overheard someone say that she was a judge and had been pronounced dead on arrival. Nurses fought to pull away a man who sobbed as he draped himself across the judge's chest. Her soulless body rocked back and forth in the tussle.

Walker tried not to be distracted by his surroundings, forcing himself to focus straight ahead. His main task was to keep his hand pressed to his victim's head to slow her bleeding. The white towel he used was now stained crimson, absorbing the woman's life as it drained from her body. Not wanting to admit it, he didn't see any way possible that she would survive.

Just as the gurney reached a set of doors, a surgeon appeared and jogged next to one of the nurses. She updated him on the victim's condition. "Patient is a 33-year-old female. There's trauma to the left occipital region and massive blood loss."

The doctor lifted the patient's eyelids and shined a

small light into her pupils. "She's concussed and showing signs of shock. Get her pumped with Misoprostol and prep her for surgery." The doctor peeled away from the fleet and went to scrub in.

To Walker, it was like being in the front row watching a scene from a movie. But the warmth on his hands from the dying woman's blood was an uncomfortable reminder that this was, in fact, reality.

In the operating room, the head nurse announced, "We need to transfer her from the gurney to the table. Keep your hand in place while we sweep her body on my count. Got it?" She looked directly at Walker. Swallowing his nerves, the paramedic pressed his hand down firmly and prepared for her signal.

"On three. One. Two. Three!" The team heaved Robin Malone's body onto the operating table in one quick and seamless motion. A single tear of sweat trickled to the tip of Walker's nose. He waited for more orders.

"I'll take over from here," the nurse barked. Before anyone could make a move, the patient began screaming, her body wrestling against theirs.

"Kevin, don't!" she shouted, as the staff tried to contain her. The nurse yanked the towel from Walker's hands. He backed away. An anesthetist injected something into the woman's IV. Walker watched as the drug took over and Robin Malone's fearful eyes began to calm.

One Hour Before...

The *bang* of Judge Evelyn Childs' gavel affirmed Kevin Dennison's life sentence. The sound signified the end of the worst time in Robin Malone's life and the beginning of the best years to come. Every person in the room was elated with the judge's ruling. Accused of everything from abduction to forcefully administering a lethal substance, Kevin's guilty verdict was long overdue. Robin let out a howl of relief. Her husband, Austin picked her up and twirled her around. Flashes of light from the media cameras blinded her. She didn't care.

Aunt Joanne, who had raised Robin, was a ball of light as she watched her niece get the justice that she deserved. Joanne stood with the newly vindicated victor, gleefully posing for pictures.

Robin had just turned to Austin when she heard a commotion at the front of the room. Confused, she looked up and couldn't believe her eyes. Kevin had jumped onto the judge's bench and grabbed Her Honor by the collar. A loud *Snap!* sounded in the courtroom. Evelyn Childs' head lulled unnaturally to one side. The bailiff charged toward the dangerous criminal and came close to tackling him. Kevin spun quickly in the opposite direction, yanking the gun from the bailiff's holster.

"Gun!" she screamed. Everyone hit the deck.

Robin watched, in shock and couldn't turn away. Kevin's eyes connected with hers through the chaos and screaming people. His arm lifted, and Robin found herself staring into the hollow end of the government issued weapon. Her brain sent the signal for her body to move, but it was too late.

Pow!

The bullet sliced the air at lightning speed. In a split second, District Attorney Katherine Palmer dove in front of Robin, shielding her from the gunfire. The .40-caliber bullet tore through Katherine's shoulder and knocked both women to the ground. The room once again exploded, this time with panic, as people tried to make their way to safety. Dennison grabbed the bailiff from behind and forced his forearm into her throat. With her own gun pressed to her head, the bailiff was now a hostage, and there was nothing she could do about it.

Austin reached for his gun but realized it wasn't there. Although an agent with the CIA, he wasn't on duty, which meant that his weapon hadn't been allowed inside the courtroom. That fact didn't stop him from charging toward the gunman.

He'd gotten only a few feet away when he heard his wife call out to him. The agent stopped in his tracks, his eyes focused on Dennison, who was quickly making his way out of the room.

"Austin, don't leave me. Please," he heard his wife say.

"Listen to your wife, Agent Malone," Kevin cackled above the pandemonium. With his arm wrapped firmly around the bailiff's neck, the fugitive kept his right arm extended with the gun ready to fire at anyone who made a wrong move.

Austin realized he had a difficult decision to make:

go after the bastard who'd just tried to shoot his wife, or stay to comfort her until help arrived. As it would turn out, he'd not have to make a decision. When he turned to Robin, there was a pool of dark blood forming next to her head. In an instant, he was at her side where he dropped to his knees. Austin had been completely caught off guard — which, in his line of work, was a rarity. He knew the district attorney had been hit, but never realized that his wife had taken the bullet as well.

Robin groaned in pain and mumbled a sentence that he didn't understand. "I'm here, Baby," he whispered, as terror began to set in. Guttural sounds escaped from the worried courtroom spectators, all in fear for their lives. Austin could only hear the sound of his wife's breath grow fainter by the moment.

Her eyelids fluttered softly. She fought hard to remain conscious. "Stay with me, Honey, focus," Austin called to her when her eyes rolled back. "We're going to get you out of here; just hang in there." The agent looked around, searching for the best route of escape.

There was suddenly a hail of gunfire and another round of screams. Austin raised his head to see Kevin and his hostage make their way from the room. By the time he turned back, Robin was no longer moving.

Chapter One

Downtown parking was always terrible in the bustling town of Belle Isle Heights, Michigan. To avoid traffic, Joanne and Robin took the People Mover, which dropped them off in front of the courthouse on St. Antoine Street. After passing through a rigorous security checkpoint, the women were directed to courtroom A12. Trekking down the long, narrow hall, they passed several people having a bad day. Most noticeable was a young man of 16 or 17 with spiked blue hair sitting with a court appointed attorney. His head was buried in his hands, the attorney giving him information he didn't want to hear. Joanne and Robin continued down the hall, hoping that they, too, wouldn't be disappointed with the ruling on their case. Inside the courtroom, they took a seat on one of the very last benches, as far as possible from the train wreck about to go down.

A small man with wire rimmed glasses brushed past them and made his way to the defense table. His name was Rayko Blu, the lead defense attorney. He stood only five feet, five inches high, but his reputation as the city's most licentious attorney made him seem more like a big bad wolf than the leprechaun that his outer packaging suggested.

Feeling her niece's growing nerves, Joanne put her hand on Robin's bouncing knee. Robin was the very core of the case they were there to witness; it was expected that she'd be nervous.

The prosecuting attorney was last to arrive. Katherine Palmer dressed in a burgundy suit with sensible heels, not a single hair out of place. Rayko Blu extended his hand; she shook it on the move. There was no doubt that she was ready to get down to business.

The bailiff entered and commanded the attention of

the room.

"All rise."

Everyone stood and watched Judge Evelyn Childs stride gracefully to her seat. The lines on her elegant face spoke of her experience in the judicial system. Robin knew she had been a hotshot attorney in her heyday. Running for her judicial seat, Childs beat out a slew of salty faced men and had been re-elected each term since.

She organized some papers in front of her and looked up to acknowledge the room.

"Please be seated."

The crowd took their seats as instructed.

"Counselors, I expect a clean case. I don't want any trouble out of either of you. Mr. Blu, you have a reputation for your outlandish behavior, so I am warning you once, and only once: do *not* bring those games into my courtroom. Finding you in contempt is just a breath away."

Rayko Blu raised his hands as if to surrender and smirked.

Robin sat at the back of the room trying desperately to keep her composure. Just a few feet away were the two individuals responsible for her attempted murder. Sadly, one was her daughter's father, and the other was her best friend of over 20 years. Her bouncing knee started again, and Aunt Joanne patted her hand tenderly.

Judge Childs asked Katherine Palmer to proceed

with her opening statements.

Katherine stood up and held a photo in her hand. She didn't speak. She instead paced back and forth in front of the jury, showcasing the photo.

"Look carefully. What you are seeing is the picture of innocence. Two little girls joined at the hip. They grew up together in a small town just outside the city. Raised by loving and hard working parents. Practically raised as sisters. They have a close bond; camaraderie, if you will."

Katherine suddenly ripped the photo to shreds, tossing the tiny pieces in the air. Some members of the jury gasped, and a buzz of soft chatter filled the room.

"Please don't feel sorry for the photo. It is a mere object that has no emotions, no feelings or tears. If you must feel sorry, feel sorry for Robin Malone. She has shed many tears and has been hurt deeply by two individuals she thought she could trust. Her life was nearly snuffed out by the greed and malevolence of her life-long best friend, Melanie Mitchell, and the man who fathered her child, co-defendant, Kevin Dennison.

"Throughout this case, you'll hear details of how Ms. Mitchell and Mr. Dennison plotted out a plan to tear the victim's life apart, just as I've done to this photo.

"The defense will try to paint the picture of innocence for these two individuals who mercilessly toyed with the emotions - and very life's breath - of a truly innocent woman. I am certain you will not be fooled. Melanie Mitchell and Kevin Dennison are cold and calculating, and their selfishness caused a best friend to betray the person closest to her," Katherine pointed to Melanie, "and a lover to betray his confidant and mother of his child." She pointed to Kevin.

"Through the course of this trial, I suggest that you do this: take off your shoes. Go ahead, just kick them off."

Spectators exchanged puzzled looks all over the courtroom. Even Judge Childs slid her glasses down to the tip of her nose, peering at Katherine, quizzically.

"Do not wear the shoes of an outsider listening to a story of strangers. Instead, step into Robin Malone's shoes. Step into the shoes of a victim whose faith and spirit has been broken. The spirit of truth. The spirit of honesty. The spirit of humanity."

Katherine scooped up the torn pieces of the photo and placed them on the wooden banister in front of the jury box. After looking each juror in the eye, she took off her shoes and walked back to her seat.

Sudden staccato applause echoed through the room.

Clap. Clap. Clap.

The source was Rayko Blu, smiling devilishly as he now stood in front of the jury. His mock applause was a segue into his own course of action. Every eye in the room was on him and prepared for a show.

Meticulously, he rolled back each of his sleeves with his fingertips. He then swirled his hands like a magician, as if a rabbit were going to pop out of thin air.

"Look closely. Do you see? No fire; no smoke and mirrors; not even a single noisemaker. All I have to present to you, the people of the jury, is facts. My friend, the prosecutor, would lead you to believe that I plan to manipulate you into believing things about the defendants, Melanie Mitchell and Kevin Dennison, which aren't true.

"Take a second and think about what she has implied. She has typecast each of you as an individual incapable of forming a solid opinion on your own, without the aid of her elaborate displays to coax you. All she has managed to do is expose her true feelings that your intellectual capacity is not up to par."

Rayko turned to Katherine and said, "Tisk tisk," wagging his finger in her face.

"Ladies and gentleman, I am no artist. I don't mix colors from a palette with the intentions of creating a false portrait. And I am not a magician with something hidden up my sleeve. What I am is a simple man; a simple man who takes evidence and allows that evidence to prove my clients' innocence."

The room waited for him to go on, but all he did was wipe his hands clean. Calmly he walked back to his seat, having said all he needed to say.

Robin could only see the backs of their heads, but she pictured Kevin and Melanie with smirks on their deceitful faces.

Wasting no time, Katherine called her first witness to the stand—Robin Malone.

Robin's mouth instantly went dry. The room was quiet except for the clicking of her heels on the floorboards as she made her way to the front of the room. *Breath in, breath out,* she said to herself. All eyes in the room fastened to her, adding to her anxiety. As the bailiff swore her in, Robin's right hand trembled when she raised it, swearing an oath to speak truthfully. She had nothing to lie about, so that was the easy part. For her, the dread came from having to look her would-be murderers in the eye for the first time in months.

Robin took a deep breath and closed her eyes. When she opened them, her gaze immediately fell on Melanie Mitchell. With a pink cardigan pulled over a floral dress and wisps of hair delicately hanging from her otherwise perfectly placed bun, Melanie looked the picture of innocence. Her body language was confident, yet humble, most likely a tip coached by her attorney.

In spite of the well-thought appearance, Robin could tell that Melanie was a wreck on the inside. Her foot tapped continuously in patterns of three. *Tap tap tap, tap tap tap, tap tap tap.* It had been a dead giveaway to her guilt since Robin and Melanie were six-year-olds. A vivid memory suddenly surfaced to Robin's mind. They'd gotten caught stealing helpings of pie at Thanksgiving before dinner was served.

"Who dug this hole into my sweet potato pie?" Aunt Joanne asked the two little girls with the evidence on their faces. Robin knew better than to lie, so she kept quiet. Melanie's foot began the nervous tap-tap-tapping, and Joanne instantly knew who the culprits were.

It was a bittersweet memory that brought a fleeting smile to Robin's lips. Focusing back to reality in a world where Melanie was now on trial for her attempted murder, Robin suppressed the childhood recollection and avoided eye contact with her former friend for the rest of her time on the witness stand.

"Hello, Ms. Malone," Katherine Palmer said softly.

"Hello." Robin's voice crackled nervously.

"Would you like to tell the court how you know the defendants?"

Robin swallowed hard. "Melanie Mitchell is my best friend. *Was* my best friend," she corrected herself. "And Kevin Dennison is my deceased daughter's father."

"I see." Katherine paced slowly. "How old was your daughter when she passed away?"

Robin forced down another dry swallow. "Just two days old."

"How was your relationship with Kevin Dennison before your daughter passed away?"

Robin glanced over at the man himself, who sat stone-faced, looking completely detached from the situation.

"It was strained. I had a very difficult pregnancy, physically. The baby wasn't developing at the rate she should have. Kevin pretty much forbade me to move forward with the pregnancy. He was afraid that our daughter would have birth complications related to the placental issues. I didn't want to have an abortion, so I chose to have her — alone."

"Were his concerns about her health validated when your daughter was born?"

"Yes, unfortunately. Gabriela was born prematurely and developed meningitis from an infection. That's what led to her death."

"I assume this is one of the reasons for the dissolution of you and Mr. Dennison's relationship; am I right?"

"Yes, one of many. Kevin blamed me for her death. He said that if I'd never had her, she wouldn't have passed away the way that she did." Robin willed the sudden pooling of tears in her eyes not to spill over. Katherine had prepared her for the difficult line of questioning, but that made the sting of reliving the memories no less difficult.

"How was Melanie during this rough time in you and Kevin's relationship?"

"She was very supportive. We spent lots of time together talking and being there for each other. She was my daughter's godmother, so the loss was huge for her. What I didn't know at the time was that she was consoling me during the day and consoling Kevin at night."

"And by *consoling*, you mean they entered a sexual relationship together, is that right?"

Robin's teeth clenched before answering, "Yes. I discovered this when I showed up at her house and found the two locked in a very inappropriate embrace."

"They were sucking face," Katherine said bluntly.

"Yes, they were," Robin nodded.

"Not long after this, you moved on to a new

relationship, is that right?"

For the first time in her testimony, Robin smiled.

"Yes. I met a wonderful man, Austin. I was in a very vulnerable position after losing Gabriela, but Austin came along and made me feel…safe. Safe to love and trust again."

"I'm glad to hear it," Katherine smiled. "The two of you have since been married?"

"We have."

"Hmm. So why it is that your husband isn't here today?"

Robin looked down at the floor before responding. "Because he and I were attacked one night while walking through the park. I was pistol whipped, and Austin was…" Robin stopped, too choked up to continue with her testimony.

"I know this is very difficult for you, Ms. Malone." Katherine handed Robin a tissue. "But please go on."

After a deep breath Robin responded, "Austin was shot."

"Please tell the court what exactly happened on the night in question."

Robin was hoping for an easier transition into the most difficult part of her testimony. Unfortunately, she wasn't given one. Through tears, she recounted the details of the life-changing event.

She reported that after dinner on the evening of March 24th, she and Austin had gone for a drive through his old neighborhood. At the end of one cul-de-sac was a tree he'd climbed to impress a girl and had broken his arm falling from it. Robin remembered appreciating the sneak peek she'd been given into his childhood.

After a half hour more of driving, they'd stopped in front of a park, not far from Robin's house. She got out first. Grabbing a box from his back seat, he rushed over, covering her eyes with his hands.

"Austin, what are you up to?" she asked impatiently.

"Nothing. I just want to go for a walk, that's all."

"I think I'd enjoy it more if I could actually see where I'm walking."

"Okay, but give me a kiss before you open your eyes."

"Austin!" she laughed.

"Just kiss me."

She leaned in, puckering up, and was surprised by a mouth full of fur. Her eyes popped open, and she couldn't believe what she saw.

"A puppy! Oh gosh, Austin, she's beautiful!"

"She's a Shi Tzu-Schnauzer mix, and she's all yours."

The puppy's tiny paws reached out to Robin playfully. Robin took her from Austin's arms and immediately began to melt.

"A puppy is a huge responsibility...so I plan to be around for a long time to help you take care of her."

The statement was Austin's way of giving Robin his letterman jacket and calling her his girlfriend. Having no objection to the notion, she offered her approval by way of a kiss. When Robin went in for an embrace, she heard a loud *pop!* Looking to her right, she saw a man with a gun push Austin to the ground. Robin backed away, but the burly man rushed her, smacking her hard across the face with the butt of a .380.

"Get down on the ground!" he screamed.

Her chin quivered fearfully, and her pulsing heart lurched into her throat. Doing as he said, she lay face down on the ground. Robin could hear his heavy breaths through the crisp night air. Lurking behind her, he seemed to be sniffing in the scent of her fear. A sinister laugh erupted from his throat, sending a chilling pang of terror down her spine. Time stood frighteningly still as she awaited his next move.

Suddenly, her ribcage exploded with excruciating pain. He had kicked her hard with his steel-toed boot causing her to dizzily fold in half. He stooped down over her continuing his spine-tingling evil laughter.

"I'm going to splatter your brain all over this pavement," he said in her ear.

His voice wasn't familiar. Robin wondered why a person she didn't know would want to hurt her. He laughed again, this time with the barrel of the gun hard on the back of her head. Robin squeezed her eyes tight, dreading the blast of the gunshot. Only that shot never rang out. The next sound she heard were his footsteps running in the opposite direction. Her head peeked up and glimpsed his face before he disappeared into the shadows.

Several minutes ticked by while she lay perfectly

still, praying that he wouldn't come back to finish her off. Once she felt it was safe, Robin tried to stand up, but her legs collapsed beneath her.

She finally managed to roll herself up onto her knees, willing away the ringing in her ears. The new puppy barked non-stop. Robin feared it was because the gunman had returned. Then she turned and saw the true reason for the incessant barking.

Austin lay in a pool of blood.

On the witness stand, Robin's voice trembled uncontrollably. Tears streamed down her face as she tucked her stress-thinned tresses behind her ear.

"Who do you feel was responsible for the attack on you and Austin?" Katherine asked.

The entire room knew the answer, but Robin responded with, "Kevin Dennison and Melanie Mitchell were responsible for this."

"At this time, your honor, I'd like to submit exhibit *A* into evidence." Katherine removed an 8x10 photo from a manila folder. She paced back and forth in front of the jury, holding the photo high enough for everyone to see. Two women in the front row cringed at the gruesome shot.

"This was taken the night Robin Malone was beaten in the park. You'll notice that the whites of her eyes are no longer white. They are blood red from the multiple blood vessels that ruptured when she was struck with the butt of the gun."

Katherine held up another photo, this time of Robin's torso, which was black and blue.

"A punctured lung, three fractured ribs, and internal bleeding were the injuries she sustained that night."

Just seeing the horrid pictures sent a flood of terror through Robin's body. She could still feel the hot breath of her wicked assailant on the back of her neck. She squeezed her eyes shut and reminded herself that she was safe and sound inside the courtroom.

"To me, this looks like the work of someone who is angry. Someone who wanted Robin to hurt very badly. Someone who was jealous that she had moved on with her life. To me, this looks like the work of a man who was bitter about the death of his young daughter and wanted revenge!"

"I object, your honor, prosecution is misleading the jury!" Rayko Blu hissed.

"Sustained." Judge Childs warned Katherine, "Reel it in, Counselor."

Katherine continued without missing a beat. "It is Kevin Dennison and Melanie Mitchell's defense that they were miles away on vacation the night Robin and Austin were nearly murdered in the park. To that, I say this: I have a remote starter on my car. So guess what that means. It means that although I'm not physically there to turn on the car with a key, I can still remotely control the situation—just as Kevin Dennison and Melanie Mitchell controlled this one.

"Melanie Mitchell admits that on several occasions, she drove Mr. Dennison to back alley meetings with a man she described as *seedy*, yet she claims having no knowledge of what their meetings entailed. Ms. Mitchell also admits to being jealous of the success and lavish lifestyle of her former best friend. Jealous enough to befriend her lover and help him remove Robin from the picture? I say so, and so does the evidence."

Katherine held up a sketched photo.

"Robin Malone provided a sketch of the attacker's face." She held up another sketched portrait. "I find it no coincidence that the sketch is an exact match to the description given by Melanie Mitchell of the man attending the meetings that *she* drove Kevin Dennison to."

Katherine held both sketches up high allowing the jurors to take in the undeniable likenesses.

"Austin Malone has spent months in a rehabilitation center where he is presently relearning to walk and function in a normal capacity. The bullet that ripped through his body never would have been fired had it not been for these two individuals." She pointed to Kevin and Melanie.

"Robin and Austin were able to escape with their lives, thankfully. But this makes the defendants no less guilty. The fact that their hired help flubbed the job was a mere setback for them. The assailant is still out there roaming the streets freely, his identity unknown. I am confident that if you allow the defendants to walk away free from this situation, they will try again and again until they find someone who *will* kill Robin and Austin Malone. They just might be brave enough next time to do it themselves," she said to the jury.

That display in the courtroom was now three days past, and the jury had just come back with a verdict.

Kevin Dennison stood surrounded by his team of high profile lawyers. Dressed in a William Malcolm Black Label suit, he looked more like the legal counsel representing him than he did the defendant. A confident smile lit his face as he prepared for a ruling that he was sure would be in his favor.

Melanie's face, however, was pale. She folded her hands behind her back to conceal their nervous trembling.

Sweat moistened Robin's clasped hands. *This is it...*she thought to herself.

"Has the jury reached a verdict?" asked Judge Childs.

"Yes, we have, your Honor," replied a juror.

The judge took a folded slip of paper from the female bailiff and cleared her throat. She handed it back, addressing the jury foreman. "How do you find?"

"On the charge of conspiracy to commit homicide, we, the jury, find Melanie Mitchell guilty."

Melanie crumpled into her chair, her face buried in her hands.

"And on the charge of conspiracy to commit homicide, we, the jury, find Kevin Dennison guilty."

The courtroom erupted with cheer, and Robin's bowed head jerked upright. She and Aunt Joanne nearly yelped with joy. Shock and disbelief registered on Kevin's face. His legal team corralled around him while the judge banged her gavel.

"Mr. Dennison," said the judge. Kevin didn't look

up. He appeared to be quarreling with his lawyers. "Mr. Dennison," the judge said more firmly.

Defiantly, Kevin turned his head in the judge's direction with flared nostrils.

"You selfishly orchestrated the murders of two individuals." The judge slid the glasses from her face. "I must say, I thank God that your plans were thwarted. Two people nearly lost their lives because of your actions, sir. That is not something that this court takes lightly. To help you clearly see the severity of your behavior, I am choosing to make an immediate ruling."

A buzz of chatter went around the courtroom. The judge cleared her throat.

"I hereby sentence you, Mr. Dennison, *and* you, Ms. Mitchell, to a minimum of fifteen years in the Jackson State Correctional facility. The next time either of you think about toying with someone else's life — don't."

Judge Childs banged her gavel and retreated to chambers.

Robin's breath seemed to leap from her body, a wave of relief washing over her. She squeezed Katherine Palmer and thanked her for doing a stellar job on the case. Because of Katherine, there was no more worry of Kevin and Melanie harming her or anyone else.

Or so she thought...

Three years later...

Robin sat uncomfortably in the conference room of

her real estate investment firm. Her face was beginning to stiffen from the pseudo smile plastered on it for most of the afternoon. Mrs. Cartwright, her prestigious potential client, was on another tangent about her grandson who'd won the spelling bee with the word *adjudicate*.

"The little darling stepped right up to the microphone and said, 'Adjudicate. A-D-J-U-D-I-C-A-T-E. Adjudicate!'" She clasped her hands together. "You should have seen him, dear. What an angel he was."

Robin simply nodded and smiled, struggling to keep her eyes open. The night before, she had been restless, tossing and turning, waking up in cold sweats. It was a wonder she made it to work at all. Mrs. Cartwright's voice was beginning to slice through the last shred of patience she had left, so she quickly attempted a redirect.

"You know what I was thinking, Mrs. Cartwright? How about we get on with the final details of the document? I'm sure your grandson has made it home from school by now. Let's get you out of here so the two of you can spend some time together."

"Yes, of course dear, down to business. Now where did I put my reading glasses?" she asked, squinting and patting the conference room table. "I could have sworn I had them right here. Oh dear," her voice crackled.

Robin leaned across the table and slid the bifocals — that were propped on Mrs. Cartwright's forehead — down over her eyes.

"Oh my, what a divvy I've been in," Mrs. Cartwright

chuckled.

"It happens to the best of us," Robin smiled. "Now, let's refocus on the final agreement that we've arranged. In this last section, I've outlined — "

Robin was cut off by a speakerphone on the table announcing that someone was holding on the line for her.

"Carol, you'll have to take a message and let them know I'll call back. I'm in the middle of — "

"They said it's very urgent, Mrs. Malone."

Robin scooted her chair back hastily as she huffed in frustration. She was on the verge of sealing the deal; whoever was interrupting had better have a good reason.

"Pardon me, Mrs. Cartwright. I'll be just a few moments."

"No worries dear, take your time. Now that I've found my glasses, I can go over the rest of the contract and see just how wealthy I'm making you," she laughed.

Robin excused herself once again, and rolled her eyes when she made it to the other side of the door. She dragged herself down the hall to her office, passing a mirror along the way. Her eyes were bloodshot, and the bags beneath them were large enough to carry groceries. A little rest was all she needed. She planned on getting it as soon as she could get the old bird to sign the contract.

After pushing through the glass double-doors of her

office, she plopped down into her cream, Italian leather chair.

"This had better be good," she said to herself before picking up the call. "Thank you for holding; this is Robin."

There was no one on the other end of the line, just the sound of voices in the background.

"Hello, this is Robin. Are you there?" she asked.

The next sound she heard was a clicking noise that reminded her of a music box being wound up. Then there was the ticking of a timer. This sound went on for several more seconds. Finally the line went dead. Eeriness washed over her, but she quickly dismissed it. There had been trouble with the phone lines since a big storm a few days earlier. She attributed this occurrence to that.

After taking a few moments to clear her head, Robin made her way back to the conference room. Walking inside, she took a deep breath and turned her stage smile on again.

"All right, Mrs. Cartwright, where were we?" she asked the empty room.

Robin looked all around, even checking behind the door, as if the woman would be hiding there. Completely baffled, she stepped into the hall. "Carol, did you see where Mrs. Cartwright went?"

Carol, who had worked for her since she opened the doors to her first office years ago where they shared a desk in one small room, walked up with a consoling look on her face. "She left right after you took that call, saying something about leaving to be with her angel."

Robin let out a long sigh and rubbed her fingers across her forehead.

"Well, that was three hours of my life I'll never get back. Call her secretary and arrange some time for us to meet again later this week. Whatever day she schedules, make sure the meeting room is stocked with Vicodin and a muzzle."

"Will do," Carol smirked.

"Forward all my calls to voicemail for the rest of the day. I've got a few errands to run, and then I'm heading home."

Robin grabbed her briefcase and jacket all in one swoop and headed to the elevator.

*

After picking up fresh flowers from the Farmer's Market and her suit from the dry cleaner, Robin finally pulled into the horseshoe driveway of her home. Managing to get everything in the house without dropping a single item was a task she'd mastered. The hanger with her suit dangled from her mouth; her coat and briefcase were stuffed under her arms; and the flowers and her keys hung on the tip of her fingers as she managed to open the top and bottom locks.

Noodles bounded over, knocking everything out of her hands. The Shi-Tzu Schnauzer mix wagged her tail giddily, pawing at Robin's legs.

"Noodles, no matter how bad my day is, you always make it better." She scratched the pup's ears and made her way into the house.

"Do I have to wag my tail and lick your face, too, to get some love?"

Robin smiled when her 68-year-old, Aunt Joanne came from the kitchen with a plate of freshly baked muffins.

"I'll scratch behind your ears and even throw in a belly rub, if you let me have one of those."

Joanne twisted her lips as if the thought was absurd. "Later on after dinner, you can eat as many muffins as you want, Muffin," she chuckled at her own joke. "Now pick up those things off the floor; I didn't spend all day cleaning for you to just come in and trash the place."

"But, Auntie, I—"

"But, but nothing," Joanne shooed.

Years earlier, after the death of their parents, Joanne had taken Robin and her younger brother in, raising them as if they were her own. Now Robin was CEO of Michigan's largest real estate investment firm and owned properties all over the state—including the million dollar house she called home. Joanne still made it perfectly clear that her niece wasn't too grown up to get put in her place.

"And make it snappy," Joanne called over her shoulder.

Picking up her belongings, she made her way to the kitchen with Noodles tagging along behind.

"So, tell me about your day." Joanne cut up potato

slices and prepared their meal.

Robin unenthusiastically plopped onto a kitchen barstool. "There isn't very much to tell besides me being exhausted and my client boring me to death with sappy stories of her grandson." Robin scrunched her nose. "What about you, you had a good day?"

"I sure did. After walking down to the market, where I bought groceries for these bare cupboards of yours," she rolled her eyes, "Noodles and I went for a walk through the park. We both got some good exercise in, didn't we, Noodles?" she said in baby talk, while the pooch wagged her tail. "I checked the answering machine when we got home. The phone lines must still be having issues from that storm, because three of the calls were hang-ups. I heard on the news that some parts of the state are just now getting their power back. I'll have to check and see if mine finally came back on."

Before starting for the stairs Robin said, "I appreciate you pampering us while you're staying here, Aunt Joanne. I'm hoping your power never comes back on and that you finally accept my offer to move in."

"I appreciate the offer, but I have a life of my own to keep up with, thank you very much."

When she turned her back, Robin tried sneaking a piece of a muffin, but Joanne, who seemed to have eyes in the back of her head, spun around, snapping her on the hand with a dish towel. Caught in the act, Robin made her way upstairs empty-handed.

Half an hour later, she emerged from the shower with tufts of jet-black hair peeking out from the terrycloth turban wrapped around her head. Too tired to dry her slender 5 foot 6 inch frame, she slid into her bathrobe and settled onto her king sized bed to unwind. Slathering on her favorite lilac moisturizer, her mind unintentionally drifted to her work, like it always did when she tried to relax.

Aunt Joanne had dubbed her a workhorse; a befitting label, given that in lieu of much sought after rest, Robin was now checking her voicemails.

"Six new messages," the automated voice announced.

The first two were from developers. The third call was from her personal assistant, Cassidy. Cassidy, her younger cousin, who was fresh out of college and staying with her while she got on her feet, was a spunky hipster who spent most evenings with music blasting from her room while she worked on oil paintings. Her voicemail said she'd be staying over at a friend's house. Robin couldn't help feeling grateful for a night bass line free.

The next call was from Austin.

"Hi, Honey. As you probably guessed, I'll be home late again tonight."

Robin sighed because it was the third night that week he'd had to work late at his law firm. He was as much a workhorse as she was.

"You know I'll make this up to you. I'm thinking a visit to the day spa followed by a night at the ballet. Granted, you'll have to do the ballet part on your own, because can you imagine me; 6-foot 3 inches tall, prancing around in pink tights and a tutu? I shudder to think."

She laughed at his corniness that never seemed to grow old. "But seriously, I miss you, Kiddo and I can't wait to see you later tonight. Love you so much. Bye."

Beaming from her husband's voice, she checked the fifth message. It caught her by surprise. She heard voices in the background, just like the call earlier; but this time, she heard a person breathing.

The breaths weren't loud or inappropriate; even still, there was something unnerving about the message. Suddenly uneasy, Robin ended the call without ever listening to the final message. Slipping further down into the comforter, she bundled up tight, warding off the creeping chill moving up her spine.

*

After breakfast the next morning Robin carted Joanne to a doctor appointment for the arthritis she was too proud to admit was setting in. The medical center was just down the street, so they didn't have far to go. Joanne sat in the passenger seat rattling on about the rainy weather made her knees achy. All the while, Robin's eyes were glued to her side mirror. Earlier that morning, she'd noticed a man jogging by her house and thought it was odd since she'd never seen him before. Now a vehicle two cars back appeared to be trailing her. The driver looked an awful lot like that same man.

Her first thought was to switch from lane to lane to see what he would do, but traffic was tight, and the turn for the medical center was quickly approaching. She stayed in her lane and kept pace with traffic, trying to think of a plan.

"Hellooo. You haven't heard a word I've said," Joanne griped.

"Just trying to maneuver through this traffic." Robin tried to hide the tension in her voice. She glanced at the rear view mirror. The suspicious driver was now one car length behind them. She began to panic.

"I was telling you about the report I saw on Oprah the other day. Did you know that if you eat—"

Joanne was cut off mid-sentence when Robin floored the gas pedal. The mystery car was nearly on her bumper. If Robin hadn't accelerated when she did, the two vehicles would've collided. Not knowing what to do next, she cut the steering wheel hard to the right and turned a corner. The tires screeched, and Joanne threw her hands up dramatically, squealing, "Oh my Lord!"

Robin hit the brakes hard, then yanked on her rear view mirror to get a glimpse of the trailing vehicle as it passed. But it never did.

"Robin, what on earth is going on?!" Joanne asked with saucer-wide eyes.

Ignoring her, Robin gripped the rearview mirror tighter and squinted, still searching for the trailing car.

"Robin Elina Malone, explain yourself!" Joanne huffed angrily to deaf ears.

Robin continued staring in the mirror, ignoring her aunt and all the angry drivers behind her. She was sure the car should have passed by now and felt a little like she was losing her mind.

"Tell me what's going on, Robin!" her aunt demanded.

As if landing back into reality, Robin made eye contact with Joanne. "I'm fine. I just—everything is ok."

After taking a quick glance in the mirror without spotting the car, Robin realized she'd been wrong about the tail—or simply outsmarted. The steering wheel slid through her hands, and she finally took her foot off the brake. Moving forward down the street, Joanne stared at her niece as if she'd grown another head. Robin gripped the wheel tight while her eyes darted from the rear view mirror back to the road in front of her.

*

After the appointment, Robin dropped Joanne off at home, and crept through bumper-to-bumper traffic, finally making it to her office. It was the end of the quarter, and her work life was virtual chaos. There were endless meetings, phone calls and emails, and she was pulled in every direction. Nagging at the back of her mind was the man she'd seen.

There was a meeting scheduled to begin in a half hour. She went to the conference room and prepared the large screen monitor for her presentation. While fidgeting with the high-tech system, she happened to stumble upon a local news station's breaking news.

If ever a human looked like a deer in headlights, Robin did now. She stared open mouthed at the screen, her mind not believing what her ears were hearing.

Frank Holland reported on the early release of Kevin

Dennison from Jackson State Correctional Facility.

"Kevin Dennison was released from prison earlier today after his legal team uncovered discrepancies in reports filed by court officials. After serving just three years for conspiracy to commit the murders of family law attorney Austin Malone and real estate investor Robin Malone, he walks away a free man."

The camera cut to a shot of Kevin flanked by the media pandemonium. He stood perfectly still and waited for a hush to fall over the reporters and spectators. When he knew that he had the crowd's ear, he finally spoke.

"I'd like to thank everyone for their support through what has proved to be a very difficult time. I have served an unfair sentence for a crime that I did not commit. Although my release is due to a technical error, I still, and have always, maintained my innocence. What this situation has taught me is that you must accept certain circumstances and handle them with dignity and integrity — even if your actions didn't warrant the false allegations against you. Sometimes, you must simply suffer the punishment."

As if looking through the camera and directly at Robin, he said, "We will *all* have our turn to suffer." Hauntingly, the words seemed to slither from his lips and crawl slowly up her spine.

"Kevin! Kevin! Kevin!" The reporters all shouted, trying to get him to answer their questions.

Frank Holland was able to speak above the rest of the pack. "Kevin, what is your plan now that you're out?"

"My plan is to make up for all of the time that was unjustly stolen from me. That is all I have to say." After giving his statement, he was whisked away into an SUV that sped off in a cloud of dust.

Robin felt like the wind had been knocked out of her as she crumpled into a conference room chair. Her worst nightmare had come true. Kevin was a free man. And he'd basically just admitted that he would resume his role in life, which was to make her life miserable.

Immediately, Robin's mind shot back to a comment that the district attorney made at Kevin's trial.

I am confident that if he walks away free, he will try again and again until he finds someone who will kill Robin. He just might be brave enough next time to do it himself...

Without warning, the speakerphone announced that her guests had arrived for the meeting. Robin had only a few seconds to get her head in the right place and try to refocus. Beads of sweat trickled down her back as she slowly sucked in breaths.

The next thing she knew, her assistant, Cassidy, along with Carol, began to escort the meeting attendees into the conference room. Robin labored through individual greetings in a fog. Then she waited at the front of the room while everyone took their seats.

Robin opened her mouth to speak, but her distracted mind swirled with the news she'd just heard. Everyone silently stared at her struggling to keep it together. Clueless, Cassidy stood at the back of the room, giving her boss the thumbs up to start the presentation.

"Hello, everyone, and thank you for joining me

today. I'd like to present you with—"

Her face quivered as she spoke, trying to paste on a smile.

"Uh, I'd like to present you with—"

Beads of sweat began to form along her brow line as Kevin's threatening statement played in her mind.

We will all have our turn to suffer...

The entire room stared at her uncomfortably. "We know you'd like to present it, so how about you get to it already." A suit at the back of the table made the snarky comment. A wave of chuckles went around the room. Robin blanched at the humiliation. She smiled crookedly and tried to continue.

The entire time she spoke, a split screen played in her mind. On one side, she saw the blurry images of the people in front of her. On the other side was Kevin's press conference playing over and over. Unconsciously, she began to speak loudly, because she heard Kevin's voice over her own.

Finally seeing that her boss was struggling, Cassidy stepped in to run damage control. She walked brusquely to the front and took over the presentation.

"Yes, as Robin pointed out," she directed everyone's attention to the monitor, "the next phase of development will require the resources that all of you here have to offer."

Robin, taking the cue, gratefully stepped aside, letting her assistant continue as if it was all a part of the plan. She felt sick; her clammy hands clasped over her mouth to keep from throwing up.

After twenty minutes of fumbling through the PowerPoint screens, Cassidy ended the session and thanked everyone for coming.

The participants shuffled out the door. Robin and Cassidy shook their hands. The gesture was an apology for the disaster they'd just witnessed. The last person was being shown out, when Robin saw a different group of visitors.

It was the press, and they were ready to pounce.

"Robin, how do you feel about Kevin Dennison's release?"

"Mrs. Malone, do you regret accusing Mr. Dennison of the attempted homicides of you and your husband?"

Questions were shot at her, and, together, they all sounded like gibberish. Robin shielded her face from the cameras, as Carol held a jacket over her boss's head. The reporters followed them down the stairwell into Robin's private parking garage. Carol aggressively swatted them away as they inched closer and closer. Cassidy was tousled about in the crowd, fighting to keep pace in the garage.

"Mrs. Malone does not have a comment at this time. Please respect her privacy!" Carol barked.

The reporters swarmed around the car. Robin dived into the driver seat. Carol stuffed Cassidy in the vehicle and slammed the door. Then she turned and began corralling the aggressive mob away from them. Flashes of light from the cameras blinded Robin, as she inched the car through the crowd.

She couldn't believe this was happening. Not even an hour ago, she had learned of Kevin's release, and already his freedom was wreaking its usual havoc on her life.

She was finally able to maneuver her way out and make it to the main road. "What's happening, Robin?" Cassidy asked, frightened.

"See if you can get hold of Austin. Tell him to meet us at the house as soon as he can."

"He's not picking up," Cassidy said, after several tries.

"Probably in court. Dammit!" Robin pounded her fists against the steering wheel.

Cassidy continued to hit the redial button. "Pick up, pick up…"

Robin darted from lane to lane making her way to the freeway with tears burning her eyes. Things were happening too quickly, and she felt like she was losing control. When she finally pulled into her driveway, she didn't even remember the drive home. She turned off the engine and sat still.

Cassidy sat quietly next to her, wishing there was something she could do.

After a while, Robin grabbed the door handle and managed to pull herself out. The women trudged through the front door. Noodles came running up to them as usual. Robin barely acknowledged the dog. Cassidy shushed her excited barking.

Joanne, tugging an apron from around her neck

asked, "What's wrong?"

Cassidy looked over at Robin, who didn't say a word.

"Your face looks like death, Robin, and I know something is going on. Now, is someone going to talk to me, or will you both just stand there looking silly?"

With Noodles and Cassidy on her heels, Robin made her way to the sofa and sat down on the edge.

"Well," she said with a deep breath, "because of some technicality, Kevin was released from prison today."

Cassidy sat down on the sofa with lowered her eyes.

"He got out this afternoon. There was a big press conference about it on the news." She nodded at the TV. "I'm sure it's on every channel."

"So that's why you were acting so strangely in the meeting today," said Cassidy.

"Yeah, I heard the news right before everyone walked in." She rested her forehead in her palm. "I should have known something like this was going to happen. It's like I could sense it; I've been feeling uneasy lately." Robin sighed. "We can probably expect a few knocks on the door from story hungry reporters."

"They can sniff around the yard like mutts all they want," Joanne quipped. "That's why God invented sprinklers."

The conversation was cut short when Robin's cellphone rang. She sprang up to answer it, thinking it was Austin.

—

"Honey, I've been calling you back to back—"

"You have? Well that's funny, because I didn't realize you even had my number," said the voice on the other end.

Ice ran through Robin's veins. The voice was one she was hoping to never hear again.

"Kevin." Her teeth clenched. "How did you get my private number?"

"Oh, come on, Robin. You were the mother of my child. I'm always going to keep up with you. Did you miss me while I was away? I missed you."

"Go to hell, Kevin," Robin said and meant it.

"There's the Robin we all know and love," he laughed. "I just wanted you to know that I'm thinking of you and to let you know that there are no hard feelings about the whole sending me to prison thing. Maybe we can have lunch sometime?"

"I'm going to tell you this once and only once, Kevin: leave me the HELL alone."

Her body shook. She could feel heat rising to her face.

"No lunch, eh? Maybe we'll do dinner instead. Either way, I'm sure I'll see you around town." Robin knew that was a threat. "I'm going to let you go now, Robin, but it was really nice catching up with you. By the way, how's that husband of yours healing up? I heard bullet wounds don't look so pretty after awhile."

Robin slammed the phone down on the table, nearly breaking it. Jerking upright in her seat, she suddenly felt the need for fresh air and a pain reliever for the splitting headache that had formed. With no word to Joanne or Cassidy, Robin grabbed her jacket and headed for the door.

Noodles whimpered when she saw this and wanted to go along. Robin didn't feel up to fighting about it, so she said, "Alright, alright," and led the pooch out the door.

There were only a few people out at the nearby dog park. Walking down the path she noticed slivers of sunlight attempting to pierce the pillowy atmosphere of gray clouds in the sky. It seemed that the conflicting sunny-gray sky mirrored her own jumble of emotions.

Face tucked behind dark sunglasses, with a ball cap pulled over her hair, Robin hoped no one would recognize her.

That hope was shot to hell when she saw a woman approaching with a small object in her hand. It wasn't until she was closer that Robin realized it was a tape recorder. The woman was a reporter.

Instinctively avoiding her, Robin tugged Noodles' leash in the direction of home.

"Mrs. Malone, please," the woman shouted. "I just need a few moments of your time."

"I have no comment about Kevin Dennison. See my publicist if you'd like an official —"

"I'm not a reporter, Mrs. Malone." Robin kept walking, picking up the pace. "Mrs. Malone, please. Kevin Dennison is my brother."

Robin stopped abruptly. Slowly, she turned around. "I'm sorry that you share a bloodline with him, but I still don't have anything to say." She started to turn away but the woman stepped in closer.

"Please, just give me a few minutes."

There was something about the way she spoke that intrigued Robin enough to want to hear what she had to say. Knowing it was a bad idea, she still stepped closer to the woman. "You have 5 minutes."

They found a close bench, and Robin let Noodles loose to run while they spoke.

"My name is Allysa Dennison, by the way," the woman extended her hand.

Robin lightly shook hands with the tips of Allysa's fingers. "Four minutes left."

"Okay. Well, I first want to apologize for everything that my brother has done to you. I'm sure my apology can't take away the past, but I wouldn't feel right without extending it to you."

Robin nodded.

"Mrs. Malone, have you ever heard of a man named Paul Archer?"

"The so-called Michigan crime boss? I thought he wasn't even a real person. Just a made up goon to tell little kids scary stories about. Why are you asking me about him?"

The woman adjusted the dark sunglasses on her face. "Paul Archer is Kevin's father."

Robin's heart sank. It was rumored that Paul Archer

came from a wealthy family and was known for his array of unethical ventures ranging from murder-for-hire to corrupting politicians. In the 90's, he was sentenced to life in prison for money laundering, drug trafficking, and being linked to several crime organizations.

Allysa pulled out a folder and removed a portrait that must have been 20 years old. Although the image was faded and the edges of the picture worn, Robin could clearly see what appeared to be 12 year-old Kevin standing next to his father. She took the picture from Allysa's hands and stared at it. It was amazing how wholesome and innocent Kevin looked with braces on his teeth and knee-high socks on. A bright smile lit his face as he hammed for the camera.

Robin handed the picture back. "Why are you showing this to me? I have absolutely no ties to your brother anymore."

"I'm not sure what you know of Kevin, but I'm sure you don't know the truth. You and probably the rest of the world," said Allysa, while placing the folder back into her purse.

"So tell me then; what's the truth?"

Allysa looked Robin in the eye. "Once Paul Archer was sent away to prison, our mother relocated to Maryland. She remarried, and that's how he became a Dennison. Feeling like he didn't fit into the new family, he linked up with his father's old contacts, and pretty much took over the family business, picking up where he had left off."

Robin swallowed hard. "So, let me get this straight;

you're telling me that the father of my dead child is an organized crime leader and drug lord, and I'm the person responsible for sending him to jail."

"I figured you deserved to know who you were dealing with. After stewing in jail for years, I don't think he'll just let bygones be bygones. I wanted to warn you. Protect yourself."

"I appreciate you telling me this, Allysa. But don't worry about me; Kevin's tricks have grown old. I won't let him get close to me."

"I wouldn't be so sure about that." Allysa stood up. "You're into real estate; maybe you should think of moving somewhere on the east coast. You know, get a fresh start and experience the life he tried to take away from you."

"I appreciate your concern, but I'll be fine," Robin reassured.

"Well, you said five minutes. Thank you for taking the time to speak with me, Mrs. Malone." Allysa began to walk away. "Oh, wait, I almost forgot." She took the tape recorder and photo out of her purse and tossed them into Robin's lap. "I recorded this conversation for you. Just in case you need a reminder of who it is you're up against."

And just like that, she was gone. Robin stood in the center of the park shivering, as much from the news she'd just heard as from the crisp fall air. As brave and unafraid as she tried to be in front of this stranger, she was feeling the exact opposite now.

On the ride home, Noodles' head hung out the

window while Robin drove dazed. Hands tight at ten and two on the wheel, her face were still flushed from the warning Allysa had just given her. She began a mental activity she'd learned in Yoga, to help regain control of her spiraling thoughts. Promptly cutting in, Noodles began to bark loudly. Robin tugged at her tail to get her to stop. "Noodles! Sit down!" she yelled, but the barking persisted.

The dog was obviously irritated by something. Robin looked out the window to see what it was. Noodles continued to bark, but Robin didn't hear any more. Her eyes focused on Austin, standing in the parking lot of the local drugstore, deep in conversation with two men standing with him.

The first man she was sure was the one who had been following her. The second was the hit man who'd put a bullet through Austin's torso. Robin's open mouth instantly went dry; her stomach churned.

Startled by Noodles' incessant barking, Austin looked up and made shocked eye contact with his wife.

Chapter Two

Joanne shuffled through the living room, and picked up an empty teacup from a coaster. Suddenly, screeching tires roared so loudly and close that she thought the vehicle would come crashing through the wall. A car door slammed, and Robin rushed into the house.

"Aunt Joanne, we have to get out of here right now!" she shrieked with tears streaming down her face.

"What's going on?" Joanne asked, startled.

"I'll explain later, Auntie, but please, we have to leave right now!"

Over her niece's shoulder, Joanne saw Austin come through the door. Noodles happily trotted over to him, but Robin screamed out as if he had tried to kill her.

Austin put his hands out in a surrendered position and slowly moved toward his wife.

"Robin, this is not what you think, I swear to God. You *have* to believe me."

Robin grabbed her aunt's hand, trying to rush her to the door. But she wouldn't budge.

"Someone needs to tell me what's going on," Joanne demanded.

Austin turned as the two men he was with in the parking lot came through the front door. He turned back to Robin's ashen, sweaty face.

"Robin, listen to me, Honey. I have to tell you something very important that you probably won't believe; but you have to hear me out." Austin pleaded.

Tears continued an endless stream down her face. She felt broken and confused. Joanne's head swiveled back and forth from Robin to Austin, wondering what was happening.

Austin tried to inch forward, but Robin screamed. "Don't you dare come any further!"

He swallowed hard, looking worn down and broken himself.

"Listen, I don't know what's going on here, but someone needs to get to explaining real fast," Joanne pushed.

"Aunt Joanne, please have a seat. I need to share this with both of you."

Joanne didn't budge. Austin lowered his head. It was a while before he spoke again. Robin sat with her hands cupping her elbows as more tears began fall.

"I love you both more than I could ever try to explain. But the truth is I haven't been completely honest with either of you." He looked back at his friends. Then he said, "I'm an agent for the CIA, and these two men are Agents Sidwell and Nettles."

The men nodded, and Agent Nettles removed his ball cap.

"I know this all seems crazy, so I'll do my best to help you understand. I work for a division of the CIA called the Cavity. We're an underground division assigned to extremely high profile security cases. About four years ago, I was put on the case of Kevin Archer, AKA Kevin Dennison. Agent Nettles was brought in three years ago and Agent Sidwell, about a month ago.

"Robin, this man was assigned to protect you, not follow you around," he pointed to Agent Sidwell. "We got a tip that Kevin's lawyers were working to overturn the judge's ruling and possibly get him out of prison. We put Sidwell in place as a precaution."

"Ma'am, I'm sorry if I frightened you. I guess I need to do a better job when I'm tailing someone," said the agent.

"The hang up calls you've been getting were from Kevin. He was just trying to get you wound up, because he knew he'd be released soon," Austin explained.

Joanne looked over at her niece, who didn't even lift her head. Austin made his way over to the loveseat and cautiously sat down beside her. Her trembling body leaned away from him.

"That man tried to kill us in the park," Robin said, referring to agent Nettles.

"No, Honey, he didn't." Austin looked up and said, "Can I have a minute alone with my wife?"

The two agents obliged and exited through the front door. Joanne stood watch like a sentinel and didn't budge.

"Aunt Joanne, would you mind?" Austin asked warmly.

The woman looked down at her niece. After a while Robin nodded, giving her approval. Joanne grabbed Noodles by the collar and headed down the hall.

Austin tried to put his hand on Robin's knee, but she jerked it away.

He sighed and continued. "Like I was saying, he was never going to kill us that night, Honey. We set up a sting for Kevin to hire Nettles as the hit man when we heard he was scouting for people to take you out."

Robin's confused head shook from side to side, and she put her palms on her temples.

"Then why did he shoot you?" she asked through

quivering lips.

"We had to make the situation seem as genuine as we possibly could. We couldn't afford for Kevin to suspect that anything foul was going on. I volunteered to take the hit."

Austin opened his shirt and showed her his wounds.

"Look. The bullet was a clean through and through—on purpose. Nettles was a marksman in the Marines. He's like a surgeon with a gun. I knew I'd be okay. He's the reason why you weren't harmed at all."

"If you call fractured ribs and a concussion unharmed," she said quietly.

Austin looked away. "He and I did have some words about how rough he was with you that night; but again Robin, we had to make the situation seem as real as possible."

"Why didn't you just tell me, Austin?"

"I would have, Robin, but that would have compromised the whole case."

She sank back into the loveseat and tried to catch the questions darting through her mind.

"Are we even *married*?" she asked aggressively as she stood up.

"Yes, Honey, we are. Not only did I risk my life for you, but I also risked my job. I could have been fired for marrying you, but I didn't care. Robin, I fell in love with you, and nothing in the world was going to take that away."

"How can you say you love me, Austin?" she asked,

heat moving across her face. "I don't even know who *you* are. Everything about us is a lie. The way we met, the job you have, our whole relationship, everything!"

"No, Robin, that's not true at all!" He stood up. "My love for you is completely real. Yeah, maybe we didn't meet by chance at a coffee shop, and maybe I don't go off to work at a law firm every day, but I am still the same person."

He took a step closer. "I'm the same man you fell in love with. I'm the same man who watches you when you sleep at night because you look so beautiful. And I'm the same man who'd do anything on earth to make you happy."

Robin paced across the room with one hand on her hip and one on her forehead.

"So, did you marry me as a part of a plan for your job?" she asked, looking into his eyes for the first time.

"I told you already, Robin. No. I married you because I love you. That had nothing to do with this case."

Robin kept pacing as more questions popped into her head.

"Look, let me get rid of the guys, so you and I can talk some more about everything. I just need to let them know that things with us are okay."

"That would be just another lie coming out of your mouth, Austin, because everything with us is certainly not *okay*."

Her angry eyes seared through him and felt like a

thousand blades.

"Maybe you need to stay away for a few days." She turned her face from him. "I need some time to clear my head."

"Robin, please don't—"

"Austin, just go! I'll talk to you when I'm ready."

Austin saw the pain in her eyes and didn't want to make it worse. Reluctantly, he agreed to give her what she'd asked.

He backed away slowly and finally walked out the door.

Robin found herself standing in the doorway of her aunt's room. Joanne patted the space next to her on the bed. Robin slowly walked over. Feeling weak and exhausted, she laid her head in Joanne's lap like she did when she was a little girl. Tears seeped out of the corners of her eyes. She didn't have the strength to wipe them away.

"You keep going like this, and I'm gonna feel like I wet myself," Joanne joked.

Robin smiled dimly while her aunt wiped the tears from her face.

"Listen here; I know you must feel confused and as crazy as a Bessie Bug. I wish I could wave a magic wand and make things better, but I can't. This is another tough storm that you're just going to have to weather."

"I've been weathering storms my whole life. Everyone I love has been taken away from me. My parents, my daughter, my best friend and now my husband; they've all been ripped away. For years I pushed past all the grief by throwing myself into my work. Some days I felt hollow, like a shell walking around with a *business mogul* mask slapped on so that I could somewhat resemble an actual person. I met Austin, and he made me feel like a human being again." Robin sat up. "Now look at where we are. I'm so tired of these horrible things happening."

"You have every right to be tired, Baby. But then what? What happens after being tired? You can't just crawl away in a hole somewhere and never face your problems. With any journey, you're going to encounter roadblocks and traffic jams all along the way. But the objective is to keep moving forward."

"How do I do that? I'm married to a man that I don't even know. How do I move forward with him? He couldn't even be truthful with me."

"Austin is still your husband. I know that what he did seems despicable, but you really have to look beyond what he *didn't* do, and focus on what he *did* do—which was take the chance to fall in love with you."

"Aunt Joanne," Robin sounded surprised, "it sounds like you've completely taken his side. Yeah, he fell in love with me, and that's great. But he also got out of bed every morning for the past three years and has walked out that door to a hidden life that I knew nothing about."

"I am always going to be on *your* side, Robin. But what I honestly feel is that Austin did what he had to do so that he could be on your side, too. He's not the first person on this earth to keep a valuable secret to himself, and he won't be the last."

To Robin, the statement seemed to have a tinge of guilt in it, making her momentarily question if her aunt was hiding secrets, too.

Robin suddenly stood up, agitated with everything. She didn't feel like discussing anything more or listening to another word of advice. Joanne watched her walk out the door briskly and close it behind herself.

*

After driving for nearly an hourly, Robin's GPS system alerted her that the final turn for her destination was coming up. She located the address and found a parking spot right out front. Getting out of the car, she stretched and massaged her tired eyes. Then she walked around to the back of her vehicle, retrieving her luggage from the trunk.

"You are about as stubborn as your aunt. I told you to call me as soon as you pulled up, so I could come out to help you with those."

Robin looked up and smiled as her baby brother came down the walk. Robert picked his sister up and swung her around in a bear hug.

"How is it that I'm your *big* sister, but I've got to stand on my tippy toes just to hug you?" She shook her head. "How are you?" she asked, pinching his cheeks — a gesture that he hated.

"I'm fine," he swatted her hands away. "Now, are

you going to let me help you with these bags, or do I have to put you in a Boston Crab and make you beg for mercy?"

She held her hands up. He plucked up the heavy bags with no problem. Robin slammed the trunk closed and followed him up the walkway. After making their way through the front door of his condo, Robin embraced her brother again. She was glad to see him. "So, Bub, how's life post-MIT treating you?"

Robert had recently received a Master's degree in Electrical Engineering and Computer Science from the esteemed institute in Massachusetts. "It's a bit of an adjustment. Life on the east coast is a lot different than here in the Midwest. I'm happy to be back in Michigan where I can eat Coney dogs and drink pop," he chuckled. "How's Anchewy doing?"

When Robert was a little boy, he had a hard time saying "Aunt Joanne," instead pronouncing it "Anchewy." After all these years, the name still stuck.

"That old ox is just fine. I'm surprised she hasn't been out here to see you yet."

"I told her to give me some time to get settled in, and that when I did, I'd invite her to stay with me for a little while."

"She'd have a conniption if she knew I was here right now. On my way up, I called and told her I would be staying with a friend for a few days, but I didn't say who. I just needed to be away from everything."

Robin went quiet, thinking of all the things she was trying to run away from at home.

"I saw the news yesterday," Robert said, referring to Kevin Dennison's release.

"Unfortunately, so did I." She went quiet again.

Robin being at her brother's home was proof enough of the stress she was under. Robert didn't want to waste the visit dwelling on those negative things, so he said, "Who cares about that? You're here now, so let's just have a good time and bring you back in from the ledge."

He threw his arm over his sister's shoulder, pretending to give her a hug. She immediately jumped up and pummeled him with a sofa pillow when she realized he'd stuck a wet finger in her ear. Playfully, they tussled back and forth. Her brother was just the therapy she needed.

Robert's phone rang. Robin let her brother up to answer it.

"Hello?" he answered, still laughing at his sister. "Oh, hi, Aunt Joanne."

Both their eyes grew large. Robert put his finger to his lips.

"No, I haven't talked to her."

He made a face at the lie.

"I really don't think you should worry. She probably just needs to blow off some steam for a little while. She'll be fine. Okay, I will. Love you, too. Bye."

Robert hung up the phone and turned to his sister. "I can't believe you've got me lying to her. And I can't believe she believed me."

—

"You've always been able to get her to believe anything you say. It's me that she sees right through. Thanks for not telling her I'm here. I just wanted to be away for a bit. Austin and I are going through some private things in our relationship. I needed a breather from that and this Kevin situation. You know her; she likes to talk about a situation until she's convinced that you're feeling better about it. That's just not what I need right now."

"I totally understand. Just, at least, send her a text or something to let her know you're okay. She sounded really worried."

"I will."

"Robin, can I ask you a question?"

"Of course you can."

"How'd you get hooked up with this jerk?"

"Which jerk are you referring to? The one I married, or the one I pissed off?"

"This Kevin person. He's definitely not someone I would have ever picked you to be with. He's low down and not your speed at all."

Robin ran her hand along his bearded face. "Honestly, it didn't start off this way. Kevin was a funny and charismatic guy. We used to have great times together. But as soon as he found out the baby was sick, and that I wasn't going to terminate the pregnancy, it changed something inside of him."

Robert shook his head, fidgeting with his fingers.

"What do you think Mom and Dad would have said

about all of this?" he asked.

Robin lowered her eyes and sighed. "I'm not sure. Sometimes I wish they were here so I could talk to them about everything and get their opinions. But other times, it's kind of a relief that they don't have to experience the heartache, you know? Even though I was only a mother for a few days, I know how loving a child so much can break your heart when you know that they're hurting. I wouldn't want that for mom and dad."

Robin looked at her brother who was quiet but still fidgeting. She asked him, "Do you think about them a lot?"

"I was young when they passed away. I try hard sometimes to dig up memories, but they are all so foggy. I thought I had lots of memories, but then I realized those were just things I'd heard you and Aunt Joanne saying about them. I still pray for them and ask them to watch over me, though. What about you?"

"Just like you, my memory is a little foggy."

"What do you remember most?" Robert asked.

"Well, with Dad, it was his laugh. He would laugh so loud and with the deepest voice. It always reminded me of thunder," she smiled. "With Mom, it's probably her always being in the kitchen, baking. I would sit and stare at her all the time. She was so beautiful, with the most delicate hands. She always painted her nails a different color every day," she smiled again. "The two of them together were amazing. I don't think I ever heard them have an argument. They were so loving and happy."

"I wish I could remember those things. You're so lucky to have specific details about them and their personalities. Vaguely, I remember being carried around on Mom's hip and Dad's loud footsteps charging through the house."

"They were great parents, and they would be very proud if they could see you right now."

She pressed her cheek to his.

"They would be proud of you too, Robin. They'll help you get through this. I know they will."

The two hugged as they both thought about their parents.

"What do you say we go freshen up and then go out for a nightcap?" Robert suggested.

Robin smiled and nodded.

*

A black sedan pulled up to the curb in a dingy part of town. Agent Nettles stepped inside.

"Teddy, my man, how's it going?" Kevin Dennison said to agent Nettles, as the two men shook hands.

"Mr. Dennison," Nettles nodded.

Kevin pulled out a cigar and leaned back in his seat.

"Light?" he asked the agent. After Nettles shook his head, Kevin tucked the cigar back into his pocket. "I heard these things are bad for you anyway."

Nettles sat across from the unsuspecting man and kept a stone face. Austin, who was miles away inside the Cavity home base of the CIA, chewed on the end of a toothpick as he listened to the entire conversation. The sound of Dennison's voice made his skin crawl.

"So, Mr. Dennison, why did you want to see me?" asked Nettles.

"Why the rush, my friend? It's been a while since we checked in with each other. Can't I just enjoy seeing your face? You've been on the run since you did that hit for me three years ago — even though you botched it. But I'm not one to hold a grudge," Kevin smiled.

Nettles didn't flinch. He kept his eyes locked on Kevin's and was prepared to take him out if he made a wrong move.

"But you know what? You're still a good man. I have another job lined up for you. This one is on a much smaller scale, so hopefully you'll be able to get it right."

Nettles sat eyeballing Kevin, waiting to hear the details. Instead he felt the car come to a stop.

"Get out," Kevin ordered.

Austin and the other CIA agents listening in were now on high alert. They'd hoped Nettles' cover hadn't somehow been blown.

"This isn't my stop." Nettles said calmly.

"Yes, but it's as far as this ride goes," Kevin smirked. "I'll contact you soon with details for the next gig. Don't go disappearing on me."

Kevin opened the door, and Agent Nettles slid out.

Kevin was behaving oddly. He had all of the agents on edge.

Hours later, Austin sat on a bench in the locker room and began to change his clothes. A few other agents filed in, chatting quietly about their day. Agent Nettles opened the locker next to Austin's and slid the wire from around his neck.

"Great job handling yourself out there with Dennison," Austin said. "You played it real cool."

Nettles slid his shirt off over his head. "We're too deep in for me to lose my cool. I'm not sure why he was acting so strange, but I'm sure we'll figure it out; me and Bessie Lou."

Bessie Lou was his nickel plated Sig Sauer X-Five that was locked and loaded at all times.

"How are things on the home front?" asked Nettles.

"Not good. Haven't seen Robin in days. She's not taking my calls."

"I wouldn't worry about it too much. These things take time. Just hang in there, and it will all work out," offered Nettles.

Austin appreciated the man's words, hoping he was right.

*

Spending time with her brother was wonderful, but Robin could no longer run away from her problems at home. She'd been away for almost a week and knew she needed to figure out her next move. Not working things out with Austin was honestly not what she wanted. But she didn't know how she'd ever be able to trust him or even how to start fresh with his true identity.

Just a few weeks ago she was living a quiet life with her husband and their loveable dog. Now she was the wife of a CIA operative and on the worst enemy list of an organized crime leader. She couldn't help but chuckle at the irony.

Her brother, although younger, was wise enough to bring up a good point. "If you have questions that only Austin can answer, then why aren't you giving him the opportunity to?"

Her only retort was, "How do I know that his answers won't be more lies?" Robert pointed out that she owed it to herself to try and find out. After several rounds of debating, she decided to give her husband a call.

The phone rang a few times. She thought it was about to go to his voicemail. At the last minute, Austin finally picked up.

"Hello?" he answered.

"Hi," she said softly.

Austin felt like he could breathe a little better now that he'd heard her voice. "Hi to you, too. I'm so glad you finally called, Robin."

She should have replied by saying something kind, but couldn't pull it out of herself. "I've been thinking a lot about things. I feel like I need to get down to the bottom of who you really are."

"Robin, you know who I am. I am your hus—"

"Just save it for right now, Austin. Meet me at the

Haberdashery Market in Royal Oak tomorrow at noon. We'll talk it out then. Okay?"

"Alright, I will. But Robin, just please know that I love you very much."

"See you tomorrow." She hung up.

*

The Haberdashery Market was only open during the fall season. It was a strip of booths that sold everything from fresh cider and donuts to squash-filled gift baskets. There was an outdoor eating area where locals gathered and sampled the goods from each booth.

Austin got there thirty minutes early. He wanted to be sure that they had the perfect area to sit while they talked. The anticipation of knowing that his wife was coming made him extremely nervous and anxious. He didn't know what she'd have to say and tried to prevent his mind from thinking the worst.

Walking through the crowd, he saw Robin looking around, searching for his face. He wanted to stand on top of the wooden picnic table and scream out her name. Instead, he waved his arm in the air until she saw him. The couple suddenly stood a few mere feet away from each other, with worlds of distance between them. Neither knew what to say, so they just stood, looking dumbfounded and nervous.

"How about a picture?" asked one of the photographers on the Haberdashery strip.

The couple looked at each other and then stepped closer together in front of the camera.

"Alright; on three. One. Two. Three. Cheese!"

The camera flashed on their insincere smiles.

"What a nice couple you make," said the photographer.

He handed them a ticket and told them where to pick up the photo. The photographer then tipped his hat and went on to the next customer.

The strip was crowded, and suddenly, it didn't seem like the best place to have a heart to heart.

Austin nervously turned to his wife. "You mind if we sit in the truck?"

"I'll follow you."

As they walked forward, Robin instinctively grabbed for his hand, but stopped herself. Out of the corner of his eye, he'd seen her pull her hand away, and it hurt him to know that she felt the need to. He opened the door for his wife, then jogged around to the other side and slid into the driver seat.

"So," he said.

"So."

He slid his hand along the side of her cheek, and she closed her eyes. His touch was gentle and warm. She hadn't realized how much she'd missed him until then.

After a long silence, she took his hand in hers, tracing her finger along the inside of his palm. There was a scar on his inner thumb; her finger danced over it slowly. Abruptly, she stopped. "Did you really get this scar from falling off your bike when you were little? Or was it from something else?"

They both knew what *something else* implied.

"I was eight years old, and Jimmie Thompson was pissed that I'd beaten him in a bike race. Laila Turner was his girlfriend at the time, and my winning made her notice me. He kicked the bike right out from under me, and I fell, palms first, onto the ground."

Robin rubbed the scar gently.

"What about this one?" she asked about a small scar on his chin.

"Fell off the monkey bars because of my sweaty palms. Laila Turner was at the park that day, too," he smiled.

Unconsciously, she smiled, and it made him melt.

"Look, Babe, I am still the man you love. When I leave the house every morning, I don't go to a law firm and try cases. I go do my job catching bad guys and keeping the world safe. I may have lied about those things, but I am still *me*."

"But why, Austin? Why did you have to lie? Couldn't you have just told me from the beginning what you do for a living? I would have been able to accept it better."

"Listen to what you're saying, Robin. There was no way I could come up to you and say, 'Hi, my name is Austin, and I've been assigned to watch you closely, because we think your daughter's father might try to kill you.' That just isn't reality."

"And what we have isn't reality either, Austin. How can it be real when it's all based on lies?"

"It's not all based on lies, Robin. I was assigned the case to protect you, yes. But everything else is real. My love is real, our life is real, and how I feel is real. The job that I go to everyday doesn't change that."

"How did you even get into this agent thing anyway? Where do you go to sign up for the freakin' CIA?"

Austin exhaled and tried to find the quickest, most simple answer that he could give. Unfortunately, there wasn't one.

"You know my dad left my mom and me when I was younger. He disappeared, and we never knew whether he was dead or alive. I ended up meeting a man in college who said he had valuable information that might help me in my search for him. I attracted his attention when logging into a chat room for people in my same position looking for a missing person.

"We met at a restaurant one night, and basically, as soon as I walked in, he started handing me drink after drink. We were laughing and having a good time, just swapping stories. I told him about the information I'd been able to dig up on my father, which at that point wasn't much. All of a sudden, he goes into this spiel about President Truman signing a national security act back in 1947. I assumed he was drunk, but after hearing all the things he was saying, it began to make sense.

"He went on about how The CIA has essentially become responsible for the safe harbor of everyone in the United States. The main focus is to depress foreign intelligence and assist the president with making decisions related to our safety. Well, there are many underground branches created with individual focuses. One in particular, called the Cavity, has a focus on missing persons and high profile security, and we also dabble in foreign trading."

Robin looked confused as all hell. Austin squeezed her hand and continued.

"The man who approached me back in college was David Bells. Remember, I took you to a barbeque at his house the year that we met?"

Robin nodded.

"He's not a partner at some law firm. He's actually the commander of the CIA's Cavity division. His expertise was in the detail of missing persons. The truth of the matter is that quite a few missing persons aren't actually missing. Lots of them have been recruited by terrorist cells to act on their behalf.

"What the terrorists do is basically abduct people and then brainwash them. They tell them that if they try to escape or contact the authorities, their families will be harmed. Nine times out of ten, the abducted person ends up disappearing and taking on these roles as operatives for foreign intelligence, just to spare the lives of their families. They are sort of downloaded into society and given tasks to carry out.

"It's a pretty effective tool, because when Americans think of terrorists, they think of someone foreign. No one would ever suspect their next-door neighbor or local handyman of being a terrorist. So essentially these foreign cells were able to find the most vulnerable point on the body of the American society, and they've exposed it."

Robin didn't think she'd blinked the entire time he was speaking. It was like he was telling her about life on another planet. Although fascinating, there was a slight twinge of fear about this whole other world that millions of people — including herself — were unaware of.

Austin took a deep breath and went on.

"When the CIA learns of a missing person, particularly ones with military backgrounds like my father, they automatically begin a search to locate them. The ones who are found are monitored to see if they've been recruited by one of the terrorist cells.

"By monitoring them, we are able to keep a steady hand on the prevention of terrorist acts on American soil. So," he exhaled, "when I started up the search for my father, the CIA took notice. After getting to know me better, Commander Bells decided that I could be a useful member of the team. Said I reminded him of himself when he was younger, and was impressed with my investigative abilities."

Robin sat back and rested her chin on her knuckles, digesting the information.

"So, did you ever find out what happened with your father?"

Austin nodded.

"My father isn't a terrorist," he smiled. "Just a scum bag. He moved to Wichita, Kansas and has been living there with his mistress. I have two little sisters I've never even met."

Robin's mind was blown. Hearing what Austin had

to say was surreal. One thing she noticed was that when he spoke about the CIA and their history, there was a spark in his eye that she'd never seen. He obviously loved his work.

Austin looked at his wife. "Well, how do you feel?"

Even he wasn't fully aware of what he meant by the question.

She sighed. "I feel better knowing the truth."

He slid his hand along her cheek and leaned down, pressing his lips to hers. Their interaction was tender and fragile, like it was the first time they'd touched.

Robin shifted in her seat. "I have another question."

"Ask me anything."

"How were you assigned to Kevin's case? He was never a missing person. Is he involved with terrorists somehow?"

"Not exactly, Honey. It's a long story, but Kevin's father was involved in smuggling illegal contraband from foreign countries. Drugs, weapons, things like that. This, of course, is a matter of national security, which touches lightly in our sector. Commander Bells worked on his father's case years ago. When I was brought in, I took over Kevin's case."

Before going further into his explanation, his cell phone rang, and he grunted out an agitated breath. He lifted his index finger and mouthed the words, "One minute."

In the shuffle of everything, Robin had forgotten to tell him about her meeting with Kevin's sister. There was much ground needing to be covered, and she felt like it would take a lifetime to hash it all out.

Robin sat back in her seat, her mind reeling. Knowing the details of why Austin had to be dishonest made the sting of it all seem not as harsh. Her palm gently rested on his knee, while he listened intently to the caller on the other end.

"I'll be there as soon as I can."

Slowly he took the phone down from his ear and slid it into his jacket pocket.

"That call was about work. I've got a few things I need to go and take care of."

Robin didn't respond, she just leaned her head on his shoulder and held his hand. "Thank you," she whispered.

"For what?"

"For coming here and explaining everything to me. Not only that, but thank you for what you do. Kevin probably would have killed me a long time ago, if you weren't here to protect me."

"You never have to thank me for that, Robin. I protect you because you are my wife, not because of my job."

She nodded because, deep inside, she believed every word he'd just said.

"I'll probably be out late working on this project, so I'll stay at the hotel another night. But if it's alright with you, I'd like to come home tomorrow."

"Home is exactly where you belong." Robin smiled.

Then she kissed her husband tenderly.

After she got out of the vehicle, Austin watched her walk through the crowd until she finally disappeared. Before heading off to his job, he took a minute to get their photo from the photo booth. In exchange for his ticket, and twenty bucks the photographer handed him a glossy print of him and his wife, smiling at the camera. He breathed a sigh of relief, feeling like things between them would be okay. Tucking the photo into his shirt pocket, he hoisted himself into his truck and sped away.

Chapter Three

Being out of the office for so long put Robin behind in her work. She spent the majority of her first day back returning phone calls and emails, while Carol helped get her up to speed.

"I've organized piles on your desk in order. These need signatures, these need your approval, and those you'll need to provide figures for," she pointed to each stack.

"Carol, you are an absolute lifesaver, my dear."

"Just remember that when bonus time rolls around," she winked. "I'm gonna head out. Charles and I are going to see Cirque du Soleil tonight."

"I hope you have a great time. You certainly deserve it. On your way out, let Cassidy know that I'll be ready in a few minutes. We're making a run to the mall."

"Don't do too much damage there," Carol warned and marched out the door.

A short while later, Robin and Cassidy pulled up to Somerlane Mall and started toward the entrance.

"Tracey's going to pick me up in a bit. We'll be out pretty late, so I'll probably end up staying at her place again tonight," said Cassidy.

"That'll be fine. I won't be here too long myself. I'm just going to run in and pick up a few things."

Cassidy's phone rang with a call from Aunt Joanne.

"Hello? Yeah, she's right here. I'm not sure, let me ask her."

She slid her hand over the receiver. "Aunt Joanne wants to know why you aren't answering your cell phone."

Robin checked her pockets and purse, realizing it wasn't with her.

"I must have left it at the office."

Cassidy got back on the line. After a series of Mmm Hmms and Okays, she slid her phone shut. "She wants you to pick up some dog food for Noodles on your way home."

"She hunted me down just to say that?"

"That, and she said to put a hat on your head because it's chilly out."

Robin shook her head at the worrisome woman, and they made their way into the mall.

*

The swishing of her shopping bags and the *click clack* of her high heel shoes were the only sounds that could be heard as Robin made her way through the parking lot. It was nearly pitch black outside. The dimly lit space seemed hollow without the bustle of customers rushing about. She hadn't meant to stay as long as she did. But the retail therapy from shopping helped get her mind off of everything else she had going on.

Austin was probably worried sick about her. When she left her office earlier that day, she never even called to let him know when to expect her home. The pricey heels she was wearing were beginning to wear out their welcome on her feet, so as soon as she spotted her car up ahead, she instinctively picked up the pace.

Suddenly, the sound of footsteps behind her fell into synch with her own. Trying to inconspicuously peek back over her shoulder, Robin gripped her car keys so that they jutted out from between her knuckles. She may have been overreacting but figured she'd take the precaution just in case. Her vehicle was just within reach, and as she nervously grabbed for the door handle, the steps behind her turned into a full out sprint in her direction.

Her heart leapt into her throat as panic surged up her spine. There was no time left for her to run. Robin swung around as her balled fists came up swinging wildly for protection.

"You're a rotten egg!" a young woman screamed playfully to her boyfriend when she slapped the door of their car.

"No fair, you cheated."

He lovingly pulled her in for a kiss, and they snuggled on the edge of the car.

Robin let out a breath, flattening her back against her car door. She pressed a palm to her forehead and chuckled at herself for being paranoid.

Good going, Robin, you almost keyed those kids to death because you're a stressed out, psycho, scaredy cat.

She watched the young couple get into their vehicle and speed away.

After sliding behind the wheel of her own car, she leaned back on the headrest and closed her eyes. It had been a long day. It was time to retreat to the safety and sanity of her own home. Still shaking her head over her excessive reaction, she slid her key into the ignition and turned the switch.

The car didn't make a sound.

Her eyebrows furrowed deeply. She tried the switch again. Still nothing. This time, she turned the key as far as it would go and pumped the gas pedal, as if that would make a difference.

"Going somewhere, Robin?" a voice asked from her backseat.

Her eyes widened. Before she could let out a scream, a damp cloth was forced over her mouth and nose. Robin's rigid body fought desperately to break away from the grip. After several seconds of writhing around, to no avail, she gradually slumped forward. The backseat passenger calmly leaned back and dialed a number on his cell phone. As he waited for his accomplice to arrive, he hummed the tune *Hush Little*

Baby in between puffing away on a cigar.

Several minutes later, two men—along with Robin's unconscious body—made their way down the potholed road of I 75 North.

"Sweet dreams, Robin..." Kevin Dennison stroked her hair.

*

Joanne had fallen asleep on the sofa. When she woke up it was just after one o'clock in the morning. Almost every light in the house was still on. She went from room to room, turning them all off. After securing every door in the house, she made her way upstairs.

Before going to bed she checked on her niece to wish her sweet dreams. She tapped lightly on the bedroom door and didn't get an answer. She knocked more firmly the second time, and the door creaked open. The room was quiet, the bed still made.

Joanne checked the guest bedrooms to see if Robin was there. Finding nothing but empty rooms she dialed Cassidy's cell phone.

After two rings, the young woman picked up.

"Hello!" Cassidy shouted over music blaring in the background.

"It's me, Aunt Joanne."

"Hi, Joanne!" The Jell-O shots she'd been slurping all night had her tipsy.

"Have you heard from Robin?"

"What?!" she shouted.

"Have you heard from Robin?!" Aunt Joanne shouted, too, but more from worry than the loud music.

"No, I haven't seen her since we were at the mall earlier."

"Did she happen to say where she was going after she left the mall?"

"All she said was that she wouldn't be there long, and that she was tired and would head home soon."

Joanne sat down on the edge of the bed and immediately knew something was wrong.

*

Robin's eyes slowly fluttered as she tried to shake away the grogginess. Extreme pressure on her head made her eyelids heavy and difficult to open. A ragged strip of cloth bound her mouth, and zip tie cuffs secured her hands behind her. From the backseat of her own car, Robin stared at the backs of two men's heads.

She tried speaking the words *help me*, but the gag held her tongue.

"Rise and shine, sleepy head." Kevin beamed from the passenger seat.

Robin's eyes widened unnaturally when she saw his smiling face.

"Surprised to see me? You shouldn't be. You know I can only stay away from you for so long, Robin. We're soul mates," he said melodramatically, placing his hand over his heart. The skin on Robin's body crawled. Kevin turned around in his seat and said, "Don't you just love road trips? I know I do. It's very freeing to drive to an unknown destination without a single care in the world. But it wouldn't be a road trip without singing a song though, right? Oh, I know, how about Bottles of Beer on the Wall? I'll start it off," he cleared his throat.

"Ninety-nine bottles of beer on the wall, ninety-nine bottles of beeeer — come on Robin, I can't hear you."

Frightened and dazed, Robin's head swirled at the sound of his psychotic voice.

"That gag in your mouth is really affecting your singing, Robin. Ugh, and you've managed to drool right through it," Kevin said, disgusted. "Don't be too embarrassed though; drooling is just one of the many side effects of the happy juice I doused you with. It's a little somethin' called Succinylcholine. Did you know that Sux is one third of the cocktail used in lethal injections? Pretty cool, huh? I had to be careful not to give you too much. We wouldn't want your heart and lungs to conk out on us, now would we?" he asked, with a devilish grin. "Then you'd miss out on all the fun I have planned for us."

Robin's body trembled, and she didn't know if it was from being drugged or from the sheer terror.

"Relax, Sweetheart. We've got a long ride ahead of us, so go on and get comfy. Well, as comfy as you can, given your current situation." He mimicked having bound hands like hers. With the palm of his hand, he shoved her in the forehead, causing her body to thrash backward. Feeling weak, Robin leaned her head against the window and tried to calm the panicked thoughts that thudded against her skull. The sheer effort was exhausting.

An eerie silence filled the car and it terrified her. She couldn't remember how she'd managed to get herself into the situation and had no clue how she'd get herself out. She pictured Aunt Joanne worrying herself sick about where she was. The stress of finding out that she'd been kidnapped would probably kill her aunt. *Just another unfortunate bonus for Kevin,* she thought. Things with Austin were just beginning to look up, but now, it didn't mean a thing. Her life would probably be over in a matter of hours — or minutes, for all she knew. Robin's eyes closed slowly as she took in the last few moments of peace and quiet that she'd probably ever have — minus the peace.

After a few miles, Kevin loaded a disc into her CD player and turned up the volume. Robin curled into a tight ball while Kevin hummed along to Carl Orff's *O' Fortuna.*

Chapter Four

They had been driving all night. The sun was beginning to rise when Robin came to again. A glimmer of hope flickered through her mind, when she thought about the other vehicles that would pass by and see her. That hope was quickly dashed when she realized that her back windows were tinted. Even though she could see out, no one could see in.

The vehicle made a series of turns and soon slowed to a stop. Her dilated eyes strained to see if she recognized the area. She didn't. The two men got out, leaving Robin alone in the backseat.

A few minutes went by. Suddenly the door she was leaning on was jerked open. Robin fell out of the car hitting the side of her face against the pavement.

"Oopsie," Kevin chuckled "You've got to be a little more careful there, Sweetheart."

Robin groaned, her face throbbing with pain. Kevin and his accomplice grabbed her under the arms and dragged her along a dirt path. The path eventually led to a set of stairs going underground. Her feet banged lifelessly against each stair in spite of trying her damndest to make them move on their own. With each step they took, she felt her face swell more, and was convinced that her cheekbone had been fractured.

Finally at the bottom, they dropped her in the center of the cement room. Kevin's accomplice immediately walked back up the stairs. Robin wanted to call out for help, but knew that there wasn't another person around for miles.

Kevin came to where she lay crumpled and kneeled down in front of her. He quietly stared at her. She listened to him breath in deeply through his nostrils and out through his mouth. His eyes were closed as he continued this breathing pattern repetitiously. It reminded her of the hang up calls she'd gotten from him.

Without warning, Kevin grabbed Robin's hair by the roots, violently sliding her across the floor. He flipped her onto her stomach and pulled something from his pocket. She heard the sound of a switchblade being flipped open and prepared for the impact.

Clip!

She felt no pain. Instead, her hands were now able to move freely. Kevin went back to silently staring at her trembling face. His hand reached out to touch her. She flinched in response. A wide smile spread across his face. He seemed pleased with her fear.

"Go ahead and relax." He settled himself Indian style in front of her.

She didn't move. One hand rested protectively over her head. She clutched at her throbbing cheek with the other.

"You're so beautiful, you know that, Robin? Just a lovely woman. And your bone structure is to die for." He nudged her swollen cheek with his knuckle.

"Oh, Robin," he sighed, "We're going to have such fun over these next few days. Or weeks. Hell, it might even be months, who knows? We've got nothing but time, my dear. Nothing but time."

Robin began to feel nauseous and trembled again. This time she knew it was from fear.

"Hey, I was thinking I would pay Aunt Joanne a visit. You know, keep her company. I'm sure she's going to be lonely without you around."

Anger swelled inside Robin when she thought of him hurting her aunt. She lunged at him wildly.

Kevin grabbed Robin by the hair again and smashed her cheek onto the cellar floor. This time, she heard the bone crack, undoubtedly confirming that it was broken. He leaned down close to her ear. "I'm guessing she'll like it rough, just like this. Unlike you," he said, and let her hair go.

Her hands instinctively cupped back over her face, which now felt like it had exploded.

"You were never really much fun in the boudoir, Robin, do you know that? I never knew why you let all of that sexiness go to waste. The sex we had was stuffy and flat out boring," he rolled his eyes. "Word to the wise, Honey; the missionary position is sooo...Adam and Eve. Don't you think?"

Robin looked in his eyes and, for the first time, didn't feel fearful. She was outright livid and too disgusted to be afraid.

"You look like you have something to say. Do share," he said pretentiously.

Kevin slid the gag down from her mouth with a sick smile on his face. When the cloth was down around her chin, she spat in his face and lifted her arms up to strangle him. With one arm, he was able to swat her away as if she was nothing. He slapped her hard in the mouth and rubbed the back of his hand.

Robin felt like a wild animal, ready to strike again if he came near her.

Kevin pulled a handkerchief from his pocket and wiped the saliva from his face. "You can take the girl out of the 'hood, but you can't take the 'hood out of the girl, I swear."

Robin lunged at him again. This time, he simply stepped out of the way, avoiding her sloppy, unbalanced aggression.

"You're making this so much fun for me, Robin, you really are."

He suddenly turned and started for the stairs.

Robin screamed out, "You can't leave me here!"

He kept walking as if she hadn't said a word. At the top of the stairs, he turned back. "See you soon, Robin—or not." The thick door to the cellar slammed shut and Robin was left abandoned.

*

Austin hadn't heard from his wife at all the day before. He was suddenly feeling anxious. She was supposed to call and let him know what time to come home since she wanted to plan a romantic welcome back for him. Things had gone smoothly during their talk, but the deafening silence now made him rethink it all.

Every few minutes, he checked his cell phone.

"No new messages," announced his voicemail.

"I know, A-hole." He tossed the phone onto the bed. This was a feeling he hadn't felt in years, probably not since high school. Waiting by the phone, wondering if the girl he liked was thinking of him like he was thinking of her. It wouldn't have surprised him if pimples started popping up all over his face.

"Come on, Robin. Just please call me, Babe."

Suddenly, Austin's phone rang. Seeing his home number on the screen made him feel like he'd just won the lottery.

"I couldn't take another second without hearing

your voice," he answered. As he listened to the voice on the other end, all the happiness he felt a second ago was replaced with confusion.

"No, she's not here, Joanne. I thought she was there at the house with you." Immediately he went into work mode. "When was the last time you heard from her?" Joanne gave him every detail he asked for. He multitasked while listening. Austin had taken his secure work phone from his pocket and was already dialing a series of numbers. He held a phone to each of his ears; the look on his face was stone.

"Put me on the line with Bells—now."

Joanne cut in, asking who Bells was.

"Aunt Joanne, I'll have to call you back." He hung up on her.

The commander of the CIA's Cavity division was on the line in a matter of seconds. "Bells," he answered.

"It's Malone. My wife never made it home last night. I know Dennison had something to do with it."

"Dammit, Malone, are you serious?! Where the hell was Sidwell? Wasn't he assigned to tail her?"

"That much I haven't found out yet, but I will definitely get to the bottom of it."

The veins in Austin's neck bulged. It was an indicator that heads were going to roll.

"Wait. What makes you think she's missing? Aren't the two of you separated right now?"

Austin was offended by the question. They were never separated, in his mind, just sorting things through.

"She was supposed to be home last night, but no one has heard from her. It's not like my wife to just disappear and not check in with someone. Especially now that Dennison is loose. Just believe me when I say, he's got something to do with her disappearance."

"I'll contact all field agents to see if anyone has eyes on the Bird."

Kevin's nickname was "Bird" because of his tendency to fly out of trouble.

"You do that. In the meantime, I'll be on my way in."

Austin grabbed his jacket and shot out the door.

*

Hours or minutes passed by. Robin couldn't tell the difference. With no sunlight to gage, the concept of time was just a distant memory for her. She hadn't moved from that spot on the floor ever since Kevin walked away, leaving her trapped.

Dangling above her was a single light bulb attached to a wire in the ceiling. As the dim bulb flickered, it became more of a nuisance than an aid. The windowless room reeked of mildew and animal feces. She looked around just as a rat scampered by her foot. In normal circumstance, it would have scared her witless. Now, she barely flinched. Imprisonment by Kevin was her worst nightmare come true; anything else paled in comparison.

Robin's head still whirled from the drugs in her system. At times she questioned whether or not she was dreaming. Her wrists were sore from having been bound, and although she rubbed them, they still hurt like hell. The drugs had dulled her perceptions drastically. In her mind, she massaged her wrists firmly, but in reality her fingers barely touched them.

Her feet were freezing, and she wondered why she was only wearing one shoe. With her stockinged left foot, she used her big toe to push the $1500 Christian Louboutin heel from her right foot. She figured there was no sense in keeping it on, especially since the heel had broken off, and the open toe did little to keep her foot warm.

Robin looked down spotting a round stain on her dress pants. She couldn't bring herself to acknowledge that what she thought was a puddle of animal urine was really her own. Her head bowed in shame, lulling hazily from side to side. "So this is it, huh? This is how the saga of Robin Malone will end," she said to herself.

Robin looked around the empty room with its dank, moldy walls and began to laugh.

"Well, I sure didn't see this coming!" She laughed harder and harder until her stomach began to hurt.

As if someone had pushed the pause button, her laughing suddenly stopped. A thought of her deceased parents crept in and sobered her up. She became overwhelmed with sadness. Not because of her current situation, but sad because of the loss of her parents. At the time of their deaths, they had been full of life and love. Now, just like theirs, her life would be cut short.

Robin lifted her eyes and saw the image of her parents just as vividly as if they were actually there.

Her mother and father stood holding hands, smiling at their broken daughter. The cellar became her childhood home, and her parents now stood in the middle of the living room. Slowly she laid flat on her back watching the pair slow dance in front of the crackling fireplace.

Her mother's small hand fit perfectly inside her father's. The sweet smell of cinnamon rolls filled the room from the magic that her mother had just worked up in the kitchen. Little Robert ran up and wiggled himself in between the couple. They all swayed back and forth to Billie Holiday's, *God Bless the Child*, the tot standing on his parents' feet.

A genuine smile lit Robin's lips. Her family was the most essential element of her life. She looked to her right and saw Joanne bouncing baby Gabriela up and down on her knee. Austin looked on lovingly, while Noodles playfully ran around in circles. Knowing that she was on the verge of death, Robin quietly accepted her fate while enjoying the non-existent presence of all those who were important to her.

Sluggishly, her eyelids blinked open and closed, her breathing grew more shallow. A single tear leaked out of her eye. Robin mumbled an incoherent prayer.

*

A plain, brown building on the eleven thousandth block of Jefferson Avenue appeared, from the outside, to be an abandoned warehouse. Little did anyone know it was the headquarters for the CIA's Cavity division, hiding in plain sight. Austin sped into the underground garage, parking diagonally in a vertical space. Two exiting agents stared at him, as he charged towards the entrance

Access to the building required a number of biometric checkpoints to confirm his identity. The first checkpoint was a facial recognition scan. Austin stood perfectly still while a neon green laser scanned a gridline pattern over his face. The system compared selected facial features with images in the CIA's database, confirming several matching points. The agent then walked into a small capsule-like booth and initiated the second checkpoint. "Please, state your name," said a flat, computerized female voice.

"Agent Austin Malone," he blurted in a rush.

"I'm sorry. Your name was not recognized. Please state your name," she repeated.

"My name is Agent Austin Malone!" he shouted.

There was a pause for processing. Then, "Please state your Cavity identification number."

Austin grew more frustrated by the second. Each minute that passed was another minute his wife was missing and most likely in harm's way.

"Agent number Alpha Mike 5623917."

"One moment, please." A series of clicks sounded; the system verified Austin's weight and height.

"Welcome, Agent Malone. Access granted."

The chamber opened, and Austin darted to the stairs.

Commander Bells, his stocky build reminiscent of Jesse Ventura, met Austin at the bottom of the stairwell. He slid a wad of smokeless tobacco in between his cheek and gum and tried to keep up with Austin's pace, briefing him while they walked.

"Look, Malone, I'd like to tell you that we've got eyes on the Bird, but that's just not the case. Several agents have made contact with us, but there are three that we have yet to hear from. Nettles is one of them. We're hoping to make contact with them soon."

"Did anything from those agents indicate Dennison was planning something like this?"

"Not a shred."

They entered a room called the Proof where several agents were working on the Dennison case. The room was a large space with scribbled up white boards and pictures all over the walls. Each field agent assigned to the Dennison detail would record his activity and send the information back to the headquarters. Internal agents like Austin would log those findings into the CIA's database.

"I know he's got my wife, Bells. He's probably been planning this since prison. How the hell was he able to get away with something like this without us finding out about it?"

For the first time, Austin felt like he didn't have control over the situation. It scared him.

"Who's to say he planned anything? He's crazy enough to pull this off simply because it's *Tuesday*. But don't worry, if he has her, we will find her."

Still seeing worry on his agent's face, Bells said, "We'll figure this thing out, Malone. We don't have time to be emotional right now. Separate your personal ties to this situation and strap on your work hat. I need you fresh, and I need you alert. You understand? Otherwise, you're off the case. You should be anyway, but you know more than any of these guys, and we need you."

Agent Sidwell came rushing through the door and began to apologize.

"Malone, I can't believe this happened. I tailed her all day! I just left for a little while to get something to drink—"

Austin jumped up and angrily charged the man.

"She needed you, and you were off getting coffee?! I could *kill* you right now!"

Commander Bells tried his best to keep the two men away from each other, but Austin was nearly climbing over him to get a swipe at the negligent agent.

"Did Dennison hire you to do this?!" Austin screamed. "You better hope you didn't sell out on us, I swear to God!"

Several other agents rushed in. It took all of their manpower to keep Austin at bay.

"Get him out of here!" Bells shouted to another set of agents that had just walked in on the commotion. The men dragged Agent Sidwell, yelling his innocence, from the room.

"Let go of me!" Austin shouted. With an angry jerk of his arm, he freed himself.

"Malone, calm down! I'll sort him out later. For now, let's just go get the rat bastard who has your wife, and bring her home."

Austin breathed in angry huffs, trying to redirect his aggression to figuring out what the hell to do next.

*

Robin opened her eyes, barely able to see. She tried to lift her head and move around, but her body felt like it weighed a ton. She was still groggy with an out-of-this-world headache.

"Hello," she called out. Her voice echoed in the dimly lit room. "Is anybody out there?" She meant it as a scream, but it came out as more of a whisper.

Footsteps walked over, and someone knelt in front of her.

"Who are you?" she asked in an almost childlike voice.

She struggled to make out the features of the blurry face. Without a word, the person simply stood up and walked up the stairs, leaving her alone again. Or so she thought. "Please, don't leave me in here. You have to help me. Please," she pleaded, weakly.

Robin's arms were bound behind her back again. She didn't remember how they got that way. She writhed and wiggled, trying to free herself, but to no avail. Her wrists began to bleed from the jarring, and trickles of sweat stung the cuts on her hands.

Ok, think, Robin, think! Where am I? What's happening? Shit! I have to remember....

The drugs had wiped out her short-term memory. The last thing she recalled was walking out of the mall.

Robin took a deep breath. "Help me, please,

someone!" Silence greeted her. She sobbed into the cool, damp ground.

A small bright light suddenly shined in her face. She turned her head to shield her eyes, but the person with the flashlight stooped, lifting each of her eyelids with his thumb.

"The sensitivity to light is an effect of the chloroform and other drugs you gave her," said the voice. "It'll wear off pretty soon."

Robin turned her head to see the person's face, but the flashlight blinded her. "Tell me who you are," she said.

The man seemed to be checking her vital signs and pulse. He ignored her question.

"If it's money you want, you can have it. I can make a withdrawal for any amount. Just let me go! We can work this out."

"You know she almost died. If I hadn't gotten to her when I did, it would have been too late to revive her," said the apparent doctor to someone unseen.

Suddenly, she felt the heel of a shoe plant itself firmly in her shoulder blade.

"Your money can't help you out of this, Robin," a different voice said.

The heel pressed harder, forcing her face onto the filthy floor.

"The doctor here is right; you almost died on us. I couldn't let that happen just yet, though, because I have plans for you — lots of plans."

Robin recognized the voice of the second man, and instantly knew she was in trouble. She breathed in chunks of dirt and gagged loudly, her lungs trying to suck in fresh air. Finally, Kevin eased up on the pressure. She coughed violently, spitting all over the ground.

He flipped her on her back and grabbed her by the throat.

"When was the last time she ate?" the doctor cut in, to keep Kevin from hurting her.

"The bitch will eat when I say she can eat." Kevin dragged her across the room and pushed her up against one of the supportive beams in the floor. Then he stomped away.

Robin heard the doctor's footsteps move up the stairs, and then the sound of the slamming cellar door. She let out a scream of frustration as her eyes began to well up. She used her shoulder to wipe away the tears dripping from her chin. She tried her hardest to focus. *Where is my purse? Is there anything on me that can be used as a weapon? Try and remember as much as you can, Robin.*

With no warning, rapid footsteps charged across the floor. Kevin yanked her up by the arm and ripped the binding from her hands. Robin kicked her legs up to resist, but he was too strong for her to fight. She screamed and kicked harder, as he forced a burlap sack over her head.

"You can't do this to me!" she squealed.

Kevin jabbed her in the throat, causing her to choke and sputter for air.

—

"You say I can't do this to you, but I just did," he said with chilling calm. "Now, I really wish you would behave. But I'm beginning to realize it's a struggle for you. Don't worry though; you'll have plenty of opportunities to practice."

"What do you plan to do with me?" she asked from beneath the sack.

Kevin walked a complete circle around her, each step nearly making her jump out of her skin.

"Just get it over with already, instead of torturing me!" she screamed.

The pacing stopped. She could feel the heat of his body looming treacherously close to hers.

"If that's what you want."

Crack!

He struck her in the head. The crunch of bone was the last sound she heard.

"Lights out, Precious."

Kevin kicked her body to the side like a ragdoll, and made his way back up the stairs.

Chapter Five

Five large men assertively walked through the entrance of Somerlane mall. Austin, Commander Bells and a small team had come to follow up on a lead. They'd run a check on Robin's recent credit card activity and identified the retailers where she'd made purchases before she disappeared.

"Alright, let's split up and cover each location. Interview any and everyone you can. Make sure you get the names of each employee who rang her up for a sale. If they aren't working today, we'll pay them a special home visit," Bells instructed.

He handed out papers to each man listing the retailer names and their locations inside the mall.

One of the younger agents joked, "I got Victoria's Secret. Anybody want to trade?"

Austin's icy stare with balled fists was enough to convince the man to set off toward his destination without saying another word.

A teenager with bright red hair and freckles stood at the counter of Techno World. Playing a video game on his phone, he completely ignored Bells and Austin when they walked in.

"I need to speak with the store manager," Austin said, leaning over and knocking on the counter.

"He's out to lunch right now, but he'll be back."

The boy must have scored a point; he pumped his fist and gave an excited, "Yesss!"

Bells dropped his badge on the counter.

"Tell your manager lunch is over. As a matter of fact, I'll do it myself." He and Austin moved toward the back of the store.

"Wait! You can't go back there," the teen's high-pitched voice squeaked.

Austin was right at Bells' side as they pushed through the doors that read *Employees Only*.

The young man tried to squeeze through the small space between them in order to get to the manager first, but he sloppily collided with their backs.

"Like runnin' into a brick wall, ain't it?" Bells asked with a chuckle.

A man in a white button down shirt with a napkin tucked into the front and a donut in one hand, looked up with total confusion on his face.

"Who the hell are you?" He jerked out the napkin.

Austin flipped open his credentials. "Your worst nightmare, if you don't give us the help we need."

*

If Joanne were to wring her hands once more, they'd probably fall off. She was worried, panicked, and could barely see straight.

"My sweet angel. What have you gotten yourself into this time," she paced.

"She's just fine, I'm sure. Probably just needed a break from everything that's been going on," Jacob Hicks, her long-time beau, supplied.

"This isn't like her at all. She lets me know if she's going to be away. I know something's wrong with that child. I can just feel it." Joanne then did something that she hardly ever did: she broke down. Jacob tried to wrap his arms around her, but she pushed him away.

"Crying won't do any of us any good," she said with a determined sniff, wiping her face. "We just need to figure out what to do to get her safely home." The doorbell rang, and Joanne shuffled over.

"I got here as soon as I could." Joanne threw her arms around Robert as tears began streaming down her face again. Seeing her fall apart was surreal for him and made him nervous. His aunt broke away abruptly, quickly cleaning her face once more. "Come on in, sweetheart" she sniffed. "Can I get you something to drink?"

"No, Auntie, I'm fine."

Robert made his way into the living room, greeting Jacob along the way.

"My, oh my. The last time I saw you, young man, you were no bigger than this." Jacob held his hand out to his knee.

Awkwardly, Robert replied, "It's good seeing you Jacob. I just wish it were under different circumstances." They all sat down in the living room. Joanne brought out a tray of unwanted tea.

"When was the last time you saw her, Auntie?" asked Robert.

"Yesterday morning, before she and Cassidy left for work."

As if on cue, Cassidy came into the room. She looked pale and exhausted when greeting her cousin.

"You really need to eat something, Sugar. Starving yourself isn't going to help us find Robin any quicker."

"I don't have an appetite, Aunt Joanne." Cassidy's eyes pooled with tears. "If I had just stayed with her, none of this would have happened."

"We don't know what happened yet, so you can't be

certain what you could have done, baby. Now you straighten your face and hush that fuss." Joanne tried to soothe the young woman's mind, but she could barely keep her own in check.

"Have you already spoken to the police?" Robert asked.

"I was interviewed a million times by some cop friends of Austin's. I wish I could give them some details that would help, but I can't. I was off doing my own thing," Cassidy lowered her eyes.

They heard footsteps in the kitchen and looked up to see Austin. "Hi everyone," he said with no emotion.

"Have you heard anything new from the authorities?" Robert asked.

Joanne and Austin locked eyes, knowing that *he* was the authority. "Yes, I've spoken to them. They gave me something that I think you all should see."

Austin crossed the room and loaded a DVD into their theater system. "This is surveillance from every store that Robin went in before she went missing."

Robin's face appeared in black and white on the screen. The video was time lapsed. Her family watched her chatting up the different sales reps at each location. She was smiling and appeared to be in a good mood. Joanne noticed that she'd actually looked better than she had in recent days. Each of them sat watching her every move, trying to see if they noticed anything strange, like someone lurking in the background. Nothing seemed out of the ordinary.

"What about surveillance of the parking lot?"

Cassidy's face brightened, as if she was the first to think of that question.

"If you notice here," Austin said, pointing to the screen, "she walks just out of range, so we weren't able to see her make it to the car."

The screen showed Robin push through the glass doors with bags in her hands. She reached into her purse and pulled out a knit cap. After tucking her hair inside and pulling up her collar, she stepped off the side of the curb and out of view.

"She put on her hat," Joanne whispered, her eyes filling with tears. Jacob put his arm around her shoulder and tugged her closer in.

The screen went blank, but everyone continued staring at it, hoping to see more of the woman they all loved. No one would admit it out loud, but they all sat wondering if they'd just witnessed Robin's last few moments alive.

*

Jacob went home. Cassidy and Robert settled into their rooms. Joanne was restless and made her way to the kitchen for warm milk. As she walked down the stairs, there was a glow coming from the large screen television in the living room. She stood on the bottom stair, watching Austin look at the surveillance video over and over. He slowed the footage down in certain spots, watching his wife glide gracefully across the screen. Joanne stepped down from the last stair; the creaking caused Austin to jump up.

"It's just me!" Joanne apologized. Austin's wide stare

slowly softened. He lowered himself back onto the sofa.

"What are you doing up, Aunt Joanne? You should be in bed resting."

"Rest? Humph. How can anyone rest knowing Robin is out there," she jerked her thumb towards the door.

"We're working on bringing her back home safely."

"Don't you do that. Don't you give me that typical response to crisis training that the government gave you. I need to hear some facts, Austin. Do you, or anyone, have any idea where she is?"

Austin lifted his head and stared at her. She searched his eyes, hoping to find an answer, or at least a bit of comfort. Unfortunately, all she saw was his sadness and worry.

"It's like she vanished into thin air."

A chill went through Joanne's body, as the thought of never seeing Robin again crept into her mind.

The stairs creaked; Cassidy joined them. "You guys couldn't sleep either, huh?" Joanne shook her head, and Austin turned back around on the sofa.

"Since we're all up, would one of you mind putting on a pot of tea?" Austin asked.

The two women moved towards the kitchen. Neither was thirsty. Austin wasn't either; he just wanted to get back to watching the video in peace. Cassidy climbed onto a barstool at the kitchen island while Joanne began boiling water. The entire time it took for the pot to boil, they were both silent. The hush that lingered in the air was one filled with questions everyone wanted to ask.

Austin opened up his wallet. Tucked into a side pocket was the picture of him and Robin they'd taken at the Haberdashery Market. His wife had never looked more beautiful to him. The glow from the sun beamed off her skin, making it nearly luminescent. Her hair was pulled into a high ponytail — a style that he loved on her. He was always impressed at how glamorous she could get when going to events, but loved that she was just as breathtaking wearing no makeup and a messy ponytail.

His heart physically ached thinking of her. He tried to refocus on the video. At that point the sun was just about coming up, and he'd officially been up for 72 hours.

Out of the blue, Robert said, "Here," and handed him a cup of tea.

"I didn't even hear you come downstairs," said Austin.

"That's because you were in the zone." Robert sat next to his brother-in-law, trying to find the right words to say.

"One thing you probably know about my sister is that she's a strong woman. She'll find some way out of this; she always does."

"I appreciate you saying that." Austin shook Robert's hand.

They both sat back staring at the video, their minds going wild.

Suddenly, Robert leaned forward as if he saw something on the screen this time that he hadn't seen before. "Rewind that." Austin took the disc back a few frames and Robert stopped him.

"Right there. Is that a laptop she has in her shopping bag?"

"Yeah, she bought it at the electronics store. Why?"

Not responding right away, Robert stood up and pulled his cell phone out. "I have an idea."

Chapter Six

Robin was awakened by a sweet scent. Her eyes fluttered and blurrily focused on what looked like a wooden bowl placed a few feet away from her. She didn't remember how or when, but her hands had been unbound and the sack removed from her face. Realizing that she could move freely, she painfully crawled over to the bowl. Without hesitation, her filthy hands began scooping up sloppy piles of peaches n' cream oatmeal, shoveling it into her mouth. Each time her jaw opened, awful pain shot up the side of her face. The muscles of her jaw were torn, tiny bits of bone protruding through them. Nevertheless, she polished off the oatmeal and the cup of lukewarm water that was with it.

She had just swallowed the last drop when she heard the door to the cellar open. She knew this wasn't good news. Looking around the open room, there was nothing to use as a weapon and nowhere to hide. All she could do was cower behind one of the wooden posts that supported the ceiling.

Purposeful were the footsteps that made their way

down the creaky stairs. Robin squinted, trying to make out the face. The poor lighting from the struggling bulb in the ceiling made it nearly impossible. The visitor was wearing heavy boots that clomped loudly with each step. He wore a hood on his head. When he stepped close to her, she saw his index finger pressed to his lips. At first, she didn't understand what was happening. But when his face came closer, into view, she almost jumped into his arms. Agent Nettles reached out and embraced her in a hug. She burst into tears of relief. "Shh, don't cry, Robin. I need you to be really quiet, alright?" he whispered.

She was trying to compose herself, but was overwhelmed by the first glimmer of hope she'd had in days.

"Where are you hurt?" he asked, spotting dots of dried blood on the floor.

Through trembling lips she said, "Mostly my face. Otherwise, I think I'm ok. But he drugged me, and I don't know what—"

He lifted his hand to silence her, thinking he'd heard a noise. After feeling secure that no one was coming, Agent Nettles finished looking her over.

"Listen, I've got to figure out a safe route to get you out of here. It's going to take me a few hours probably, but I promise you, I'll get you out of here." Robin clasped her shivering hands together and nodded. The agent removed his overcoat and slid his hoodie sweater over his head.

"Here, wrap yourself up in this. If you hear anybody coming, you'll have to find somewhere to ditch it—

quick. Don't leave any evidence that I was down here." She scanned the room and saw an empty vent that she'd be able to quickly tuck the sweater into.

"How is my family? Do they know where I am? What about Austin?"

Nettles kept an eye on the cellar door. "No. They don't even know where I am. I'm deep under cover, which means my communication's been very minimal. No wires, no cell phones, nothing that could blow my cover."

It was disheartening to know that her family was still in the dark and no doubt worried sick. Robin focused on getting out of there so she could be with them.

"Take this."

Nettles pulled out a small black tool that looked like an L wrench.

"Use it if you have to. Hold it in the palm of your hand with the flat edge sticking out. If anyone comes near you, press the tip with your thumb like this."

He demonstrated how to thrust the tool forward while pushing a small button on the tip. Suddenly the thin tool ballooned out with razor blades that would sever anything. He tapped the tip of the weapon, and the razors retracted back into the slits on each side.

"After you've hit him with it, get away as fast as you can."

Nettles handed her the knife. She tucked it into the inside of her sleeve.

"I'm going to map things out, but I'll be back as soon

as I can." He headed for the stairs. "Try to keep warm and focus your mind on getting the hell out of here."

"Thank you so much," she whispered, through teary eyes.

"I'll see you soon. Don't forget: thrust, jab, and run. Got it?"

"Got it."

He smiled at her and quickly shot up the stairs.

*

Robin's house was like a command post, with people walking around in just about every room. Austin and Robert stood at the front door, waiting to brief Bells on what they'd learned. Joanne, coming down the stairs, looked bewildered by the people crawling everywhere.

"What's going on, Austin? I take a nap for an hour, and I wake up in a police precinct. Why are all these officers here?" Her eyes widened. "Oh, my God, did something happen to Robin?"

"No, no, nothing like that. They're just searching for clues that could lead us to her."

Just then, Bells walked up the driveway, and Austin rushed Joanne off so that they could get down to business.

"So, what's this new information you've got?" asked Bells.

Austin introduced Robert. "Robert, this is a friend of mine, David Bells. He is working with these officers to bring Robin home. Bells, this is Robin's brother, Robert."

Commander Bells nodded, and Austin showed him in. Robert pressed *play* on the living room entertainment system. The surveillance footage of Robin began to play. Robert froze it on a frame of her walking out of the electronics store carrying a plastic bag.

"You see this?" he said, pointing to the grainy image of the bag. "The logo on the box inside that bag is for a Hartrige TX 2. It's a computer system that works kind of like a laptop, but has capabilities like a phone. You can dial out and dial into it without having to run a program like Skype or other VoIP software. I worked with one in college, so I'm familiar with its capabilities."

Bells looked at Austin. "You dragged me over here so this kid could tell me about his glory days in college?"

Completely disregarding his statement, Robert went on with his point.

"This system has a chip in it that works like a locator. Even if the computer is turned off, you can track its location."

Suddenly, the gist of Robert's story became perfectly clear.

"It was developed by one of the guys in my class at MIT. He came up with the idea after misplacing his laptop and not having the money to get a new one."

Bells jabbed him on the shoulder. "Nice work, kid."

"Alright, so how do we find this thing?" asked Austin.

"We'll just need the serial number on the unit she bought. The guys at the electronics store should be able to look it up for us and get us the coordinates. If she's still in the same place as the computer, it will take us right to her."

Austin grabbed his keys off the coffee table. "I'll drive."

The three men barged into the electronics store where the redhead was once again playing a game on his phone. He looked up wide-eyed when Austin, Bells and Robert walked in.

"Yeah, it's us again," Bells smiled.

The young man tucked his phone onto a shelf behind the counter and straightened his shirt.

"Oh, hi fellas. What brings you in again?" his voice shook.

Austin pulled out the receipt they had confiscated on their last visit.

"I need you to look up the transaction from this receipt and get me the serial number for this one."

"Now, that, I can do," redhead said confidently.

Grabbing the receipt, he stepped over to a monitor and began typing in information. A short while later he turned the screen toward the men so they could see what he'd found.

"Okay, here's your serial number right here."

Robert jotted down the numbers and made his way around the counter.

"Hey, you can't come back—"

The young man cut himself off when he saw Bells eyeballing him.

Robert turned the monitor back around and used the system to access the Internet.

"On the Hartrige website is a search tool where you plug in the serial number, and it spits out the system's geographic location."

His fingers were lightning fast as he keyed in the only shot he had at finding his sister. The progress bar at the bottom of the screen moved slowly while the computer did its work. Finally, a small map appeared, and everyone lit up.

"It's in Sandusky, a few hours away," Robert said. Adrenaline pumped through his veins.

"The chopper will get us there in 30," Bells said. They all darted towards the door.

*

It seemed days since Nettles' secret visit, but it was just a few hours. Robin was going insane waiting for any sign from him. She dozed in and out of consciousness a few times but tried to shake away her fatigue. Feeling like it was only a matter of time before she would get out alive, Robin pictured all the things she'd do once she was back home, surrounded by family again. She closed her eyes and ran her hands up and down her arms to keep warm.

Without warning, she heard the heavy cellar door fly open. Footsteps came rushing down the stairs. Not knowing what to expect, she quickly slid her hand into the sleeve of her shirt, searching for the blade Nettles had given her.

Too late, she realized she was still wearing his sweater. She tried hard to pull it over her head and toss it to the side, but the person came charging toward her, snatching her up from the floor. She took a breath to scream, but a hand slapped firmly over her mouth.

"Shh, it's me, Nettles."

Her body relaxed, and he took his hand away.

"Listen, we've got just a small window of time, so focus and get ready to move. Listen to my voice at all times, even if you can't see me. You understand?"

She nodded.

"Stay close behind me."

They ran for the stairs, and he led her by the hand.

A sharp wind from the fall air stung their faces as they moved up out of the cellar. Robin's eyes were weak causing her to squint from the sunlight. She kept her head low and positioned herself behind the agent so that he blocked her from the cold air rushing down the stairwell. Her shoeless feet felt heavy, like blocks of ice, as she inched upward.

As soon as they made it to the top of the stairs, Nettles said, "Ready?"

She took a deep breath and mustered up every ounce of strength that she could find. She nodded. "Ready."

Nettles turned forward and shifted into a runner's stance. After a deep breath he yelled, "Go!" Robin literally ran for her life. Still holding hands, their bodies moved as a unit down a dirt path. Her vision was blurry from the wicked wind blowing in her face, but she tried her best to forge forward.

Nettles stopped. They crouched behind a thicket of bushes. They checked to make sure that the coast was clear before darting toward Robin's car. The agent took one step, and Robin stepped quickly behind him. Expecting him to move forward again, she stepped and collided into the back of his unmoving body. Robin bounced back hard, and her hand lost its grip with his. A red mist sprayed in front of her eyes; she was momentarily dazed.

Like a puppet on a string, Nettles tipped around toward her as if he couldn't keep his balance. A tiny hole had appeared in the center of his chest and with each step grew larger.

He had been shot.

Pow! another shot rang out.

Robin shielded her ears from the horrific sound while screaming a bloodcurdling cry. Nettles' muscular body tipped forward like a tree that had just been chopped down. The whole earth seemed to shake when he thudded down right in front of her.

"Nooo!" She dropped down to her knees.

The wounded man tried to speak, but foamy red bubbles took the place of his words. His mouth moved back and forth like a fish gasping for water, until finally he became still.

Robin buried her face in his chest, pounding wildly

on the ground. Nettles had risked his life to save her; the guilt was overwhelming. She sobbed hard, clenching at the dead man's clothes. The shooter was probably seconds away, but she was stunned motionless by this surreal scene in front of her. She lay on the ground, clinging to the agent's unmoving body.

Suddenly, Kevin grabbed a huge chunk of her hair and dragged her back towards the cellar.

"You mangy dogs always find a way to get out!" He gripped her hair even harder. Robin heard ripping sounds as hairs were yanked out at the root. Kevin was angry; she could almost smell the adrenaline rushing through his veins. She didn't put up much of a fight. Her eyes stayed locked on Nettles' body lying deserted on the ground. The further Kevin dragged her away, the smaller Nettles' body grew in the distance, until she could no longer see him.

At the cellar, Kevin kicked her forward, making her walk down the stairs. Her body was weak, like it had given up hope. He kicked her in the back, and she went tumbling down the remaining stairs. Robin hit the bottom hard; her body writhed in pain. Kevin stood back with his arms folded watching like it was a show.

"Now, why would you try and pull a stunt like that, Robin? I can't believe you would do something so stupid! Look at all this I've laid out for you," he said with spread arms as he looked around the room. "Why on earth would you want to give this up?!"

Robin already knew that Kevin's screws were loose. But after seeing what he was capable of, she now realized he didn't have screws all together.

"You had sex with him, didn't you? Tried to woo him with your feminine wiles, huh?"

He reached for her legs, and she snapped them closed like a vise.

"*Now* you want to close them? I wish you'd had the same integrity before you bedded the help," he said, disgusted.

Kevin began pacing the floor with his hands clasped behind his back. Robin slid herself away from him and propped her back against the beam in the middle of the room. She stared at the psychopath who had her captured in a living hell. As she looked at his villainous stride, hatred welled inside of her.

"Why, Kevin? Why are you doing this? What could I possibly have done to you that would bring us to this point? It doesn't make sense." She shook her head. "Nothing with you makes sense. I've done nothing to you!"

Kevin charged over and grabbed her by the throat.

"You *did* do something to me, Robin! You want to know what that something is?"

She looked into his angry eyes, and he hissed, "You breathed."

Robin lowered her head, feeling like a fool for expecting to get a real answer out of him. She even let out a slight chuckle at her own expense.

"Something is funny to you?" He leaned down close to her ear. "I'll give you something to laugh about."

She closed her eyes, a shudder coursing through her

body.

Chapter Seven

The chopper glided smoothly through the air. Each man on the team was briefed.

"According to the pilot, the laptop is in this area. We'll be touching down in a few minutes. We'll have a two-man team covering each sector, and we'll sweep the premises, fanning out. A ground team is arriving soon as back up. Use your radios to keep in constant contact, and fire away at the Bird if he's in your sights."

Austin sat with his head down trying to prepare for whatever was waiting below. Bells elbowed him in the side and held up one thumb, the Cavity signal for victory. Austin nodded at his commander and took a deep breath.

The long stem grass whipped heavily as the chopper lowered. Each man checked his weapons and gear, preparing to dispatch. Bells crouched down in front of the door, gripping the long handle. The aircraft rocked from side to side and finally touched the ground.

Bells pulled the door open. "Go! Go! Go! Go!"

The men jumped out one by one, spreading out over the area. Austin was first to hit the ground, darting forward leading the pack with his Glock in his right hand and a radio in the other. His eyes were zeroed in on the building that potentially held his wife.

They all reached an old cabin. Austin kicked in the front door. Several other agents secured the rear. Austin barely breathed as he scanned the rooms for his wife. He was prepared for the worst but anticipated the best. Each person shouted "Clear" when a room had been swept. No sign of anyone.

The radio crackled out a message.

"We've got something out here. You fellas need to see this."

Austin raced down a dirt path that ended at the cellar door. Bells and the agent who made the call met him out front, and led the way down the wooden stairs.

Spots of blood dotted the floor. Austin tried not to make assumptions about whose it was. Flashlights focused on a large lump covered in newspaper in the corner. A knot formed in Austin's throat as he stepped forward to see what was underneath.

The agent asked Austin, "Are you sure you want to see this?"

Austin reluctantly nodded. The agent snatched back the paper and turned away from the gruesome sight.

"Dammit!" Bells yelled. He swung an angry fist.

Agent Nettles' crumpled body lay lifelessly in the corner. His eyes were still open, his mouth slightly gaped.

Heaviness lingered in the air as the agents processed their loss. One of the men fingered with a charm on his necklace that bore the image of Jesus hanging on the cross. That man closed Nettles' unseeing eyes and said a silent prayer.

Austin trudged up the cellar stairs, feeling momentarily defeated. He couldn't shake the thought that if Nettles was in that condition, Robin would probably be worse off. An agent a few feet away waved his arms in the air, signaling that he, too, had found something. As the devastated husband walked closer, he saw his wife's abandoned car, the backdoor wide open.

"We found the computer system still in its box." The agent lifted the box in the air.

Austin sighed. "Send it to forensics and check it for prints."

He went around to the front of the vehicle and placed his hand on the hood. Cold; it hadn't been driven in a while. Bells looked around in the back seat.

"This your wife's purse?" Bells asked, holding a leather handbag in the air. Austin nodded and felt queasy.

"We'll get all this stuff packed up and see what we can find. Don't give up hope, Malone. Look at it this way; if she was dead, we'd have found her right there next to Nettles, but we didn't. That means she's still out there, and we're going to find her." Bells clapped a firm hand on his agent's shoulder. They got back to the hunt.

*

The train station was bustling. Robin was pushed forward through the crowd. Kevin draped a long jacket over his forearm to conceal the gun he pressed into her back. He had mildly attempted to spruce her up by placing sunglasses over her face to hide his abuse, and giving her too small shoes for her calloused feet. The oversized clothes he'd dressed her in were a welcomed change from the soiled ones. He'd instructed her not to make eye contact with anyone and to keep moving forward. As she made her way through the throng of travelers, her heart skipped. An armed guard was ahead.

Kevin had her gripped tight, but she thought that if she could get the guard's attention, she might have a chance of getting away. They walked closer and closer until she stood just a few feet away from the guard. Her eyes rolled to the side to see if Kevin was looking.

He leaned in close to her ear. "If you even think about it, I will put a hole through the back of your head. Don't end up like your friend back at the cellar."

Robin closed her eyes, recalling the impression of Nettles' blood spattering against her face. The threat was enough to keep her in line. Kevin walked past the guard and smiled. The guard smiled back pleasantly and walked in the opposite direction. Robin choked back tears and prayed for a miracle.

*

The forensics lab was filled with agents spraying chemicals and dusting for fingerprints on the possible evidence they'd brought back from the cabin. Robin's personal affects were cut into pieces small enough to fit under microscopes and in test tubes.

Austin sat in the Proof room, staring at the photos of Dennison on the walls. Bells came in and took a seat next to him.

"What have we found so far?" Austin asked.

"Well so far, we've checked the little bit of surveillance Nettles had, but it wasn't much. He didn't wear a wire, so the only audio we have is from bugs he'd set up on Dennison's phone. That turned up nothing more than a few conversations between Dennison and some reporters trying to run stories on him."

Austin got up from his seat to stretch his legs.

"We did find one thing I thought was interesting. Have you ever seen this picture before?"

Bells held up the picture of Kevin Dennison when he was a young boy.

"No, I've never seen this," Austin shrugged.

"Take a closer look at the kid in the picture." Austin held the picture closer and studied the boy's features. As if a monster had leaped out of the photo, Austin jumped back when he realized the boy was Kevin.

"Where did you find this?" he asked, baffled.

"It was in your wife's purse."

"Why in the hell would she have a picture of *him* in her purse? This doesn't make sense."

"We'll see if we can find out how she got it. In the meantime, why don't you go home and try to get some rest. There isn't much more you can do here tonight."

"I'm not leaving," Austin contended.

"That wasn't a request," Bells said, as he stood up and started towards the door. "A dull pencil does me no good. Go home. Get some sleep and come back tomorrow when you're sharp and more alert."

Austin huffed a sigh and walked out the door. He had no intention, however, of going home. He sneaked the Dennison photo and made a copy. Something Bells said stood out to him, so he decided to go check it out.

*

The WKRP news lot had parking spaces lined against the side of the building, each posted with the photo of a local news anchor. He breathed a sigh of relief when spotting Frank Holland's filled space, since that's who he needed to see.

Inside, the news studio was a maze. There were long hallways with doors that led to God knows where. Searching for studio C, he wondered if the floor plan was purposely confusing in order to keep the public away. Austin finally found himself standing at the front desk.

The receptionist was unimpressed as Austin tried to slick talk his way inside. "Let me guess: Beautiful?"

The large eyed woman peered at him over her glasses. "Excuse me?"

"Beautiful, right? It's the scent of the perfume you're wearing. I only know because my wife wears the same kind," he smiled.

"Sir, how can I help you?" the receptionist asked, with a roll of her eyes.

"Well I—"

"Mr. Malone?" Frank Holland cut in. Austin smiled and walked toward the reporter as if they were old pals. He turned back to the receptionist. "Thanks,

Brenda. This is just who I was looking for." The woman twisted her lips and eyeballed the men as they walked down the hall.

Frank Holland felt almost like a hostage when Austin gripped him by the arm and walked him out of Brenda's earshot. "Mr. Malone, what are you doing here?"

"Frank, I need your help. Something has happened to my wife, and I was hoping you could help me."

Genuine concern spread across the reporter's face. "I'm not sure what good I'll be, but I'll help as much as I can. What happened?"

"Frank, my wife has gone missing, and I believe that Kevin Dennison is involved in her disappearance."

The reporter's eyes grew large; he cupped a hand over his open mouth.

"Wow, I truly don't know what to say. I'm very sorry to hear about your wife."

"I've been working with the police on potential leads. We obtained some voicemails left by you on Mr. Dennison's phone. It sounds like you were planning to do an interview."

"Yeah, we were supposed to meet up and do the second portion of an interview on location. But he suddenly disappeared and stopped taking my calls."

"Did he mention anything about going out of town?"

"No, nothing."

Austin slid the copied picture of Kevin and his father out of his pocket and showed it to the anchor.

"The police found this picture of Kevin Dennison in my wife's belongings. Have you ever seen this photo, or do you know why she would have it?"

Frank took the picture and stared at it for a while. He then shook his head from side to side.

"No, I'm sorry. I have no idea why she would have this."

He looked at the picture once more. Suddenly, his face brightened, and he snapped his fingers.

"Wait a second. The building in the background looks familiar. This is where we met to do the first part of the interview. His family owns a stable out in the country where they raised horses when he was young. The camera crew and I met him out there just a week ago."

Austin lit up; this was a new lead that he desperately needed.

*

With a sack over her head, Robin was wedged into a small space in the back of a pickup truck cab. Kevin sat in the passenger seat, a small Mexican man at the wheel. They had been driving for an hour, and Robin's body ached all over. Making matters worse, she had to use the restroom. Knowing what her only option would be, she squeezed her legs tight and tried not to focus on it.

"Después de manipular mi negocio con la niña, usted puede contar con ella."

Kevin spoke fluent Spanish, and whatever he'd just

said, made the driver perk up.

"Ay, espero con interés a ella!"

Both men laughed loudly. Robin had no clue what they were saying but she knew it couldn't be good. The men continued to chat. She lay uncomfortably in the back.

What are they going to do with me? I have to find some way out of this...

Suddenly, Robin heard something that made her heart skip a beat. The siren on a State Patrol car, whooped loudly behind them. A voice on a bullhorn demanded that they pull over. Kevin and the driver argued, while their vehicle slowly veered to the side.

Kevin jerked the sack that was over her face. "Don't make a sound, Robin! Don't you dare make one sound!"

He turned back around in his seat, while the driver rolled down the window.

"Good evening, officer. Did we do something wrong?"

The trooper shined a flashlight in the men's faces. He looked at the driver and back at Kevin. "You boys know you have a taillight out?"

The officer leaned into the window, and Robin tried to be still. She thought of screaming for help, but Agent Nettles came to mind. He had suffered for trying to save her. She didn't want to force that same fate on someone else. She wouldn't have put it past Kevin to kill the patrolman. So, she kept quiet.

Suddenly, Kevin perked up. "Brubaker?" he said.

The trooper broke into a wide smile and made his way around to Kevin's window. "Man it's been years since I've seen you. How has everything been?" he shook Kevin's hand.

Brubaker was a cop that Kevin's father had corrupted years ago. Recognizing him, Kevin felt like he'd just hit the jackpot.

"Things are great. Just heading in for the night and trying to stay out of trouble."

The men all laughed. Robin couldn't believe that this was happening. Did Kevin have *everyone* in his pocket? Tears stung her eyes as her last bit of hope began to wane.

"Well, fellas, I'm going to head back to the station, but it was good seeing you. You be careful going home. There are a lot of crazies out on the road at this time of night." Robin was in the vehicle with King Crazy himself; it would be hard to find worse.

The trooper made his way back to his vehicle and swooped off into the night.

As the trio pulled back onto the road, Kevin leaned back and slid the sack up just enough to see Robin's eyes. "Good girl. Remind me to give you a treat later for being so well behaved." He licked his lips and the driver laughed at Robin's expense.

*

Twenty or more men crouched in the woods surrounding the stables. They had a clear view of the ranch-style home that sat just a few feet away. Looking through infrared goggles, Austin was clearly able to see the outline of three human bodies. A surge of hope coursed through his veins, as he looked at the bright red images.

Austin's radio chirped with a message from Bells.

"Malone, we have eyes on the Bird, and it appears that the package is with him. Do you copy?"

Austin allowed himself a smile, hearing the confirmation he'd been hoping for. Frank Holland's lead had been a long shot, but now it proved to be worthwhile.

"Copy, loud and clear," Austin responded.

"Everyone is in position and ready to go. Tell your men to move only on my signal."

Austin held up a clenched fist, signaling the other men to hold their positions. Anxiety mounted as he waited for the signal from his commander. The woods were completely quiet; the only sound was the howling wind. Austin's heartbeat thudded in his ears. He tried to pace his breathing. It was do-or-die time, and he was prepared for either one.

Suddenly, a bright red flare shot into the air. Like a runner at the official blast of a gun, Austin raced toward the front of the house, ready to charge in. A battering ram leveled the front door. Shattered glass echoed from the agents entering through the windows. The house was an open floor plan; Austin ran directly to the spot where he'd just seen the bodies on his screen.

As if expecting their arrival, Kevin waited in the center of the living room, his right arm locked firmly under Robin's neck. He stood behind her with a gun to her head, her arms tense and stiff at her sides. Kevin squeezed her close, providing cover for himself against the armed men.

Austin's heart pulsed in his throat when he saw his wife.

"You okay, Baby?"

His weapon was drawn and pointed at Kevin's head.

"Peachy keen," Kevin laughed.

Robin stood perfectly still and didn't open her mouth.

A loud *Boom!* sounded in the room next to them and someone let out a scream. "Rendirse! Rendirse! No hurt me! Por favor!" Kevin's Mexican comrade had been leveled by one of the agents. He begged the officers to spare his life. Robin's eyes followed the cowering man as they marched him out the door. Kevin glanced at him with disgust.

Unaffected by his friend's capture, Kevin refocused on the situation in front of him.

"Well, well, well. Look at what we have here. A good ol' fashioned stand-off," he said drolly. "I bet the two of you missed each other, didn't you?"

Tiny red lasers bounced all over Kevin's body; agents were ready to fire. Austin inched forward, keeping his gun pointed at the man's head.

"You come any closer, Romeo, and I will shoot your

precious Juliet right in the temple." Kevin smiled wickedly and rubbed the barrel of the gun against Robin's head. Austin had no choice but to stay where he was.

"It appears that we are in a position to do some business together, Mr. Malone. I have something you want," he tugged at Robin's hair, "And you have something I want," he gestured towards the door. "Now we just have to come up with a creative way to make us both happy."

Austin didn't respond at first. The massive bruising on his wife's face distracted him. With effort, he concentrated on keeping his aim at Kevin's head, focusing on the crazy man's eyes. "I think we may be able to work something out," he managed to reply

Kevin put his mouth close to Robin's ear. "Aww, isn't he romantic? I'll bet he's willing to do anything to save his damsel in distress." Still looking up at Austin, Kevin licked the side of Robin's face and smiled.

Austin nearly went ballistic. He stepped closer and slid his finger into the loop of the trigger. "Ah, ah, ah. Get back, Jack," Kevin said melodically.

Bells stepped in to gain control over the explosive situation. "Kevin, let the woman go. We can work this out as men. Like you said, we'll find a creative way to—"

"Who is this person?" Kevin asked, as if Austin would actually answer him.

"My name is David Bells, and I'm a commander with the CIA."

"CIA?" Kevin laughed as if this news was amusing to him.

"My mother would be so proud knowing I've attracted the attention of the Feds. Although I'm thrilled to have met you, Mr. Bells, my business here is not with you. So if you'll please—get the fuck out."

Still holding his position, Austin said, "He's right, Bells. Everybody out! This is between us." Bells hesitated at the request. "Give us a few minutes to talk this out," Austin said to his commander, eyes always trained on Kevin.

"Malone, are you sure you want to—"

"Just go," Austin said firmly. Battling in front of everyone wouldn't help things. Bells relented and decided to trust his agent's judgment. He gave his men the retreat signal. Slowly, they all backed out of the room. The dancing red dots were gone.

"Ahh, that's much better. Gives me a little room to breathe," Kevin boasted.

Robin's knees were beginning to give out. Kevin gripped her tight to keep her on her feet.

"Let my wife go, Dennison."

"Let her go? But we're having so much fun together," he kissed the side of her forehead. "You know, you really had me fooled for a while there, Austin. Or should I say, *Agent* Malone. A CIA agent? I never would have seen that one coming. Especially given how easy it was to have someone pop you at the park that day. From what I hear, the bullets missed your major arteries by mere millimeters."

"Maybe you would have seen it coming a little better if you hadn't hired an undercover CIA agent as your hit man."

A look of surprised confusion flitted across Kevin's face. Austin could tell that he hadn't yet made that connection.

"You didn't know? Yeah, Kevin, the man you hired to *pop* me was an agent. Those bullets missed my major arteries because they were supposed to. That agent is dead now because of you. I'm sure I don't need to tell you the penalty for killing a federal agent, but I will anyway. Life in prison. That's the price you'll pay for what you've done." Austin laughed and said, "Look on the bright side; being sent back to prison will give you the chance to reconnect with your old cellmates. I heard you guys got pretty close on those dark and lonely nights." Austin taunted further.

Robin had never seen this devious side of her husband. He clearly knew how to play along with Kevin's psychotic mind games; it was jarring for her to witness. The reality was that he was doing his job — the job she hoped would save her life — and he was doing the hell out of it.

Surprisingly, Kevin was speechless. But not for long. "If your little friend was indeed an agent, then he deserved to die." Kevin leaned his head down to Robin's. "Unfortunately, now you'll have to witness your husband suffer the same fate as his friend."

Using her body to shield himself, Kevin raised his gun to fire off a shot at Austin. With lightening speed, Robin slid Nettles' blade from her sleeve. His instructions played through her mind as she executed them: *Thrust, jab and run.*

With a scream, Robin gripped the knife firmly in her hand and plunged it deep into Kevin's abdomen. Her next moves played out in slow motion in her frazzled mind. She pushed the button on the tip, and used her body to push Kevin away. Startled he let out a painful roar as the razor-sharp blades sliced into his lower ribcage.

He reached out to grab her, but Robin leapt away to safety. Austin fired a shot that hit Kevin in the shoulder and knocked his feet out from under him.

Taking that cue, Bells and the rest of the team swooped in ready for war.

Thankfully, the war was already over. Kevin lay wailing in pain. Austin kicked the gun away from his palm. Then, calmly, as if from the CIA manual, he leaned down over Kevin and cocked his arm back. All his pent-up rage took its revenge in the blow that he thundered down onto Dennison's jaw. Rubbing his fist, Austin sprang up and wrapped his arms around his wife.

Her knees completely gave out, but it didn't matter. Austin lifted her up, squeezing her tighter than he ever had before. Tears streamed down her face. She held him as tight as she could. There had been a point where she thought she'd never see him again. But there he was, holding her in his arms; her hero, who had just saved her life.

Trickles of blood lined Kevin's lips; still he laughed his insane laugh again. While several agents picked him up from the floor, Austin gave in to the taunt and went back for more. He stormed over to the man, jabbing him hard in the ribs, knocking him back to his knees.

"Laugh now, mother fucker!" Austin spit, with several agents looking on.

Kevin's wind was gone, but as soon as he caught his breath, incredibly, he began laughing yet again. After everything he and his wife had been through, Austin was done. He pulled his Glock out and held it firmly at the center of Kevin's head, ready to make the final move of this perverse game. Bells stepped close to him and tried to jolt him back to reality.

"Wait a minute, Malone. I know you're upset, but let's just think about this. Don't take this situation into your own hands and make it worse. He'll get what's coming to him. Just don't do it this way." Austin's steady and unmoving hand still held the gun in place. It was as if he was in a trance and couldn't snap out of it.

Still laughing, Kevin said to Robin. "If he kills me, how will you ever see Gabriela again?"

Shocked chills coursed down Robin's spine.

"Stop it, Kevin. You know Gabriela is dead," she said through trembling lips. She was livid with the fact that he'd mention her daughter's name in the middle of all this.

His chuckles went on, even as Austin's gun rested on his skull.

"What makes you think she's dead, Robin? The fact

that someone *told* you she was? You know better than that," he sneered.

Robin's whole body began to tremble as she stepped closer to him. Her mind swirled while trying to focus on what he was saying.

"He's just toying with you, Robin. Don't let him do this," Austin said over his shoulder, with his finger on the trigger.

"Did you ever see her body, Robin? Did you see her buried in the ground?"

Robin's mind went back. She tried hard to recall exactly what had happened. After Dr. Resnor told her Gabriela hadn't survived, she talked her out of viewing the body one last time. She'd said that the stress of seeing her lifeless baby would have been too hard on her, that she should remember the few quiet moments they'd shared. The doctor suggested that she allow the hospital to make the final arrangements.

Robin was in no state of mind at the time to question her and agreed to the suggestion. She didn't even choose to have a formal funeral. She was so numb that she never thought twice when the hospital sent her daughter's remains directly to the cemetery.

Austin, seeing the turmoil Kevin was putting his wife through, said, "That's it!" He cocked back the chamber of his gun. Robin screamed, "Wait!"

She stormed over to Kevin and grabbed his jaw, firmly holding his face towards her.

"Are you telling me that my baby is still alive, Kevin?"

He smiled viciously at her; she backhanded him hard across the face.

"Is Gabriela alive?!" she screamed.

Smugly he replied, "What do you *think*?"

As if her anger was a pool of lava, she erupted. "Kevin, what the hell have you done with my daughter?! What have you done?!" she screeched, grabbing at his throat.

Completely unaffected by her emotional display, Kevin grinned happily while two agents snatched him up and finally carried him out the door. Robin tried lunging after him, but Bells caught her by the waist and held her back.

"What have you done with my baby?!" she still screamed. Austin holstered his Glock and took his wife to his chest, muffling her sobs. "Austin, we have to find her!"

"Robin, he may have been making that up, just to —"

"But what if he wasn't, Austin?! What if Gabriela is out there somewhere? We *have* to find her!"

She began weeping harder, and he held her even tighter. Austin exhaled, dreading the next battle they were about to face.

Chapter Eight

When Austin pulled into the driveway, the front door sprang open. Aunt Joanne was never one to move too quickly, but when she saw her niece sitting in the passenger seat, she rushed across the front lawn to the vehicle.

"Robin!" Joanne squealed, as she pulled open the car door.

Robin leapt out of her seat and threw her arms around her aunt.

"Oh my Lord, my baby is home!"

Joanne placed her hands on either side of Robin's face and cried. "I knew it. I knew the good Lord would bring you back to me. And here you are. Looking just as precious as the day you were born."

They embraced again. Nothing in the world could have torn them apart.

"Come on in here; let's get you out of this cold."

Joanne led Robin by the hand up the walkway. Inside, her family circled all around her. Robert and Cassidy stood beaming; Jacob clasped his hands and smiled. Even Noodles trotted up with her usual jolly greeting.

Robin couldn't think of a better way to be welcomed home than being with the people she cared for the most. Aunt Joanne looked her niece over from head to toe, watching her hugging and crying with her family. Her eyes caught the massive lump on the side of Robin's face. "My Lord. What did he do to your face?" Tenderly, she cupped her niece's cheek. As if a record had just scratched in the middle of a song, everyone in the room turned and stared.

"Let's not worry about any of that right now, guys," Robin said, trying to lighten the mood. "The most important thing is that I'm home and here with all of you."

Her hand warmed as Joanne squeezed it affectionately and kissed her on her good cheek. The excited brood all stood bundled closely together at the door and enveloped Robin in a group hug. Finally, Robin broke away from the pack. Everyone followed behind.

"Well, are you hungry? You look like you haven't eaten in days," Joanne said to her niece. It wasn't until the statement came out of her mouth that she realized how insensitive, yet hauntingly accurate she was.

"Actually, I am. And I'm in the mood for some of your squash soup," Robin smiled.

Joanne clapped her hands in the air. "You're in luck, because I have a big container of it in the freezer!"

The sound of clanking pots soon sounded from the kitchen while Joanne prepared the meal. For Robin, home couldn't have been more inviting. As she took a seat next to her brother on the sofa, her eyes glanced slowly around the room taking in the calm and peacefulness. Noodles came and sat on her foot. She did that anytime she was feeling neglected.

"I missed you too, Noodles," Robin said to the pooch, winning a lick on the fingers.

Being stripped of her freedom for those few days gave her a new appreciation for her life and the people in it. Every now and then she looked up and caught a member of her family staring at her. Their minds were a sea of questions that begged to be answered. When the time was right, she would be sure to answer each one. But at this point she wasn't ready, and even had a question of her own. *Where is my baby?*

Joanne emerged carrying bowls of piping hot soup. "Robin, this one is yours right here," she pointed to the largest bowl. "I sprinkled toasted crackers on top just the way you like it."

Robin took her bowl and sat back comfortably against the sofa cushions. She had just raised the spoon to her lips when Joanne cleared her throat. Everyone bowed their heads while she said grace over their meal. "Heavenly Father, we thank you. Thank you for this time, and thank you for bringing Robin home safely."

Joanne's prayer continued and was more fitted for the benediction of a church service than it was for grace over supper. Given the circumstances, no one was going to complain.

With her head bowed, Robin's eyes looked over and caught a glimpse of her husband. His shoulders hung low as if the weight of the past few days was resting on them. A portrait of strain and worry was painted vividly on his face, and she knew exactly what was on his mind. The question of whether or not Gabriela was alive was eating at him just as much as it was her. Robin's eyes closed as she prayed for the strength to make it through whatever would be next.

" —in Your name we pray, Amen."

"Amen," they all said in unison.

Everyone started in on their meals as Robin shifted on the sofa. The spoon swirled aimlessly through the bowl. She had no appetite now.

"Too hot, isn't it?" Joanne asked, when she saw that her niece wasn't eating. "I'll tell you what; how about I put an ice cube in it, and let it sit on the counter for a while to cool off?"

"How about you wrap it up for me and save it for tomorrow? I'm a little tired, and should probably head upstairs," Robin yawned.

Robin went around the room, kissing and hugging everyone good night.

Joanne clasped her hands as she watched her niece walk up the stairs, and thanked God that she was safe and sound.

Passing through the empty hallway, Robin suddenly felt uneasy about being alone. Thankfully, she heard Austin's voice moving up the stairs behind her, asking if she needed anything.

"Hey, Babe. I just wanted to check on you and make sure everything is all right. Do you want me to —"

"Babe, I need you," was her response, as she held her hand out to grab his.

Her body melded into him. His body became like a support beam, steadying her. From behind, he slowly walked her into the master bath. She stood still while he peeled off the layers of hospital clothes she was wearing.

Black and blue marks dotted her body from the gruesome beatings she'd endured. Austin knelt and gently kissed each bruise, then leaned his head on her stomach. Robin closed her eyes, grateful to be home with the man that she loved.

They sat and nestled on the side of the tub while water filled the basin. Neither of them spoke. Their touch was conversation enough. Austin's arms were wrapped protectively around her waist; her head leaned against his. Perfect was the temperature of the water when she stepped in and slid down up to her neck.

Robin soaked in the jasmine scented bubbles. With a cup in his hands, Austin leaned her head back as the cup filled with water. Slowly, the fresh water streamed through her hair as he poured it over her scalp. Over and over he washed her tresses until the cloudiness of filth had disappeared.

After washing away all of the residue from her unwelcome time away, Robin wrapped herself in a robe. The couple made their way to the bedroom and cozied up close together.

"You have no idea how happy I am to be here with you. I didn't know if you'd ever let me come back home. Then when I almost lost you, I realized that no place would ever feel like home again if I didn't have you to share it with," Austin said.

Robin smiled and scooted in a little closer. His hand grazed her cheek, and she winced.

"Robin, please tell me what all he did to you."

Details of what occurred those few days had only been given to Commander Bells and the doctor at the hospital. And that was for good reason. If Austin knew of all the things she'd gone through, he would have killed Kevin on sight—not that she would have had a problem with it.

"Just like I told Joanne and the rest of the family, none of that matters now, Honey. These bruises will heal, and life will go on. Instead of us dwelling on what happened, let's move forward and focus on the future. We've got some questions to ask, and Kevin is the only person who can answer them."

Austin rolled away from her and sat with his back up against the headboard.

"He's being transported up to Jackson tomorrow morning. It'll take a few days for him to be processed, but after that, I'll go and pay him a visit."

"Let me come with you," Robin said to him.

Austin's jaw clenched when he thought about his wife being in the same room with that monster again. "I'll have to think about it. In the meantime, let's do like you said and not focus on it." Robin agreed and slid down under the covers. Rolling over to turn off the lamp on the nightstand, she noticed her pocket calendar flipped open. In a bright red circle was Gabriela's name with, *B-day* written next to it.

Tomorrow was Gabriela's birthday.

*

The sun shined intrusively through the blinds, irritating Robin's eyes. Her clock read 6:03. Austin lay curled up next to her in bed. She'd been awake the entire night, unable to rest. *How do you know she's dead, Robin?*" Kevin's statement had played in her mind the whole night through.

Relentlessly, she relived that conversation and dissected it word for word.

"Did you actually see her body?"

The truth of the matter was that she hadn't. And that fact alone was doubt enough. Today was her child's birthday, and her heart skipped at the fact there was a chance she was alive to see it.

Slowly, Robin crept out of bed, trying not to wake Austin. He stirred, then rolled over and cradled a pillow in his arm. Robin noticed how innocent he looked while sleeping, a stark contrast to the bone chilling aggression she now knew he was capable of.

She snuck out of the room and made her way downstairs to the kitchen. She didn't know exactly what she was looking for, but after making a few phone calls found herself on the afterhours line with the medical examiner's office. Surprisingly someone was in early and picked up.

"Wayne County ME's office," the voice on the other end droned.

Robin hadn't come up with a clear, convincing explanation for calling. She fumbled through her greeting.

"Hi, my name is — uh — I'm looking to find information about — "

The words weren't coming to mind quickly enough. She was frustrated.

"What can I help you with?" the voice asked.

"My child died, and I'm wondering if I can get a copy of her autopsy report. The hospital gave her a burial, but I never saw her body. I know it sounds strange, but I really need to make sure that she—"

Feeling a breath on her neck, Robin turned to find Austin standing behind her.

"I'll have to call back later," she said and slid the phone down from her ear.

"Robin, what are you doing?"

"I have to know, Honey. I have to know if Gabriela is dead or alive. I figured if I got hold of someone at the medical examiner's office, they could tell me if an autopsy was performed. From the autopsy, maybe they can tell me if the remains that were buried were actually Gabriela's."

"Why were you trying to do something like that alone? Honey, I told you we would figure things out together, and I meant it. I'm working with Bells on some things that will help us—"

The sound of breaking glass filled the room. The couple turned to see Joanne standing with a hand clasped over her mouth. She had dropped her coffee mug at Robin's words.

"Did I hear you right?" she whispered. "Gabriela is alive?"

This was the last thing that Robin wanted. It was bad

enough she had to be burdened with hopes that may have been false; she didn't want Joanne going through that same thing. "Auntie, please. Sit down so I can explain." The older woman didn't move. She kept a trembling hand over her mouth as she tried to steady herself at counter.

"Please, just have a seat, and I'll explain everything, Auntie. Please."

The phone on the wall rang. Austin snatched it up.

His face was like stone as he turned away from the two women. Robin quickly explained to her aunt as much as she could, while Austin listened to the call. He disappeared from the room for a while and then came rushing back in.

"Get dressed," he said, and turned to hurry away.

"What's going on?" asked Joanne, following him out of the room.

"We all have questions, and now we're about to find some answers."

Less than an hour later, they pulled up at the Pine Ridge Cemetery. The grass was healthy green as they walked across it, making their way to the main entrance. Pine Ridge was owned by the hospital. The land was purchased by now-deceased mayor C. J. Young who had donated it to the NICU. Having experienced the death of his grandchild, he wanted to ensure that the resting place for small children would be special. Colorful tombstones with balloons and whimsical characters could be seen for yards in the distance as they walked closer to the gatehouse.

Commander Bells walked toward them. There was a thin, wiry man with him. Bells shot Austin a look that both Robin and Joanne noticed. He wasn't happy to see the women there, for obvious reasons.

"Good morning, everyone. This is Mr. Ransom Pounds. He's the groundskeeper here at Pine Ridge. He's given his okay to the contractors, and they'll be arriving soon," said Bells. Robin was confused as she shook the men's hands, still in the dark about what was happening. Austin pulled the two ladies to the side and explained the situation.

"The commander made arrangements with the city to have Gabriela's body exhumed. I have no idea what we're going to find, but we figured this would be the best place to start." The women clutched close together in preparation of what was about to go down.

"Now, you listen to me, both of you. Stay as far back away from everything as possible. It was a bad idea on my part to even bring you here, but you deserved to know the truth."

In a matter of minutes, men equipped with tools and shovels swarmed over the grounds. Robin took in every detail. A bright yellow and black wheel excavator beeped. The letters CAT on the side of the truck caught her eye. Slowly the long arm reached in, pulling out piles and piles of earth, dumping it to the side. The machine was uncovering a secret that, for years, Robin had never even known existed.

Suddenly, a tiny casket appeared. It was hauled into the air by massive straps attached to one of the machines. Pain surged in the pit of Robin's stomach;

she turned her face away. Joanne hooked arms with her niece and held on to her tightly. Austin and Bells stood next to the construction workers, watching them direct the box onto the ground. The experienced machinist was able to gently lower the casket without disturbing any of the precious contents, which may or may not have been inside.

Several men walked over and worked to pry open the miniature coffin. They all stepped back quickly. Austin and Bells both stepped forward and peered in, neither knowing what to expect inside. Joanne clenched Robin's arm tight; they both held their breath.

Austin's body suddenly jerked angrily. He looked extremely pissed off. Bells shook his head from side to side and grabbed Austin's shoulder. Without even realizing that she was in motion, Robin dashed across the grass to the casket. She stood suddenly still at the edge of the open tomb and closed her eyes, preparing herself to look in the coffin.

Her eyelids snapped opened. The vision in front of her was almost too unbearable. Breathless, she stared down at the tiny body in the casket. Austin was at her side and tried to shield her face, but she wouldn't turn away. As if watching herself in a movie, Robin screamed, reaching down into the casket, pulling out the remains.

Baby Wets O' Lot smiled raggedly in Robin's shaky hands.

Gabriela was no more dead than that doll was alive. And now Robin had to find her.

*

Ransom Pounds sat in an interrogation room. A generic cola trembled in his hands. Bells and Austin watched the groundskeeper from behind the one-way mirror, while he fidgeted in his seat.

"I doubt he'll give us anything. I'm sure Dennison paid him off well enough to keep his mouth closed."

"We'll see about that." Austin stalked out the door.

Bells saw the agent appear in the interrogation room. Austin was known for putting on charm that could make the most hardened of criminals soften up. A smile crept across Bells' face as he watched his agent in action.

"Mr. Pounds, I should apologize to you. I didn't realize they'd given you that off brand beverage. I ordered us lunch and made sure to tell them to bring us the good stuff."

"No worries, mate. It's actually quite enjoyable."

Ransom's Australian accent seemed even heavier than Austin remembered. He wondered if that was on purpose.

"I do appreciate you coming down here. We just need to clear up a few things and ask you a few questions. We'll be out of your hair before you know it," said Austin.

Ransom reached up, running his hand over his shiny bald head. "That shouldn't be too hard, now should it?"

Both men laughed and Austin continued on.

"About four years ago is when you would have

gotten the remains from Beaumante hospital for this medical file." He handed Ransom Gabriela's hospital paperwork. "Do you remember setting up that pick up with the staff there?"

"Come on, bloke. You can't expect me to remember a pick up from that long ago. Besides, I have hardly anything to do with what comes in. All I do is arrange the time and make sure my men are there to have the plots ready. That other end of things is out of my control."

"Well, you see, Ransom, that's where I'm having a hard time believing you."

Austin opened a manila folder and pulled out a statement sheet.

"I spoke with the staff at the hospital, and guess what they told me? They told me that you personally were there to collect the remains and transport them to the grounds that day."

Beads of sweat began to form on Ransom's forehead; Austin knew he was beginning to get somewhere.

"Now why is it that you personally took on this particular pick up, Mr. Pounds? What was so special about this one that made you do more than simply arrange the time and prepare the plot?"

"I—I really don't remember what could have—"

"Come on, Ransom, I thought we were better than that. You are in an interrogation room right now, which means you're speaking to a man who can recognize when someone is lying to him."

"Well, good onya mate for possessing that skill, but I'm giving you good oil here. I don't remember what the circumstances were that—"

Like a bolt of lightning, Austin shot across the table and knocked the man out of the chair. Ransom lie pinned against the floor with the agent's forearm locked securely over his throat. Bells thought about going in and defusing the situation, but the lying little bastard that Ransom was needed to feel every bit of this wake up call.

"Tell me where the girl is, Ransom! Where is the girl?!"

Austin's bulging arm pressed down even harder on Ransom's throat. He finally relented.

"Alright, mate. Alright," Ransom rasped.

Austin plucked the man up from the floor and pushed him by the shoulder down into the seat.

"Tell me what you know."

Ransom rubbed his neck as he turned his head to the side and cleared his throat.

"Look, mate. I really don't know where the baby is..."

Austin motioned like he was about to get up again, and Ransom quickly said, "BUT, I will tell you what I do know."

Austin settled back in his seat. Ransom went on.

"What usually happens with the little ones is that the families get the remains and send them to the funeral parlor to get them prepared. In severe cases where the little ones are small, like stillborn babies or preemies, the families often don't have funerals. They send the remains directly to us, and we handle the burial. The families say their goodbyes privately at the cemetery rather than having a service."

The man paused, and Austin said, "Go on, Ransom, I'm listening."

"I was contacted by a man who basically told me there was going to be something special with this particular pick up. He told me not to ask questions and to just turn my head the other way, if you will. I told him to rack off, but he sent his goons to make sure I got the message loud and clear."

Austin's blood began to boil. He kept himself in the seat with difficulty.

"The mother for this little one was told that her daughter's body had already been given to us to transport to the cemetery. I have no idea what really happened with the little girl. I was instructed to turn my head the other way, and that's exactly what I did. When we picked up the shipment, it was already sealed off and ready to go. I swear on my grandmother's grave, mate, that's the honest-to-God truth."

"Who was this man that contacted you?"

"Well, he didn't exactly leave his business card."

"Would you recognize his voice if you heard it again?"

"I'm not quite sure, bloke; it's been awhile, but I'll give it a try."

Austin stood up from the interrogation table and stared at Ransom, disgusted with him. He exited the room and arranged for him to meet with an audio specialist. While Ransom listened to audio of different men's voices, Bells and Austin made their way down to the forensics lab.

"What do you think; he telling you everything?"

"Yeah, he doesn't know anything else, I'm sure."

"Little twerp. You should have let him sweat a little longer."

"What pisses me off is that Dennison was able to orchestrate all of this right under our noses. I did some digging around; guess who disappeared a few weeks after Gabriela *died*. Dr. Resnor, Robin's OBGYN. She retired and no one has heard from her since. I'm sure that she, and God knows who else, was in Dennison's back pocket on this. If you think about it, it had to have involved tons of people to pull this off. The doctors, nurses, everyone who would have had access to Gabriela."

"Maybe not; he could have simply been banging her at night, just like he was Melanie, for all we know. This guy seems to have the golden penis that makes women do anything he asks. It could have been a Bonnie and Clyde thing with them pulling off a baby heist; who knows. He has the manpower to strong-arm people into doing what he wants, given his family ties. Don't worry; we've got agents interviewing everyone possible so that we can get some answers. We'll catch up to Resnor and see what we can get out of her." Bells packed a wad of smokeless tobacco into his cheek before saying "Look, I know what today is for you and your wife. Why don't you go home and be with her? I'm sure she needs you."

In all that had happened, it almost slipped Austin's mind that today was Gabriela's birthday.

"I'll give you a call if anything happens around here," Bells reassured.

The house was quiet when Austin walked in. Noodles trotted up to him, and he patted her on the head. After pouring fresh water in her dish, he made his way upstairs, where he found Robin on the edge of the bed brushing her hair. He walked over and sat on the floor beside her feet.

"I know how hard it was seeing those things today, but you were brave about it. You handled yourself really well, Sweetheart," Austin said. Robin didn't respond. She instead squeezed the handle of the brush and continued to stroke her hair. "We're working on a few leads right now that might give us some answers on a few things."

"She's four years old today," Robin said softly. "I hope that wherever she is, she's having birthday cake and ice cream, and that she has lots of toys." Robin smiled as the image of those things played in her mind. Austin sat quietly at her feet, not knowing what to say.

"We need to get answers, Austin. I'm ready. I'm ready to see Kevin. I know you think I can't handle it, but you have to trust me. Just let me meet with him one time."

Austin looked into his wife's eyes, unable to deny

the inevitable.

*

Jackson was tucked neatly away in the woods of southern Michigan. The calm, winding roads were a deceiving overture to the ugliness held inside the prison walls. Robin fidgeted with the strap on her seatbelt while Austin drove. The closer they got, the more she tried not to talk herself out of going. For the whole ride, Kevin's sinister grin played repeatedly in her mind, and she tried not to let it bother her.

"You alright?" Austin asked, sensing that she was having second thoughts.

"I will be as soon as I get some answers." He nodded and squeezed her hand. Gravel on the road leading up to the guard shack crackled beneath their tires. A uniformed officer checked their identification and then gave them instructions on how to get to the main entrance.

"You go straight ahead, and you'll see a sign directing you where to park. Once you get into the lobby, there will be someone there to get you signed in. You all are about the fourth set of visitors Dennison has gotten today, so don't be surprised if you have to wait a while."

Robin was sure that his visits were from reporters, looking to conduct interviews. It made her sick knowing that his treacherous actions garnered him so much media attention, which he loved.

She and Austin entered into the lobby. Robin found herself surprised by how clean it was. There were little pumpkins and squash placed strategically in honor of the fall season. The scent of spiced cake wafted through the air. A female officer at the front desk was warm and pleasant. She very well could have been the receptionist in any doctor's office.

"Welcome, Agent Malone," she said to Austin, after identifying his credentials. "You and your guest can step right this way. We need to check your weapon and remove your belt. Please review this list, and make sure you don't have any of these items on your person."

There was a list posted on a wall showing items that weren't allowed in. Robin thought about the fact that she'd love to smuggle in a machete, and go Lorena Bobbitt-style on Kevin when the guards weren't looking. Just the thought gave her a chuckle that she very much needed.

Once signed in, they were led down a long hall and shown to a private interview room. The couple waited while a clock on the wall ticked loudly. Robin was just beginning to worry that something had gone wrong with the plans, when the door opened, and Kevin came shuffling through.

As soon as he entered the room and saw their faces, he lit up.

"Robin, Austin!" he beamed, as though they were old friends. The guard led him over to his seat and chained him to a hook that protruded from the table. The shackles weren't nearly as horrific as the ones he'd kept Robin in, but they did the trick. Kevin's arm was in a sling; a large bandage wrapped around his midsection. Robin felt a certain satisfaction. The husband-wife duo had done a real job on him, and he deserved every bit.

"They told me I was having an interview. But I didn't realize my two old pals would be the ones facilitating it. How ya doin', bud?" Kevin smiled at Austin.

"Cut the crap, Kevin. You know why we're here," Austin scolded.

"Too soon, huh?" the inmate joked.

Austin felt his pulse begin to quicken as his fists clenched.

"Wow, Robin. What happened to your face? You're looking a little swollen around the cheek area."

He looked at Robin's flared nostrils and knew he'd gotten under her skin, which was exactly where he wanted to be.

The agitated woman picked up her large bag and plopped it down onto the table. She then unzipped it slowly and kept her eyes locked with Kevin's. The inmate smiled when he saw what she was pulling out.

"I've always thought you were a bit immature for your age, Robin. But now you're playing with dolls?" He chuckled to himself and shrugged his shoulders.

Baby Wets O' Lot was splayed across the table as Robin reached into the bag again. This time she pulled something out that wasn't so funny.

Instantly, Kevin's face stiffened and his jovial demeanor disappeared. His eyes stared down at the photo of 1-day-old Gabriela lying in an incubator.

"Where is she, Kevin?" asked Robin.

She slid the photo closer. His eyes followed it across the table.

"Where is Gabriela?" she asked again.

His face seemed to soften, and for a split second Robin thought she might have gotten through to him. "She's in heaven with the angels. And she's also in your heart," he said with a flutter of his eyes. A flash of anger rippled through her skin, but she suppressed it and tried not to erupt.

"Kevin, you're never going to get out of this place after everything you've done. You might as well just tell us where she is," Robin said.

"We already know about you threatening the staff at the hospital, and making the swap at the cemetery. We know everything," Austin added.

"I guess you got me there. You've got me pegged and have my MO all figured out, huh?" Kevin asked with a shrug. "So after discovering all of this, why is it that you still don't know where Gabriela is?" The couple sat speechless.

"Just like I thought; you don't know as much as you think you do." As angry as they were, they knew that he was right. They were chasing the wind trying to find clues and kept coming up empty handed.

"What do you want, Kevin? What do we need to do to get you to talk?" Robin asked out of desperation.

"I'm glad you asked. I'll tell you exactly what I need

you to do. Are you listening?" He leaned over and whispered, "Go. To. Hell."

Kevin began cackling like a witch. Austin called for the guard to come and remove him.

"Kevin, please don't do this! Just tell me where she is! Please, Kevin!" Robin pleaded.

Austin held his wife around the waist to keep her from chasing Kevin back into his cell. Robin listened to his psychotic voice echo off the walls as he was escorted back behind bars. Tears rushed down her face. She felt like her hope had been ushered out the door with him.

"What are we going to do now?" she asked through tears. "He's the only one who can help us."

"We don't need him." Austin placed her head on his chest. "I promise you, we'll find her."

As Robin clung to him, he squeezed her tight and gained just as much comfort from her as she did from him.

On the way home, Austin checked in with Bells to see if there had been any new leads. The commander informed him that the case was still at a standstill, but suggested they meet. As a father himself, Bells couldn't imagine the turmoil that Robin must have been in. He wanted to assure her in person that he was working hard toward the safe return of her daughter.

They all arrived at the couple's home at roughly the same time. Joanne stood expectantly in the doorway, waiting to hear the details of the prison visit.

"Before you whisk her away, can I steal her for just a few moments?" Bells asked.

Joanne stepped back and fiddled with her watch, signaling to him that he shouldn't take his time. He nodded graciously.

"Robin, I just wanted to say to you that I admire you. I don't think even the toughest man could have endured everything that you have and handled it this well. Please know that it will not all be in vain. We've got a team of the best, and we'll get down to the bottom of things."

"I appreciate hearing that," she responded.

"I have to tell you. When Austin was assigned to this case, I knew that he would handle it with the proper care and attention that it deserved. To say that he put his whole heart into protecting you is an understatement. You *became* his heart...even in spite of me warning him to stay away. When I said that we have a team of the best, I meant it. And you've got one of the best there is, standing right here next to you," Bells said, looking at Austin.

For years, Bells had been like a father figure to him. The Commander taking the time to share his feelings was an honor that Austin genuinely appreciated.

"Your aunt is eyeballing me, and since I don't want to get on her bad side, I'll keep my promise and let you go be with her."

"Well, again, I appreciate everything that you all are doing and have done. We'll see this thing through to the end," Robin said, and turned to walk away.

"Oh, wait. One last thing, Robin." Bells pulled out the photo of Kevin Dennison standing next to his father. "We found this in your belongings at the cabin."

Robin snatched the photo from his hands and felt as if a light bulb had clicked on over her head.

"Oh my gosh! I completely forgot about this! That woman Alicia…Alice…Allysa…yes, Allysa Dennison! She gave this to me. I was out at the park with Noodles, and she came up—"

"Wait a minute, slow down," Austin said, putting his hands on her shoulders. "Who is Allysa Dennison?"

Robin looked confused. If anyone should know who Allysa was, it would have been the two of them.

"She's Kevin's sister. She met me in the park one day and—"

"Robin," Austin cut in. "Kevin doesn't have sisters. He came from a family of all boys."

She squinted, because what she was hearing didn't make sense.

"The tape recorder!" she blurted out.

Robin turned and darted up the stairs to her bedroom. She remembered tossing the recorder into her jacket pocket after she and Allysa had met. The two men were on her heels, while Joanne was left baffled, standing alone in the kitchen.

Robin stumbled into the walk-in closet and began pulling clothes off the hangers. She couldn't remember exactly which jacket she had been wearing, so she tore through every item and checked the pockets.

"Robin, tell us what you're looking for." Austin's pulse raced.

"She gave me a tape recorder, and it had our entire conversation on it. I know I left it in a pocket of one of my jackets," she said quickly. Bells and Austin joined in the search.

"I found it!" Robin shouted. She held the recorder high in the air as if she'd just found gold. Her anxious hands trembled as she pressed the play button. They all stood quietly, listening to the entire conversation between the women. Austin put an arm around her shoulder and squeezed, letting her know that this might just be the break they'd needed.

"Let's get this down to the lab right away." Bells pulled the recorder from her hands. "Do you think you'll be able to work with a sketch artist and get us an accurate description of this woman?"

"I'm pretty sure, yes."

They made their way out and Bells called ahead telling the agents at the lab to prepare for the incoming evidence.

*

Robin sat in an interrogation room with a sketch artist, trying her best to provide every detail she could recall.

"She was about 5'5, 5'6 with a wide frame. She wore dark sunglasses, so I didn't get to see the color of her eyes. I remember that her hair looked odd and stiff. Now that I think of it, she was probably wearing a wig."

The artist's hands moved delicately across the sketchpad at Robin's description.

"Were there any distinctive marks? Any tattoos, scars, or physical deformities?

"No, nothing like that. Everything all happened so quickly, though. I should have paid better attention," Robin said, beating herself up.

"You're doing fine, Mrs. Malone. Just take a deep breath and take your time."

Austin stood with his arms folded across his chest, listening to his wife's voice. Even from behind the one sided mirror, he could see the hope dancing in her eyes. Bells came in and briefed him on their progress.

"We've got our men looking into the manufacturer of that particular brand tape recorder. The audio department is running the tape through the voice analysis database to see if we come up with matches. Was she able to give some clear details on the description?" he asked, looking at Robin.

"Yeah. It isn't much, but we'll have a little something to work with. In a photo lineup she was able to identify Jack Mueller. He's a veterinarian who worked on the horses that Kevin's father bred. When she was locked away at the cabin, he had been treating her. I've already put the call out, and as soon as he surfaces, we'll pick him up." Austin took a deep breath. "I'm really having a hard time understanding who this woman could be, though. I mean, what's her angle? Did Dennison hire her for some reason just to jerk my wife around? Something just doesn't seem right. I want to hear the tape again."

While Robin continued working with the sketch artist, the two men walked down to the audio lab. Foam lined the walls, with speakers placed in each direction, like a recording studio. An audio specialist sat in a booth and played the now infamous tape over and over while the men listened in. The specialist slowed the tape down and was able to pick out specific sounds and isolate them.

"So she's out at a park, and this woman comes rushing up, basically begging her to hear her out," Bells said, more to himself than to Austin. "This mystery woman gets her to listen, and then she records the whole conversation. Why is that?"

Austin squinted, trying to think of this person's angle.

"Robin said that the woman seemed anxious and very concerned. Her description of the female sounded as if she was wearing a disguise. Maybe she had to conceal her identity because she was afraid."

"Of who though? Her brother that she's not even related to?" asked Bells.

"Yes, that's exactly who. Think about it; she's trying to warn Robin of potentially being in danger. Which means that if she's caught helping her, she'd be in danger too."

"But why take the risk to warn someone you don't even know about a man that you aren't related to?"

"Unless..." Austin said.

"Unless what?"

"Unless she had news big enough to warrant taking the risk."

Bells smiled because he was beginning to catch on.

"Knowing that this woman's baby was alive and well would be enough to make a person take a risk like that, especially if she were a mother herself."

"Yes. In so many words, she's trying to send Robin a message. Lenny, run it back one more time," Bells said to the sound tech. His heart began to pound.

"You're into real estate; maybe you should think of moving somewhere on the east coast. You know; get a fresh start and experience the life that he tried to take away from you."

The men looked at each other at the same time, as if Allysa Dennison had just spoken to them personally.

"'Move to the east coast to experience the life that he tried to take from you.' She's trying to tell her that Gabriela is somewhere on the east coast!" Austin darted out the door.

Bells right behind him, they made their way to the Proof Room. Surveillance photos hung from the walls, and Austin began pulling them down to look at them more closely. He remembered that when he was first assigned to the Dennison case, he had done a background check on all of the Dennison family members.

"Bingo!" he said, thumping a stack of papers. "Kevin's mother divorced his father and relocated with her new husband to Maryland — on the east coast."

Austin heard Robin's voice in the hallway as she walked with the sketch artist. He shot through the door and charged towards her.

"I think we found something."

Chapter Nine

Usually Robin could hardly sit still on a plane. The anxiety of flying would overwhelm her before takeoff. This time, however, she seemed to have tunnel vision and focused only on the possibility of bringing her daughter home. As she sat peering at the clouds through the thick windows of the plane, she couldn't help thinking about how far she had come.

Just a few weeks ago, the death of her daughter was a memory that she often fought to suppress. Now she was on a roundtrip flight that she hoped would turn their family of two to a family of three. Austin sat next to her, resting his chin on his knuckles. She reached her hand up and slowly massaged his head. It was a move for him that was the equivalent of catnip.

"I'm sorry," she said to him.

"Sorry for what?" his eyes closed, reveling his massage.

"I'm sorry for ever doubting you."

Austin shifted in his seat and turned to face her. "Look, you have nothing to apologize for, Robin. Let's just focus on our future together and on bringing our daughter home."

She loved it each time he referred to Gabriela as his daughter. He leaned his head on hers, and they remained silent for the rest of the flight. They both knew that this journey wouldn't be an easy one, and they mentally prepared for the ordeal that lie ahead.

*

The plane had a smooth landing. Robin and Austin made their way through the Baltimore Washington International Airport with their carry-ons in tow. A CIA field agent was assigned to meet them and provide them their lodging and transportation arrangements. As the couple approached the luggage carousel, they spotted the agent right away.

Agent Gregory Mcclain stood six feet, five inches tall and looked like he could have been the twin of Michael Clarke Duncan's character in *The Green Mile*. The man stood out in the crowd as he held a sign in the air with the last name *Malone* on it. Austin walked up and shook the agent's hand.

"Good to see you again, Agent Malone."

"Likewise. Meet my wife, Robin Malone."

"No introduction is necessary. I've heard a lot about you, Mrs. Malone," the agent said while shaking Robin's hand, "You're a hero for your will to survive all that you have. I'm a little tempted to offer you a spot on my team. We sure could use a strong woman like you," he smiled.

Robin blushed.

"Your sedan's waiting out front. Here are the keys to your room at the Monaco Hotel in downtown Baltimore. If there are any special accommodations you need, please let me know, and I'll get it taken care of."

Austin shook the man's hand once more and thanked him for everything that he'd done. Mcclain nodded at Robin and made his way to the front exit.

They gathered their luggage and Robin turned to Austin. "The Monaco Hotel? Wow, that's pretty swanky."

"Well, you are a celebrity and all," he smiled and hoisted up his bags.

The couple found the waiting sedan out front. They loaded their luggage into the trunk and got settled inside. While Austin plugged the coordinates of the hotel into the vehicle's navigation system, Robin peered into the rearview mirror. Agent Mcclain sat in the driver seat of a black sedan, waiting to trail them.

"He's assigned to our detail to make sure we don't run into trouble while we're out here," Austin explained, when he saw she'd spotted the agent.

Robin licked her lips as she buckled her seatbelt. She then prepared for a ride that she hoped wouldn't be a bumpy one.

Twenty minutes later, Austin slid the key into the hotel door and a green light flashed, allowing them access inside. Robin was speechless as she walked into the stunning hotel suite. The drapes were drawn, displaying a full view of the city. She walked out onto the balcony and peered at the twinkling lights all over town. It was 10 o'clock at night, and the Baltimore harbor shimmered beautifully, reflecting the celestial glow of the moon.

Austin walked up behind his wife and slid his arms

around her waist.

"This is just beautiful, Honey," she whispered.

"But not as beautiful as you are," he said, with his nose buried in her hair.

She turned around to face him, and he kissed her on the lips. He kissed her again more passionately, but she pulled away. Robin tried creating a romantic state of mind, but she couldn't get past her feelings of angst. Austin knew that she was worrying about how things would turn out. He watched as sadness filled her eyes.

"Come here." He grabbed her by the hand, leading her over to the bed and kneeled in front of her while she sat on the edge. "Tomorrow will be a very big day for us. We don't know what's going to happen, but we have to go into this with clear minds and prepare for every possibility."

"Austin," she exhaled, "What are we going to do exactly? We can't go showing up at Kevin's mother's house and expect her to just hand over our child — if she's even there. We're just operating on a hunch, and it all feels so rushed."

Her eyes lowered.

"Who says we can't do just that? Who says that that's not exactly the way that things will work out? The reality is that we don't know for sure, but we'll find out soon. Worrying about how it's going to unfold is fruitless and will do nothing but give you gray hairs," he tugged at her hair.

She smiled softly, and he ran his fingers along the side of her face.

"Look, I know I can't keep you from worrying or thinking about those things, but I can do my best to put a smile on your face for the time being. Whatever awaits us tomorrow will happen tomorrow. Please just allow me to do what I can to get you through the night."

Her almond eyes peered up at him. "What do you have in mind?"

"Well, let's do something fun, like...go dancing. We haven't been in a while, and you know we always have a great time. We'll get freshened up and enjoy an evening out on the town like old times. What do you say?"

He raised his eyebrows looking for her response, and finally she said, "One dance couldn't hurt."

The Harbordine Jazz Club sat in a strip just off the water. The hostess led them to a table near the stage. A few heads turned as the couple made their way down the aisle. Robin suddenly felt self-conscious, thinking that they were staring at the bruising on her face. Her fingers slowly slid up and shielded the side of her cheek. Austin tugged her hand down and whispered," You look absolutely beautiful." She clasped her hands and smiled at the fact that he always seemed to know what was going on inside her mind. The hostess informed them that the waiter would be right over.

"So is that a CIA thing?" Robin asked.

"Is what a CIA thing?"

"Being able to read my mind."

Austin chuckled at his wife. "No, that's an, *I love my*

wife and know her well, thing."

The waiter cut in, introducing himself, and they each placed a drink order.

"Long Island iced tea for me," said Robin.

Austin raised his eyebrows and mockingly applauded.

"I'll have a club soda with a twist of lemon."

The waiter gathered their drink menus and announced that he'd be right back.

"You're pretty brave ordering a drink like that. Normally a wine cooler has you talking in circles," Austin chuckled.

"Yeah, well I'm talking in circles anyway, so I figured what the hell."

The house lights went low as the Damon Warmack trio took the stage. The band began to play one of Robin's favorite tunes, and her body swayed from side to side as the melodies filled the air.

"You remember our first date?" she asked sweetly, with her head cocked to the side.

"Yes, I do, and I remember that you were late."

"Not on purpose," she laughed. "That night started off horribly. Everything that could go wrong did, and fast." She slid her hand across the table to touch his. "But who knew that by the end of the night I would be on my way to falling in love."

Austin looked into his wife's eyes and delicately caressed her thin hands. He stood from the table, held his hand out to her, and said, "How about we fall in love all over again?"

Robin slid from her seat and followed her husband out into the middle of the dance floor. Every eye in the room watched as the pair locked fingers and slowly began to move. Hailing from the mid-west, their style of dance was a whole new vibe for the east-coasters patronizing the club. Their steps moved in synch as they *cha-cha-cha-ed* together over the hypnotic rhythms. Austin twirled his wife around and even dipped her a few times, just for show. He was extra careful not to aggravate any of her injuries.

The band took notice, and the saxophonist walked out onto the floor, serenading the couple as they danced. Robin felt as if she were floating on air, moving in her husband's arms. Austin looked at his wife, feeling like she was the only person in the room. Even in the dim lighting, her face glowed, and to him, she had never looked more beautiful.

When the song came to an end the entire room applauded. Robin went laughing back to her seat as her husband tightly held her hand. "You can still move with the best of them," Austin said, making her smile.

The waiter returned with their drinks, and they toasted them in the air. "To us," Robin said. They clinked their glasses.

She took one sip and squinted as the beverage made its way down. Austin chuckled at her, and she swatted his hand.

"It's so good to see you laughing and having a good time like this. I've missed spending this type of quality time together," Austin said.

Robin smiled at his sentiments and agreed. "When we go home, we'll make sure we make nights like these a priority. Deal?"

"Deal." He kissed the back of her hand.

After a few more dances and a lot more laughs, the couple finally made their way back to the hotel.

Robin walked with her arms looped through Austin's and leaned her head on his shoulder. She couldn't have imagined a more picture perfect evening and thanked him for bringing her out.

"I know I gave you a pretty hard time, but I'm glad you talked me into coming out tonight. You knew exactly what I needed."

"Yeah, it's that CIA thing again," Austin smiled.

"Well, there's this Robin thing I've been meaning to show you. I'll give you a sneak peek as soon as we make it upstairs."

Coyly she grabbed his hand as they stepped into the elevator. On the ride up all twenty-two floors, the couple made out like they were teenagers. It felt like ages since they'd been together last, and they were both well past ready. They tumbled out of the elevator doors and continued their steamy session out in the hall. Robin finally tugged on Austin's hand and they turned, making their way to the room.

Once inside, Austin ran his fingers through her hair as she kissed a path leading up to his neck. His hands felt like butter sliding along her body, and she seductively arched her back. Robin stepped back and slowly began to undress in front of him. The balcony door was open so she crossed the room to close it.

"Outside is just fine with me." Austin ran up behind her.

As Robin looked over the balcony, she saw the black sedan with agent Mcclain sitting inside. Like a slap in the face, the reality of why they were there hit her hard and shifted her back to reality. She turned to face Austin, and he knew just that quickly that her mind was back in turmoil.

The good man that he was, he pulled her in close and wrapped his arms around her. After kissing the top of her head, he ushered her inside the room, closed the balcony door, and tucked them both into bed.

"Let's get some rest and try to relax; tomorrow will be here before we know it."

*

The next morning, Robin woke up to the smell of brewing coffee. Austin's spot in the bed was empty. She heard the shower running. She must have slept hard, because she never even heard him get out of bed. The Long Island iced tea she had the night before was probably to thank for that. Robin rolled out of bed and shuffled over to open the curtains. Rays of sunshine flooded the room; birds chirped happily on a nearby ledge.

She wrapped herself in the hotel's plush bathrobe and pushed open the doors to the balcony. It was a beautiful day. Robin found herself smiling. She peaked over the balcony's ledge and saw the black sedan, sitting sentinel down on the street below. Her shoulders were tense; she rolled them backwards, taking a few deep breaths of fresh air.

"You out here giving Baltimore a show?" Austin asked from behind her with a cup of coffee in his hands.

She smiled as she grabbed the cup from him and took a sip. Immediately her face scrunched unpleasantly.

"Blech. What happened? They run out of cream and sugar?" she walked back inside.

"After the way you were sucking down those Long Island's last night, I thought you would need something strong."

Robin playfully elbowed his stomach and gave him back the cup.

"Room service will be up with breakfast in just a bit. By the time you get out of the shower—"

BOOM!

A loud explosion rocked the entire building. The fire alarm sounded in the hallway, and the sprinkler system instantly kicked on. Robin squeezed her hands over her ears. Austin went to look out over the balcony.

"Oh my God…" he said.

Robin ran out through the doors and saw that the black sedan agent Mcclain had been in was now roaring with flames. Immediately, Austin ran to get his gun and then slid on a pair of jeans. He began shouting something to Robin, but she couldn't hear him over the sound of the alarms.

She happened to glance down at the street and saw two men with guns run toward the entrance of the hotel. She felt dizzy and nearly lost her balance when she saw that one of the men was Kevin Dennison.

"Robin, we have to go. Now!" Austin barked.

She tried her best to run, but her feet felt cemented to the ground. Her hands reached out to her husband, but he had already run out the door.

"Austin wait! Please! Austin!"

Robin's body began to shake as she covered her ears again.

"Robin! Robin wake up!"

Austin shook her by the shoulders trying to wake her. Her eyes popped open, and she let out a frightened scream.

"It's okay, Honey. It's okay. You're here in the hotel with me, and you're safe."

It took a few seconds for the dream to fade away and reality to set in. She threw her arms around his neck and clung to him shakily. Her body was slick with sweat when Austin cradled the back of her head in his hands.

"It was just a dream. You're all right, Honey."

*

An hour later, Robin walked into the lobby wearing a black turtleneck sweater, black jeans, and heavy black boots. Austin stood to greet her and did a double take.

"You look like you're dressed for a jewelry heist. We're just missing the black ski mask."

Robin couldn't help snorting out a laugh when she realized he was right.

"We'll be leaving in a few minutes. Are you sure you won't try to eat at least a little something?"

"No, I don't have much of an appetite." she responded, slinging her purse over her shoulder.

"I don't need you passing out on me, so take a bite of this bagel while I get the car."

Austin handed her the bagel and went to the valet podium. Robin ate a few bites, threw the rest in the trash, and walked to the front entrance. She breathed a sigh of relief at the sight of Agent Mcclain's black sedan out front, no flames shooting from it. Before she knew it, their car was at the curb, and she went to meet Austin.

"You ready?" he asked, as they buckled up.

"As ready as I'll ever be."

They drove out of the city and traveled up through Baltimore's countryside, trading the fast pace of the city for long winding roads. Most of the homes were made of solid brick. The real estate agent in Robin automatically appraised them for no less than six hundred thousand dollars. The real estate was prime, in one of the nation's first suburbs.

Robin rode the entire way in silence. Her palms began to moisten. Her mind raced with thoughts of how things would pan out. She slid a small picture of Gabriela from her pocket and rubbed her fingers across the child's face. Butterflies filled her stomach, and she took a few deep breaths.

A large "Welcome to Roland Park" sign sat at the corner of one of the streets, and Robin knew they were getting closer to their destination. They entered a garden community inside the Roland Park district, and the navigation system announced that the address was just ahead. Robin filled her lungs with air and slowly exhaled to calm her nerves. Austin looked over at his wife, giving her hand a squeeze as he pulled up to the curb.

"This is it," he said and put the car in park.

She looked up at the row of large homes. "Which one is it?"

"The one over there with the pumpkins on the stairs. 226 is the address."

Robin looked at the massive home and wondered if her daughter was actually inside. There was only one way to find out. She prepared herself to go in.

"You don't have to do this if you don't want to, Robin. I can go in and handle — "

"If my baby is in there, Austin, I want to be the one to go in and get her. I'm ready."

She looked him in the eye, and he could see that she was, indeed, ready and wasn't going to back down. He walked around to open her door. Robin stood. The heavy fall wind whipped her hair. Heading up the driveway together, Austin turned and gave a hand signal to the agent in the waiting car. Robin made her way up the front stairs of the home. Austin held her hand tight.

A brass knocker hung on the front of the door. Robin reached up to grab it, hesitating a brief instant. She took a deep breath, and then knocked as hard as she could. The house was quiet. She listened for movement inside but didn't hear any. Austin pushed the doorbell as they stood on the porch waiting.

After a while of no response, Robin turned to her husband. "Now what?" They hadn't counted on this development; Austin had no idea what to do next.

"I guess we'll just wait in the car for a little while. If no one comes home soon, we'll leave a note."

"A note? What are we going to say, Austin? 'Hi, I'm your granddaughter's mother, so if you don't mind, leave her by the front stairs with her luggage, and we'll be by to get her later. Thanks!'"

The couple stood bickering on the front porch and didn't notice that someone on the other side began to unlock the door. The large door slowly creaked open, and Robin's words cut off mid sentence. An older woman appeared, framed in the over-sized doorway, and greeted them pleasantly.

"How do you do?"

Robin stood speechless. She had gone through countless scenarios of what she would say. But now that she was standing there in real time, no words were coming to mind. Austin cut in to help her out.

"Hello, madam. We are looking for Mrs. Caroline

Dennison. Is she home at the moment?"

The woman's face wrinkled oddly, and she looked away.

"No, she isn't. I'm so sorry to inform you, but Mrs. Dennison passed away early last year. Finally lost her long battle with cancer."

Robin felt as if she'd just been hit with a sledgehammer. All hope of finding Gabriela had been snatched away just that quickly. Oddly enough, she began to think about Kevin. His antics since getting out of prison made perfect sense now. He was in prison at the time of his mother's death. And Robin was the reason that he wouldn't have been at her side when she passed away.

Everyone stood in the doorway staring at each other, until Austin finally broke the silence.

"Well, we appreciate your time, ma'am. We're sorry to have bothered you."

The woman smiled pleasantly and closed the door.

Robin stood staring at the door as if the woman was still there. Austin put his hand on her shoulder. "Come on, Honey. Let's go."

Finally she managed to turn around, and force her feet to march down the stairs. She felt completely emptied out. Once back inside the car, she and Austin sat in silence. He had told her all along not to get her hopes up; she wished she had listened.

"Robin, I—"

"I know what you're going to say, Austin, so just

save it," she snapped, hurt in her voice. Her eyes began to pool, and she lowered her head. "I should have listened to you and not expected too much."

He put his hand on her knee. "Actually, I was going to say that this isn't the end. We'll keep trying and following every lead until we find her. This was just the starting point. Let's mark this off the list and move on to the next plan."

"Austin, I'm sorry, I didn't mean to snap at you on the porch. I just—"

There was a light tap at the window, and Robin looked up to see the woman who had informed them of Mrs. Dennison's death. Robin quickly cleaned her face and rolled the window down.

"I realized that I was completely rude. Were you friends of Caroline's?" asked the woman.

"No, I uh—we know her son, Kevin," Robin stuttered.

"I see. Well, there's no sense in you all sitting out here in the cold. Won't you come in for tea?"

Robin turned to look at Austin, who said, "We'd love to."

*

Inside, the house was immaculate. Modern furnishings gave the newly renovated home a polished look. The woman seated them on the sofa and went off to get a tray of tea. Robin looked up at the photos on the mantel and didn't see anyone she recognized. Her eyes scanned the large room, and she realized that she didn't know whose home this was.

Has the house been sold to a new owner? Does Caroline's husband still live here?

The woman reentered the room and set the tray of tea down in front of them. Robin noticed that she remained standing after serving them, and thought that it was odd.

"My name is Isabel, by the way. I was Caroline's head housekeeper for over thirty years."

That's one question answered...now tell me where the hell my baby is, and I'll be on my way...

"Nice to meet you, Isabel. My name is Austin, and this is my wife, Robin."

"How do you do?" she said with a nod. "Yes, it was quite awful when Mrs. Dennison passed away. We all thought that she would pull through, but unfortunately that never happened. She was the kindest woman you'd ever meet. When you find a bright soul like that, you assume they'll live forever," she smiled at one of Caroline's photos.

"We're very sad to hear about her passing. From what we hear from her son, she was a very fine woman," Austin offered.

Robin kept to herself the fact that she'd always thought Kevin was the lovechild of Medusa and Satan himself.

"So tell me, how is Kevin fairing these days? We were all devastated when we heard that he was overseas during the time of her passing and couldn't make it for her funeral."

"You know Kevin; always on the move," Austin said with a nervous chuckle. His job made him quick on the draw, fortunately.

"Always into something different, that one is," Isabel smiled.

Robin and Austin had finished their tea, and Isabel called for someone to clear the tray away. A young woman in a maid's uniform appeared and shakily reached for their cups. She quickly gathered everything on the tray and made her way back to the kitchen. There was something odd about the woman, but Robin couldn't put her finger on what it was.

"Caroline's eldest son, Marcus, will be here in just a little bit. He always brings the grandchildren over to visit their grandfather. He suffers from dementia and barely recognizes them some days. It's pretty painful to see," she said, with her eyes lowered.

As Isabel spoke, Robin caught a glimpse of the young maid in the doorway of the kitchen, peeking out. When Robin looked up at her, she quickly jerked her face away and moved towards the sink. The teacups clinked in her hands as she rinsed them out before placing them up on the counter.

Suddenly, Robin felt like she'd been hit with a ton of bricks.

"Oh my God, it's her," Robin said in the middle of Isabel speaking.

"I beg your pardon, dear?"

Robin stood up and looked directly at the maid, who with her back turned now stood perfectly still.

"It's Allysa."

Austin stood next to his wife. His hand instinctively inched up toward his back where his Glock was hidden.

"Yes, dear, that is Allysa. She's one of the maids here on staff. How did you—"

Slowly, Allysa turned around and looked Robin in the eye.

Suddenly, the front door to the house flung open and in tumbled a young family. A small boy of 7 or 8 years old darted off into the family room while his father called after him, telling him not to run. The earth stood still as Robin looked at the mother – and at the toddler in her arms. The four-year-old wriggled in her mother's arms, because she wanted to go play with her brother.

"Alright, alright, you can get down, but be careful and no running, okay?"

The sweet little girl smiled up at the woman and excitedly scampered off to the other room.

Robin's heart pounded through her chest. Gabriela had been in the same room as her, and she prayed to God that what she'd just seen was real.

The husband began helping his wife out of her jacket as he greeted Isabel pleasantly.

"Sorry we're late, Isabel. Janice wanted to stop at the Roland Park Mall. You know how hard it is to tear her away sometimes."

The woman playfully scoffed at her husband as she fixed her hair over her sweater. "Don't listen to him, Isabel." She stopped, realizing they had visitors. "Oh, I'm so sorry. I didn't realize you had company."

The couple had just walked into the middle of all hell breaking loose and now were about to become part of it.

"I'm Janice Dennison. Pleased to meet you." She extended her hand out to shake Robin's.

Robin's eyes were a pool of tears, focused on the precious child playing in the other room.

"What's going on here?" Marcus Dennison asked when he sensed that something was wrong.

No one responded. Isabel looked confused as to why Robin was suddenly crying. "I can explain," Allysa spoke up.

Everyone in the room turned to her, waiting to hear what she had to say. Everyone except Robin; her eyes were still trained on her daughter. Allysa's glare turned cold as she stared at Marcus Dennison. The man was genuinely confused as he stared open mouthed back at her.

"I know about everything, Marcus."

"You know about what, Allysa?" he asked.

Allysa walked up until she was just a few feet away from him. Then she said, "Four years ago, I was here in the house when you got a visit from your brother, Kevin. I overheard a conversation that the two of you had about a certain *package* you were expecting to receive." Marcus' face began to stiffen, and Austin noticed the malicious resemblance that he shared with his brother.

"Now is not the time, Allysa" he warned through gritted teeth.

"There is no better time than now. Everyone needs to hear the truth," she shot back.

The truth brought Robin's attention back to what was transpiring in front of her.

"Marcus and his wife couldn't have a second child, Mrs. Malone. This was around the time Olivia was born."

Robin noted that Gabriela had been renamed.

"Kevin came here to the house and spoke to his brother about the complications that your baby was having, saying that he could use that to his advantage. I heard them plan to steal Olivia away from you by faking her death."

Robin labored not to correct her on Gabriela's name.

Janice Dennison was stunned as she turned towards her husband.

"But... this can't be true, Allysa. Marcus' good friend down at Shriners Adoption agency worked out the adoption for us. That's how we were able to get Olivia. Tell her, Marcus. Tell her about the agency," Janice pleaded anxiously to her husband.

Marcus simply stood in front of Allysa with a threatening look in his eye. He took a step toward her, and Austin said, "I wouldn't do that if I were you."

Agent Mcclain then walked through the front door and blocked it with his massive body.

"This is my friend, Agent Mcclain, and he's here to help us get to the bottom of things," said Austin.

Reassured, Allysa went on.

"I'm sorry to tell you this, Mrs. Dennison, but you didn't get Olivia from some *agency*. She belongs to this woman right here," she pointed to Robin.

Janice Dennison stared at her husband as if he were a complete stranger standing next to her. Her hands cupped tightly over her mouth as she shook her head from side to side.

"Marcus, how could you?" she whispered, shoulders slumping.

The angry man didn't respond. He continued staring straight at Allysa with his fists balled tightly.

"You bitch!" he growled and suddenly lunged at the young woman.

He had barely moved when Austin chopped him in the throat. Marcus doubled over, and Austin hit him again with an upper cut to the jaw. Agent Mcclain rushed into the quarrel, and Janice Dennison screamed, begging the men not to hurt her husband.

"Please wait!" Janice said, her body trembling. Her heart was torn between saving the man she loved from a beating and turning on him herself.

Austin and Agent Mcclain wrestled Marcus to the ground and handcuffed him. Unexpectedly, he turned his aggression to Robin, while the men kept him pinned.

"We did that child a favor by rescuing her from a piece of filth like you! What kind of mother lets something like this happen to her only child?!" Marcus jabbed. Without warning, Austin delivered a blow the side of his head that knocked him out cold.

Robin stood back and watched as Agent Mcclain called out on a radio that they had a kidnapping suspect in custody. Before she knew it, the house was crawling with agents who questioned the still-stunned Marcus and broken Janice Dennison extensively.

Robin sat alone on the sofa, her head reeling. Just a few feet away, Janice Dennison recounted to an agent the story of how she thought she was legally adopting her daughter. A twinge of pity touched Robin's heart for her. For four years, Janice had raised Gabriela as if she were her own. She had been the one there for midnight feedings, and she was the one potty-training and spending mother-daughter time with her. It hurt Robin to admit that this other woman mothered her daughter.

Robin had gone through the heartbreak of losing a child; the reality was that she was there to impose that same pain upon another mother. The situation was horrendous all around. Robin felt sick to her stomach.

Allysa came and sat next to her on the sofa. Robin squeezed her hand.

"I don't know how to thank you, Allysa. All these years I've been mourning the death of my daughter. And now, because of you, I no longer have to. There are no words that can express to you how—"

Abruptly, the situation all came down on Robin at once, and she broke down. She cried for every day that she didn't get to be with her daughter. She cried for Janice Dennison. She cried for all the hurt and deceit that everyone involved had been through. Robin never could have imagined that so many ugly things would come from the birth of something so precious.

"I only did what I should have done a long time ago, Ms. Malone." Allysa said to her.

Robin felt a hand on her shoulder and looked up to see Janice Dennison standing in front of her, offering a box of Kleenex.

"I am so very sorry. Please understand that I had no idea what was going on. My husband and I had been trying for years for another baby. I didn't even think twice about it when he said he had a friend who would help us out. He handled the paper work and before I knew it, she was here." She sat next to Robin on the couch. "Looking back on it now, I know I should have asked more questions. It's just that, at the time, I didn't feel like there was a need to. I was just so happy to be getting the daughter that I'd always wanted. It seemed too good to be true. But I wanted it to be, and so..."

The three women looked up as Marcus Dennison was carted out the door in handcuffs.

"I did this for you, Janice! I did this because I love you!" he shouted, as the agents ushered him out.

Janice turned her face away from her husband and wrapped her arms around herself. Her life had just been turned upside down. Ironically, only Robin could understand the turmoil of the betrayal she was feeling.

As the women sat next to each other, Robin leaned in and squeezed Janice's hand. The room fell silent.

Janice stood up suddenly and took a deep breath. "You have waited long enough, Robin. – May I call you 'Robin'? - Let me introduce you to… *your* daughter."

Robin's heart skipped as she heard the words come out of the woman's mouth. Slowly she stood up and followed Janice to the playroom upstairs. Austin's eyes caught his wife's as she moved across the room. She nodded her head, and he gave a supportive smile.

In the hallway, Janice called her son and told him to go with Isabel, who was waiting for him. "Mommy needs you to go downstairs for just a little bit. Isabel will take you to get some ice cream, okay?"

The little boy nodded, and the housekeeper guided him down the hall, leaving the women alone.

Janice held Robin's hand giving it a firm squeeze. The two then entered the room and stood a few feet away from the playing toddler.

"Olivia, come over here, sweetheart. I have someone I'd like you to meet," Janice said.

With a doll in her hand, the child came running over and stood directly in front of Robin.

"Olivia, this is Robin. Can you say hello?"

With the sweetest eyes, she looked up and said, "Hi, Robin."

Her voice was perfect, like an angel's. Robin knelt down in front of her daughter.

"Hello, Olivia." Her words were breathy as her eyes

pooled with tears.

"Are you crying?" the sweet child asked, her face filled with concern.

"Yes, I'm crying. But only because I'm very happy to meet you."

Gabriela's tiny hand reached up and touched her mother's cheek for the first time. A few tears spilled out of Robin's eyes, and the toddler wiped them away with her fingers. Her hand was warm against her mother's skin. Robin felt like she was in one of the many dreams she'd had about that very moment with her daughter. Only this time it wasn't a dream. Gabriela was there in the flesh, and Robin could hardly compose herself.

"Want to play with my toys?" Robin smiled at how generous she was and noted that Janice had done a great job teaching her to share.

"Yes, Honey, I'd love to play with your toys."

Gabriela grabbed her mother by the hand and led her over to her dollhouse. Robin stared at her tiny face that looked exactly like she had imagined. Bouncy curls spilled from the ponytail pulled high on top of her head. She had a tiny button nose and a smile that could light up the world.

As the tot struggled to open the door on the dollhouse, she furrowed her eyebrows. That was the same face that Aunt Joanne made anytime she struggled with something. Robin smiled and kissed the top of the child's head.

She turned to the door and mouthed the words, "Thank you," to Janice Dennison. The woman nodded her head, as she witnessed the touching scene.

*

Robin held a sleeping Gabriela on her chest for the flight back to Michigan. The tot was pooped out from saying all her good-byes to her adoptive family. Robin had stayed in Baltimore for three weeks and finally felt secure bringing Gabriela home. Both mothers agreed it would be best to split Gabriela's time between both families, until she was able to adjust to life with her real mother. Janice would fly out every other weekend to visit and would bring her son, Tyler, when she could. To save further confusion, Robin begrudgingly decided to refer to Gabriela using her adopted name, Olivia. It was a small sacrifice in exchange for the treasure that she was gaining.

Chapter Ten

"To be quite honest, I am sick of seeing you here in my courtroom," Judge Childs pined to Kevin. "Either you have a fixation with seeing women in robes, or you are just as insane as your behavior has been, and I'm inclined to believe the latter."

Kevin wore his usual smug expression as the judge continued to throw the book at him.

"Your actions have been downright animalistic, and since you've behaved like an animal, I will treat you as such. For the remainder of your natural life, you shall be kept at the Jackson State Correctional Facility without parole. Be thankful, Mr. Dennison, that capital punishment is illegal in this fine state of Michigan. Because if it weren't, I'd put the needle in your arm myself."

The judge banged her gavel, and the courtroom erupted.

Austin held his wife firmly and shouted, "We did it!"

"It's all over now!" Katherine Palmer, the DA said, with a high five to Robin.

This was it; the end of the worst time in her life, and the beginning of some of the best years to come. Robin let out a howl of relief as Austin picked her up and twirled her around. Flashes of light from the media cameras blinded her, but she didn't care. Every person in the room was elated with the judge's ruling and seemed to let out a collective sigh of relief.

Robin was wrapped in her husband's arms when she heard a commotion coming from the front of the room. She looked up and couldn't believe her eyes.

Kevin had somehow managed to jump onto the judge's bench and had grabbed Her Honor by the collar. A loud, "Snap!" sounded in the courtroom, and Evelyn Childs' head lulled unnaturally to one side. The bailiff charged Kevin and came close to tackling him. But Kevin spun quickly in the opposite direction while yanking the gun from the female bailiff's holster.

"Gun!" she screamed, causing everyone to hit the deck.

Robin felt as if she were watching a train wreck and couldn't turn her eyes away. Kevin's eyes connected with her across the chaos and screaming people. In a split second, his arm lifted and Robin found herself staring into the hollow end of the government issued weapon.

Her mind blocked out all the noise, and time stood still. Her brain sent the signal for her body to move out of the way.

"Pow!"

Too late.

Chapter Eleven

The weight of uncertainty hung over the shoulders of everyone inside the trauma ward's waiting room. In addition to Robin Malone's family, Timothy Palmer, the husband of District Attorney Katherine Palmer, and officers of the CIA and sheriff's office were all on pins and needles, waiting to get word on the fate of the victims.

Austin stood staring through the waiting room window. He saw nothing but the image of his wife as she lay in his arms fighting for her life. Over the years, Dennison had taken her through the wringer, trying to tear her life apart. The fact that his antics towards Robin seemed to be merely for the sport of villainy put an extra zing on the situation. The trial and sentencing should have marked the end of his tyranny. As Austin looked down at the streets that Kevin Dennison now roamed freely, he realized it would take more than justice to get rid of him.

Cassidy, with Aunt Joanne and Robert, sat quietly next to him. Cassidy's hair hung loosely around her face, her button down shirt stained with sweat. Joanne had aged 10 years over the past few hours. Her sunken eyes reflected the same grim mood that everyone else was feeling.

A team of two doctors and a chaplain walked into the room. Everyone tensed as they stood. Katherine Palmer's husband cut through all pleasantries. "How is my wife? Can I go in to see her?"

"She's in stable condition," one of the doctor's

responded. "We were able to —"

Timothy cut him off, already heading down the hall to find his other half. The doctor dashed to catch up.

Austin couldn't help thinking that if Katherine was in stable condition, the chaplain was there for Robin. He tried hard to mentally prepare for whatever news was about to be delivered to him. Dr. Arnold Chalks stepped forward, making eye contact with him. A nauseating lump immediately rose in Austin's throat. Robert put his arm around Aunt Joanne's shoulders. They stood holding each other closely.

Before speaking, the doctor sighed. "Mrs. Malone was shot through the cartilage of her ear. The bullet is now lodged at the base of her skull."

Joanne's knees nearly gave way. Austin reached out and held firmly to her trembling body. They listened to what the doctor had to say next.

"I know you'd like a prediction of her outlook, but at this time I don't feel confident in providing one."

The chaplain's presence had already given them an idea of what her outlook was. Tears instantly pooled in Joanne's eyes, her fears of the worst being realized.

"There is massive swelling to her brain, so we had to remove a portion of her skull to alleviate some of the pressure. Once we get the swelling under control, we'll be able to get a better gauge on exactly where we stand. Her vitals aren't ideal, but after the swelling recedes, we should feel confident enough to begin the removal process of the bullet."

The doctor took a step closer to the family. He

softened his voice. "She had a few things work in her favor. Passing through the first victim slowed the bullet significantly. Once exiting Mrs. Palmer's shoulder, it splintered, leaving a portion in the cartilage of Robin's ear. The other portion passed through, eventually piercing her skull. Thankfully, that area of bone is one of the most solid in the entire human body. It kept the bullet from traveling through to her brain."

Aunt Joanne unconsciously smiled. She had always joked with Robin that one day her hard head would get her into trouble. This time, it was helping to save her life.

Cassidy said, "She'll be able to survive this and live a normal life, right? Gabrielle Giffords, the congresswoman in Arizona, was able to—"

"Right now we've got a close eye on her," the doctor interrupted. He didn't want to give the family a false sense of hope, but didn't want to dash their hopes completely either. "When the time comes, we'll go in to remove the remaining pieces of the bullet. Our biggest focus at this point is making sure she doesn't develop an infection."

Just the thought sent a chill down Joanne's spine.

"We'll do our best to control the situation with a focus on getting her to the best possible point of health."

"Doctor, we appreciate all your efforts," said Austin. He paused, trying to find words suitable. There were none. The doctor, who had experienced this uncomfortable silence many times before, said, "Time will reveal the answers to all the questions you may have. For now, you should use a bit of that time to go home and rest. We'll be in touch every step of the way."

Austin had no plans to leave the hospital until he could do so with his wife at his side. He shook the doctor's hand anyway and thanked him again.

"I was hoping he'd come out and say she was okay. She's already been through so much." Hope faded from Joanne's voice. "Just yesterday she was so happy, saying how she was ready to move forward with her life. Now, she may not have a life to look forward to at all."

Joanne, with ever-wringing hands, lost all control of her emotions. She broke down in the middle of the waiting room. Her lips trembled as Cassidy, Robert and Austin encircled her in an embrace. Seeing Joanne crack struck a pang of fear deep in the pit of Austin's stomach.

"Robert, why don't you take the girls home? I'll stay here tonight and call you guys with any new developments," Austin suggested.

He was prepared for a protest from Joanne, but surprisingly, she didn't have one. She simply grabbed her handbag from the floor and, for what was probably the first time in her life, didn't put up a fight. Austin watched the threesome make their way down the hall where they were ushered by an officer to a private exit out of the hospital.

Turning around, Austin noticed that the waiting room had cleared out. He appreciated the solitude. Feeling drained, he slid down into a seat and settled in.

He noticed there was a Michigan Sentinel newspaper on the table in front of him. On the front page was an article in which the mayor spoke about the trial.

"Kevin Dennison's trial has been epic for the city of Belle Isle Heights — and not in a good way. Dennison has waged terror on Robin Malone, who is a beloved and respected member of our community. I know that Dennison will be found guilty of his actions, and when he is, we as the citizens of Belle Isle Heights will rejoice alongside Robin Malone and her family."

Austin tossed the paper back onto the table and slid further down in his seat. As if on cue, Mayor Urrond Daltry arrived on the scene. He gave someone an earful on his cell phone. "How the hell did this happen? She was supposed to be secured! Get the Commissioner on the gotdamn phone!"

The mayor's aide paced frantically alongside his boss, whose face was now drained of color.

"He's unavailable?! The world is crumbling all around us, and you're telling me he's unavailable?! I don't care if you have to rip his ass off the toilet or from inside the slut he's screwing, you just make sure you get a hold of him, NOW!" He looked like his head would pop.

His aide handed him a handkerchief to wipe the sweat from his balding head. In a childish display of frustration, he snatched it and tossed it to the floor. The disgruntled mayor suddenly saw Austin sitting at the far end of the room. His demeanor quickly changed.

"Have him call my cell," he snapped into his phone.

The not-so distinguished official got control of himself and walked over to Austin to offer words. "Agent Malone, if there's anything you need, please let me know. I'm certain your wife will come out on top of this situation. Be secure in knowing that I've got people on the case trying to locate Dennison. We'll get him," the mayor reassured. His eyebrows then creased with anger. "This situation does nothing for the terrible image that the rest of the country has of our city. We need to turn this thing around and get the heat off of us."

The mayor suddenly looked down at Austin's clothes, which still had his wife's blood on them. The city's image should have been the least of anyone's worries, but it was evident that Mayor Daltry was blind to such a notion. It was a few months before the election, and Austin knew that the mayor's concern was more for his campaign than it was for his wife, Katherine Palmer or Judge Childs. To his relief, Daltry's cell phone rang, and he scuttled off to a different area of the trauma ward where he could berate whoever was on the other end of the line in private.

Hours later, Austin found himself in the vacated waiting room, trying to collect his thoughts. All he could think about was little Olivia, who would one day learn that her father had shot her mother in the head. Although the little girl didn't yet know that Austin wasn't her real father and that Dennison was, he knew that day would come. It added to his current dread. His thoughts began a downward spiral that he fought hard to control.

What if Robin doesn't make it? Olivia doesn't deserve to

lose her mother. What will life be like without her?

Knowing the danger of the unhealthy path that his thoughts were on, Austin immediately switched gears. Flipping on the television, he hoped for a moment's escape from it all.

Unfortunately, he wasn't granted one.

Local news reporter Frank Holland broadcasted live in front of the Belle Isle Heights Municipal Court where it had all occurred. "Just hours ago, this building was the scene of a horrific tragedy. Judge Evelyn Childs was murdered in cold blood, and two victims were gunned down, all at the hands of Kevin Dennison, who at this time remains at large. District Attorney Katherine Palmer and real estate investment mogul Robin Malone were taken to Beaumante Hospital where there has been no word on their present conditions."

The camera cut to a scene where an eyewitness recalled her perspective of the events. "It was awful," she said. "I saw Kevin Dennison jump down from the judge's bench, and then he wrestled the gun away from the bailiff. I'd never heard gunshots before in real life." She looked at the ground. "When they rang out, all I knew to do was hit the floor. He took that poor bailiff as a hostage, using her for cover to get away. It happened so fast, but it seemed to go on forever in our minds, because we were all petrified. It is a very tragic situation all around."

"Bailiff Cynthia Jerome was taken at gunpoint by the assailant into an abandoned police vehicle outside the courthouse. If you have any information on the whereabouts of Kevin Dennison or Cynthia Jerome, please contact your local police department," Frank Holland reported.

Suddenly, the mayor's sullen face appeared on the screen. He stood outside the hospital entrance to address the media. "This is a sad day for the city of Belle Isle Heights and the state of Michigan, respectively." Already, Austin could tell that the speech was going to ride the hell out of his nerves. He sat back and clenched his teeth. "Snatched from us was one of the finest judges ever to take a seat at the bench. We will miss her sorely. You can rest assured that Kevin Dennison will be held accountable for his heinous actions. You must also know that the acts of this one unscrupulous individual in no way reflect the conduct that we, as members of this community, are accustomed to.

"Our city has a spirit that cannot be broken by the will of this evil man who has tried to destroy us. So we must band together and stand strong. The Sheriff's Department and I are exhausting every possible resource to ensure the capture of Kevin Dennison, and the safe return of Bailiff Cynthia Jerome." He gazed proudly at Commissioner Ronald Imes, who he'd ripped to shreds just hours before.

"I am more than confident that our police department and sheriff's office will bring this situation to an end as quickly as possible. Our history shows that when circumstances are difficult, we pick ourselves up and fight against all adversity. It is now that I implore you to join with me in sending prayers to the families of the victims—"

Austin turned the power off, fighting the urge to smash the television to pieces. The more Daltry showed up in the news, appearing to control the situation and show signs of humanity, the better his chances were of winning the votes of the city. He hated that the situation was becoming an instant campaign for the mayor's re-election. The political fabric of the matter was blaringly insignificant to Austin as his wife's life hung in the balance.

His mind went back to the day he found Robin paralyzed under Kevin's grip when he abducted her. Austin remembered having a clear shot at him. He could have blown the man's brains out. Commander Bells had talked him out of it. He'd been furious with himself ever since for not finishing this all back then when he had the chance.

Thinking of what he should have done wasn't going to get him anywhere. Austin suddenly stood up and decided to pay a visit to someone who deserved it.

*

"Baby, we did it!" Bailiff, Cynthia Jerome giggled. Kevin Dennison had just tossed her onto the bed of their ratty motel room and unbuckled his pants. "You were amazing back there! I was so turned on when I saw you jump Childs' bench and grab her by the neck. *Snap!*" she demonstrated with her hands. "You snapped it like a twig. I loved it!"

Cynthia jumped up and grabbed a bottle of the cheap champagne she'd purchased. She pushed him onto the bed. Crawling her way up Dennison's body, she kissed him all over. With his hands folded behind his head, he smiled, basking in the woman's praise.

She rose to her knees. "You slid the gun away from me so smoothly. Steadily your arms lifted, and you squeezed the trigger." With one eye closed, holding the champagne bottle like a gun, Cynthia mimicked the moment when he'd popped Katherine and Robin, all in one shot. "Pow! It was beautiful! When you grabbed me from behind, I had to keep myself from smiling. It felt amazing being in your arms and *finally* feeling you close to me."

Crawling seductively on top of him, Cynthia straddled Kevin and kissed him hungrily. In response, he ripped off her shirt. She squealed with excitement.

"I need to know; when did you first notice me?" she asked as he kissed her breasts.

"C'mon on, you can't expect a man like me to sit through months of a trial and not notice the most gorgeous woman in the room. I couldn't keep my eyes off of you. That's why I started writing you. I was hoping you'd be just as interested in me as I was in you," he charmed.

The naïve woman was flattered by his sentiments, blushing as she lay on his chest. "I was very excited when you wrote me. I'd felt a connection between us all along and felt like I'd never be able to do anything about it. And yet, here we are—finally," she sighed.

Cynthia looked into his eyes and kissed him passionately, releasing months of building tension. Kevin flipped her over on her stomach, and then kicked off his pants and underwear. Slowly he pulled a switchblade from his pants pocket, concealing it from her view.

Snip! Kevin cut off the sides of her lace pink underwear and slowly pulled them from between her legs. Already she was dripping with lust. "Now you and I can be together forever," she panted breathlessly as he entered her. He growled with bliss. Cynthia moaned loudly, in disbelief that she was living out her fantasy with the notorious Kevin Dennison. She didn't regret agreeing to help him escape because it meant having him all to herself. Cynthia grabbed his hand, and slid his fingers into her mouth just to feel as much of him as possible.

Kevin flipped her over on her back so that he could look her in the eyes. Lustily, she smiled while he stroked, harder, quicker. She couldn't seem to get enough.

Unfortunately for her, he'd had enough. Kevin was on the verge of climaxing and needed something to push him over the edge. He leaned down to her face and slid his tongue wildly over her lips. "Open your eyes," he whispered as she moaned beneath him. She did as she was told. Kevin smiled with anticipation of what was to come next.

"You know why they say you should never play with fire?" His body pumped aggressively. Her eyes squinted inquisitively, uncertain of a response. "Because you'll get burned…"

From the corner of her eye, Cynthia saw a flash of light. Suddenly a searing pain swept across her scalp. Her eyes flashed bright with fear.

Kevin had lit her hair on fire.

The sound of her voice screaming in agony pleasured him to the point of climax. His body writhed along with hers. The small flame licked dangerously close to his face. The rush was welcomed. His hands held her firmly in place, fascinated by the sight of her melting skin. The monstrous scent of her cooking flesh filled the room. The mad man knew the memory of that moment would never leave him.

*

Katherine Palmer was in the middle of giving the nursing staff a courtroom-worthy argument on why it couldn't "possibly be necessary to take this much blood from me!" when Austin walked into her room. The nurses were nervous, failing at a rebuttal with the city's most acclaimed attorney — and they should have been. Katherine had just taken a bullet but could probably still go a few rounds in the ring with Manny Pacquio before showing any signs of weakness.

"Austin," she smiled as two nurses retreated with tails between their legs.

Austin walked over with a genuine smile and placed a hand on her good shoulder.

"How are you feeling, Katherine?" he asked softly.

"Pfft. This little thing? It's just a flesh wound," she gibed. "The doctor says it was a through and through and didn't hit any bones or major arteries. They can just throw a band-aid on it and let me be on my way, if you ask me."

Austin admired her strength and chuckled at her belief that that would actually happen.

Katherine's smile faded. "How's Robin? I've been asking questions, but no one is telling me anything."

Austin pulled a chair close to her bed and slid down in the seat. "Well, that's probably because there's not much to tell. She's alive, but that's all we know right now. The bullet broke into pieces inside her. They're waiting for her swelling to go down before they can operate. Now it's just a waiting game to see how things will pan out."

Katherine pursed her lips, sincerely disturbed by the news. "How's everyone holding up?"

His shrugging shoulders implied that they were as well as could be expected. The district attorney reached her hand out to his. "Think about all she's been through, Austin. She'll get through this too, just like everything else." He squeezed back and patted her hand with a gracious smile.

"Any word on where Dennison is?"

His face hardened. "No. It's like he vanished into thin air. I'm itching to get out there myself to find him, but my priority is to be here for Robin."

"As it should be," said Katherine with a nod. "We'll find him; he's finally going to pay for everything he's done."

Austin didn't need reassurance on that. He planned to find Kevin if it was the last thing he'd ever do.

A nurse walked in, cutting off their conversation. This time she brought along muscle to help persuade Katherine to provide more blood. Austin chuckled; he knew it wouldn't make any difference. He slid his chair out. "I don't want to hold you up. I really just wanted to thank you for what you did today. If you hadn't blocked Robin the way you did, she may not even be alive right now. There are no words I can say to explain how grateful I am."

A smile took over Katherine's face. "You and Robin are like family, and as you know, protecting each other is what families do."

Austin couldn't help thinking that protection was exactly what the nursing staff would need from Katherine Palmer, if they tried poking her with more needles. As he made his way out of the room, she said, once again, "We'll get him, Agent Malone."

He relished the thought.

Austin wandered through the halls of the hospital for hours thinking about the hell that his wife had gone through. Even up until the day before the trial, she was up in the middle of the night in a cold sweat, worrying over the outcome.

"Don't worry, Honey, justice will be served," Austin had assured her. Now, almost 24 hours after that declaration, she lay dying in the hospital while her attempted murderer was on the loose. The rage that Austin harbored against him warned the universe itself that when he finally got his hands on the scumbag, he would make him pay — in blood — for all he'd done.

Austin rounded the corner back to the waiting room and saw the surgeon looking for him. "Do you have news on my wife?" He hurried over to where the doctor stood.

"Yes, I do. There was a small window where the swelling receded; we took advantage of it and made an extraction. I'm sorry that we didn't have the opportunity to call you first. But we really needed to capitalize on the opportunity to operate before the conditions changed. Thankfully, the procedure was successful.

Austin breathed a sigh of relief.

"However, we did run into a minor problem."

His chest went tight again.

"When trying to remove the bullet, we found it had weakened and splintered in several sections. We were able to successfully remove the larger pieces, but there is still a smaller portion that we felt was too risky to maneuver. We decided to leave it in place, at the base of her skull."

Austin didn't know how to respond. "So…what now? Will it ever move?"

"The positioning of the remaining fragment is favorable; however there is a small chance that it could shift in the future. The odds are encouraging enough to move forward with allowing her body to force the foreign matter out naturally."

Robin walking around with shrapnel in her head was not exactly the outlook Austin wanted. But the fact of the matter was, she'd survived—shrapnel or not.

"There is one other thing," said the doctor. "In order to do the surgery, we had to halt the blood flow to her brain. This basically means that we placed her into a medically induced coma. By inducing the coma, we are essentially shutting down the brain function, giving it time to heal without the body overexerting itself to aid in the process. We're going to leave her in that state for a few days."

"Can I see her?"

"She needs her environment to be as sterile as possible right now to prevent infection. It will be a while before you'll be able to physically be at her side. But we are working to ensure you'll get that opportunity." The doctor looked around before making his next statement. "Agent Malone, I've followed the Robin Malone case for years, and I know how much she's already been through. We're not going to let her down. We'll handle things on this end. You go and handle things out there," he pointed out the window.

Austin had been itching to get on the case, so that's exactly what he did.

Chapter Twelve

This Saturday morning was understandably different than the rest. For Aunt Joanne, there would be no Saturday breakfast with Robin and Olivia. Their weekly tradition had been brought to a tragic and abrupt halt that she hoped wasn't permanent. Sleeping just down the hall was a child who had no idea the turmoil her family was going through. Even more tragic was the fact that it was all at the hands of the child's own father.

Their family endured many setbacks over the years, including the death of Robin's parents, yet nothing had affected Joanne as severely as the thought of losing her beloved Robin. For her niece to pass away after winning so many battles against Kevin Dennison would seem glaringly unfair and like a waste of an extraordinary life. Joanne felt obligated to pull from deep inside and be strong for the rest of her family, even if she couldn't do it for herself.

From down the hall, little Olivia called out to her great-aunt who shuffled into her room.

"Well, there's my sweet baby girl. How are you feeling this morning, precious?"

The almost 5-year-old smiled and embraced her in a big hug. Joanne couldn't help thinking about how much Olivia reminded her of Robin at that age. They were both precocious and loving, with smiles that lit up the universe. Joanne squeezed a little tighter that morning.

"Guess what, Auntie!" Olivia beamed.

"What?"

"You have to guess," she giggled.

"You really want me to? Okay, let's see. Umm, you bought a giraffe and you're keeping him in the bathroom as a pet?"

"Nooo," the little girl snickered.

"Oh, I know. You want to borrow the car so you can take your new pet giraffe out on the town. Am I right?"

"No, silly," Olivia laughed again.

"Well, I give up."

"It's Saturday! Me, you, and mommy get to go eat

pannycakes!"

Joanne forced a smile. "Well, I guess you're right, it is Saturday, little Miss Olivia. I'm looking forward to going and getting some *pancakes* with you." She paused. "But mommy won't be able to come with us this time."

Olivia's face wrinkled, as if her mind couldn't compute how she could have Saturday breakfast without her mother.

"Why not?"

This was an age-old question, yet in circumstances like these, it became no easier to answer.

"Well, my sweet shuga, she had a doctor's appointment. She's sad she's not able to make it to breakfast with us, but she told me to make sure I tell you to have a good time. Also, she said if you're good, we could stop by the penny candy store on the way home. How does that sound?"

To Joanne herself, it would sound much better if her niece really was at a doctor appointment, rather than in the hospital fighting for her life.

"That sounds good," Olivia smiled. "Maybe we can go tomorrow."

Without letting on that something tragic happened, Joanne said, "It may be longer than that. The doctor is checking your mommy out because she isn't feeling well. It's going to take him a little time to make sure she's nice and healthy. In the meantime, you get to stay here with me and Uncle Jacob."

"Yay!" the little girl shouted as she climbed out of bed. She grabbed her great-aunt by the hand. "Let's go pick out something for you to wear to breakfast." Joanne chuckled at her tenacity, and then grimaced when she recalled looking like a circus clown the last time she let the tot pick out her clothes.

On the way to her closet, Joanne heard Olivia shout, "Mommy!" The child ran up to the television where Jacob was watching the morning news. A recent photo of Robin displayed on the screen as a news anchor spoke about the tragic details from the night before. Joanne quickly charged over to the television and ripped the cord out of its socket. She turned and glared at her beau who whispered, "I didn't know she was awake."

Joanne looked at him with fiery eyes and then ushered the impressionable child out of the room.

"Mommy was on TV, Aunt Joanne, did you see her?"

"Yes, I saw her, honey," she said flatly. "Now let's go and get ready for breakfast."

The family matriarch fought the lump rising in her throat as she steered Olivia down the hall.

*

Austin hadn't realized he'd fallen asleep until his ringing cell phone jolted him awake. It had almost been a week since the shooting. Robin was still in the medically induced coma. Each passing second was agony for him. He tried to fill the time by tracking clues that would help him get to Dennison. The agent's body ached as he reached for his cell phone from the coffee table that had files and photos scattered all over it. While rubbing the back of his neck, he saw that the call was from Commander Bells. He hurried to pick it up.

"Agent Malone," he answered, hoping Bells hadn't already hung up.

"How you holdin' up?" asked his boss.

"Still no word from the doctor yet. So, I guess I'm doing as well as can be expected." Austin stretched his legs, and shook his foot to wake it up.

"Just know that you aren't going through this alone; you have all of us here to support you." Austin appreciated the kind words. "Well, you know I wouldn't call you unless I absolutely had to." Bells paused and Austin knew something serious was on his mind.

"What's up, boss?"

Bells took a few seconds before speaking again. "I don't want to get into the details over the phone, so I'm going to need you to meet me downtown."

"Where at?" was Austin's response, as he jumped to his feet.

"The sheriff's department..."

Bells' trailing voice was a definite signal to Austin that something was up. It didn't seem like something good.

Austin sped through the streets, rushing to meet the commander. He slid into a spot on Beaubian Street and noticed a specific set of unmarked vehicles parked in front of the building. That meant only one thing: the mayor was there. Austin instantly became suspicious about what was really going on. With clenched fists, he walked into the sheriff's office and was immediately shown back to a private room. The conversation inside came to a halt when he entered. Staring back at him was Mayor Daltry, Commissioner Ronald Imes, Commander Bells, two Michigan State Police detectives and two sheriffs.

Austin glared coolly at Bells, wondering why he hadn't given him a heads up about what he was walking into. He also wondered what cockamamie excuse he'd be given as to why he was called so late to a meeting that had clearly been going on for a while without him.

Mayor Daltry took it upon himself to say, "I'm glad you could make it, Agent Malone. I'd like you to meet the task force assigned to investigate the escape and whereabouts of Kevin Dennison. This is Commissioner Imes," he said as the commissioner extended his hand. The rock hard look in Austin's eyes made the man retract his hand, fearing he might not get it back. In spite of the awkward exchange, the mayor continued. "These two men are detectives Jake—"

Without regard for the mayor or anyone else in the room, Austin turned and said to his boss, "What are they doing here? We've been working on the Dennison case long enough to not need the help of the local authorities."

Bells, feeling his agent's frustration, said, "The mayor and commissioner are here to offer assistance on the case and to find—"

"We appreciate your concern, but this case is under the jurisdiction of the Central Intelligence Agency," Austin directed his statement toward the mayor. "We'll inform you of any information we feel you need to be aware of."

"Now, see, that's where you're wrong, Agent Malone." The mayor stood. "This case has now become the shared jurisdiction of the sheriff, state police, and any other authority I see fit." He handed Austin a signed court paper that verified his statement. "I didn't invite you here as an agent on this case. I brought you in solely as an advisor."

Austin felt like he'd been slapped in the face.

How the hell can they make me an 'advisor' on a case that I've lived and breathed for the past five years of my life?!

"Now, I know you have personal ties to this case, but I can see to it that you are removed if you feel that your emotional capacity isn't up to par."

Austin had just been threatened to stay in his lane. It wasn't an easy pill for him to swallow. From this point forward, he would be held under the thumb of the oily city official.

Commissioner Imes attempted to ease the tension. "Gentlemen, this case is personal to us all. I'm sure we can work together to locate Dennison and put him behind bars, where he belongs." Imes' summation of putting Dennison behind bars was further proof to Austin that they didn't belong on the case. Kevin Dennison needed to pay in blood for all the things he'd done. Austin knew that he was the only one willing to make that happen. The agent wondered what deplorably slimy deal the mayor had cut to get control over the investigation. Until he could figure out some red tape that could keep them out of his way, he decided he'd have to keep his mouth shut.

Mayor Daltry, knowing he'd just trumped Austin, said to him, "Now that we have a better understanding, we can fill you in on our latest findings." He took his seat while nodding his head. The sheriff called for someone named Artie on the radio.

A chubby man with adult acne walked into the room carrying a tray of items marked as evidence. The eyes of everyone in the room fastened on the objects when the man laid them out on the table.

"This is Artie Camille, one of Michigan's finest forensic scientists," said the mayor. Austin was aware of who Artie was; he'd worked with the CIA before. He was glad to see him, because Artie knew his stuff.

Looking down at the items on the evidence tray, Austin noticed there were words scribbled with a magic marker on a brown paper bag. Artie picked it up and said, "The paper bag is a low grade brand that can be found in any store from here to Timbuktu." He added, "The marker used was Crayola jet black, which again is sold at countless retailers. It'll be hard to track back to a specific store, but we'll see what we can do."

Austin was confused about the items sitting in front of him. No one had explained what they were.

"Right away I noticed that the person who sent this wasn't shy at all about leaving forensic evidence behind. We were able to lift some pretty clear prints. I sent samples of everything to the lab to see if we could get a hit in CODIS or IAFIS, and this morning the results confirmed they belong to Kevin Dennison."

Instantly, the hair on the back of Austin's neck began to rise.

Commissioner Imes said, "Agent Malone, this package was delivered to the front desk of the sheriff's department. It was addressed to you."

"Is this how it came?" Austin asked, looking at a large envelope with his name on it.

"Yes. The package came through the U.S mail, of course, without a return address. We've already brought in the mail carrier and the workers at the post office, but it appears they don't have any involvement."

Artie handed Austin a pair of gloves and pointed to a small box on the table.

Lying next to the box was the paper bag with a note that read: *Here's to another hair-raising experience.*

Bells nodded to Austin to open the package. Once the agent laid eyes on what was inside, his blood began to boil. It was clumps of human hair that appeared to be singed.

Austin, now furious, said, "He's toying with us, as usual. It's his MO."

"There's more." Artie handed a small jewelry box over to Austin. "We received another package." The mayor and other men eagerly waited to see what was inside.

Flipping the top on the small velvet box revealed the severed tip of a human finger, placed in the tiny slot where a ring would normally be. Mayor Daltry squeamishly looked away. Austin noted that it wasn't just the man's political structure or moral decorum that was weak.

Artie looked at Bells. "We've received confirmation that the fingertip belongs to Bailiff Cynthia Jerome. The good and bad news is that she was alive when the fingertip was severed. So, hopefully this means we will locate a human being once we find her, and not a corpse."

Instantly, the mayor became angry.

"Why in the hell didn't I know about this latest bit of information regarding Cynthia Jerome?" He looked around to see who was responsible for keeping him out of his own loop. Commissioner Imes sat closer to the edge of his chair wondering why he hadn't been briefed on that information, either.

"Well, Mr. Mayor, this and all other cases involving Dennison have been handled by the CIA — up until this point," said Bells. "With all due respect, sir, we wanted to keep this bit of information locked up tight. Kevin Dennison is a powerful figure with known ties in the city. We felt it best to maintain the integrity of the case by keeping the details as close to the vest as possible. Any details being leaked to the press could set off another hailstorm of panic and negative attention."

Bells' assertion of negative publicity was the only thing that kept him from being reamed out by the mayor.

"This man is an animal. We need to get him off the streets right away," Daltry said firmly. He then leaned forward and placed his balled fist on the table. "What in the hell has made this bastard so angry? We need to get inside his head. If we know what makes him tick, we'll have a better chance of finding him."

As much as Austin loathed Mayor Daltry, he had to admit that he had a point. Kevin's behavior over the years had escalated from minor felonies to brutal violence, and it was all unwarranted. "At this point, I think it would be best to bring in a forensic psychiatrist to help us get a better understanding of things," Austin suggested.

Every head in the room nodded, agreeing that it was the decision needing to be made.

"I'm glad to see you're on board with your role in this case," said Daltry, making it clear that Austin should have limited involvement. He spoke to everyone else. "Now let's set our hands to purpose, and see to it that we find Dennison and Miss Jerome. We cannot allow him to make a mockery of us or this city."

The mayor delegated teams assigned to different tasks, purposely leaving Austin's name off the to-do list. Looking at his watch, he stood up and said, "I've got matters of the city to attend, but I'll be in touch. I want to know updates every step of the way. We'll meet up every few days and compare notes of what we've found in the field."

As if he were a celebrity, he slid on a pair of dark shades and strode out of the room with his entourage of one, Commissioner Imes, following close on his heels.

"Why'd you let me walk blindly into that battle zone

back there? You all have had this information for days now, and I didn't know a damn thing about it. What the hell is going on?" Austin asked Bells as soon as they walked out the front door of the sheriff's office. Bells didn't respond right away, waiting until he knew for certain that they were out of everyone's earshot.

"I knew you could handle yourself against those clowns, Malone. If I had told you what was going on, you would have reacted in a way that would have gotten us both kicked off the case. What I'm doing is playing their game and being clearheaded, because you can't be right now. I couldn't give a damn about what protocol the mayor or anyone tries to put in place. But what I do care about is the integrity of this case, and the only way I can ensure that it's handled the right way is for me to be on the front line with my eyes and ears open. How do you think Artie was the forensic scientist put on the case? It was because of my suggestion. We're still calling all the shots, Malone. But we have to play their game, just for a little while, so they won't get in our way."

"So, I'm off the case entirely?"

"Come on, Austin, you have to be realistic. There was no way you could be on the front lines of this case without getting your emotions wrapped into it. Daltry is keeping you on merely as an advisor, but like I said; we'll do what we do, no matter what he says. I'll be the eyes and ears in there, but in the streets, we'll play it how we see fit."

Austin didn't like the situation, but he trusted Bells and was confident in choosing to go along with his plan.

Chapter Thirteen

Cynthia Jerome sat uncomfortably with her mouth, hands and feet bound. A trail of blood dotted a pattern from her head all the way down her right arm. Her fingertip had been raggedly severed; her hand and scalp throbbed mercilessly. For hours her muffled screams were heard by no one. She'd tried everything she could think of, even drudging up memories of the *What to Do If You're Taken Hostage* training she'd gone through in the academy, yet she still was unable to free herself. Her body reeked of exhaustion from the sheer effort.

The young bailiff recalled her graduation day from the academy and the proud look on her mother's face. She'd never seen her mother smile so much. Thinking of her mother's certain broken heart when learning of her daughter's torture and death made her sob hard. When the motel room door slammed, her body shook with fear. She tried her damndest to clean her face, not wanting Kevin to see that she had been crying. Any emotional display had set him off in the past, so she worked to avoid it happening again.

"Honey, I'm home," Kevin said pretentiously when he entered the room.

Cynthia didn't respond and turned her head away from the sound of his voice.

"I ran some errands today," he kicked off his shoes. "Seems there is always much to do but little time to do it. Do you ever feel like there just aren't enough hours in the day?"

His speaking to her as if they were a happily married couple sharing the details of their day baffled Cynthia. The ugly truth was that she was a hostage who'd been savagely burned and had a piece of her body chopped off. The last thing she wanted was to casually engage in senseless banter.

"Are you hungry?" he asked, pulling the gag from her mouth.

She was afraid to say yes, afraid he'd feed her poison, for all she knew. But death was a welcome option for her at that point, so she was willing to accept whatever would help the process along. "Yes, I'm hungry."

Kevin sighed as he tore open a plastic cup of tropical mixed fruit. He scooted a chair close to her and fed her the syrupy fruit piece by piece with his fingers. She felt like a child. She'd never experienced such humiliation in her life.

Once the cup was empty, he dutifully wiped her chin and gently cleaned her face.

"I picked up a few things while I was away," he beamed. "Let's see; I got some food, a few magazines, and look," he said, grabbing a newspaper and holding it up. "I made the front cover of the Michigan Sentinel."

Cynthia wondered if he actually expected her to be able to see the paper through the black eye he'd given her the night before, or if he was simply being cruel, as usual.

"They picked the worst photo of me." Kevin slid

down onto the floor next to her feet. "The headline reads, 'Escaped Convict's Path of Destruction.'" He smiled wickedly, pleased by the ominous accolade.

"'Path of Destruction' — I like that. When they write a book about me one day, I hope they use that phrase as the title. It has a certain *je ne sais quoi*, don't you think?" Cynthia nodded in agreement, and he smiled at the confirmation. "There's no doubt that I'm a household name these days. Little kids will probably look up to me and name their little toy soldiers after me. It makes me feel so...proud," he beamed.

Cynthia had no doubt that he actually believed his delusional thoughts.

"When I was little, I used to wonder what the point of life was. I mean, think about it; you go to high school and then to college. Maybe get married and have kids, but then what? It's like it's all for no reason. I thought there would be nothing left to look forward to. But one day I realized there is certain power that life gives you to want to discover new things and new feelings. Think about it; how many people can say that they took someone's life with their bare hands? Not many, that's for sure." He grinned and said, "But I can. I find a way to do the impossible and the unimaginable, and I've come to understand that it's my talent."

There was a look of pure bliss on his face. He was brilliantly psychotic, and Cynthia found herself intrigued by his psyche. She didn't understand how he could seem so sane sometimes, like when he'd gently bathe her or brush what was left of her hair. He'd go from that extreme to believing that he was a role model for murdering people. She was baffled by it all.

"I'm probably going to go into the books of Michigan history, if not U.S history. You think?"

Cynthia rolled her good eye. He instantly became enraged. "Are you even listening to me?!" he screamed as he jumped to his feet. He grabbed her by the head and punched her hard on the area that had been burned. She screamed in agony.

"Why are you doing this to me?!" she foolishly asked. "I've only tried to help and love you, Kevin. Why would you want to hurt me after all of that?! I put my job on the line; I risked everything to help you be free and now you—"

"Blah, blah, blah," he mimicked as she began to cry. "You're in this situation because you wanted to be, Cynthia." She shook her head from side to side, and he said, "Yes, Honey, yes you are. You wanted to be with the infamous Kevin Dennison and experience life walking on the edge with the man himself. Now you're getting to do exactly that."

"Kevin, please, just let me go."

"Let you go? You want to leave me? What is it with you women always wanting to leave?!" he shouted. "It was the same thing with Robin. I took her to this nice cabin in the woods where there was no one else but me and her, and she tried to escape from me the whole time. She's my child's mother, for goodness sake. You'd think we were better than that."

Cynthia remembered from court that Kevin had kidnapped Robin and locked her away in a cellar secluded in the woods. She also remembered hearing about her being tortured for days at a time and Kevin drugging her so that she couldn't fight him off. The young bailiff wept for herself and hoped that somehow he'd let her go free. Quickly, she devised a plan to play on his emotions by agreeing with the events as they happened in his world.

"Kevin, I know how good you were to Robin and that she was ungrateful for all you'd tried to do. But I am not that way. I don't want to leave you. I want to be here with you," she said nervously. "Just not like this, being tied up. Please believe me when I say that I will never treat you the way she did. But when you have me tied up, it doesn't allow me to treat you the way that you deserve."

Almost instantly Kevin's aggression seemed to calm. Sensing that she was on the verge of breaking through to him, she pressed on. "You're an amazing man and anyone would be lucky to be with you. Robin was a bitch for ever taking you for granted, Kevin."

Suddenly, he leaned down so that his eyes were level with hers. She tried mustering a smile to make it appear that her sentiments were genuine.

"So you're saying that Robin is an evil and vile woman that you hate?"

Cynthia nodded emphatically. "Absolutely. Absolutely she is."

Kevin was quiet as he peered into the glassiness of her emerald green eyes. A single tear trickled down her face, resting on the apple of her cheek. With that, he simply stood up and walked away. Cynthia let out the breath that she'd been holding as tears of relief began to fall. The psycho seemed to respond well to flattery. Her plan from that point forward was to be as supportive of him as she needed to be, until she could find a way out.

As if somehow reading her thoughts of freedom, Kevin swung around and powerfully backhanded her, sending her flying backwards.

"Take it back, bitch! Take it all back! Don't you DARE speak about Robin that way!"

Through her grainy vision she saw Kevin angrily scramble away and pick up a shiny object. Enraged, he charged back over to her and yanked her head back. She cowered on the floor begging for mercy, and wondered what was in his hand.

"You have a filthy mouth, Cynthia." He pried open her lips and grabbed her tongue while she struggled beneath him. "We have to do something about that..."

*

Austin had been home from the meeting for over an hour, yet the car still idled in the driveway. The day hadn't treated him well. He knew that the lonely silence of his family-less home would be no better. He was tempted to pay a visit to the hospital just to watch over his wife. But the compounded nuisance of local cops swarming the halls and his wife's ever-pending prognosis warned him not to.

There was loads of stress needing to be unleashed; he knew of only one place to release it. His Coldplay CD had just switched to the second round of repeats when he pulled out into the street. After several security checkpoints, Austin hustled to the CIAs Cavity headquarters weight facility. The room was empty and smelled of testosterone from the other agents who, just like him, used the room as a source of stress relief. His leather, fingerless gloves squeaked when he pulled them over his massive hands, preparing to pound out his aggression.

Austin lay flat on the weight bench, flashes of his wife's distorted face haunting him. He easily lifted the 180 pounds of weight mounted on the rack. Rep after rep, he pushed up and down, each time harder and faster than the last. The agent wished he could bulk up on the mental strength that his wife's condition drained from him.

Startled, he saw a face appear upside down above him. It was Commander Bells. With a loud *Clunk!* Austin dropped the weight onto the rack. He sat up, using his forearm to wipe the beads of perspiration that dotted his face. "How's your wife?" Bells asked, sliding smokeless tobacco into his cheek. Gulping water, Austin shrugged, "Still a waiting game." His curt response indicated his lingering frustration over the meeting with Daltry earlier.

"Well, keep me posted, and let me know if you need anything."

Austin nodded, and the commander turned to leave. "What happened earlier was fucked up, Bells," he said suddenly.

The commander ran his tongue over his teeth, careful not to rush his response. Slowly he turned back around. "Let me take this opportunity to remind you that you are my agent. Not the other way around. It's my job to make hard-hitting decisions, even when they don't benefit you, Malone. I'm not going to let you stomp around here throwing a hissy fit just because you aren't getting your way. What's *fucked up* is your wife lying in the hospital because of a lunatic out on the loose. Now, you can sit there and sulk some more, or you can get your pansy ass up off that bench and help out like you're supposed to."

The reprimand more mirrored a father scolding his son than the clash of pride that it appeared to be. Austin knew that he deserved to be put in check. His getting up and following the commander to the Proof room affirmed this.

Both men walked into the evidence room that had files scattered across the table. They burrowed down into the mass of work and set their minds in motion.

"Now, let's see," Bells tapped his chin with an ink pen. "The question that has been burning in my mind is: what was his angle? Did he *intend* to kill Childs, Kat Palmer, Robin and then escape? Or was it more a decision made in the moment?" The questions were said more to himself than to Austin.

"There's no evidence to show that his actions were premeditated. I honestly feel that the judge handed down the decision, and he just snapped. Did he think it through to the end of whether or not he'd make it out of the courtroom? Only he would know the answer to that. At this point, I don't think it really matters."

"But it does matter," Bells retorted. "And the reason

why is this: how was it that he was able to escape a courtroom in broad daylight from a scene that was televised all over the country?"

Bells had a good point.

"So, you're thinking he had help. Someone on the inside helped him get away? If that's true, who could it be? Who would be foolish enough to get involved?"

"Well, you know Dennison has friends in high and low places. Who knows what goons he had working for him. I think we should look at the history of every security guard, inmate, and worker of any kind that he came in contact with while in custody."

"I'll pull some records and see what I can find."

An agent walked into the room, unaware that Austin had now joined Bells. It was Agent Sidwell. Austin's jaw clenched at the sight of him. A year ago Sidwell was assigned to tail Robin when Dennison was released from prison. It was his job to protect her, yet somehow he was MIA when she was kidnapped. Sidwell was interrogated and interviewed dozens of times by the CIA's version of Internal Affairs and was cleared of any wrongdoing. He received nothing more than a mildly angry slip of paper in his file in return for his costly negligence.

Austin didn't care if the Pope himself had cleared him; in his gut, he still felt like Sidwell was hiding something and didn't trust him.

"Oh, I didn't realize you weren't alone," Sidwell said to Bells. "I'll just bring these files back later on." Bells, who was all about business and not emotions, said,

"No, show me whatever you need to show me. There's no reason to wait." Sidwell's eyes lingered over Austin, whose gritting teeth were heard by everyone in the room. Sidwell fumbled through explaining a warrant discrepancy with another case, while Austin's eyes burned into the side of his head.

After covering his information with Bells, Sidwell cleared his throat. "Malone, I just wanted to say that I'm sorry to hear about—" He cut himself off when seeing the bulging veins in Austin's neck. With a dry swallow, he abandoned his useless condolences and exited the room.

Bells didn't bother lecturing Austin on letting go of his heavy feelings towards Sidwell—even though he knew those feelings did more harm to him than good. Instead, he let Austin focus on the case, hoping that getting one step closer to capturing Dennison would help alleviate some of his stress.

Days later, Bells and Austin found themselves on a stretch of land just north of Interstate 75. When they arrived on the scene, the sheriffs were dusting an abandoned vehicle for prints. Commissioner Imes was there and briefed them on the scene.

"We have confirmation that this is the vehicle used by Dennison to escape from the courtroom." He led the men over to the vehicle that had been torched and was still smoldering. "It was set on fire using an accelerant, most likely gasoline from the smell of it. We'll need to wait for the evidence report from forensics to confirm."

"There isn't much here but a charred frame. Why are you so sure that this is the vehicle Dennison used?"

asked Bells.

"Because he left his calling card." Imes walked over to a table they'd set up for bags of evidence. He picked up a license plate and showed it to the agents. "It's registered to the local PD and has been confirmed that it belongs to the stolen vehicle. Also, it was the only thing we found that hadn't been burned. Dennison is doing everything he can to prove that this is his work."

"Then why torch the car in the first place?" Bells questioned.

This time it was Austin who responded. "Because he can. Torching the car is his way of giving us the finger. You need to do a search to see if he has any known allies in this area. This place is too random for him to be out here without having a specific reason to be. You should get an APB out on him and alert the locals."

"Already in the works," Imes responded.

Austin walked over to the car and bent down to look inside. "Any signs of Cynthia Jerome?"

"Not yet, but we're still collecting evidence."

Austin wouldn't have been surprised if they had found her body in the trunk of the car. He knew that since Kevin had no more use for her, he'd dispose of her the first chance he got. The agent sympathized with Cynthia for getting dragged into the situation. With no idea that she was an accomplice, Austin and the rest of the men felt a sense of urgency to find her.

Like vultures on a carcass, Austin saw several news vans swoop in with story-hungry reporters ready to pounce. "Could this be the vehicle used by Kevin

Dennison to escape police custody?" one reporter shouted. Local officers rushed over to the forming mob of camera crews. "Stay back!" the officers warned, to keep the open scene contained. Austin and Bells used tarp and anything else they could find to form a visual barrier around the evidence. They didn't want details leaked to the press, who would undoubtedly misconstrue facts and send the public into further panic.

Mayor Daltry's car pulled up onto the gravel, his aide rushing around to open the door for his disgruntled boss. He charged towards Commissioner Imes dramatically. Austin was pissed with this display, since it obviously pointed to the importance and severity of the scene, further encouraging the media's curiosity.

"It's Dennison's get-away vehicle isn't it? Did you find Cynthia Jerome? How far do you think he got from here?" Imes tried his best to keep up with the mayor's multitude of questions, but it was impossible. Bells and Austin let the mayor continue ranting to the Commissioner while they thought about what the next move would be.

Austin's phone rang. His face turned sallow when he saw the number on the screen.

Bells stopped in his tracks, figuring that the call was from the hospital.

"I'll be right there," said Austin after a few minutes of listening to the caller. His skin was now slime green when he turned back around to face the commander.

"I've got to go," was all he said as he slipped the

phone from his ear. He nervously started towards his vehicle. Bells didn't need to ask him what was going on; the haggard look on the man's face told Bells that there had been a new development with Robin.

Austin blew through the halls of Beaumante Hospital like a storm. The doctor had been uncomfortably vague when he'd told him to come immediately. Austin's worried eyes bounced on the room numbers, searching for the right one, his heart pounding through his chest. Anytime Robin was involved in an equation, the stakes, along with his blood pressure, seemed to rise.

Dr. Chalks exited Robin's room just as Austin rushed in. With an extended hand, he spoke a greeting to the agent. Austin didn't hear a word. He breezed into the room, holding his breath with anticipation of what he'd find. Upon rounding the corner, he found himself shocked to see his wife sitting upright in bed. Her head was heavily bandaged and had swelled to an abnormal size. Even through it all, Austin could see the woman he'd fallen in love with. Not known for being emotional, he was completely out of character as his eyes began to well.

Butterflies fluttered wildly in his stomach when he walked over to her bed. She looked up with fear lingering in her eyes. It was all the invitation he needed to wrap her in his massive arms. Relieved, he was careful not to squeeze too hard, but couldn't help the need to be close enough to feel the life pulsing through her veins. Finally he took a step back. "You scared me for a minute there. But I should have known that you weren't leaving me anytime soon."

Robin stared at Austin as if she were surprised to see him. The truth was she couldn't remember his name.

"How are you feeling?" he asked, after another embrace.

"I—" she stopped, her throat too dry to continue. The doctor handed her a Dixie cup of water that burned her throat when she drank it.

"Better?" asked Austin.

She nodded, unsure of what to say next. Braving the silence, she croaked, "The doctor said I was in an accident and that you would explain it all once you got here." She squinted, still trying to recall his name.

It had never occurred to Austin that she wouldn't remember what happened. For him, the memory had been mercilessly seared into his mind.

"Well, Honey," he hesitated, "...you were shot."

Her eyes widened in horror.

"How did this happen? Who would—"

Suddenly, blurry images began to flash in her mind. Robin rubbed her neck, trying to focus on the flood of random memories that came rushing back at once.

A horrifically gruesome memory clawed at her on the inside. Kevin Dennison's steady hand raised; the gun fired. *Pow!* Suddenly feeling a hand on her shoulder, she jerked away from the memory and back to reality.

Austin's concerned faced stared down at her. Robin's eyes began a pitiful pool. "I remember," she whispered.

Some part of him wished she could have held on to the bliss of being uninformed for just a little longer. The dismay painted brightly on her face reminded him that, unfortunately, life didn't work that way.

"Everything will be okay, Honey," he squeezed her hand."

A snicker crept from her lips. Even she didn't know why.

Austin said, "Aunt Joanne and Gabriela are on their way here. Robert is bringing—"

Robin suddenly let out a full-blown laugh. The laughing continued; she couldn't seem to control herself. Austin's worried eyes begged for a reason.

Dr. Chalks, spotting her dilated pupils said, "I'll need to run tests, but I believe she may be affected by something called Pseudobulbar Affect. It's a condition where sufferers have sudden outbursts of involuntary emotional displays. This is common in individuals who've had brain injuries. Picture it like improper wiring; a flip on the light switch, but the toilet flushes sort of thing," he said, checking her over.

Austin exhaled, feeling slightly relieved. This wasn't the worst that could happen, but in the scope of everything else that had happened to her, the effect of the lightweight blow still registered.

"Mommy!" Olivia's voice suddenly squealed as she bounced into the room. Robin's swollen face instantly lit up.

"My baby...Oh my gosh, my baby!" Robin squeezed her daughter tight.

Dr. Chalks looked concerned over the energetic tot who, with the help of her father, scaled her mother's bed until she was nestled securely in her arms. Robin didn't feel an ounce of pain, only love. Joanne shuffled over, joining in on the affection.

"Robin, you sure know how to scare me half to death," she leaned down, with a smile, to kiss Robin on the forehead. Looking over her aunt's shoulder, Robin noticed her brother standing safely at a distance, not wanting to pull, tug or unplug the wrong thing.

"It's okay," Robin said to her brother, who she knew was afraid. "I won't bite, I promise." Braving his fears of seeing his sister in pain, he inched close enough to plant a kiss on her cheek.

"Mommy, is your head okay? Your face doesn't look nice. You got a owie?"

Robin smiled. "I sure did get a owie, but it feels much better, now that I see you." Olivia giggled, and so did Robin, but only from her condition.

"So when will you let her out of here so we can take her home?" Joanne asked Dr. Chalks, ready to take her niece home that night.

"Well, Mrs. Malone is in pretty good condition. If she keeps going at this rate, I can see her going home within the week."

Joanne clasped her hands and everyone breathed a sigh of relief. Austin's phone rang. He stepped away from the group to answer it.

"It's Cynthia Jerome," Commander Bells blurted out.

Plugging a finger in his ear Austin said, "I thought we'd already confirmed those prints. We got the hit in IAFIS—"

"You don't get it. We think she helped him plot the escape."

Rage boiled in Austin's stomach. His joyous moment had just had a healthy dosage of salt poured all over it.

*

With a deep gash on her tongue, Cynthia sat in the bathtub. Kevin sponged water over her body. She'd learned to appreciate the calm times, even though his touch felt like acid against her skin. Currently, he was on a rant about yet another newspaper article.

"Guess who got to go home from the hospital?"

Even though it was a rhetorical question, Cynthia knew better than to not answer him. "Robin?"

"Yes, Robin is exactly right. You know, sometimes I feel like she's a cockroach that I just can't seem to squash. Have you ever had someone like that in your life?" he asked nonchalantly.

There was no way she would tell him that she was staring her vermin in the face. Instead she replied, "You'll get her."

He smiled at her confidence in him, and rewarded her by caressing the soft skin on her breast. "You're right, you know. It's only a matter of time before I put an end to the Robin Malone chapter. I've had enough fun with her." He looked at Cynthia and chillingly asked, "How long do you think we'll have before it's time I put an end to me and you?"

Dread locked her mangled tongue in place at a question impossible to answer. She knew that her days were numbered, but forcing her to think about it was almost as horrendous as the end itself.

The scent of her fear wafted pleasantly to his nostrils. Kevin kissed her forehead and smiled. "Let's not think about that right now. There's another target in my sights that's as hard to get rid of as the other one." He referred to Austin. "I've got a few special things lined up for Agent Lover Boy, though. I can't wait to see how they play out."

Cynthia knew that he was up to no good. She desperately wished she could scream out so that someone could save her and the lives of everyone else that hung in the balance.

Chapter Fourteen

Austin's eyes were on fire after having gone through file after file. He and the task force worked tirelessly to figure out Kevin Dennison's whereabouts, all to no avail. One after another, each of the avenues they pursued turned cold. Stacks of papers were strewn about the room, leaving the agent half buried beneath the wall of useless information.

His current focus was on a pile containing every shred of information about Cynthia Jerome's life. It included driver's licenses, computer passwords, names and numbers to all her friends and relatives. The abundance of information at his fingertips still meant nothing. Not a single lead to Dennison's location had come of it. An 8 x 10 photo of Cynthia's face was tacked to a corkboard. "Why'd you get yourself involved in this?" Austin asked the photo. Cynthia's unmoving eyes stared back at him, providing no answers. The wheels turned quickly in his mind while he summoned his infamous gut to kick into action.

The agent realized just how exhausted he was when he almost admitted gratefulness for the extra help of Mayor Daltry's task force. They'd found the potential link between Dennison and Cynthia. After reviewing media footage of the courtroom on the day of the escape, they noticed how the interaction between him and Cynthia seemed choreographed and stiff. He didn't know how he was able to miss it himself. The fact that the case was so close to home was obviously affecting his judgment and meant he was less sharp.

Looking at the open files of information showing the damage Dennison had done to Robin made Austin feel like he had failed her. All under his watch, his wife had gone through unimaginable terrors and had come close to losing her life several times. Even though he'd helped her escape the gloomy fate, he still held himself responsible for allowing the tragedies to occur in the first place.

Accepting his mental berating as a cue to take a break, he eased out of his seat and hunted for a vending machine. He had managed to make a few acquaintances in his recent long hours at the sheriff's department. On his way to the main area, Austin stopped and shot the breeze with a few of the officers.

From the corner of his eye, he saw a woman walk into the station. With a shawl over her shoulders and cane in her hand, the woman moved strangely as she made her way to the front desk. The officers around him chuckled at something, but Austin missed it. His attention was honed in on the woman. There was something about her that he couldn't put his finger on. Something was off, drastically off. A crooked smile decorated her oddly shaped face as she reached inside the vinyl backpack slung over her shoulder. The officer at the front desk was laughing with the officer next to him when he happened to glance at the woman who now held a manila envelope in her hands.

Austin's hand had already reached for his gun when the woman looked up and saw him staring at her. Kevin Dennison winked his heavily made-up eyelid at Austin and darted out the front door.

"Dennison!" Austin bellowed as he gave chase.

The curly brunette wig on Kevin's head bounced when he jumped the flight of stairs and out the doors. Austin's heart pounded in his throat. He came within inches of the psycho. It might as well have been miles. At 1 o'clock in the afternoon, the downtown streets were filled with city workers who breaked for lunch.

Kevin carelessly tore through the crowd, knocking over a woman and sending papers flying from her briefcase.

With his gun out and ready to fire, Austin drew close enough to hear his prey's quickened breaths. "Give it up, Agent Malone!" Kevin taunted, "You will NEVER catch me!" Austin's teeth gritted at the maniacal cackle from Dennison's lips. Radio in hand, Austin called for backup, hoping his team was near.

"Suspect is heading northbound on Larned Avenue wearing a blue dress and black wig! Suspect has been identified as Kevin Dennison! I repeat, suspect—"

A city bus blew its horn at an individual standing too far in the street, interrupting Austin's call for help. The agent grunted with frustration and made the call again. "Do you copy? Suspect has been identified as—"

"Copy that, Agent Malone. Officers en route," the radio crackled. In the distance, Austin heard sirens wailing. Every muscle in his body screamed as his pace kicked into high gear. Kevin Dennison was just a few feet away, almost close enough to reach out and grab. Austin's gun lifted; he took aim and prepared to take the shot.

Kevin seemed to sense the danger. He was desperate to not be taken down by a man whose wit, he felt, paled in comparison to his own. Ever the clever one, Kevin did something that made Austin's stomach turn.

A group of elementary school children prepared to load into a school bus after a field trip. In desperation, Kevin reached out and snatched a first grader from his place in line. All of the children began to scream. The child dangled from Kevin's arms as he mad dashed down the street. Austin was forced to lower his weapon, but continued to charge forward. He needed to gain control of the situation, quickly.

Dennison, knowing the vulnerable position Austin was in, taunted him even further.

"What are you going to do now, Agent Malone?!" Kevin was barely winded as the screaming child cried out for help from within the grip of his arms.

Austin wondered where his backup was. Bullets of sweat shot out of his pores. "Put the boy down!" he shouted. "Don't be stupid, Dennison!"

Those were the wrong choice of words to say to a man who considered the term insane a compliment. *If stupid is what he wants, stupid is what he'll get.* As he reached an intersection, Dennison cocked the boy back in his arms. Then as if he were a discus, he hurled the child high into the air and jetted forward down the street. Everything dropped to slow motion. The boy's body flailed wildly, grasping at the air. Inevitably, gravity took its place and pulled the frightened child back down to the earth.

For as long as Austin lived, he would never forget what happened next.

A bicyclist rounding the corner found himself face to face with the tiny human tumbling from the sky. The impact of their two bodies colliding created a bone-chilling crunch. It stopped Austin cold. Not wanting to see the aftermath, the agent's eyes instead searched for Kevin who had just disappeared around a corner.

Damn...

"What the hell happened?!" Mayor Daltry screamed at the roomful of officers who all looked defeated. "So you mean to tell me, he walks right through the front door, hands us evidence, and then walks right out?! What do we have, a bunch of circus clowns on duty here?!" The mayor spewed potent venom as he paced and loosened the tie around his neck. "How did the little boy even get involved? The press will have a fucking FIELD day with this!" His face was the deepest shade of red; veins dangerously bulged in his neck.

"With all due respect, sir, Agent Malone was the one who spotted the suspect and chased him on foot. We were dealing with a crowded street in broad daylight, so our circumstances were less than ideal. Other officers were en route to join in the pursuit, but the incident with the child brought the pursuit to a halt," Bells supplied.

The mayor knew that Austin had done above and beyond what was in his power to do, but that fact did little to clear up the aftermath that he felt would compromise his re-election. "Have there been any sightings of Dennison since then?" he asked a tad more calmly.

"No, sir," a sheriff responded. "A few blocks from the chase, we found women's clothing that had been dumped in a trash can. We believe it was the disguise Dennison used."

The mayor vigorously shook his head, trying to rid his mind of the knowledge that one man, dressed as a woman, would single-handedly be responsible for his failure to be re-elected. With nothing further to do or say, Mayor Daltry stormed out of the room with his aide scampering behind him.

At 4 o'clock the next morning, Austin sat watching surveillance video of when Dennison entered the sheriff's department. He and Bells were side by side watching, for the hundredth time, the phony woman walk up the steps and in through the station doors. The ill-fitted dress and orthopedic shoes he wore were probably more for his own amusement than anything else. The sheriff at the desk had barely acknowledged the hardened criminal hand feeding him critical evidence. He was too busy chuckling with the person next to him.

"This is exactly why I didn't want the locals being involved. If the officer had taken just a split second to pay attention—"

"You can't think about that now," Bells cut in. "He got one over on us, and there is nothing we can do about it."

Austin continued to stew as he rewound the tape again. "What made him brave enough this time to show himself on camera? The only thing in the manila envelope was Cynthia Jerome's courthouse identification card. He wanted to taunt us so badly with it that he'd risk capture?"

"He's trying to prove that he's smarter than us. That he can walk right into the lion's den and come out unscathed," Bells supplied.

Austin played the tape and stopped in the spot where Kevin made eye contact with the camera. Devilishly, he smiled up at it, making his way deeper under Austin's skin.

"This is his favorite game to play," said Austin. "I can't wait to nab his wacky ass."

"And that's exactly what we're going to do." Bells stood up and stretched. "Any word on how the little boy is doing?"

"Couple broken bones. Some scrapes and bruises too, but he'll be fine. A few uniforms went to the hospital and gave him an honorary badge and invited the media to participate. That part undoubtedly was Daltry, trying to run damage control," Austin huffed.

"I hate the idea of waiting around for something else to happen and chasing our tails. We have to figure out a way to draw him out again," Bells yawned. Physical and mental fatigue weighed on them both.

"The forensic psychiatrist should be getting back to us soon with his findings on the case, right? Hopefully, he can give us an angle that we aren't seeing. If we can get in his head and understand what makes him tick, it'll be easier for us to hook him. I'm sure he'll resurface soon though, because that's the way he is. Bastard can never stay away too long. When he does show up again, we better make sure we're ready for him," said Austin.

*

Austin met up with Bells at the Cavity. Bells sat behind a desk when Austin came through the door, looking worn.

"Get any rest last night?" asked the commander.

"I'll rest when I have Dennison in my sights again."

Bells nodded.

"I ended up doing a little investigating, though. Regarding Cynthia Jerome's potential involvement, I found a few things that I thought were interesting," said Austin.

Bells leaned back in his chair and propped his feet up on the desk. He knew that his agent was going to produce his usual golden nugget from thin air. He was interested to see what he'd found.

"She helped him with everything. And when I say everything, I mean details from the exact timing of when to storm Crenshaw's bench, down to the exact type of police car they'd need to escape in." Austin tossed a small stack of papers to his boss. "They'd been sending notes back and forth for the last couple of months of the trial. It's clear to any person reading them that he was playing her like a fiddle, and she fell for it."

Bells read the scribbled letters, penned on everything from chewing gum wrappers to paper towels and shook his head in disbelief. "How the hell this guy managed to wrangle her into his snare of treachery is beyond me. You're right, she fell for it big time. She'll probably end up paying for it with her life, if she hasn't already."

Austin sat down and said, "It doesn't surprise me that he was able to talk his way into getting help, but something else is off, and I can't put my finger on exactly what it is."

"My question is," said Bells as he took his feet off the table and leaned in closer to see the handwriting, "how did you get your hands on this stuff? We didn't find a shred of this anywhere."

Austin didn't admit that before they'd had the chance to get the search warrant on Cynthia's apartment, he'd already picked her locks and found the notes in a box under her bed, along with a collection of sex toys. With a sly smile he responded with, "I have my ways."

Bells shook his head, unable to deny that Austin was a crafty SOB. "I'll find a way to slide this into the evidence docket. Was there anything else you managed to get a hold of, sticky fingers?"

"Not at this point, but I'll keep digging," Austin smirked. "In the meantime, I'm hoping the psychiatrist will have something for us to work with. We have an appointment to meet him in an hour."

The classroom on the Belle Isle Heights University campus was empty. Dr. Blake Ivory scrawled words on the chalkboard. The balding professor, whose everyday attire was a bow tie, blazer and slacks, stood no taller than five feet six inches high, making his appearance that much more peculiar. Six foot three inch Austin towered over the man as he strode into the classroom and extended his hand.

The little professor jumped, startled to see the agents standing there. "Agent Malone, you're awfully quiet for a man of your stature. I didn't hear you come in," Blake's voice crackled. "I see you brought along a friend." Blake shuffled up to Bells and seemed to examine his face. Bells leaned backward to avoid the man who was clearly an invader of personal space.

"Have a seat, gentlemen," he gestured to the lecture hall seats. "That is, if you can fit." He chuckled at himself, and Bells made a sour face.

"Were you able to examine the information I provided you?" asked Austin, ever ready to get down to business. Blake nodded his curly-haired head up and down and slid a folder from his briefcase.

"Indeed I have, Mr. Malone. As soon as I looked at Mr. Dennison's rap sheet, I saw right away that he was showing classic signs of sociopathic behavior."

"Pfft, well, there's something we didn't know," Bells scoffed.

Blake looked at him over the top of his glasses. Bells could tell he was performing some type of psychological personality analysis on him when he responded to the comment with, "Mmm Hmm."

"As I was saying, his patterns of sociopathic behavior have been textbook, actually: not recognizing the rights of others, viewing his self-serving behaviors as permissible, etcetera, etcetera. He appears to be charming, yet his behavior has been covertly hostile and domineering, viewing his victims as merely instruments to be used."

Austin hated the fact that his wife had been one of his instruments. From reading the letters between Kevin and Cynthia, it was clear that she had been as well, and there was no telling how many countless others. "Does that explain why his aggression has drastically evolved over the years?"

"Funny you should ask that." Blake licked his thumb to help him turn a page. "Sociopathic tendencies are fairly common and don't usually have the ability to be impartial with regard to who their victim is. But with Mr. Dennison, this appears to be the case when it comes to who has become his most cherished target, Robin Malone."

"How so?" Austin sat forward in his seat.

"Sociopaths typically have an inability to understand or feel genuine emotion. For them everything is an act. A snub, if you will, or a denying or blocking of one's wishes, although it is an emotion, usually initiates rage. In return, a sociopath responds with anger and, most times, acts of violence."

To Austin it sounded like Blake was talking in circles and hoped he'd bring his point to light.

"In the instances involving Mrs. Malone, Mr. Dennison has shown actual emotion towards her, even though that emotion is anger. In any usual circumstance, the sociopath will commit a violent act and will feel vindicated and outright bored with that particular subject or victim after having committed the act. They have a natural need to conquer and manipulate many, rather than focusing on one. His zeal for the demise of Mrs. Malone leads me to believe that there is something more that we aren't seeing."

"So, what you're basically saying is, the books make you think he's a sociopath, but his behavior with Robin makes you feel like there is an additional issue there?" Bells tried to cut through the heavy wording the doctor used.

"To put it in laymen's terms, yes, that is what I am saying. If I may, I'd like to request information from his medical records as well as his family history. I want to dig a little deeper on this one. Once we understand more, we may even be able to come up with options to help him manage his behavior better. Maybe medication, rehabilitation, and things of that nature can help him recover."

"The only thing that will help him is a bullet," Austin said matter-of-factly. "We're not here to rehabilitate him; we're here to get inside his mind so we can find him and take him down."

"So be it," Blake said with a shrug as he placed his papers back in his bag. "I am merely fulfilling my duties as a doctor. You can fulfill yours however you see fit."

"Anything you need is at your fingertips with regard to his files. I'll personally see to it that you get the information you need," said Austin.

The agents both thanked Blake for his time and made their way out the door.

*

Kevin walked into the hotel room where Cynthia shivered in the corner. She expected him to either start ranting or beating her. That had been his usual routine over the past few days. He surprised her by doing neither. As if coming in from a long day of work, he walked into the room, slipped off his shoes, and sat down to watch TV.

"Our time together is almost up."

Cynthia would have taken another beating in place of hearing such dreadful words.

Chapter Fifteen

It had been weeks since Robin was released from the hospital. She was getting stronger by the day. She'd slowly been working on a few issues she was having with forgetting minor things, like the location of the bathroom, or which day of the week it was, but overall there were drastic improvements.

Robin walked over to the glass window of her living room and peered at her reflection staring back. On the outside she was perfectly put together, covering up all of the tragedy that had happened to her over the course of the years. She was trying to move forward with her life, but a constant voice in her head nagged, saying that she couldn't move forward until Kevin was put away. As much as she had overcome, she still had to admit that the uncertainty of knowing when tragedy would again strike, by way of Kevin's hand, made her uneasy.

Robin glanced over at Olivia who had just put hair bows all over Noodles' head, oblivious to her mother's frustration. Olivia looked up, with a worried frown. "Are you crying, Mom?"

The youngster and her furry companion hopped up onto the sofa, settling in next to her weeping mother.

"I'm not crying, really, Honey. I'm just happy. Happy to be here with you, and happy to be alive and well."

"I'm happy you're here too, Mom. When you were at the doctor, it was lonely and different than when you're here."

Noodles, convinced she was human, couldn't be left out of the conversation. She agreed with Olivia's statements by jumping up and licking Robin on her chin. Robin laughed, rubbing the pooch behind the ears.

"Well, Honey, you won't have to worry about me going away like that for a very long time, I promise."

As Robin embraced her child, she thought about Kevin's vengeance for her and hoped she hadn't just told a lie.

*

Austin and Bells were forced to sit through yet another meeting with the mayor and Commissioner Imes to update everyone on the progress of the case, which, unfortunately, wasn't much.

"Cynthia Jerome was key in helping Kevin Dennison plan and plot the escape. We have elevated her to a suspect and have an all points bulletin out on them both. Looking through her prior phone records, we see that she was very close with her mother and other family members. We've tapped their lines to see if she makes contact. So far nothing has turned up," Bells informed them.

"How did your meeting with Dr. Ivory go?" Mayor Daltry fiddled with an ink pen.

"He confirmed sociopathic tendencies but feels that there's something more beneath the surface and wants to dig deeper into his shell."

"There's nothing inside Dennison's shell but a nut, because that's exactly what he is," Daltry scoffed.

Bells continued, "Dr. Ivory is looking into his medical history now to see if there are any underlying issues there."

Daltry dramatically leaned back with his hand on his forehead. "And then what? What if there is an underlying issue? It still doesn't tell us where Dennison is or how to find him. So, who cares about that?"

Austin cut in. "That's where you're wrong, Mayor Daltry. Looking into Dennison's medical records gives us not only insight into his behavioral patterns, but it can provide new leads. For instance, if he's on medication for an illness, he'll obviously need to get a prescription filled. This gives us the opportunity to canvas drug stores or medical suppliers who have recently had transactions with that particular drug. There are endless leads and possibilities out there that we can follow. "

The agent suddenly felt like he'd wasted his breath. Daltry wasn't a cop, or investigator, and trying to make him think like one was pointless. As far as he was concerned, Daltry didn't belong on the inside of the case. Austin didn't feel the need to explain anything else to him.

"The press is going crazy with this story. Every time I turn the channel, there is a new story running about how we look like assholes sitting on our thumbs, while he's running amuck in our town. Enough is enough. Do whatever you have to do to find him," the mayor said firmly. Austin was sick to death of hearing the same speech from him over and over and hated having to point out that they were clearly exerting all of their efforts to find the criminal.

Daltry rambled on, but the agent had already checked out. His mind was now focused on something that sent his head reeling. On the monitor in the corner of the room was the image of the front desk of the sheriff's office. Standing in the center of the screen was Dennison dressed in the same type of dress and bad wig as before. Austin couldn't believe he would be so brazen as to pull the same stunt again. He wondered if his eyes were playing tricks on him. When he saw the pseudo woman pull yet another envelope out of her bag, he knew that it was his guy.

This time Austin wasn't going to let him get away alive.

"Stay here," his voice boomed to everyone in the room. He charged out the door, leaving everyone to question what was happening. Bells' eye caught the monitor, and he immediately shot to his feet, pulling out his weapon. Both men moved quickly down the hall as Austin cocked his gun. They blew past a gang of sheriffs just outside the locker-room and finally found themselves standing just inches away from the man who'd turned the city and Robin's life upside down.

Dennison was in full-on character as he hobbled towards the door, even stopping to allow a couple to go around him. Austin quietly moved up behind the man and placed the barrel of the gun firmly to the back of his head.

"Make a single move, and I'll blast your brains all over this room," Austin said calmly.

Shockingly, Kevin didn't move an inch, doing exactly as he was told.

"Put your hands on your head and get down on the ground!"

Kevin moved slowly, keeping his hands in full view.

Instantly, Austin sensed that something was off. Everything seemed easy. Too easy. Furthering the peculiarity was Kevin's severely shrunken frame and nervous body language.

"Please don't hurt me," said a woman's voice as she inched towards the ground.

Austin hit the roof. "Who the hell are you?!" he screamed, rolling the woman onto her back.

"Please, sir, don't hurt me!" she pleaded with big eyes. "I was paid to bring this envelope here."

"What envelope?!" Austin grabbed her firmly by her arm, plucking her up from the ground. His usual reputation for smooth interrogational skills was being shot to hell as he fought back the urge to hem her up by the collar.

"It's right there on the desk." The woman nervously looked around at the room of people who stared at her.

Bells made his way over to the package. Austin kept the woman firmly in place.

"I didn't think I was doing anything wrong. I needed the money, and it seemed pretty easy so—"

"You needed the money?" Austin asked. He yanked up the sleeve on her dress, exposing track marks on her arms. Instantly, she burst into tears. "You didn't *need* that!" he scolded without a single pang of sympathy for her. "Not only have you put your own life in danger, but you've involved yourself in a federal case that's much bigger than your crack head can understand!" He jerked her arm.

Bells took a step closer to his agent as a gentle reminder to reel his emotions in. He understood the man's frustration but couldn't afford to let him escalate the already fragile situation. A crowd of officers and civilians had formed, and they were watching every move being made. Mayor Daltry was among them. "What the hell is going on, and what are you doing to that woman!" he shouted from a few feet away. Austin ignored him as Bells picked up the envelope. Flipping it over, Bells pulled on a pair of plastic gloves and carefully removed the contents. He and Austin were surprised to find a neatly typed letter.

I've decided it's time I do something nice for someone other than myself. It pleases me to say that I have a present for you, Agent Green.

A surge of anger rolled through Bells' body as he continued to read.

Cynthia Jerome wishes to confess to aiding in my courtroom escape. I have come to realize that she should be punished for her role as an accomplice. Currently, she is in a position that forces her to think about her foolish actions. She will be out of her misery soon, so if you have any last words for her, you still may have time.

But you better hurry...

"Dammit!" Bells yelled. Curious eyes stared at him. He noticed a logo at the top of the page for the Imperial Motel and then looked up at Austin. "Let's move out."

*

The team, comprised of CIA agents, the local PD, and Belle Isle Heights sheriffs, swarmed around the filthy motel. Dicey looking individuals hung out on the stairs blasting music, openly consuming illegal substances. One by one, each person was removed, every room in the motel cleared out. The team of heavily armed men radioed back and forth making sure the scene was contained.

Receiving the green light, the men stormed the stairs with battering rams and firearms in tow. They prepared to enter the fourth floor room that belonged to Dennison. Agent Malone had a debt to settle with him. He was first in line, hoping to get the opportunity. The chances of Kevin being at the scene were slim, but Austin didn't give up hope.

Austin gave the signal for the team to rush in. He stood back as two officers swung a battering ram, and watched as the flimsy door tumbled down. *Here we go...*

He stepped inside the room, ready to shoot at anything that moved. Moving swiftly, the other officers fanned out through the dingy room looking for Jerome and Dennison, senses alert in the volatile situation.

"Cynthia Jerome, are you in here?" Austin shouted, approaching the closed bathroom door. No sound came from the room. He shouted out to her again. "Cynthia, this is Agent Austin Malone, and I am here to help you. Open the door and walk out slowly with your hands on your head."

Still no sound.

An officer confirmed that the closet and entire room had been swept, finding no signs of anyone. Austin turned to Bells who nodded, giving the signal for the men to enter the bathroom.

"Wait!" Austin suddenly shouted, before they could charge the door. An eerie feeling washed over him; he urged everyone in the room to be silent. "Shh."

The adrenaline-filled room of officers all stared, eyeing his peculiar behavior. Fanning the flames of their curiosity, the agent moved closer to the door, placing his ear against it. No one moved as he slid along the frame with his eyes closed. He got down on his hands and knees and reached inside his back pocket, pulling out a silver tool. He opened a flap on the instrument and a tiny mirror appeared. With steady hands, the agent slid the mirror slowly under the small space between the door and the floor.

Twisting his fingers gently caused the mirror to

rotate, giving him a 360-degree view of the room.

His body froze. The mirror was dangerously close to snagging a thin wire that ran the width of the door. By moving even an inch, he ran the risk of setting off the trip and blowing himself and everyone else in the room to pieces.

The next thing he saw in the mirror was Cynthia Jerome's horrid reflection staring back at him. Her mouth was gagged and wires crisscrossed in front of her as a barricade to keep her secured in the bathtub. Tears stained her face; her naked body fought to keep perfectly still.

"We've got explosives," Austin said. Bells quickly got on the horn, requesting a bomb technician.

"Cynthia," Austin's voice boomed. "I know you're in there, and I know that you can't speak. I see the wires, and I know exactly what will happen if I touch them, so I promise you I won't do that. There is a team of people on the other side of this door all fighting to get you out of there. Just know that we're here to help."

Austin wiped the newly formed beads of sweat from his head and quickly devised a plan.

"Cynthia, I need you to help me out so we can get you out of there. I'm going to ask you some yes or no questions. I want you to blink once for yes and twice for no; do you understand?"

She blinked once, and he began.

"Tell me, is there more than one wire in front of the door?"

One blink.

"Is there white clay on the ends of the wires?"

Another blink.

"Okay, Cynthia, you're doing great. Besides the wires, is there anything else I should be concerned with?"

One hard blink.

Austin angled the small mirror around and tried to view as much of the room as possible. That's when something caught his nostrils and made him feel sick to his stomach.

"Cynthia, is the tub you're in filled with accelerant?"

One long blink.

Austin swore under his breath. The men around him all cringed. He and everyone else now knew that Cynthia was literally sitting inside a bomb. The slightest motion would be enough to trip the wires and level the entire floor of the motel. This was an evil like none Austin had seen before. Dennison's antics had crossed the point of insanity. Being on the outside witnessing his mental spiral was chilling.

"Listen, Cynthia. I'm going to get you out of there even if I have to bust through the walls to do it. Just hang in there with me, all right?"

Her tired eyes blinked, and this time she kept them closed. Austin carefully retracted the mirror and rolled up onto his feet. The wheels in his mind were turning as he cut through the crowd of staring officers. Without saying a word, he started towards the door. Bells was right at his side, trying to tap into his plan of action.

"I've already called in the bomb squad. But something tells me you don't plan to wait that long. What's your game plan, Malone?" he asked, nearly jogging to keep up with him.

"My plan is to get her out," Austin stated as a fact.

"Well, why in Sam Hill didn't I think of that?" Bells said, as if the plan would simply be that easy. Although joking, somewhere in the back of his mind, he knew full well that Austin would do exactly as he said.

Up ahead, Austin spied the utility shed he'd seen when they entered the motel. The shabbily constructed shed sat in the middle of the motel parking lot, looking like it hadn't been used in years. With one powerful kick from the heel of Austin's boot, the door splintered from the hinges and eventually fell completely off. He saw exactly what he was hoping would be there.

"Grab the other end," he said to Bells. They hauled a large extendable ladder out of the shed. Weighing easily upwards of 100 pounds, the men effortlessly trotted with it across the lot and around to the back of the building. Counting the rows of windows from the outside, they were able to pinpoint the one belonging to the bathroom that Cynthia was in.

With a loud thud, they propped the ladder up against the side of the building; a crowd of people looked on. Without pause, Austin began making his way up, while Bells got on his radio calling for backup. Onlookers watched the agent fearlessly scale the ladder, wondering what was happening.

Austin reached the 2 x 2 foot window and pulled the mirror gadget from his pocket. He grabbed a thick razor instrument from the utility belt around his waist. With the razor, he cut a small circle into the glass of the window and poked it out with his thumb.

Inside the room, Cynthia Jerome was startled at the glass hitting the floor.

"Cynthia, this is Agent Malone. I'm going to get you out of there in just a little bit. But I need you to tell me; are there any wires or other obstructions blocking the window?"

With his mirror extended as far out as possible, he was able to see two firm blinks of her eyes. That was exactly the news he was hoping for. Using his palms, Austin pushed upwards on the window. It had been painted shut and wouldn't budge. In his utility belt was a small flat head screwdriver. He used it to chip away the coat of paint that sealed the bottom of the window.

Cynthia was nervous listening to the sounds outside the room. Her face was heavily stained with tears and dried blood. She didn't feel like she could keep her body upright any longer — even though she knew what the sudden movement would mean. Almost the instant the thought crossed her mind, she heard a loud *Crack!* and the sound of the window clunking upward.

"Cynthia, hold on tight, I'm almost there."

She wanted to shout at him to hurry up because she couldn't take it any longer, but she couldn't even do that. A sudden loud crash came from Austin tossing the windowpane to the ground. The breath of the agent drew closer as he hoisted himself in through the small space and crawled into the room.

Before turning his attention to her, he went cautiously over to the door and sized it up. There were three invisible wires crisscrossed in front of the door, each with detonators peeking out from the white clay. Kevin had done a shoddy job with the explosives, but shoddy or not, they would have been effective. Austin shook his head, knowing that if they had opened that door just an inch, many lives would have been lost that day — including his own. Gently, he snipped the wires with a wire-cutter and carefully disassembled the contraption.

Finally, he turned to face Cynthia Jerome. The woman had been brutally beaten and tortured, evident from the burns on her scalp and black and blue marks covering every inch of her exposed body. The fluid in the tub was cloudy from the blood that had seeped out of her wounds. Kevin had sadistically wound wires all over her body and connected them to a detonator on the door. Row upon row cut deeply into her skin, leaving marks that would probably never fully heal. The mere sight of it was agonizing. The agent couldn't imagine how painful it must have felt.

A haze of hopelessness lingered in Cynthia's eyes as Austin made his way over to her. Suddenly, her head hung low from a combination of fatigue, guilt, and shame. It was her own decisions that had caused her to be in that position, and she felt like a fool.

Austin found himself sympathizing with her. He knew that even after all this, she'd still have to face charges for her role in Kevin's escape. The torture she'd been through could have easily been punishment enough, but the justice system wouldn't agree.

As he kneeled by the side of the tub, he said, "I'm going to use this tool to cut the wires off of your skin. You'll feel some pressure and tugging, but I'll be as gentle as I can." The agent couldn't help remembering that he'd said those very words to his wife just weeks before, when he cleaned the wounds from the bullet that Cynthia helped Kevin put in her head.

The agent worked a path down the front of her body, breaking through the wires, trying not to clip her skin. By the inert look on her face he could tell that she was beyond the point of pain and most likely going into shock.

Austin cut the final wire and slowly slid her out from the cocoon they had formed around her body. Like a rag doll, she drooped forward. He pulled the gag from her mouth.

"You're okay now, Cynthia," he said softly.

Without warning, the woman let out a bloodcurdling scream as she sobbed in his arms. Austin stood perfectly quiet, imagining the stories of terror that each of her tears told. Her body trembled wildly against him. There was nothing he could do to repair the pain and fear she'd experienced — just as he couldn't for his own wife.

After a few moments, Austin spoke calmly into his radio, asking that someone bring in dry towels. The door creaked open. Before the individual could step inside, Austin said, "Drop them on the counter and close the door — quickly." The agent didn't want to put her through the humiliation of having other people see her in her current condition. Although she was unable to articulate it through words, Cynthia squeezed him as tight as she could to indicate that she was appreciative.

Austin's long arm reached up and plucked a towel from the counter. With one swoop, he draped it over the back of her body and lifted her from the tub. Shakily she stood on the wet tiles of the floor, the strong scent of the accelerant burning both their eyes.

"I'm so sorry," was all she could utter as he wrapped another towel around her.

"You're safe now, Cynthia."

"No, Agent Malone, you don't understand," she sniffed. "This all happened because of me. I helped Kevin escape. I knew what his intentions were that day in the courtroom, and I'm the one who helped make it all happen. Your wife never would have been shot if it hadn't been for me."

Austin was well aware of everything that she was saying. Even though hearing it from her aggravated him, he took solace knowing that his job that day was to find and rescue her, and that's exactly what he'd done.

"I know what happened, Cynthia. We're going to get you cleaned up and have you checked out by a doctor. That's our focus right now."

Cynthia was baffled by his reaction. She couldn't understand how he could be kind after what she had done.

There was a tap on the door.

"I need to step out for just a few minutes; but I'll come right back, hopefully with a fresh change of clothes for you, okay?"

She smiled appreciatively. Her mouth was sunken in from Kevin knocking out her front teeth. Seeing the shakiness of her legs, he sat her down on the toilet and helped her lean on the side of the counter for support.

"I'll be right back." He quickly opened the door and closed it behind him. The dingy motel room had been cleared out, and the only people inside were now Austin and Bells.

"She okay?" Bells asked. Austin shook his head from side to side, and moved closer to the commander.

"He's out of control, Bells. You wouldn't believe the things he did to her. Just knowing that Robin experienced some of those same things—"

"Now is not the time to think about that, Malone. There is a distinctive line that separates your work from your wife. I know that those lines have been blurred, but you've got to do your best to differentiate between the two. Keep your mind focused on *this* case."

Austin nodded, knowing that Bells was right. "She admitted to everything. She—"

Suddenly, screams erupted from outside the building. Their radios blared loudly on their hips. More voices screamed. Terror gripped Austin by the throat. The agent darted quickly to the bathroom. Cynthia was gone. Running to look out the window, he saw Cynthia's mangled body on the ground, a crowd of people looking on. Her unseeing eyes stared up at him, her gaped mouth shaped into its final horrid expression.

"Dammit!" Austin shouted, dashing towards the door. With each step he took down the stairs, the realization set in that he was rushing for no reason. She was already dead, but his sense of urgency still wouldn't leave him. He had every reason in the world not to give a damn about her, but couldn't help the fact that he still did.

"Stay back!" He tried to preserve the scene from the gawkers. Once making it over to her, he knelt down and looked at her fragile face. Her towel had come undone during the fall. He pulled it up higher to cover her bare body. Blood slowly seeped onto the pavement. Austin understood that he was witnessing her paying the price of crossing Dennison's path.

*

Cynthia Jerome had described him as fearless when he'd taken charge of his destiny that day in the courtroom. Fearless is exactly the way Kevin Dennison felt as he walked the streets of downtown Detroit. Dressed in a black wig, women's clothes and lipstick, he couldn't help but marvel at his genius. He walked by stand after stand filled with newspapers that talked only about him.

"I can't wait to see what they'll write once they find out what I've done to the bailiff and, hopefully, to Agent Malone."

As a neighboring city to Belle Isle Heights, which he

had now made infamous, Detroit felt as much pressure to capture the maniacal man as they did. "Come and get me," he whispered, knowing that no one would do such a thing, because they had absolutely no idea who they were dealing with. Kevin vowed that he would never be a prisoner again.

*

The night was pitch black and moonless, but the bright lights used to illuminate the crime scene lit the sky above. Nearly every guest of the motel, as well as gawkers from the streets, lined the sidewalks, watching the police teams work. Technicians and officers carried bags of evidence, the news crews zooming in for closer shots. Radio and news vans from all over the country were there to get a glimpse of Kevin Dennison's latest handiwork.

Three hours after Cynthia's suicide, her body was still lying out on the pavement. Her body itself was evidence, forcing the medical examiner to process it out in the open. Officers lined the perimeters, pushing the spectators back. The growing crowd was becoming too much to control.

Breezing onto the scene came Mayor Daltry, a look of utter dismay on his face. With the public eye staring directly at him, he put on a façade of sorrow for the death of the young woman, even though he couldn't have cared less for her. His face creased deeply as he approached the hail of flashing police lights. Commissioner Imes gestured for Daltry to join him, Commander Bells, and Agent Malone in the command post.

When Austin looked up and saw the mayor coming his way, he immediately put his head down and pretended to be on the phone. The gritty official's face was the last one he wanted to see.

The mayor was wise enough to cover his mouth with his hands before he spoke, so that the news cameras couldn't zoom in on what he was saying. "So, I guess tonight you're Barnum and I'm Bailey. Oh, and the dead body and crime tape are the spectacles under the big top of our grand circus, huh?"

Even Commissioner Imes, who usually let the mayor's jabs roll off, looked like he was seconds from pummeling him.

"That rat bastard has done it again. He's outsmarted each and every one of us. We're looking like complete and utter fools out here, just like all the times before. I am at my wits end trying to figure out how one man can be responsible for so much destruction!"

The mayor's voice and evident anger had gotten louder than he'd expected. He was forced to tone down when people's heads began turning in his direction. "I bet he's somewhere laughing his ass—"

"If you say one more word, I swear to God, I'm going to wrap my hands around your throat and squeeze until those beady eyes of yours pop out of your head." It wasn't until he saw everyone stare wide eyed at him that Austin realized he was the one who'd just made the threat. His jaw was clenched tight, and if Daltry even moved wrong, the agent was prepared to make good on his promise.

The mayor couldn't chance taking a public ass

whooping. He shut his mouth like he was told.

Bells stepped in. "This was out of our control. We had the scene secure, but there was no way of knowing she'd pull something like this."

Daltry was itching to make a snarky comeback. But Austin's eyes hovered threateningly over him, just waiting for him to say something out of line. The mayor bit his tongue.

The men looked up and saw the uncoordinated stride of Dr. Blake Ivory shuffling toward them. He could barely contain the news he had. The awkward professor began his conversation by pushing his glasses closer to his face with his index finger. Then he proceeded to blow everyone's mind.

"I came down as soon as I heard about what happened. I found some things I think you all would like to hear." He was almost giddy over his findings and couldn't wait to divulge. Blake handed Austin a slip of paper and began explaining its meaning. Everyone listened in.

"I did some digging into Dennison's medical and family history like I told you. What I found was this; when Mr. Dennison was a child, he apparently had some behavioral issues in school. Initially, his mother thought he was acting out because of his father going to jail. After receiving daily calls from the school about his inappropriate and awkward behavior, mostly toward his female classmates, she became suspicious that something else was going on. It wasn't until speaking with the principal directly that she found he had done specific things like burn a girl's hair with a cigarette lighter. On another occasion, he poured just enough ammonia into a classmate's drink that she got sick and had to be sent to the school nurse. He was expelled from school, and that's when his mother took him to a doctor to be examined. This is what they found," Blake said, sliding another paper into Austin's hands.

"His physician was deeply concerned with the violence he was exhibiting, and felt it necessary to put him through a series of tests, both written and biological. The results of the biological test came back showing that Mr. Dennison has an additional X chromosome."

Austin and Bells glanced at each other, and Dr. Ivory continued on.

"Women have two X chromosomes and men have XY chromosomes. In Dennison's case, his profile would show as XXY. The addition of this X gene made his levels of estrogen much higher, causing him to grow breasts at a young age. What his mother thought was childhood chubbiness was instead the effects of the abnormal gene on his body. Turns out, he was vigorously teased about it by his classmates and mostly expressed his aggression about it toward females. The doctor ordered testosterone injections to help balance out his levels. The problem is that over the course of time, Mr. Dennison got his hands on the hormone and started to do the injections himself. This means that he now has abnormally higher levels of testosterone.

"High testosterone in itself is not necessarily a dangerous thing, but when it's combined with low levels of serotonin—which males with additional X chromosomes have, the results can be monstrous. Testosterone is widely associated with dominant behavior, but serotonin keeps the testosterone levels from peaking. When serotonin levels are low, the individual becomes frustrated and their behavior becomes aggressive, even sadistic. This explains Dennison's inability to control himself and the fact that he has immense hatred toward women. It all stems back to his childhood," Blake Ivory smiled as if he'd said something to actually be happy about.

"I knew he was a nut," Daltry jabbed.

Everyone ignored the statement and focused their attention on Blake.

"His very private family was careful to shield his condition from ever being exposed. They had the means and the money and used it to shut mouths all over the city. By doing so, they inevitably cleaned up all of Dennison's messes, sending the message to him that everything he did was untouchable." Blake's eyes shifted to Cynthia's body. "There is your collateral damage."

This news gave Austin an even greater sense of urgency to find Kevin and put him down like the rabid dog he was.

When Austin got home that night, Robin wrapped her arms around him. For the longest time, they stood in the doorway of their home, not wanting to let each other go. If anyone understood the gut wrenching awfulness of the situation, it was his wife, who too had fallen prey to Kevin's wickedness.

"I'm so sorry for what happened to Cynthia. It's an

absolute pity that she had to die that way." She caressed her husband's face.

Robin, wasn't privy to the exact details of the case and had no idea that it was because of Cynthia's help that she, herself, was almost killed just weeks before. Austin realized that even if she had known the full scope of the details, his wife would probably still have compassion for the loss of human life.

Austin himself had tested the boundaries of his professionalism just by putting his life at risk to rescue the rogue bailiff. The easy choice would have been to allow Cynthia to feel the full wrath of the punishment she'd brought upon herself. But he couldn't allow Dennison to force him to sacrifice the integrity with which he tended his job simply to punish a woman too foolish to realize what she was getting herself into.

"Still no one knows where he is?" Robin asked.

Her husband responded by clenching his jaw and bending down to unlace his work boots. They still had spots of Cynthia's blood on them. Robin helped him peel off layers of clothing soaked through with the accelerant and by the storm that had rolled in and washed away valuable evidence from the scene.

Peeking out from his abdomen was the scar left behind from a bullet he'd taken years earlier working the Dennison case. Looking at the scar and thinking of the slew of other physical and mental scars Kevin had inflicted, Robin suddenly said, "I can't take this anymore. We have to do something."

Austin already had a plan of action in mind. "We need to bait him and draw him out. He loves the limelight, so I think we should give him exactly what he wants."

Austin strode across the room and searched through the contact list in his phone. Robin wondered what he was going to do. Seconds later, the agent was on the line with Frank Holland, the head anchor of the WKRP news station in Belle Isle Heights.

Hearing the reporter's voice on the line, he said, "Frank, this is Agent Austin Malone. How would you like to have an exclusive?"

Chapter Sixteen

Three days later, Robin sat in the makeup chair at the news station. Her stylist fiddled with the new pixie cut she'd given her. The cinnamon spice dye job helped mask the misery that had happened to her in the weeks prior. The atmosphere buzzed with chatter of her presence in the studio. It was exactly the response she expected, and she hoped that the same energy would resonate with the viewers who'd watch the show. Having been all over the news for years gave her the advantage of being able to capture the public's attention, which would be needed to pull off the stunt that was planned.

A stage manager popped his head into the makeup room. "Mrs. Malone, we'll need you on set in five minutes."

Robin smiled graciously and took a deep breath. The stylist packed up her things and made her way out just as Austin walked in. He shut the door behind himself and stood behind his wife to prep her.

"You ready to do this, Honey?" He kneaded her shoulders.

Sitting in the chair, she responded to his reflection in the mirror. "Absolutely, I am. We've tiptoed around Kevin for way too long, so now it's time we fight dirty."

Austin agreed. "That's very true. I just want to make sure you understand that by baiting him this way, we stand a chance of getting bitten. We're doing this interview and going on camera just to draw him out from hiding. We need to be prepared when he shows up. He won't like this, and I know he'll do something to prove it to us."

Robin understood the dangers of walking into the lion's den, and mentally prepared herself for shaking the beast awake. "Let's just get it done." She stood up and walked out the door.

Frank Holland greeted her warmly as she stepped onto the set, taking a seat under the impossibly bright lights. Sound technicians hooked them both up to microphones. Frank said, "Robin, you know it's an honor to have you here in the studio. For years the city has wanted to hear your view on things with Kevin Dennison. I'm so glad you chose our show to help make that happen."

"I appreciate hearing that Frank, and I'm happy to be able to finally give the people what they want."

Nearly all of the employees at the station, as well as Austin and Commander Bells, stood watching from the other side of the set as the two prepared to go on the air. The station's signature theme song of patriotic-sounding horns played. Robin watched a man with cue cards count down the seconds until they were live on the air.

Three. Two. One. Showtime...

"Hello, and welcome to the segment that we like to call *Being Frank, with Frank Holland*. I am your host, Frank Holland, and I have with me one of Belle Isle Heights' most recognizable faces: real estate investor Robin Malone. Robin, thank you so much for joining me in the studio today."

"Frank, the pleasure is all mine," she smiled warmly.

"Now, let's get right down to it. It has been just a few months since you were senselessly gunned down in a court of law by Kevin Dennison, who is still somewhere out there on the streets. The people of Belle Isle Heights are wondering how you and your family are coping with this situation."

Looking supremely confident, Robin responded, "Frank, I'd first like to thank the people of the town for sending such wonderful messages and showing such an outpour of support to me and my family. We truly appreciate it. And to answer your question, we are not merely coping with the situation, instead we have chosen to rise above it and view it for what it was: a failed attempt at dimming a light too bright to be snuffed out by violence."

"You have gone through having your child stolen away from you, as well as having stared death in the face, but somehow you've still managed to come out on top. What do you say to the viewers who question how you've been able to persevere?"

"I say that when you have purpose in life and the will to live, no one can take that from you, no matter how hard they try. Kevin Dennison and every attempt that he's made to bring me and my family down is pathetic. I'd like to point out that he doesn't deserve the credit he's being given. He hasn't stolen my life at all. What he's done is made me value it, and the people in it, much more."

"The next question on everyone's mind is, why? Why do you think he's tried this hard to silence you? Is there any reason that we, on the outside looking in, aren't aware of?"

"Frank, as much as I'd like to, I can't even begin to understand Kevin's motivation for trying to bring me harm. It's kind of like someone taking two slices of thin bread and trying to make a soup sandwich with them; it just doesn't make sense."

The two of them laughed as the eyes of the entire city looked on.

"Well, I have a few guests on satellite who may be able to weigh in on things. Live, in our state capital is District Attorney Katherine Palmer, who was the lead prosecutor on the Dennison trial. Katherine, thank you for joining us."

The sound in her ear was slightly delayed so it took her a few seconds to respond. "I'm very thrilled to be here, Frank. And I'd like to add how wonderful you're looking, Robin. I'm so happy to see how well you've pulled through."

Robin smiled appreciatively. Frank introduced the next guest. "Also with us via satellite is Rosetta Barnes, a former classmate of Kevin Dennison, as well as Dr. Blake Ivory, a forensic psychiatrist, both here to share their points of view. Thank you both for being here."

They smiled. Robin looked past the sea of bright lights to see Austin standing close to the largest camera, rooting her on.

"Katherine, not only were you close to this case in the legal sense, but you were also dragged into the inferno of this man's hatred when he opened fire on you as well. How does it feel to be a victim of such a tragedy?"

Katherine laughed. "Frank, you know me much better than that. I am not a victim and could never be, even if I tried. To piggyback on what Robin said earlier, the situation that happened doesn't define me. This was merely an event in my life that occurred at the hands of a coward. When justice finds him, it will do much more damage to him than he could have ever done to me."

"I see.

"Dr. Ivory, based on the facts of the case and knowing the injustices that this man has caused, what say you in regard to motivation behind such villainy? I want to know; do you think he's just plain crazy?"

With a heavy dose of his signature awkwardness, Blake pushed his glasses further up his nose and said, "Well, Frank, as a professional, I'm disinclined to refer to any individual as crazy. But I do feel that Mr. Dennison is exhibiting classic signs of narcissistic and psychopathic behavior. He has a fascination with being in control of situations and individuals, and he'll stop at nothing to keep his vicious tentacles tightly grasped around anyone he chooses. The problem is never his subject; the problem is always him."

Frank nodded. "Rosetta, you went to grade school with Kevin Dennison and shared classes with him for almost eight hours a day. Tell us, has his behavior always been this erratic and compulsive?"

Rosetta was a paid actress from California who had never met Kevin Dennison a day in her life—but the public didn't know that. She and everyone else on the show had been coached to berate him, and that's just what she did.

"Absolutely not, Frank, it was the exact opposite. Kevin Dennison was a loser." Everyone on the panel laughed and the actress went on. "I'm just being frank, Frank. The things he's done to Mrs. Malone are absolutely sickening. His behavior now is a stark contrast to the person he was when he was younger. I can remember countless times his mother bringing a change of clothes up to the school because Kevin had wet himself. Granted, we were kids then, but even still. I truly believe he's channeling his aggression, for all of the times he was bullied for being overweight and wimpy as a child, toward Mrs. Malone."

"Well, Dr. Ivory, what do you think? Is it possible that the pain and misery Kevin Dennison put so many people through could be payback for bad memories of his childhood?"

"Absolutely, Frank. What you have is a psychopath who's trying to disavow, if you will, a prior history that has haunted him for many years. Kevin Dennison's father, Paul Archer, was a very powerful man in his heyday, and history shows that he was relentless in expecting his son to follow his lead. Studies have shown that a desire for parental acceptance alone is a huge factor in an individual's need to compensate for an attribute they may be lacking. Which, in the case of Mr. Dennison, was his lack of power and respect for himself. His violent behavior today is his way of manufacturing the power he didn't have in his youth."

"What the doctor is trying to say is that Kevin Dennison is nothing more than a spoiled brat who preys on women in order to make himself feel more like a man," Rosetta snuffed. Everyone laughed.

Austin watched the monitors knowing that although his tactics were unethical, they would still garner the results they wanted, which was to lure Dennison out from hiding. If Kevin was nothing else, he was proud, and it would be that pride that would make him surface.

Just a few miles away, the man himself sat fuming, listening to the group who openly berated him. This time he was in a posh hotel, laying on high quality sheets as two women crawled all over him. Emotion wasn't evident by looking at his face, but his insides felt as hot as lava. There was no doubt for him that Robin and Austin were behind the charade he'd just witnessed. He vowed to himself that they would pay for humiliating him.

*

Robin and Austin sat in the back of the black SUV that escorted them back home from the news station.

"You did a great job, honey. You were very natural. Definitely would have pissed me off if I was the poor bastard," Austin said with a laugh.

"We did what we had to do. Now I guess we wait to see what happens."

"Waiting is the last thing we need. We have to prepare and continue to trail his scent while we do it. As a matter of fact..." Austin suddenly shouted out to the driver. "Mack, we're going to take a little detour."

A half hour later, Robin found herself standing in front of a large unmarked building out in the middle of nowhere. With high heels on, she tiptoed across the gravel lot. Austin held her hand to keep her steady.

"What are you getting me into this time?" she asked as they walked through a set of jet-black doors.

With a smirk on his face, Austin led her down a hall and finally into a large open area that looked like an arena. Multiple types of terrain had replaced the ground. There was a pit of sand in one space, in another area was a sandbox filled with mud. All around the room were posts shaped like human torsos.

"Welcome to the CTH, better known as the Cavity Training Headquarters," said Austin. "This is where we come to prepare ourselves for physical combat."

"In other words, here is where you're taught how to beat the hell out of someone," Robin smirked, sliding off her shoes. "What are those pits and different surfaces for?"

He grabbed her by the hand and led her out to the center of the open space. "When you encounter someone that you need to defend yourself against, nine times out of ten, the area you're in won't be a beautifully shellacked gymnasium floor with soft mats for you to fall on. Sometimes you're out, and it's raining and muddy; or you're on a street with rocks and broken glass. You have to be prepared to defend yourself in every situation no matter what the conditions around you are. Even if it's snowing."

Austin pushed a small red button on a nearby post, and snowflakes began falling from a machine built into the ceiling. Robin looked up in the air as the cool flakes fell on her face, melting against her warm skin. Her husband began to walk a circle around her as if to instigate a physical altercation. Her eyes followed him. He slowly stalked her, and she placed her feet in what she thought was a fighting stance.

Taking one large step forward, he swept his foot into the back of her leg and caught her in his arms before she hit the ground.

She was startled as she stared up at him. "You always have to be prepared, Robin. You never know when your opponent will strike." He helped her back to an upright position and began walking a circle around her again. Not wanting to be caught off guard again, Robin loosened her neck and balled her fists. This time he walked right up to her and stood just a few inches away from her face. Fists still in a ball, she swallowed hard, trying to figure out what he would do next.

"Boo!"

Robin jumped high in the air, and Austin laughed at

her.

"That was not funny," she sulked, with a punch to his arm.

"You were so worried about trying to figure what was up my sleeve, that you didn't even look at the danger right in front of your face. This is how Kevin works, Robin. He's very cunning and quick thinking, and we have to figure out a way to be one step ahead of him at all times. We can't be so fearful of what comes next that we —"

Mid-sentence, she cut him with a quick jab to his gut. Although his iron abs did more damage to her fist than the other way around, he still smiled and said, "Now, that's more like it." A smile spread across her lips. She bounced up and down like a fighter who'd just won a championship round.

He chuckled at her, "Come on, Champ, let's see how your skills are with chuggin' slugs."

"Chugging what?" she asked as he picked up her shoes and took her down a long hallway.

"Slugs." They walked into a room with targets mounted 360 degrees around them. "We need to see how well you can shoot."

"A gun?"

"No, a rubber band," he said, and she punched him again.

They walked up to a booth, and he looked her hands over.

"Let's start you off with a .22-caliber."

Against a long wall at the back of the room were rows and rows of handguns. It reminded Robin of the shelves of balls at the bowling alley. Austin picked out the weapon he wanted and brought it over to her. He handed her the weapon butt first, and she looked at it like it had a contagious disease.

"Don't I need some gloves, or earplugs or something?"

"If someone approaches you on the street and tries to hurt you or Olivia, will you have time to say, 'Mister Robber, hold on just a moment so that I can put on my protective gear'?"

Robin snorted out a laugh.

"Okay, shoot...at the target, not at me!" Austin took a step back. Robin took a deep breath, lifted the gun with her right hand, and squeezed the trigger.

Click! Click! Click! She pulled the trigger over and over; the weapon still made the same noise. Her eyebrows creased. She tapped at the back of the gun with the palm of her hand.

"There are no bullets in the gun, Robin." Austin held the clip high in his hand.

"How was I supposed to know that?!"

"Because you are always supposed to be aware of what's going on, I just told you that. You need to not only keep track of your own rounds, but also the rounds of your enemy. Besides that, the fact that there was a big empty space at the bottom of the gun should have tipped you off." He slid the clip in, locking it in place.

___

281

He then stood behind her and showed her how to aim the gun at the standing target.

"Extend your right arm, but don't lock your elbow. Now take your left hand and push it firmly against the bottom of the right to keep it steady."

She slid her finger into the loop of the gun and he said, "Never ever put your finger there unless you're ready to fire. Otherwise, keep your index finger extended along the side of the gun like this." He demonstrated in the air with his own hands; she copied his movements.

"You see how my feet are gaped but not side by side? This gives me a better range of motion and flexibility. Keep your upper body squared with your hips, and when you're ready, fire at the target."

Austin stepped back and watched his wife squeeze one eye shut. Then when she felt confident in her preparation, she fired.

Pow!

The sound rang loudly in her ears and a puff of grainy smoke plumed into the air. Her eyes stung as she coughed the sulfur from her lungs, jiggling a finger in her ringing ears.

"Not quite the way it looks in the movies, is it?" Austin asked, completely unfazed by the sound or the gunpowder. "This is what happens in real life. Your hands hurt from squeezing the trigger, the sound blasts in your ears, and sometimes you don't even hit your mark." He pointed to her still intact target.

Missing the target ticked her off. She lifted the gun

and tried again and again. Austin stood watching her with his arms folded. He was witnessing, in full force, one of the reasons he'd fallen in love with her. She had a drive and hunger for success deep inside of her that was attractive as all hell.

After unloading half a clip, she finally landed a bullet on the crotch of the target.

"It's not his head or heart, but if you shot Kevin there, I'm sure it would hurt him just the same." They laughed.

The pair stayed at the facility for almost three hours, shooting still and moving targets. By the end of the night, he'd taught her to shoot with both her right and left hands, with weapons ranging from .22 to .50-calibers. Her fingers were numb and bruising from the kickbacks on the bigger guns, but she proudly wore the marks like a badge of honor.

Walking toward the waiting SUV, Austin said, "You did well in there today. We're going to come more often to get you more comfortable."

Robin knew the reason behind his plan. What neither Robin nor Austin realized, was that danger would come knocking sooner than they'd expected.

Chapter Seventeen

The Frank Holland interview struck a chord all over the city. The media ran with the story, some using it to highlight the effects of bullying. Mayor Daltry was up in arms about the wagging tongues that spoke of him losing control of Belle Isle Heights. *Paltry Daltry* had become his nickname. He blamed Dennison for it all. But, the mayor finally calmed himself enough to reach out and ask Austin to meet with him privately.

The meeting place was on the tarmac of a small airport in lower Michigan. Austin noticed a charter plane with propellers in full swing as he approached the mayor and his aide who followed behind his boss like the frightened puppy that he had become.

"Agent Malone, I'm very pleased that you made it. We'll be meeting in flight today. But I'll be sure to have you back before dinnertime." The mayor extended his hand to the stairs of the plane. Austin wondered what shenanigans the mayor had planned.

On the airplane, the two men were given headsets that they used to communicate during the 25-minute flight.

"You know, I really admire you, Agent Malone," said Daltry, looking out the window. "You've been pouring your blood, sweat, and tears into this case, and I don't want that to go unnoticed." The mayor looked down at his own ring-less finger. "I can tell you truly love your wife. In fighting for her, I see an aura of resilience around you that anyone can spot from a mile away. It's very inspiring, actually. Kind of reminds me of myself when I was younger."

There were deep lines on the mayor's face that told stories of the things he'd seen and done while in office. Years of political mayhem had been his only companion in life, and Austin sensed that the man wanted more. But with a personality like his, there was only room in his life for his beloved career, for which he was willing to lie, squander and cheat.

"Son, I asked you to meet me because I need a favor."

Austin stretched out his neck and sat back, only half-heartedly interested to hear what the mayor had to say.

"We both have things that we need to happen with this case. I need to make sure it isn't messy and that we get things rectified quickly. I also need the public eye to see what I want them to see; the trash behind the scenes needs to stay hidden. You want closure for your wife and family. We may have different paths of getting there, but essentially we want to arrive at the same destination. So, I think we should work together."

Austin humored him by saying, "But, Mr. Mayor, we *are* working together. You've appointed me as the lead consultant on the case, remember?"

The mayor chuckled and said, "You and I are no more working together than this airplane has feathers. You think I don't know all the things you all are doing behind my back? I know, but I don't care about all that. What I care about is the way it looks, and it looks to me like your very public way of handling things isn't a good fit with the image that I'm trying to project to the city," he said, referring to the Frank Holland interview. "The point is, this has to look good, and at the end of it all, I have to look good. You can do whatever the hell you please with this case as long as those terms are met."

"So the favor you need is for us to stop doing interviews, or is there more that you want from me?" Austin asked bluntly.

"You'll find that out in just a few minutes."

Looking out the window, Austin saw a landing strip ahead. On it was a black town car. Daltry smugly looked on knowing that the mysteriousness of the situation irked the agent. The plane soon landed, and Austin followed the mayor onto the tarmac and into the waiting vehicle. Sliding into the back seat, he glanced at the car's lone occupant and did a double take, in utter disbelief.

It was Paul Archer—Kevin Dennison's father. Austin immediately reached for his gun.

"That won't be necessary, Agent Malone," said Paul. "Please, come." He gestured for Austin to slide in closer so that Daltry could get in next to him. Never one to let his guard down, Austin pulled his gun out anyway, and rested it on his knee.

"I'm sure you're wondering why you're here," Paul said. "I'm sure you're wondering why I'm here, too," he smiled, showing cracks at the corners of his eyes, which reflected his age. "I am here because my son has caused many, many problems."

The man was soft-spoken and gentle in demeanor as he sat wearing his prison blues.

"As his father, I have strived his whole life to mold him into a more refined and sophisticated way of living. The family business in politics is what I tried to push him toward, but he has his own mind and reacts impulsively. Rather than accept the path that I'd laid out for him, he instead has taken it upon himself to behave savagely. As you can tell, this does not please me."

It was not lost on Austin that Paul Archer's only political ties were in strong-arming and paying politicians to do his bidding. It sounded like Archer found this level of hoodlum more suitable than Kevin's more violent approach.

"I understand that my friend, Mr. Daltry, is in a very tricky position with the re-election just around the corner. My son's behavior is causing a hiccup in a plan that I've invested in for years. I don't want this venture to suffer over his actions. And so, I find that I have come to a point of closure with regard to cleaning up my son's messes."

Suddenly, everything made sense to Austin. He shook his head as the realization of what he'd just learned set in. Mayor Urrond Daltry was nothing more than a puppet. Paul Archer served as the brass and funding behind him, backing the man even from behind prison walls. It was clear that he was the decision maker and was truly the one running the city.

"I am prepared to do whatever is necessary to bring my son's era of tyranny to an end. I would like to extend my resources to you, Agent Malone, to see that this happens quickly. I have provided Mayor Daltry's aide with all of the information regarding offshore accounts that fund my son in his endeavors. The quickest way to bring him back to Michigan, if he has ever left, is to cut off his money supply."

Archer's jaw clenched as he said, "He is but a spoiled child and will come here to gain access to the safety accounts I've put in place for him. The only way to retrieve the money is to present the key to the bank official, who would then grant him access to the safe. I've made arrangements with the financial institution to notify me when he arrives to make the collection. Once we receive word of his arrival, that's when you come in and do whatever you please with him."

"You think your son is stupid enough to stroll into a bank, hand someone a key, and think he'd get away without immediately being reported to the police the minute his face is seen?"

"I don't believe I was clear before, Agent Malone. The banker, as well as the bank itself, is on my payroll. My son could walk in there with his rap sheet and social security number plastered on his shirt, and no one would touch him. That is, until now. As I stated before, I gave them instructions to alert me once my son has arrived so that we can handle the situation."

Paul Archer was handing over his son's life with a bow, all in the name of politics. It was at that moment when Austin realized Kevin Dennison was the successor to a family of poisonous snakes. Without regard for another word coming from Archer's mouth, the agent pulled the handle on the door and pushed Daltry out of his way.

"Before you go, Agent Malone, I will leave you with this: A gem is not polished without rubbing, nor a man perfected without trials. I have been through hell and back, yet I have remained. My son has had trials of his own, and yet he remains a fool. The time has come that his foolish deeds no longer go unpunished."

The words fell from the man's mouth so coolly that Austin expected ice crystals to form on his lips.

"Keep your resources to yourself, Archer. Your son will fall, and I won't need your or anyone else's help to make that happen."

Austin climbed out of the car, realizing there was now nothing left in this world that could surprise him.

*

In spite of the unpleasantly surprising evening, the next morning started off well. Austin had cleaned Robin's wounds, and they both noticed that the area became less tender each day. It was Olivia's birthday, and her bash was scheduled for that afternoon. He and Robin had barely spent time alone together. He hoped that would change after the party.

Olivia was still in bed. The couple decided to get an early start, making breakfast and getting decorations put up around the house. Austin stood at the counter scrambling eggs, while Robin sliced a loaf of rye bread for toast.

"This is really nice," Austin smiled.

"What is?"

"You know, us making breakfast, things being normal for longer than two seconds. Well, as normal as they can be, I suppose. I'm here whipping up a gourmet meal, and you are burning toast like usual."

Playfully, she punched him in the arm and then snuggled up to him at the counter.

"Things are going to be even better than they were before," Robin assured her husband. Then she asked suddenly, "Do you remember how it was when you were a kid? There were no cares in the world. Nothing was ever so serious that you had to stress. Food was always cooked and waiting piping hot on a plate for you; there were no bills to pay, or responsibilities to think about." Robin spread butter on the bread. "It would be nice to have that feeling again."

"You wanna be a kid again? I think you're forgetting the challenging aspects. Like how frustrating it was learning to tie your shoes. Or how you always had to go to bed early and miss out on all the fun stuff. Also, you never got to do any of the cool adult things." Austin leaned in, sliding his hand up her thigh.

"Okay, maybe there are a couple of fun things I like about being an adult," she smiled. "I hope Olivia is enjoying her childhood and that she stays a sweet little girl as long as possible. There's an innocence about her that I want to preserve; you know what I mean?" Robin looked down at the floor. "I don't want her to know about Kevin. Ever. I don't want her to know who he is, or the things he's done. But I don't want to lie to her, either."

"Honey, we've got plenty years left of her being the sweet little girl that we want her to be. We don't have to decide right now how, when, or even if we'll tell her about him. Tomorrow's worries can wait. Let's just get through these days first." He pulled her in for a kiss. "Now, let's get back to that adult stuff we were talking about."

Robin slid her arms around his neck, and he hoisted her up onto the kitchen island. Her thighs were smooth and warm as his hands glided slowly up and down each one.

"Uh, I'm sorry to break up the party, but some of us actually like to prepare our food on these surfaces, and we'd appreciate you not doing *this* all over it," Joanne said snidely as she strode into the room.

Feeling like two kids who'd just been caught, the pair moved in opposite directions from each other, snickering under their breath.

"Good morning, Aunt Joanne." Austin leaned down to kiss her cheek.

"Your lips have seen enough action for one day." Joanne brushed past him to take over scrambling the eggs in the pan.

"So, what all do we have left to do for the party?" she asked the couple. Before either of them could respond, Joanne answered herself. "I've got Jacob picking up the balloons at noon. The cake was made last night, so I just have to get the icing on and decorate it. Oh, I've also got to remember to get her presents from the basement and wrap them up," she whispered so that Olivia, upstairs, wouldn't hear her.

"Geez, Auntie, is there anything left for us to do?" Robin asked.

"Sure is; you can stay outta my way."

Robin should have known that would be the response she'd get.

As the women chatted about the details of the day, Austin walked over to the sink. Something caught his eye in the window. Noodles, who was normally in constant overdrive, was lying on her side out in the yard.

"How long has it been since you let Noodles out?" he asked Robin, wiping his hands on a towel.

Robin, trying to continue in the romantic vibe he'd created earlier, grabbed his waist and said, "A little while ago. Just let her play in the yard for a bit. She'll be fine." Using his apron, Robin looped the ties around her fingers and playfully tried to reel him towards the staircase. She went in for a kiss, but he leaned back and kept his eyes focused outside. The look on his face made her worry.

"What's wrong?" She moved next to him to look out the window. Without saying a word, Austin charged out the door. Robin fell in step behind him. The closer they got to the dog, the more alarmed they became. Jogging to the center of the lawn, they knelt by Noodles. Her sad eyes stared up at them as she whimpered in pain.

They looked her over for animal bites but didn't see any wounds. Austin's gut chimed in. He knew there was something more. Immediately he scooped the ailing dog into his arms and rushed to the garage. "Someone fed her chocolate cocoa," he said to Robin who had spotted the same candy wrapper he'd just seen.

Robin's heart sank when she turned and saw Olivia standing on the deck watching the spectacle. "I'll get her," Robin said as she slapped on a smile.

"Where's Daddy taking Noodles?" Olivia asked. Austin continued to the garage.

"Oh, Daddy's just taking her for a vet visit. Now let's go back inside and help Aunt Joanne with breakfast, okay?"

Olivia had a sense that something was wrong, but her mother's optimism lured her into believing otherwise.

*

Austin sat in the waiting room of the veterinary clinic alone. Over the past few months he'd spent more than his share of waiting on the final word from a doctor about someone he loved. He was at his wits end at this point and beginning to feel run down.

In his line of work, he was exposed to tragedy on a daily basis. The pain of tragedy striking close to home was never dulled by his professional experiences. Cutting off his morose line of thought, the veterinarian walked in. She pulled a surgical mask from her face.

Austin stood to his feet. "How is Noodles?"

"We are pumping her system with meds to flush the toxic material from her body. But we also had to do an emergency extraction."

The doctor reached into her pocket and pulled out a plastic baggy with a ragged slip of paper inside. With her gloved hands, she reached inside, gently pulling the frail note out.

"I found something very interesting inside your dog's stomach."

Austin's internal antenna rose as he took the small paper from her hands. Gently he turned it over.

One bitch down, one to go...

Every inch of Austin's body screamed with rage as he tried to not rip the paper to shreds. The only thing stopping him was knowledge that the note was now evidence that could possibly lead him to Dennison.

*

Austin came in through the garage, body drained, face echoing the same. It was 8 o'clock at night, and Olivia's birthday party had long been over. The house had already been cleaned from top to bottom, leaving no evidence that a party had ever been there. Missing his daughter's party hurt him deeply, but not as much as the news that he carried would hurt his family.

As soon as she saw the morbid look on Austin's face, Robin knew that Noodles was dead. Immediately, her eyes filled; Austin couldn't look at her. It would break his heart to see her cry.

"How did this happen? What would chocolate even be doing in our—"

Before even finishing her statement, Robin realized exactly who was responsible. Her sorrow for the dog instantly turned into rage towards Kevin.

"He hates me so much that he'd do this on Olivia's birthday?" she asked angrily. "Why is it not enough that he's done his best to ruin my life? Why does he have to try and ruin hers, too?" Placing her hands on either side of her head, she said, "This is crazy. You should have seen how happy she was today, Austin. There wasn't a single worry in her mind. Now I'm going to have to explain to her that her best friend in the world is dead. This is just too much."

Austin wanted to comfort his wife, but he was too incensed to even take a step. Even Robin herself was too drained to say anything more about the situation. Like all the times before, she felt defeated at the hands of Kevin Dennison.

The only positive for Austin was the horrific confirmation that Kevin was in the city. Days earlier, the agent had put in a call to his good friend, John Walsh, and set some plans into motion. He was hoping that the effort would pay off soon and aid in the man's capture.

*

Kevin Dennison sat in L. Gino's Coney Island restaurant having the Paul Bunyan breakfast. The low cut shirt that his waitress wore made her breasts nearly pop out. She enjoyed teasing him with the view. His eyes followed her every move. She turned, smiling coyly at him every so often. The young woman couldn't have been more than 22 years old, but the sexual chemistry she exuded was sophisticated beyond her years.

Kevin wanted her, and knew that by the end of her shift, she'd be leaving with him.

He had just stood up to pull his wallet out and motion for the check, when he overheard something that grabbed his attention. On the flat screen television in the corner was John Walsh, from the show *Most Wanted,* introducing the next segment.

"On August 29th, Kevin Dennison escaped from a

Belle Isle Heights Municipal courtroom. What you're about to see next will be the disturbing images of the events that unfolded leading up to that day."

Actors, who looked nothing like the true characters, began to play out the scenes as they happened over the course of years. They first depicted Kevin and Robin meeting at a business function and becoming lovers. Soon after, a small child was born, and Kevin's character was shown shouting and being verbally confrontational toward the mother. The next scene was the baby being stolen from the hospital in the middle of the night. Robin's character was distraught and soon found herself in the snare of the kidnapper as well.

Fake-Kevin wrestled fake-Robin into a pit out in the middle of the woods and was shown torturing and beating her. The actress cowered in fear and it brought back all of the delicious memories that Kevin had of that time. In real life, a smile spread across his face, and he enjoyed the powerful portrayal that he was given. The rise in his pants over the scene was evident.

The final scene was of the infamous day in the courtroom that he'd escaped federal custody, almost taking Robin and Katherine's lives in the process. The screen showed screaming people running for their lives as he fled with his hostage and sped off in the police vehicle outside the building. A real mug shot of him appeared. He noted that even in the prison jumpsuit he was wearing, he looked absolutely dashing.

"Kevin Dennison is a very dangerous man, and I caution you to be on the lookout. If you have any tips on his whereabouts, please call the number listed at the bottom of your screen."

Kevin, whose appearance had changed due to a haircut and dye, felt like he'd just received an award for most villainous. His chest puffed greatly with pride. He wanted to stand up and applaud the valiant effort put forth by Agent Malone, even though he knew the plan to nab him would never work.

Oblivious to the story that had just played, the young waitress strode over and handed him the bill. Scribbled across the top was her phone number, and the name *Nikki*, with hearts in place of the dots on the i's. On cloud nine, he leaned in close and whispered something in her ear. With a girly giggle, Nikki nodded and announced to her manager that she was taking a break.

Minutes later, she found herself in the alley behind the restaurant. With her panties slung around her ankles, Kevin Dennison had his way with her.

*

Olivia sat on her mother's lap. They both looked heart-wrenchingly sad.

"So, that means I will never be able to see Noodles again?" asked Olivia through tears.

"No, Honey, it doesn't mean that at all. Look," Robin said, pointing to a picture on the mantel, "We still have pictures and videos, and anytime you miss Noodles, you can look at those to make you feel better."

Olivia's eyes, although still sad, showed a small spark of gratefulness.

"Mommy?"

"Yes, baby?"

"Why do bad things happen?"

The question was one impossible to answer. Robin did her best.

"Well, honey, I think that without bad things, we wouldn't be able to appreciate the good things. Noodles' passing away is very sad, but it's a part of life. At least we got to have her here for a little while. Other things might happen that won't seem so good, but you'll get stronger and learn how to handle them."

Olivia nodded, as if the concept made perfect sense to her. Robin felt like she'd just ushered her daughter one step further away from the very innocence she'd been fighting so hard to preserve.

"I guess it's kind of like your head, Mommy. You hurt your head and it was bad, but you had to cut your hair and your face looks much prettier."

Robin melted as she squeezed her precious daughter. Aunt Joanne, who was eavesdropping from just outside the door, felt proud listening to them both sounding wise beyond their years. She was happy to be there to witness the tender moment and wondered how much longer she'd be around to witness more of them. A secret she'd been holding on to ate at her from the inside. Like all the times before, she kept quiet, waiting for a better time to share her news.

Chapter Eighteen

Sitting in a sea of paper had become a staple in

Austin's life these days. He was close to exhausting every avenue that would help him locate Dennison and needed a break in the case.

Flipping through files, Austin looked at contacts and women who had come across Dennison's path at some point in his life. What stood out to the agent was that Kevin hadn't had long-term relationships. Through college, Kevin's only consistency with women was multiple counts of sexual assault filed against him. The cases had been thrown out, each due to insufficient evidence — a deal most likely worked out by his father.

There was suddenly something that caught the agent's eye. A photo of Kevin Dennison cradling a drink in one hand and a pretty girl in another, leapt off the pages. Other college kids at a frat party surrounded the two. Austin wondered how he had missed this before. Jumping out of his seat, confused, he paced across the floor, rubbing his head. Suddenly, things that made no sense before had just become crystal clear.

Austin looked at his watch, slid his phone to his ear and headed out the door. "Boss, I've got something huge." The agent's pulse raced. He'd just gotten the break he needed.

*

Katherine Palmer had just returned from a litigation meeting when her secretary informed her that Agent Malone was there to see her. She'd forgotten all about their meeting but was glad to see him. Besides helping out with the Dennison case, she looked forward to catching up with the agent and hearing about the progress with Robin's health. Austin walked into the room with a big smile on his face, and she extended her arms.

"Agent Malone, it's always good to see you," she said as they embraced. "How is my girl Robin holding up?" Katherine took a seat behind her desk. She extended her hand to the seat across from her, and Austin sat down. "My wife is made out of regenerative material. No matter what happens to her, she always bounces back."

"I'm so glad to hear that. She really is such an inspiration." Katherine laughed and said, "I wish I could bottle up the resilience she has and drink it every day."

"Well, Katherine, we owe much gratitude to you. You saved her life. I mean, how many people do you know who would jump in front of a bullet for another person? I don't think I know any. Not besides you." Austin's smile was tight. Katherine beamed at the compliment.

"Like I told you before, you and Robin are like family, and I was just doing what came naturally."

"Yes, you were," the agent smirked.

"So, how is the case coming? Are you any closer to finding that scumbag, Dennison?"

Austin stood up and walked over to the large floor length window and peered out at the view of the city. With his hands in his pockets he said, "Still having a hard time setting eyes on him, but we'll exhaust every lead until we find him. We did find a few interesting things though."

"Oh?" Katherine said, reading over papers.

"Yes, we sure did. Taking a deeper look into his past, we found that Dennison had a way of wooing and coercing women into helping him with his dirty work."

Katherine put her pen down, now listening more intently. Austin continued staring out the window.

"It seems that every woman who crosses his path first finds themselves in his bed. Then they end up helping him with tasks like fudging paperwork, giving him access to secure data, - you know, things of that nature."

Katherine sat perfectly still. Austin went on.

"Not Robin, though. She was the only one who didn't fall for his trickery and didn't cave in to his demands. That's why he's got a hard on for her so bad. She's the beast that he could never seem to tame."

Katherine swallowed hard when the agent turned and walked slowly over to her desk. Just over her head were degrees she'd gotten from Michigan University Law School and an encased copy of her passing score from the Bar exam. Austin tapped them individually. "I've heard some stories about the wild parties that went on at the Mich U campus. Must have been good times, huh?" he smiled.

Katherine still hadn't moved an inch. Only her eyes followed him around the room.

"What year did you come out again? '98, '99? Must have met a lot of people during that time."

Tiny beads of sweat formed along Katherine's

forehead. She fidgeted uncomfortably.

"I...uh, should really get started on these files, Agent Malone."

Austin stepped away from the display and sat down in the seat across from her. "I don't want to take up much more of your time, Katherine. I pretty much just wanted to fill you in on the progress of the case, and let you know how well Robin is healing." The agent stood up and walked towards the door. Before reaching it, he said, "I do have one question for you, though."

She looked up and peered into his eyes.

"Why'd you do it, Katherine?"

She instantly stood from her desk, organizing a random stack of papers. "I appreciate you stopping by, Agent Malone." She tried to rush him along.

Austin reached inside his bag and pulled out a file. He dropped it onto her desk. The pleasant look on his face quickly disappeared. It was replaced by an icy stare that she'd never seen from him before. Her flared nostrils and pooling eyes did nothing but make the agent angrier.

"Have a seat, Katherine."

"But, I need to—"

"Sit your ass down!" he shouted, spit flying from his mouth.

Katherine's lips pursed tightly. Her trembling legs sat on the edge of the seat.

Flipping open the folder, Austin pulled out a log of Kevin's visitors from Jackson Correctional facility.

"You went to see him when he was convicted for trying to kill me and my wife. You created the loophole that eventually led to him getting out of prison. If you hadn't done that, he never would have kidnapped Robin or nearly killed her at his sentencing."

Austin reached inside the envelope and pulled out the college photos he'd found of the two. After digging around, he had gotten his hands on more incriminating photos of Katherine perched atop the very desk where she now sat trembling. Kevin Dennison's face disappeared between her legs, her head thrown back in the heat of passion.

Katherine slammed the folder shut. "How did you get these?" her lips trembled.

"Tapped into your *private* security system and got these stills." Austin pointed to the security camera aimed at her desk. "None of that matters at this point, Katherine." He took a step towards her. "You orchestrated the release of that animal back onto the streets, and I want to know why."

A single tear trickled slowly from her eye. Shame hovered over her face and finally, she fessed up. "The plan was for him to take Cynthia as a hostage, using her to get out of the courtroom. That was it. I was just as surprised as everyone else when he raised the gun and pointed it at Robin." Now the attorney was full-blown crying as she tried to explain her actions. "When I saw he was going to shoot her, I realized the mistake I made trying to help him. I did the only thing I knew to do, which was to protect her life."

Her eyes searched Austin's for signs of sympathy.

All she found staring back through them was disgust.

"Because of you, my wife was kidnapped." He took a step closer. "Because of you my wife was abused." He took another step. "Because of you my wife has a bullet in her fucking head!"

They now stood nose to nose. Before doing something to her that he'd regret, Austin turned to walk away. But he couldn't do it. He needed answers and found himself charging back towards her. "I want to hear it out of your mouth, Katherine. Tell me, why!"

Commander Bells and a group of agents walked in. They stood sentry over the agent who looked like he would blow at any moment.

"I wouldn't have this job if it wasn't for him!" Katherine shouted. Then her head hung low. "After passing the Bar, I looked for work but couldn't find anything. I was turned away left and right no matter what I did. Kevin's family had serious pull in the city, so he was able to get me in the door. He didn't even ask for anything in return. We had been friendly ever since college and were used to looking out for each other.

"So, when he started getting into trouble, I felt obligated to help him. You have to understand that I was only acting in the best interest of my career and family. There was no way I could say no to him." Her eyes begged for sympathy. The roomful of officers offered none.

"When I tried his case the first time, he had tons of evidence stacked against him. I couldn't exactly do a sloppy job of prosecuting him. But I was able to leave a trail of technicalities and paper errors that would lead to his release. I swear to you though; I thought he was going to leave the city when he got out, because he said he was bored with it. I had no idea that his plans were to kidnap Robin."

More tears tumbled down as she pleaded for Austin to believe her story.

"You caught him after kidnapping Robin, and I knew for sure Judge Childs was going to throw the book at him. I didn't want him to spend the rest of his life in prison. So, I made him swear that if I helped him get away, he would leave for good and never look back. I set it up with a court officer to have a waiting car outside the court. The rest, he did on his own, including killing Judge Childs."

Austin paced the floor, to keep from laying his hands on her. "Where is he, Katherine?"

"I don't know."

In an instant, he was on the other side of the room, shouting in her face. "Where the hell is he?! I know he's been contacting you, so tell me where he is!" His fist pounded the desk.

"I don't know, I swear to God, I don't know!"

"Do realize you're going to jail? You're an accessory to murder and attempted murder, Katherine. You may as well have pulled the trigger and shot Robin yourself. Look around; all of this is now shot to hell," he referred to her job as district attorney. "When you go to prison, you'll be cohabiting with all the women you've put away. Imagine how they'll feel seeing you walk in wearing the same uniform as them. You are no different than them now. And they are going to prove that to you, night after night," he said viciously. "From where I stand, you have nothing left to lose. Your job is gone, and once your husband sees these pictures, I'm sure he's going to leave, too. So, why are you still protecting Dennison?"

Katherine pounded her palms against her head and finally spoke up.

"I don't know his exact location, but...he calls me every now and then. He asks about updates on the case and if you guys are on his tail. I have no idea when his calls are going to come in, and they normally don't last long." Katherine closed her eyes. "That's all I know, I swear to you."

Austin massaged his eyes. Bells, standing in the doorway, looked on at the sad sight. Katherine Palmer was an excellent attorney, with a loving husband and bright future. It was a tragedy to see that she'd thrown it all away.

"I didn't mean for Robin to get hurt," Katherine said pathetically. Austin turned his back to her as officers walked over. They cuffed and Mirandized her as she unsuccessfully continued pleading her case. "I swear I didn't mean for Robin to get hurt!"

The strong willed woman fought against the officers. They carted her past the seething agent and out the door.

Bells walked over to Austin. "We're thinning the herd. Pretty soon we'll have every one of his allies turned against him. He'll be backed into a corner, just where we want him. When he sees his resources drying up left and right, he'll be forced to pop up somewhere. And that's when we'll nab him."

Austin brushed past him, and stalked out the door.

*

It was late when Austin got home that night. He'd tried to quietly creep in without disturbing the girls, but Robin was still up waiting for him on the sofa.

"I finally told Olivia about Noodles."

Sighing deeply, Austin pulled off his jacket and sat down next to her. "How'd she take it?"

"Surprisingly well. She was sad, but then easily seemed to understand that shit happens."

Austin chuckled, even though Robin wasn't making a joke of it.

"Looks like you've had a long day," she said to her husband, whom she'd only seen in passing over the last few days.

"Yeah, you could say that." The agent took a breath deeper than he even thought possible. "I arrested Katherine Palmer today."

Robin's shocked expression was expected.

"She's been helping Dennison this entire time. You know I can't get too much into detail, but what I'll say is that if she hadn't helped him, he'd still be in jail right now."

Apparent by her gaped mouth, Robin's shock hadn't worn off. Austin felt like he'd snatched off a Band-Aid, only to have the wound bleed fresh again.

Dazed she asked, "Does she know where he is?"

"According to her, she has no idea. She only helped him plan the escape with the expectation that he would go somewhere far away."

"Do you believe her?"

"Even though her reasons for helping him were bogus, I truly do believe that she isn't aware of his location. Of course we'll still go through her computer and phone records to see if we can lock in a specific number or address that he may have contacted her from."

"I trusted her," Robin whispered. "I trusted that she truly wanted to help me win and put him away." Robin shook her head, trying to make sense of the situation. There was no sense to be made. Exasperated, she said, "It's like he owns everyone in this town, and they're all in on his vicious jokes except for us. When does it end?"

Austin saw the embers of hope for Dennison's capture dim from his wife's eyes. He wished he had the words to reignite it. "I don't know, honey. I don't have those answers yet. But I'm working as hard as I can to figure it out."

The two looked up to see Joanne standing at the bottom of the stairs.

"Sorry, Aunt Joanne, I didn't mean to wake you," said Austin.

"Wake me? Humph, all I was doing was tossing and turning. I overheard what you said about Katherine. It's a shame she would be so foolish. Just makes me want to shake some sense into her." Moving towards the kitchen, her house slippers dragged along the hardwood floor.

"I want to do much worse than shake her," Robin jabbed, with a roll of her eyes.

"This makes you feel like you can't trust anybody." Joanne shook her head. "But I won't give up hope. I know there are still good and honest people out there, and they're going to help us bring him in, I know it." Austin nodded weakly. Joanne asked, "Have you gotten any rest? Your eyes are as red as the devil."

"I feel like we're on the verge of something breaking, so I've got to keep pushing through," Austin yawned.

"Well, if you're keeling over dead from lack of sleep, you won't be much help to anyone. Some lavender tea will do you a world of good. I'm gonna make you some right now." Joanne shuffled into the kitchen.

Austin looked at Robin. "The luggage under my wife's eyes says she could use a cup, too."

She pinched him on the bicep.

"I picked up something for you today," said Austin. "I want to give it to you now while I'm thinking about it." Snatching his backpack from the floor, he grabbed Robin by the hand and led her upstairs. Aunt Joanne, thinking they were up to no good, said, "Don't be up there all night getting yourselves in a huff. I don't want this tea going to waste."

Austin waved her off, telling her she had the wrong impression. At the top of the stairs, he led his wife into the bedroom and closed the door. He then sat her down on the bed and unzipped his backpack.

"If we weren't already married, I'd assume you were getting ready to propose," Robin smiled.

"I've got a proposal of sorts, but not in the way you're thinking." He pulled a square, black case from his bag and held it out in front of her. "Touch it."

Robin's slender fingers rested on the top of the shiny box, and the top popped open. She peered inside and saw the pearly handle of a .22-caliber handgun. Her smile faded. "You got me a gun?"

"Yes, I got you a gun. You can keep it here in the house for protection. This case is designed for you and you only. It's programmed to respond only to your touch. You don't have to worry about Olivia accessing it at all." He demonstrated his point by closing the case and touching it himself. The box remained closed. To further prove his point, he shook it up and down and dropped it on the floor. "It's completely safe to have here."

Robin, impressed with the high-tech device, still felt contempt for its reason for being there.

Austin's face angered. "Katherine Palmer is proof positive that you don't know who you can trust. Since things are a little hot right now, I think its best we keep our guard up."

Robin swallowed hard. Apparently being an enemy to Kevin Dennison meant being an enemy to many others as well. "Will this all end soon? I don't want to live my life like this. I *can't* live my life like this."

"Honey, I can't promise you anything. But you know

that I am doing everything I can to bring this thing to an end. Until that happens, I need to make sure you're safe. I don't ever want to come close to losing you again."

Robin stared at the box for a while and slowly pulled it from his hands. Austin cupped her cheeks, thinking about what his next move would be.

Chapter Nineteen

It was a week later that Austin came up with an idea that was as out of the box as the entire case itself.

"So, let me get this straight." Bells rubbed his bald head. "Katherine Palmer won't be charged with any crimes at the moment because we want to keep her involvement tight-lipped. We'll still have her in our custody, but she'll be kept in a separate area of the correctional facility away from the other inmates. Do I have it right so far?" he asked with a hint of sarcasm. Austin nodded, and he continued. "This arrangement is all in exchange for help with setting up a sting for Dennison?"

Austin nodded again and elaborated. "Right now, we've got guys looping a connection between her cell, work, and home phones. In the event that he calls her on either line, it will ring to her private cellblock where the agents will monitor the conversation and hopefully track his location."

"And what will stop her from blowing our cover and telling him to run from here to Jerusalem when he calls?"

"There is no way we can guarantee she won't do that. But unless you've got any better ideas, this is the one we're running with."

In all his years of service with the CIA, Bells had never seen anyone with as much determination as Austin. If nothing else could be said about his agent, Bells knew that he would pursue his target until his dying breath.

"Alright, let's give it a try," Bells said with a resigned shake of his head.

Austin turned to leave. Bells stopped him. "Before you get this started, there is one other small lead to follow. You won't be happy about it, but the time has obviously come for us to walk down that path."

"But, I don't think it's—"

"It's time," Bells said, gently cutting him off.

The agent's jaw clenched, even though he knew the commander was right. For this difficult task, he would need to enlist the help of his wife.

At the county jail, Robin sat with her knee bouncing nervously. She and Austin waited to be called back to meet with the prisoner. Unconsciously, her slender fingers made their way to her mouth. She chewed the tips of her nails. Gently, Austin slid her hand down and held it in his palm.

"Relax, Honey. This will be no sweat. You've known her for years, so it should be easy to talk to her."

Robin cocked her head to the side. "Easy to talk to her? I wouldn't exactly call conversing with someone who betrayed my trust easy."

"Just trust me on this, Honey. You'll be fine. We need her help, and I think she'd be more willing to share information with you than with anyone else. She owes you."

Robin looked into his eyes, her leg bouncing again. He patted her hand and pressed a kiss onto the side of her cheek.

"She's ready to meet you," said a female guard. She then led them back to an interview room. The pair were shown into the room, and told to wait until the inmate was brought down. Moments later, Robin looked up and took a deep breath.

Melanie Mitchell walked into the room, facing her former friend she hadn't seen in five years. There was a jumble of emotions between the two: confusion, pity, anger. Breaking the tension, Melanie took her seat at the interview table. "Wow. The infamous Robin Malone," her eyes shifted, "...and the almighty Austin Malone. Here you are, sitting in the living room of my home here in Hell. While I'd like to embrace you with a hug, something tells me you wouldn't trust me enough to be that close." Melanie smirked. Neither of them cracked a smile.

"That may be true, but it would be for good reason, wouldn't it, Melanie?" Robin coolly replied. There was no question that all pleasantries had been skipped, and the women were now on guard.

Melanie smirked again. "So, what brings the two of you here? I thought I'd never hear from you again. Since coming here, I've written you many times and never received a single response back, Robin. You did receive my letters, didn't you?"

"Yes, I received them."

"Did you at least read them?"

"I didn't see a need to," Robin lied.

Melanie lowered her eyes. "Being behind bars and having nothing to focus on, besides the reason that you're here, really gives you a great ability to articulate yourself. I hate knowing that my articulation to you was all in vain."

"I'm glad you've have time to reflect while you're here, because that's precisely what jail is designed to do. Don't sit there and try to drum up sympathy, Melanie. Let's not do this," Robin warned.

Robin was suddenly angrier than she thought she'd be. Austin made an effort to stay out of it.

"Look, Robin, what I did to you back then was wrong, and I've apologized. Sleeping with Kevin and betraying you were out of line, and I'm aware of it. There were demons that I was dealing with; at the time, I thought they justified my behavior. I now know otherwise. In the letters I wrote, I tried explaining that to you—"

"Melanie, I couldn't care less about any of that at this point. To prove how unaffected I am by your past choices, I'm going to overlook the fact that you left your attempted murder charge towards me off the list during your little apology."

Robin's coolness stung.

"All right, Robin; we'll do this your way. For the record, I had *nothing* to do with his plans to hurt you. But since you're not here to make peace about that, then why are you here?"

Robin looked at her husband before responding. "We're here because we need your help."

Melanie laughed at the statement and sat back against her seat. With raised eyebrows she asked, "And what, exactly, could I possibly help you with?"

Robin paused before answering. "I'm sure you've heard about the things that Kevin has done to me and my family. He's still out there somewhere, and we need to track him down."

Austin finally spoke up. "We're searching for potential leads by contacting people that he may have been in contact with."

Melanie looked appalled at Austin's insinuation that she would have a clue where he was.

"Uh, if you haven't noticed, I've been in jail for the past five years. I didn't get released on the same *technicality* that he did," she used air quotes. "How would I have the slightest idea where he is?" She looked from Austin, to Robin, back to Austin again.

Robin said, "From what I remember, the two of you had gotten extremely close. I couldn't imagine that your going to jail would stop a person like Kevin from reaching out to you if he wanted to keep in contact."

Melanie lowered her head and shook it back and forth. She smiled, but what she had to say next was no laughing matter. She reached into the flap on her bright orange uniform and slid out a photo of a young boy. He looked to be around 4 years old. Melanie held the photo just inches from both of their faces. "This is Kevin Dennison Jr., mine and Kevin's son."

Robin's heart fluttered unnaturally. She turned to Austin who was equally stunned.

"It wasn't until coming to jail that I discovered I was almost two months pregnant. I tried reaching out to

Kevin every way I could. I wrote letters, had people on the outside contact him; none of it mattered. He wanted nothing to do with me or our child."

As Robin heard the words coming from Melanie's mouth, the realization set in that the boy in the photo was a sibling of her own daughter. She sat in shock, as Melanie continued on.

"He never wanted me, Robin. He only used me to get to you. Kevin knew that being with me was the only thing that would get under your skin." She smirked and said, "He lived to get a rise out of you. It's like he was addicted to evoking emotion out of you any way he could." Her smile faded. "Now my son is being raised by my sister and has neither parent in his life."

Melanie leaned back, and Austin saw a small tattoo on the side of her neck. He recognized it as the marking for a well-known female gang. The scars on her body and hollow look in her eyes meant she'd had to join one, just to survive prison life.

"So, again, I have absolutely no idea where Kevin is, but I do hope you find him. I have a few words for him that I'd like to get off my chest."

"I'm sorry to hear about your son, Melanie. No child deserves to be born into those circumstances," Robin offered.

The woman thumbed her nose and leaned forward. "Don't worry about my son. He's in good hands. When I finally do get out, I'll make up for all the time I've lost with him."

"If Dennison contacts you for any reason, Melanie,

please see to it that you notify me." Austin handed her his card.

She sneered, "I'll tell you one thing right now; you better hope you find him before my people do."

Austin nodded, and Melanie stood up from her seat. She turned to call for the guard, but slowly turned back.

"Just so you know, my attorneys are working on an appeal, and I might be getting out of here soon. Maybe when I'm out, we could set up something with the kids sometime. After all, they are each other's family." She smiled at Robin, who felt sick to her stomach, and walked out the door.

Robin and Austin found themselves inside the car sitting outside the correctional facility. Austin looked over at his wife, who looked like she'd just taken a beating.

"You okay?" he asked softly.

Her unblinking eyes were glued to the dashboard. They were beginning to burn. "I'm...I don't know what I am. Confused? Angry? Sad? Those are all words that come to mind, but none can even come close to describing how I feel." Rubbing her eyes to moisten them, she looked at him. "It feels like cameras should be following me; like my life is a drama miniseries." Imitating a television announcer, she said, "'Stay tuned to find out what will happen on the next episode of Damsel In Distress, starring the damsel herself, Robin Malone.'"

The couple laughed until tears formed in their eyes.

"My daughter has a brother that she doesn't even know exists. That poor boy has a father who doesn't want him. This just isn't right," her smile faded.

There were no words Austin could offer that would sweeten the situation. Instead, he offered a pat on the hand. His cell phone rang, as it usually did at inopportune times. Robin nodded for him to answer it. The call was from one of the agents monitoring Katherine Palmer's line.

"We've got something. Can you meet us down at the correction facility?"

Austin motioned for Robin to stay inside. He slid from behind the driver seat and closed the door behind him.

"I'm already here, working on another lead. What's up?"

"Meet us in the C. A. Young sector."

Minutes later, Austin tore through the halls. Entering an abandoned cell designated as a communications room, he saw Bells and two other agents coaching Katherine, who sat in the cell across from them. One of the agents was Sidwell. Austin tried to ignore the hatred that pooled in his belly when spotting him.

Using only hand signals, Sidwell motioned for Austin to put on a headset and listen in to the call that had just come in. Voices soon filled his ears.

"Lovely day, isn't it, Kat?"

Hearing Kevin's voice, a shot of adrenaline blasted through Austin's body.

"I didn't think I'd be hearing from you for a while. You up and disappeared on me," said Katherine, sassiness lurking in her voice. "You're doing well, I hope."

"How else would I be besides well?" Kevin asked confidently.

"I know you can take care of yourself. I just worry when I don't hear from you for long periods of time. Especially since the heat's been on you so tough lately. I'm not sure if you've seen it, but there was a whole segment about you on Most Wanted."

Kevin scoffed. "That was nothing but amusement for me."

Austin listened in, realizing he was witnessing the intimacy of two lovers. Katherine tried to appear as if her concern was a part of the ruse to reel Kevin in. It was evident that her concern was genuine.

Sidwell wound his hand, guiding Katherine to pump him for more information.

"Where are you, anyway?" she asked casually.

Perfectly sidestepping the question, he answered, "I'm around. You know, just keeping my head down for now."

"Maybe we can find a way to see each other. I don't have much going on around here besides muddling through case files. I know it's different, but...it might be nice."

Katherine had just laid down the bait, and the agents all hoped he'd bite.

"You're right, Kitty Kat, that is…different…."
Kevin's voice trailed off and went silent. Katherine
looked up at the agents to see if they'd lost the call.
They stared back wondering the same thing. They
needed just a few more minutes before the trace could
connect.

"Are you there?" she asked calmly.

"I'm here. But where are you?"

"What do you mean? I'm at home. That's where you
called me, remember?"

The line went silent again. The usually steel-nerved
attorney now found herself feeling anxious. Kevin's
guard seemed raised unusually high, and she hoped he
wasn't on to her. Suddenly, he asked, "What are you
doing right now?"

After a few seconds of fumbling for words she
responded with, "I, uh, am just watching the polls for
the mayoral elections."

Bells gave her thumbs up for thinking so quickly on
her feet.

"You are? What channel?"

Alarm spread around the communications room
over Kevin's sudden line of questioning. "Channel
Four. I'm watching channel four."

Seconds of silence passed. "Who's leading in the
polls? I want to know the exact percentages."

Alarm had now turned to panic, knowing that Kevin
sensed something was off.

"Why do you care about the polls, Kevin? You don't

even follow politics." Katherine tried sounding relaxed.

"Answer my question, Katherine. Tell me the exact percentages."

She hesitated, searching for words. After a few embarrassing and panicked seconds, Kevin interrupted her saying, "You really are a disappointment to me, Katherine. And by the way, say hello to Agent Malone for me." He hung up.

"Kevin, wait!"

Hearing the *Click Click* of the line as it disconnected in her ear pushed her anxiety over the edge.

"Dammit!" she screamed, tossing the phone to the ground. "Do you know what this means?! Now I'm on the wrong side of Kevin's hit list. He knows I'm helping you, and now I'm a guaranteed target!" With her hands on her forehead, she paced back and forth in her cell, as panic flooded her veins.

"He knew something was wrong. How the hell did he know?" Bells asked, rhetorically.

Austin pulled the headphones from his ears, and couldn't help eyeing agent Sidwell. He still didn't trust him and hoped — for Sidwell's sake — that he wasn't the rat who tipped Dennison off.

"She did something out of the norm by asking to see him. He's methodical in everything he does, and knows that she is, too. Even the slightest deviation from her normal behavior sent up a huge red flag. He knew he was being squeezed," Sidwell offered — a little too quickly in Austin's eyes.

Bells turned to the agent running the audio. "Did you get a track on his location?"

The agent shook his head. "Somehow he manipulated the analog signal, making it bounce all over the place. We couldn't pinpoint where it originated. All I can tell you is he's in the Metro area."

Close enough to catch... Austin thought.

While two agents worked to control Katherine, who was having a nervous breakdown, Austin stood up and charged out the door, setting his mind on a plan for smoking Dennison out.

It was evening by the time Austin and Robin returned home after two failed visits that didn't produce the results they were hoping for. When they walked through the door, Joanne and Olivia were in the great room engaged in a round of Uno. The playful laughs erupting from the room were a welcome break for the couple, whose heads were still reeling.

"Daddy, I beat Aunt Joanne three times!" Olivia beamed.

"That's because you cheated. You know I don't have my glasses on, so forcing me to play a game involving color and small numbers is no fair," Joanne joked, tickling the little girl.

Austin brushed a kiss on Olivia's face as Joanne struggled to get up from the floor. Robin helped her up. Brushing invisible dust from her slacks, she said, "It's someone else's turn to get beat up now. I've had all the Uno I can take for one day."

Robin took her aunt's place on the floor while Olivia

shuffled the cards.

Seeing the forlorn looks on their faces, Joanne said, "It looks like I'm not the only one who's taken a beating today. I take it your visit didn't go so well?"

With Olivia there, Robin couldn't elaborate with the choice words she preferred to use. Instead, she rolled her eyes, indicating that the day hadn't been positive.

"Sounds like that's a conversation we'll need to have over spiked tea. I'll go and put on a pot," said Joanne. She exited the room just as Olivia screamed *Uno!* She chuckled all the way to the kitchen.

Austin slid down onto the sofa, flipping on the television to get caught up on the polls. In just a few hours, a new mayor would be elected. Although the result wouldn't matter one way or another, the agent was still interested to see how things would turn out.

Frank Holland's face appeared on the screen. From behind the desk at the news station, the anchor chatted with a reporter at the campaign headquarters of Mayor Daltry. With music blaring in the background, the reporter had a finger plugged in his ear. Visible behind him, Daltry, confident in a win, prepared to head over to the swanky Ponchartrain Hotel where he would give an acceptance speech.

"The vibe in this room is one of excitement and imminent victory. With only a few hours remaining until the polls are closed, the mere 3 percent lag in votes is the only bone of contention in this room for the Daltry camp. Judging by the grin on the incumbent mayor's face, he is certain that he will pull through for the lead," said the reporter on the scene.

"Let's go over to Harvey Tolver's camp, where, I'm sure, they're hoping you'll be proved wrong," Frank Holland said from the studio. "Devin, how are things on that side of town?"

Austin noticed that the scene on the opponent's side was a stark contrast to mayor Daltry's. For one, it wasn't flashy or overtly arrogant, which, for Austin, was nice to see.

"Hopeful. Harvey Tolver, along with his wife and two young children are feeling positive that the outcome will continue in their favor. The small margin by which Tolver leads has been more than enough to keep the fires of hope burning bright," said reporter Devin Harlen.

The camera zoomed in on the background where Harvey Tolver quietly watched the poll monitors with his family. A little girl around the same age as Olivia climbed into her father's lap, and he smiled at her. From what Austin knew of him and his work in the city, Tolver appeared to be a real family man. Austin admired his wholesome quality. Although the man's political views were admirable, Austin hoped that he wouldn't be elected. The agent didn't want to see the destruction that would surely ensue. He knew that somewhere Paul Archer was lurking, ready to manipulate and control whoever the victor would be.

Joanne strode into the room with a tray of tea and announced that it was Olivia's bedtime.

"Aww, can't I stay up just a little while longer?" the little girl pleaded.

"Yes...when you're older, you can stay up as late as

you like, but as long as you're my sweet 5-year-old, you'll have to go to bed at a decent hour. Now say goodnight to your mom and dad. I made you some warm milk to have before I tuck you in."

The little girl bounced over to each parent, and they kissed her goodnight.

"Mommy, we'll play Uno again tomorrow, right?"

"Yes, we will, and I'm going to be ready to win." Joanne ushered the child up the stairs. Robin turned to Austin, "That little girl is a card shark. I'm glad we weren't playing for money, or I'd be in the poor house." Austin smiled and made a note to brush up for when it was his turn.

Robin moved over to her husband and rested her head on his shoulder. For nearly a half hour, they sat together in silence. So much had gone on around them. They forced themselves to enjoy being still for those few moments.

It was Austin who broke the silence by asking, "How did it feel seeing Melanie after all this time?"

Robin thought about her answer. "I'm still not sure. I mean, I've known her since I was six years old, so it's hard not to care for her. I'd be lying if I said I wasn't interested in seeing how she looks, or how she's surviving. But the lingering revulsion for all she's done kind of taints the sentiment that should be there."

Joanne walked in and sat on the sofa next to Austin. Inviting herself into their conversation, she said, "Her mind was poisoned, Honey. Maybe sitting in jail was the antidote she needed to get her mind right. Who knows, maybe in the future, you all can work towards rebuilding the foundation that you once had."

Robin thought about the news that Melanie had saddled her with.

"Whether I like it or not, we just may have to work together, Auntie. As it turns out, Olivia has a brother, Kevin Jr., which means we all are family now."

Joanne tried to form a complete sentence with the jumble of words zipping through her mind. "Wait a minute, you said she—how did you—are you telling me that—Lord!" Joanne sat back, feeling as if the wind had been knocked out of her. "Two babies," she whispered. Her mouth kept opening to speak, but closed again, not finding words suitable to describe her thoughts.

"She offered to have the kids spend time together. I just don't know how to feel about it all. The situation is something that no five year-old should have to wrap their mind around." Pulling herself up onto her feet, Robin said, "I'm done thinking about it for today. I'm going to bed." Joanne tried to ask more questions, but Robin's mind was too warped. She'd had enough. She blew a kiss to her family and hauled off up the stairs.

Joanne and Austin sat in silence, still in shock, thinking of how to keep their family from crumbling.

Suddenly, Joanne turned to him, her face sallow and misted with sweat. "Are you all right, Aunt Joanne? You don't look so—"

"I need you to listen to me, Austin. I have something that I need to tell you about Robin." Joanne swallowed hard as she fiddled with the hem on her dress. Austin knew that her announcement wasn't going to be good. He fought with himself to tell her to hold on to it.

"It's been too long that I've kept this secret from her, and I feel like I can't keep it any longer."

Before she could go on, Austin's phone rang with a call from Commander Bells. Knowing that it could be important, Joanne sighed. "Go ahead and answer it."

He put the phone to his ear, his mind racing inquisitively.

"Agent Malone," he answered.

"Did you see what just happened with Harvey Tolver?"

"Last time I looked he was leading by a small margin."

"Turn on your television. He's on every channel."

Austin did as he was instructed. Harvey Tolver stood behind a podium with his hands gripped on the sides firmly. What Austin thought would be the man giving a victory speech turned out to be much worse.

"I won't be before you long. I first want to thank my family and the Tolver campaign for all of the hard work and sacrifices they've made over the past few months. I'd also like to thank the voters for finding value in me, and working to elect me as the next visionary in the city.

"It is with a heavy heart that I announce my withdrawal from the election. I know this comes as a shock, and I apologize for any inconvenience that I may have caused. Thank you." Tolver grabbed his wife by the hand, and hurried off the stage.

News reporter Frank Holland sat flabbergasted watching the live occurrence. This was evident by his loss of words when the camera shot back to him in the news studio.

"I, uh, am probably just as shocked and astonished as all of you by Harvey Tolver's sudden, um...announcement. The mayoral candidate who currently holds a lead in the ballot has provided no explanation for his shocking decision in the eleventh hour. Devin, you have been there on the scene the entire night. Did you see any indication that this announcement would be made?"

The reporter shook his head, "No Frank. Everyone in this room is in complete and utter shock. Tolver has been positive and even addressed the crowd with his signature thumbs up, indicating his awareness that he was close to the finish line just under an hour ago. We saw him get pulled into a private meeting moments before he made the announcement, but we don't know the details of that conversation or with whom it occurred."

The reporter wedged himself forward in the crowd of people who flanked the former mayoral contender. They unsuccessfully tried to get answers as he and his family were whisked into a waiting car.

Austin flipped off the television, almost able to smell the pile of crap that spattered the situation.

"Someone got to him and has scared the shit out of him," Bells said.

It only took one guess for Austin to realize who that someone was.

Twenty Four Hours Earlier...

Mayor Daltry exited the elevator and went into his office. He carried a pile of papers in his hands. He grumbled to himself about an article in the newspaper and looked up to see his aide sitting at his desk — with a gag in his mouth. The man had a black eye and blood trickling down his face. With a wide-eyed stare Daltry had no time to react. A fist thundered down out of nowhere, striking him on the jaw. The mayor fell flat on his face, groaning in pain.

Through his grainy vision, he saw a pair of shoes walk around him. A person slowly bent down next to his face. "It's nice to finally meet you in person," Kevin Dennison said to the ailing mayor. He nudged the mayor with the heel of his shoe, and pushed him onto his back.

"So...it seems *Paltry Daltry* is nothing but a weak old man. At least that's the way things look when you're in a standing position watching the man himself crawl like an animal on the floor. From the way you charge around town, I expected something more. Perhaps I was expecting someone with a backbone. But all I see is a spineless jellyfish, too weak to defend himself."

Mayor Daltry had never been so afraid in his life; his heart pounded through his chest. "Please, don't hurt me. I am friends with your father and—"

"Friends? You call what you are to my father a friend? On the outside looking in, the relationship appears to be more of a puppet/puppet-master type of thing, don't you think?"

Daltry didn't respond. Kevin said, "Oh, I guess you thought I didn't know about your dealings with my dear old dad. Well, just like you, I have friends, too, who keep me informed on important things like these." He looked at the mayor's aide who sat with his head down. "My *friend* has filled me in on a lot, like you and your pathetic team turning Katherine Palmer against me."

Daltry glanced up at his aide, feeling betrayed.

"Tell me, Daltry; is it true that you are in cahoots with my father to have me plucked off the scene?"

From all he'd learned of Kevin over the past few years, the mayor knew that lying to him would be a very bad idea. So, he replied, "Yes, Kevin. Yes, this is true. Your father has worked hard over the years to have the city run smoothly under his control. You're throwing monkey wrenches in the plan. He felt it would be best to remove you from the situation."

Kevin wickedly grinned. "I'll be sure to have friends on the inside pay a visit to my father and clear up the notion that he is in control of anything." He rolled the mayor up into a sitting position and leaned on the edge of his desk.

"Things were closing in on you one way or the other, Kevin. Between your father and Agent Malone, who has a bug up his ass for you, you were going to fall and fall hard." The mayor rubbed his throbbing jaw.

"Yet, here I am. Inside the mayor's office tugging on

the puppet strings and in control yet again. Don't worry about my father though; he will be dealt with soon."

Daltry knew that Paul Archer's days on the earth had just been numbered.

"With my father out of the picture, you're going to need an alliance to aid you financially in your next term as mayor — and I'd be happy to offer that alliance to you, Mr. Mayor. Don't worry about your opponent, Harvey Tolver. I will see to it that he doesn't succeed in the election."

Daltry, knowing that Kevin had clear motives behind his generosity, asked, "And what will you get out of this deal?"

Kevin smiled bright. "I'm so glad you asked." He took a knife from his pocket. "I have a score to settle with Agent Malone, and I'm going to need your help to do it."

The mayor hung his head low, knowing he was about to sell his soul to yet another devil.

Chapter Twenty

Two months after Harvey Tolver disappeared off the face of the earth, the town and nation still talked about it. Mayor Daltry pushed full steam ahead in preparation for his swearing in ceremony. Ever the flashy one, he planned a celebratory parade for the morning of, which would "give me the opportunity to shake hands with the voters who supported me."

At five a.m. on the day of the parade, Austin sat on

the edge of his bed, trying to wake up. Robin lay next to him wondering why he was up so early.

"How did you sleep?" she asked.

"Didn't get much rest. I got a call from Mayor Daltry late last night. He put together a security detail for the parade and wants me to be a part of it. Thinks Dennison might do something to ruin his moment, so he requested that I be at his side."

Robin huffed and sat up. "Of course the thought of not having a stupid parade didn't cross his mind." She leaned up and kissed him on the back of his shoulder. "I'm sorry you have to be a part of that mess."

"I'll just go down and scope things out, in case Dennison does decide to make an appearance. Shouldn't be gone too long, maybe a couple hours."

"That's fine. Me and Olivia are meeting up with Cassidy and Aunt Joanne for a trip to the Charles Wright Museum."

"That should be a good time. If the parade doesn't go too long, maybe I'll join you all for a late lunch."

Robin kissed him and tried pulling him back down into bed.

"Nice try, sexy," he laughed. Austin got showered and headed off to the arduous task of protecting a man he loathed. He had no idea he was walking into a trap.

The streets of Woodward Avenue were lined with families toting cameras and tiny American flags. Austin, along with Bells, walked behind a slow moving Chrysler convertible that carried the reigning mayoral champion. Mayor Daltry waved to the citizens and plastered on a smile as the agents followed, scanning the crowd. Officers stood on rooftops radioing back and forth about potential disturbances. Aside from an antsy horse marching with the sheriff, nothing was out of order.

"Is this what my career has been reduced to? Playing security to assholes?" Austin asked frustrated. "I'm not exactly feeling as if I'm fulfilling the duties I had in mind when signing up for this job either," Bells quipped. "But, it is what it is, and if it means potentially running into Dennison, then so be it."

From behind dark aviator shades, Austin continued down the street with his teeth clenched tight.

*

Robin had just come from the shower when she heard the door to her bedroom slam shut. Olivia giggled, and she wondered what the little girl was up to. With a towel draped around her head, Robin walked into her bedroom and found Olivia playing hide and seek with Austin. The little girl giggled and said, "Come out, come out, wherever you are!"

Austin popped up from the far side of the bed and sent Olivia into hysterics. Only it wasn't Austin who popped up—it was Kevin Dennison. Her daughter smiled, and he tickled her belly. "Look who decided to join us!" Kevin beamed. He looked at Olivia and said, "What do you think? Should we tag your mommy and make her it?"

Olivia giggled and nodded her head, obviously

enjoying the game. Robin's feet were cemented to the floor as she stood watching the maniacal man work firmly in his element.

"You cut all your hair, Robin. I like it! It looks really good on you, even with that big scar on your head," he smiled.

Random images flashed in Robin's mind of Kevin shouting and striking her across the face. Her perception of reality was rattled; she blinked hard, questioning if he was truly there in the room. "Kevin?" she asked skeptically.

"In the flesh." He ran his fingers through Olivia's hair.

Panicked and still feeling too heavy to move, Robin shouted, "Olivia, go to your room, now!"

"But why, Mommy I want to play hide and seek with—"

"Go, NOW, Olivia!" she screamed.

Olivia quickly twisted the knob and ran crying to her room. Kevin looked on with a smile.

"Why so mean, Mommy?" he mocked. "The fun part is just about to begin."

In a flash, Robin dove over to the nightstand where Austin had put her gun. She yanked open the drawer just as Kevin leapt over the bed toward her. Scrambling quickly, she reached inside, but the drawer was empty. "You'll never get away from me this time," Kevin hissed, closing in on her. Before he could take another step, Robin ripped the drawer from its track and swung around with all her might. She hit him point blank in the temple. Momentarily stunned, he stumbled to the ground and she leapt over him.

That was for the bullet you put in my head...

Wearing only a bathrobe and a towel wrapped around her head, Robin realized she was in a vulnerable position. She needed to get to Olivia fast. But while Kevin was down, she needed to take advantage of the weak moment and make sure he stayed down. Looking at him lying dazed on her floor, she unleashed fury from deep inside.

"This is for taking my baby away from me!" she shouted, with a kick to his chin. "This is for stealing me from my family!" she stomped on his chest. "This is for trying to ruin my life!" She kicked him square in between his legs and wished she had on steel toe boots. Kevin writhed on the floor like the snake he was. Robin marveled the sight.

She looked up and saw Olivia standing in the doorway.

"What's happening, Mommy?"

"Olivia, go and hide, honey! Go right now!"

The little girl ran away, and Robin tried to run after her. She'd taken only a few steps when Kevin's hand reached out, wrapping around her ankle. With what seemed to be superhuman strength, he dragged her by the foot down to the floor where they tussled back and forth. He was still hurting from the blows Robin had dealt him, and she used it to her advantage.

Using the side of the bed for leverage, Robin pressed

her back firmly to the mattress and fought hard to keep him from flipping her over. Her feet kicked wildly, aiming at his head, stomach and anything else that would hurt him. Kevin was able to block her wild striking and dragged her back down to the floor, smacking her head hard against the wooden side table. She felt nauseous as bright blood from her wound began to pour out.

The madman laughed maniacally. Robin realized that his display of pain was just an act.

"You think you can hurt me, Robin?!" he shouted, banging her head against the floor. "You can't hurt me! You can't touch me! You are nothing!"

The bath towel she was wearing graciously provided a small cushion between her head and the floor. In the tussle, the bottom half of her bathrobe had been ripped almost completely off. Seeing her bare body suddenly on display, Kevin grabbed her by the waist and thrust her onto the bed. Wildly he climbed on top of her, pinning her wrists to the mattress while his knee kept her thigh pinned in place.

"This is what you want, isn't it, Robin? You want me." He smiled down at her as if she were a lover, waiting to be devoured by him. Robin saw the psychotic look in his eyes and knew she had to think of something fast. Pressing the weight of his body onto hers, Kevin leaned down to kiss her face, and Robin saw the opportunity she'd been waiting for. As soon as his face was within a few inches of hers, she jerked her head forward and heard a *Crunch*. It was the cartilage in his nose. She knew this time he really was hurt.

Blood spouted from his nostrils and for a split second he loosened his grip. That was all the time Robin needed to maneuver out from under him and make a break for the door. Unnerved, she rolled off the mattress with Kevin right on her heels. On the nightstand was the wine glass that she'd drunk out of just the night before. She grabbed the long stem and hurled it at his head. The glass shattered on his face, severely wounding him. He agonizingly howled in pain.

The sound was music to Robin's ears as she darted out the door. Her pulse pounded wildly. She needed to get to Olivia before he did, and needed a weapon to fend him off. Running down the hall, she was sure to keep looking back to see if he was behind her. She never saw him come from the room. The glass had wounded him badly, and she used the precious few seconds of a head start to her advantage.

*

Joanne and Cassidy pulled into the horseshoe driveway of Robin's home and honked the horn. They were running behind and didn't want to be late to view the new exhibit at the museum. From behind the wheel in the driver's seat, Cassidy impatiently tapped her fingers.

Joanne shook her head. "I don't know why you thought that child would be ready. You know Robin has time impairment when it doesn't involve her work. Been that way since she was born," she informed.

"Aunt Joanne, that doesn't help us right now when we're running behind."

"You should have known better than to show up on time. The right thing to do would have been to show up early and coax her into getting ready. Haven't you learned anything in all this time you've been working for her?" Joanne teased as she opened the car door. "Now you watch and see how it's done. I'm going to go in there and tell her that everything fits perfectly and that her makeup is flawless. That'll have us out of here, and driving down the highway before you know it."

"If that's what it takes, then so be it," said Cassidy. Joanne, with flaring arthritic knees, hobbled out of the car and up the path leading to the front door. She fumbled for a while, searching for her key and finally got it into the lock. The woman disappeared inside; totally unaware of the warzone she was heading into.

*

Austin stayed at the mayor's side during the parade, fulfilling his unwanted duty. Daltry's normally animated persona was notches higher that day as he greeted the throngs of citizens. The parade seemed to go on forever in Austin's mind. He felt trapped in a *Twilight Zone* episode.

"I can hear your complaining all the way over here," Bells said, walking beside him.

"This was a complete waste of time. Daltry probably put us out here just to force us to witness his gloating first hand."

"Be that as it may, it's almost over. We can soldier through a little while longer."

Hearing his wife's voice was about the only thing that would make suffering through his current task bearable. His earpiece linked to his mobile phone, Austin pushed a button and speed dialed to Robin's cell. After a few long rings, her voicemail picked up, stating that she couldn't come to the phone, and to leave a message. Feeling disappointed, he didn't follow the instructions, and hung up. Like a sulky teenager, the agent hid his frustration behind the shaded obscurity of his sunglasses.

*

Joanne stepped into the quiet house and wondered why it was so dark. All the drapes were drawn, which to her was a tragedy, since it was such a nice day out. She called out to her niece, and then to Olivia when she didn't get a response.

A few of Olivia's dolls were scattered around on the

floor. Never one to pass up an opportunity to straighten up, Joanne knelt down and began plucking the toys up one by one. That's when she heard a roar so terrifying it made the blood curdle beneath her skin.

"Robin, you bitch! Where are you?! You can't hide from me!" Kevin's voice was deep and grotesque, almost like a being from another world.

Joanne dropped down on the floor and lay perfectly still. She could feel his rage, heavy in the air, like a blanket draping over her. His booming voice drew closer. She stayed down behind the sofa, hoping he wouldn't see her. His footsteps paced into the room, stalking his innocent prey. Robin's glass had sliced the edge of one of his eyelids. Warm blood made his vision cloudy but wasn't enough to stop him. He slowly scanned the room, searching for her.

Joanne was beyond petrified. She squeezed both hands over her mouth so her frightened whimpers wouldn't escape. Kevin's heavy breath hissed in her ears, and she prayed that Robin was somewhere safe. Suddenly, the world stood still when she spotted Olivia nestled into a ball under the kitchen island. The little girl had tears streaking down her face and terror in her eyes. The last thing Joanne wanted was for Kevin to see her. She needed to divert his attention.

By the fireplace, just a few feet away, was a toolset with a poker. If she could manage to crawl over undetected, she'd be able to use it on him as a distraction long enough for Olivia to get away. She didn't know what the plan would be after that, but it was a starting point. Kevin bellowed Robin's name again as Joanne began slowly crawling forward. Each inch that she moved felt like a mile, and her mind raced with thoughts of what would happen if he found the little girl.

She was now almost an arm's length away, still inching forward. Kevin, momentarily disinterested in Robin, now began to call Olivia's name. His voice calmed. "Where are you, Olivia? I just want to play with you, like we did before."

Joanne panicked as Olivia made eye contact with her. With trembling hands, Joanne put an index finger up to her lips, telling Olivia to stay quiet. The little girl, now frightened of the stranger she'd played with earlier, nodded and balled into a tighter knot. She was nearly sobbing. Joanne pleaded with God Himself for Kevin not to hear her.

Unable to control his anger any longer, Kevin shouted, "Olivia, I'm going to kill your mother if you don't come here NOW!"

Joanne was out of time. With speed she didn't realize she still had, she dove over to the fireplace and ripped the poker from its place. The tool kit came clanking down loudly, and Kevin swung around on his heel. Holding the poker like a bat, Joanne swung it at him and landed a shot square on his chin.

"Go, now, Olivia! Run!"

Olivia got up from her hiding place and disappeared down the hall. Kevin wiggled his jaw back and forth and rubbed his chin. He turned to face Joanne directly and gave her a slow, wicked grin.

"Dear, sweet, Joanne. It is a pleasure seeing you again."

Joanne squeezed the brass handle of the poker tightly and kept her eyes on him.

"When did you get here? I didn't even know you were home," he said casually, closing the space between them. Joanne couldn't let him distract her. She kept her feet planted firmly. She wouldn't let him back her into a wall. She couldn't.

"Now, you listen to me. You have done this family enough harm! I swear to the good Lord almighty I will use every ounce of strength and every breath in my body to keep you from harming any one of us again. You need to just go on and get out of here!"

Kevin was genuinely impressed with her spunk and feistiness. But impressing him was as far as it went. He wasn't leaving.

"Aww. That was precious," he smiled. "Now, I'm going to need you to put that weapon down." In an instant, his demeanor changed. A horrid scowl now appeared on his face, registering pure evil. Joanne was chilled to the core, but she didn't let him see an ounce of her fear.

"If you take one step closer to me, it will be the last one you ever take," she threatened.

Now fed up with her defiance, Kevin decided it was game over for her. With a roar, the man charged like a bulldozer, ready to destroy her in his path. Joanne meant what she'd said to him. As soon as he took a step, she hoisted the poker high in the air and stabbed it down, spike first, into his foot. The two collided with brute force, both falling to the ground.

With a high-pitched scream, Robin shouted out in horror, having just run into the room. Her aunt's unmoving body lay crumpled on the floor. Kevin rolled around next to her, desperately trying to wrench the poker from his pierced foot.

*

Normally, Robin returned missed calls from Austin right away. The fact that she hadn't yet didn't sit well in his gut. Seeing the stony look on his face, Bells knew that something was on his mind.

"What is it? Did you spot something in the crowd?" Bells asked.

"No. I've called Robin, and she hasn't called me back. That isn't like her."

"You said she's out with the girls, right? I'm sure they're fine. Probably just out having a good time. Let her enjoy herself."

Austin's keen sense of danger and uncanny ability to sense anything amiss nagged at him. The sun beat down on his skin; the blustery wind blew on his face. All the while, his mind churned. The mayor had orchestrated the parade detail with high security, involving an unusual bulk of police, sheriffs and CIA officers. This left the rest of the city vulnerable as the multitude of cops lined the streets solely for the protection of this one man.

Austin pulled his phone out and tried Cassidy's number. His pulse quickened. The line rang and rang with no answer. He swore loudly to her voicemail recording. Bells, now also on high alert, stopped walking and stood next to his agent who grew more anxious by the moment. Mayor Daltry spied the men from his place atop the convertible. He ordered the driver to hit the brakes. "Commander Bells, Agent Malone, is there a problem?"

Neither man responded. Daltry persisted.

"I asked if there was a problem. This is highly unethical to be on the phone while on official duty," he seethed. "In case you need a reminder, you are here because there is a maniac running loose in our city. I'd hate for your personal matters to distract you from ensuring the safety of our citizens."

Mayor Daltry assumed his reprimand would snap them back into action. But when the two stayed firmly in the street, with Austin dialing yet again, the mayor fought back the urge to throw a tantrum. He had been ordered by Dennison to keep Austin away as long as possible, and he knew he'd be a dead man if he didn't keep that promise.

Daltry climbed down from the vehicle and approached just as Austin got an answer on the line.

"Hellooo," Cassidy sang casually, smacking on a piece of gum.

Relieved to hear her voice, Austin asked, "Cassidy, where are you and the girls? I've called Robin several times, and she hasn't texted or called me back."

"Well, your wife wasn't ready when we got here, and Aunt Joanne went in to get her a while ago. I've been sitting outside for forever waiting on them to come out. They're probably in there flapping their gums, as usual, not caring about the fact that we're unfashionably late."

There was now no doubt left in Austin's mind that Robin was in trouble. He began trotting away, with Bells at his side.

"Where are you going?! I am ordering you to remain here and do your jobs!" the mayor demanded. He didn't care that the entire city would see him in a screaming fit with the two agents. His fate would be grim if he let them out of his sights. He did all he could to stop them.

"Cassidy, stay where you are," Austin warned. "Do NOT go inside the house. I'll be there as soon as I can."

Oblivious to the imminent danger, she said, "It's really not that serious for you to come all the way home, Austin. I'll go in and get them on track, as usual." Cassidy opened her car door. "No, Cassidy! Listen to me. Do not—"

Mayor Daltry snatched the phone from Austin's hand and smashed it to the ground. "There! Now you can do your job without interruption."

Austin snapped. Knowing what was coming next, and no longer interested in stopping it, Commander Bells calmly took one step to the side, out of his agent's reach. In the blink of an eye, Austin spiraled out of control, like a whirlwind, all over the imprudent mayor. With one blow, Austin knocked him and one of his teeth to the ground. He then climbed on top of the mayor and delivered a blow that sent blood and another tooth flying from his mouth. Policemen dashed forward. Austin didn't care. He now had the mayor by the neck, squeezing the life out of him.

"It doesn't matter," Daltry sputtered through bloody lips. "Dennison has probably killed your wife and daughter already."

Austin's eyes widened in disbelief.

"What did you just say to me?" He loosened his grip on the mayor's throat.

"You heard me. Your wife and daughter are dead. Dennison has no doubt carried out that task by now."

Austin realized he'd been set up.

"You did this?!" he shouted, banging Daltry's head against the pavement. "If he has touched even a hair on their heads, I swear to God I will—"

Bells, knowing that they were wasting time on the wrong person, pulled his agent up. "He's not important right now, Malone! We've got to get to your family. There's no time to waste on *him*."

Austin delivered one last blow to Daltry's ribcage and charged off to find his wife and daughter.

*

Robin, who was still naked under her shredded robe, couldn't believe her eyes. She didn't know if Joanne was dead or alive, and she didn't see any sign of Olivia. The poker in Kevin's shoe had pierced through the bones of his foot. He still struggled to remove it. While he was down, she needed to find Olivia and get her out of the house.

The concern for her aunt grew stronger when she saw that she wasn't getting up. Turning her back to her unmoving aunt to go in search of her child was probably one of the most difficult decisions she'd ever made, but it was one that was necessary. But before she ever had the chance to look for her baby, she heard a knock on the door and Cassidy's high-pitched voice.

"Joaaanne, Robiiin. What are you guys doing in there?! Open up," she knocked.

Robin's eyes shot over to Kevin. He'd finally managed to wrestle the poker from his foot. With a mischievous grin, he hobbled his way to the door as Robin screamed out.

"Run, Cassidy! Run and get help!"

On the other side of the door, all Cassidy heard was muffled gibberish.

"What? I can't hear you. Can you just open the door and let me in?! Hurry up, because I have to pee!" she danced around.

Kevin was more than happy to oblige her request and quickly swung the door open.

"My goodness, what took you so long?" she complained, stepping obliviously into the room.

The first thing she saw was Robin shivering with her hands covering her private parts. Cassidy's eyes then shifted to Aunt Joanne, sprawled in a heap on the floor. Suddenly, the door slammed shut, and Kevin Dennison stepped out from behind it. "The more the merrier," he said. Cassidy screamed as Kevin grabbed her by the hair and yanked her in front of him. He held the fireplace poker by each end, using it to choke her. It kept her frozen in his control.

"Don't hurt her, Kevin!" Robin shouted.

"Hurt her? Why would I do a thing like that? My goal is not to hurt; only to please." He stroked the side of her face. Cassidy tried to turn her head away. He pressed the tool deeper into her throat, causing her to cough.

"She has nothing to do with this, Kevin! Let her go!"

To prove to Robin that her plea had fallen on deaf ears, he tilted Cassidy's head back and lustfully sucked on her neck. Biting down firmly, he kissed and licked a line from shoulder blade up to the back of her ear. Feeling her writhe beneath him merely turned him on.

To his surprise, Cassidy stomped the heel of her boot down hard into his already wounded foot, and sunk her teeth into his forearm.

"You bitch!" he growled, trying to shake his arm free. Like a Pit-Bull, Cassidy locked her jaws in place, and shook her head from side to side to make it more painful for him. She stomped on his foot again, and he released his grip, doubling over in pain. She broke free and darted to Aunt Joanne's side.

"Aunt Joanne, get up!" she shouted, shaking the woman vigorously. Joanne didn't move or make a sound. The next sound Cassidy heard was the *Ping!* of the fireplace poker when Kevin struck her in the head with it.

"Noooo!" Robin shouted, helplessly. Things had spiraled dangerously out of control. She desperately needed to get Olivia out of the house. As if hearing her thoughts, Kevin leapt over to the bodies of Cassidy and Joanne. He held the poker high in the air and said, "Call Olivia right now. If you don't, I will drive this spike directly through your precious aunt's heart."

"Kevin, please don't," Robin pleaded as she fell to her knees.

"Do it now, Robin!" he shouted, unmoved by her tears.

Robin didn't feel like there was an ounce of energy left in her whole body. Somehow, she managed to lift her head and weakly call her daughter's name. "Olivia, come here, sweetie," she said in a hoarse whisper.

"Do it again," Kevin demanded. The poker lurked dangerously close to Joanne's chest.

Tears had her blinded. She called for Olivia again. "Olivia, come on out, Sweetheart. Come to Mommy."

Everything in the house was silent. Then emerging from the library came the frightened footsteps of Olivia running to her mother. Robin wrapped the little girl in her arms and kissed her harder than she ever had in her life. "Are you hurt anywhere, Honey?" Tears streaked Robin's face. With a small jewelry box and baby doll nestled in her arms, Olivia said, "No, Mommy, but I'm scared."

Robin's heart shattered as she held her shivering daughter in her arms. A trickle of blood ran out of her nose. "I know you're afraid, Sweetheart, and I am, too. But everything is going to be okay."

"Well, isn't that touching?" Kevin mocked. He

slowly made his way over to them. He knew he was now in total control of the situation and turned up the animation just for kicks. "Olivia, do you know my name?" he asked sweetly.

The little girl shook her head and turned her face away from him.

"Robin, why haven't you told our daughter about me?"

Robin squeezed her daughter tight and kept Olivia's face tucked into her chest.

"Well, Olivia, I'm going to let you in on a little secret."

Robin knew exactly what he was going to say. She hated Kevin for being so evil.

*

Bells and Austin sped down the interstate with sirens blaring. Every minute ticked by like an hour in Austin's mind. From Bells' cell phone, he'd called Cassidy and Robin's phones, as well as their home phone, all to no avail. His blood boiled like lava when he thought about the danger they were in. "That slimy sonofabitch! He set this all up! Why would he even..." Austin cut himself off, too angry to even see straight.

"What exactly did Daltry say?" asked Bells.

"He basically acknowledged that Dennison had harmed my family. He stated it as a fact, like he was in on the plan."

"Are you sure he wasn't saying it just to piss you off? I mean, the history between the two of you—"

"Bells, just drive and get me to them as fast as you can," Austin interrupted.

The Commander didn't press the issue further; instead, he got on his radio telling backup where to meet them.

*

The home on 587 Clarkston Drive was quiet, with the exception of one sole voice. Kevin Dennison leaned on the edge of the sofa for support, trying to fill Olivia in on his identity. "So, you know that tall man who comes home every day with the thick black hair?"

"You mean Daddy?" Olivia asked innocently.

"Well, that's all a part of the big secret. He's not your —"

"Enough, Kevin!" Robin shouted. "That's enough. You don't need to do this. She's innocent in all this, and you know it. Think about her and think about your son."

Kevin looked sincerely perplexed. "You know I don't have a son, Robin. So, why would you say such a thing?"

Robin knew she'd hit a nerve. She continued talking to keep him busy with her words while her mind tried to work out a plan.

"You do, Kevin. His name is Kevin Jr., and he lives with Melanie's sister."

His face scrunched as if her name didn't ring a bell.

"I know you remember Melanie Mitchell. She was my best friend who you slept with and coerced into helping you have me killed." Even in the midst of such a serious situation, Robin couldn't hide the disgust in her voice. "When she went away to prison, she was already pregnant with your child. You're the father of a 4-year-old son."

Kevin was genuinely stunned and taken aback by her revelation. For a brief moment she saw his face soften. He looked like the normal human being she remembered him to be years ago. When she'd first met him, he was charming and funny and extremely thoughtful. Her mind briefly flashed back to memories of them laughing together and talking about life. She desperately hoped that there was a shred of that man left inside of him, and that that part of him would somehow let Olivia go free.

Unfortunately, that man was long gone. The animal in him reared its head. He darted upright. "Since I have a son of my own, I guess there won't be a need to keep this little bastard around!" he growled, yanking Olivia from her mother's grasp.

At that moment Austin busted through the front door with a gun in each hand. Robin jumped up from the floor, and Olivia screamed out for her father.

"Daddy, help!" she shrieked, clutching her toys for safety.

Austin's eyes locked on Dennison like a missile honed in on its target.

"Oh, goody, daddy's home!" Kevin shrieked like a child.

"Put my daughter down, Dennison, or you won't be

alive long enough to hear the bullets leave this chamber."

"Your little threat was cute and all, Agent Malone, but something tells me you aren't going to do anything of the sort. You couldn't possibly risk harming this baby girl just to square off with little ol' me, now would you?"

Austin inched forward. Robin tried to cover her body with the strips of fabric hanging from her robe.

"This whole situation seems awfully familiar to me. Does it to you, too?" Kevin turned to ask Robin. Turning his back to Austin was a sign that he couldn't care less about the man having guns in his hands, because he knew he had something in his own that was more valuable. "I remember now. This is kind of how it all went down at the cabin. Only you were right here." He yanked Robin by the hair and wrapped his forearm around her neck. Olivia was squeezed tighter in the grip of his other arm. She squealed in pain.

Bells suddenly appeared, moving in from the kitchen. His gun was drawn as well.

Upon seeing the commander, Kevin said, "This really is like old times."

Bells saw the two unconscious women by the fireplace and slowly tried to edge his way over.

"Ah, ah, ah, everybody stays exactly where they are," Kevin said to keep Bells at bay. "This is my show. You, sir, better not move a step closer, or I will crush her throat with my bare hands."

Austin didn't know which *her* he meant, but it didn't

matter.

"So, what now, Dennison? What is your plan from here? It's not like you're going to walk out of that door alive — especially not with my family," Austin informed him.

"Wrong again, Agent Malone! That's exactly what I'm going to do. It's what I do best. I come as I please, and I go as I please. And there is not a damn thing you can do about it."

Austin hated the man's cockiness. His hands tingled with the urge to strangle him dead.

This time, it was Robin who spoke up. "Austin, he wants me and Olivia...so I think you should let him have us."

The agent looked at his wife like she'd lost her mind. She continued, "We can't keep living like this. He's going to keep coming for us, and he'll get us every time," she tearfully pleaded. "It's better if we just go with him now to avoid the hassle."

"Robin, you are a lying, conniving slut! I don't know what plan you're trying to concoct, but it will not work on me, my dear," Kevin quipped. The room fell silent and everyone in the room recognized the WTF look that Austin shot his wife.

Kevin broke the silence. "BUT, since you offer the idea of such generosity, Robin, I believe I may just have to take you up on your offer." Over the top of Olivia's head, Kevin said, "Agent Malone, your wife has foolishly suggested a course of action that I find works well in my favor. So I see it only fit that I honor her request. I realize that by possessing such precious cargo, I am in a position to walk right out that door. There is nothing you can do but watch."

Robin added, "Yes, that is the best thing. Austin, if you have men outside, order them to stand down." WTF showed on his face again, and she yelled, "Do it now!" Her husband got on his radio, doing exactly as she instructed.

What the hell are you doing, Robin?! You better have a plan somewhere in all this... Austin thought.

"Now, tell one of the men to leave a car for us with the door open." She turned her head a little toward Kevin. "This way we can get in and just go, far away from here."

Dennison smiled at the idea and enjoyed seeing her rebel against her husband. "You heard the woman," he said with a grin. Austin made the call. Robin softened her voice and said, "We don't need anything to slow us down, Kevin. Olivia has an armful of toys that I know will get in the way. Let me just take them from her and toss them to the floor. That's it, and then we can leave."

Hearing her mother's statements, Olivia squeezed the items closer and cried out to her father. "Daddy, no! I don't want to go with him!"

"Olivia, Sweetie, you don't have to be afraid. Mommy is right here with you. We're going to go on a little trip, but everything will be okay, I promise. I just need you to hand me your toys, Honey," Robin said gently.

"Mommy, I don't want to go!"

"Olivia!" Robin shouted, "Give me your toys, now! I said everything would be fine!" She had never shouted at her child like that before. Olivia sobbed, loosening the grip on her possessions. Robin cried, too, as she maneuvered the items from her daughter's hands. "Thank you, Sweetheart," she whispered. "Thank you so much."

In a flash, Robin dropped the doll on the floor and grabbed what Olivia had thought was a jewelry box. The instant that her fingers touched the case, the lid popped open. The next few seconds played out in extreme slow motion in Robin's mind.

Her hand reached inside the case and wrapped firmly around the butt of the small gun. With Kevin still taunting Austin with his pompous smile, Robin lifted the gun and placed it under his chin. She whispered in his ear, "It's going to be very hot in Hell."

Then she pulled the trigger.

Pow!

Kevin never knew what hit him. His body began to topple over, and Robin swiftly snatched Olivia from his grasp. The weight of his falling body dragged them both to the floor with him. Robin shielded Olivia's head with her hands, and cushioned the girl's fall with her own body. In an instant, Austin and Bells were at their sides, Kevin's body twitching next to them.

Austin scooped his wife and daughter into his arms. They both clung tightly to him. Olivia said, "Daddy, I'm scared." He held her even closer. Robin's half covered body shivered. Bells took off his jacket to cover her with it.

Robin touched the back of her child's head that was now coated in warm blood spatter. "Olivia, I didn't mean to shout at you, Baby. I was just trying to make us safe," Robin said through tears. Olivia turned her face towards her mother. "It's okay, Mom. We're safe now, and everything is okay, just like you said."

Robin smiled, grateful that her words had come true. She collapsed against her husband's chest and closed her eyes.

Chapter Twenty One

Day by day my family has gotten stronger. Austin and I have taken Olivia to see a child counselor to help her deal with the trauma of seeing a man killed right in front of her. Not just any man—her father. But we're still working our way up to letting her know that particular detail.

It's been difficult shielding things from her, especially with the way the media has been involved. Just the other day, Frank Holland ran a story to show the growth of the city since the events last year. A special segment was devoted to Mayor Daltry who was finally exposed as a fraud. Police had tapped him for his dealings with both Dennison and Archer. He got nothing but a slap on the wrist and a removal from office, which I thought was far too lenient.

Katherine Palmer is still awaiting trial for her role in Kevin's release from prison. She'll have another trial for his escape from the courtroom that day. Ironically, she has Kevin's previous attorney, Rayko Blu representing her. It remains to be seen how low they'll slither to try and keep her out of prison. To hear Aunt Joanne tell it, Katherine is better off behind bars, cause if she were to ever get a hold of her, there'd be some serious smoke in the city...whatever that means.

Speaking of the old bird, with the exception of a nasty gash and plenty of bruises, she and Cassidy both ended up being just fine. I should have known it'd take more than a bump on the noggin to keep Cassidy's motor mouth from running.

Now, to Austin my sweet, sweet husband. He does his best to make sure Olivia and I are in a good place. It's tough for him sometimes when he hears us crying at night with night terrors. It kills him that a man as powerful as he is doesn't have the power to take away his family's pain. I think he handles it all well and keeps us close to him as much as possible. He's hard on himself a lot, feeling like he could have done more to protect us. But like I always tell him, "You gave me the tools and the guts to do what I did that day. If it weren't for you, Kevin would have won a long time ago." He's still having a difficult time seeing it that way, but he'll eventually come around.

As for me, some days are good, and some, I can barely drag myself out of bed. But, somehow I find the strength to do it every single time. I've come to realize that I'm heavily scarred from so many horrid memories in my life. But when I look into my daughter's eyes and see her strength and promise, it pushes me to be strong so that I can be the best mother for her. She deserves it. The other day she asked when I'd have a baby brother or sister for her. I couldn't bring myself to tell her that she already has a brother she doesn't know about — and a new baby on the way. Austin and I are going to keep the news to ourselves. For a little while, anyway. We figure our bun in the oven will be a nice Christmas surprise for the entire family.

Melanie and her son are still being kept at arm's length for now. She was released from prison a few months after we went to see her. We've spoken on the phone a few times, but that's as far as our communication has gone. I don't trust her enough to allow my emotions to be susceptible to her, despite the blood relationship between our two kids. Until I can figure out what to do with her, I've decided to leave her in a box, far enough away to go unnoticed, but close enough to access when, and if, I ever decide to be closer.

As I sit here and write in this journal, the word that continuously comes to mind is grateful. Yep, even through all that, I'm still grateful. Grateful to be alive. Grateful for my family. Grateful for whatever purpose my life has. The Man upstairs wouldn't have brought me back from the brink of death for no reason. So knowing that, I make sure that I spend my time figuring out what His plan for me is.

Maybe one day I'll write a book about my experience. It'd make a hell of a story, that's for sure! Until then, I've decided I'm perfectly happy living in the moment — finally.

Epilogue

Irene Jessup had been waiting by the phone for hours. Her husband's platoon had been out to sea for three months, and today he was coming home. Her foot patted nervously. The grandfather clock chimed 11 times. Her eyes shifted to the mantel and the photo of Charlie in his dress blues. A wide smile spread across her lips. She always thought he looked so handsome in his uniform.

"My sweet Charlie. I've got a lot to fill you in on," she sighed, patting her baby bump.

The smell of sweet bread filled the air. It was Charlie's favorite, with mint ice cream, which she'd also just made from scratch. Etta James pined in the background for a love finally realized, and Irene grew more anxious as the minutes ticked by.

Finally, the 32-year-old heard a car door slam in front of her house. She started to spring to her feet, but a wave of nausea lapped over her. She was forced to take her time. As she made her way to the door, her heart fluttered just like it had the day she'd met Charlie years ago.

It seemed just yesterday she sat at the dance with a cast on her ankle from a cheerleading accident. Charlie was smooth as silk when he strode over to her and asked her to dance. She giggled at him, and it was all the invitation he needed to make himself at home in the seat next to hers. Seventeen years later, she was his wife, awaiting his arrival after way too much time at sea.

She flung open the front door and shouted Charlie's name.

"Charlie! I'm so glad you're—"

Her face dimmed. Two men in uniform headed up her front porch. Neither of them was her husband. One of the men looked at her barely visible pooch and shifted his eyes over to his friend. A sinking feeling nagged at the pit of Irene's stomach as she stood in the archway of the door.

One man was white with a long nose and freckles, and the other was black with a hook-shaped scar on his right cheek. As they got closer, both men removed their hats. Then Irene knew that Charlie was dead.

*

The navy seamen sat admiring the modest home of Irene Jessup. Neither man spoke as the new widow poured cups of tea in the other room. The painful silence was an unpleasant reminder of the task that they had been sent there to do. Irene soon shuffled into the room with a full tray, fighting through another wave of nausea. "Please keep your seat," she directed as one of the men stood to help her. "With your husband away at sea, you get pretty good at being able to maneuver around on your own." The gracious hostess' smile faded quickly when she realized she'd be doing things on her own from now on. After serving the men the best cup of tea they'd ever had, Irene finally sat down, no longer able to put off hearing details that she didn't want to hear.

"Mrs. Jessup...I assume you know why we're here," said the man with the long nose who never actually introduced himself.

She nodded, and her hands nervously began to wring.

"We'd first like to say that your husband Charlie was a good man who died serving his country—"

"How did it happen?" Irene cut in.

The men looked at each other. Long-nose swallowed a sip of tea before speaking again. "Friendly fire."

Irene's eyebrows raised and then furrowed. "Friendly fire? What does that mean? That whole statement is a conundrum. *Friendly* fire? Since when did someone being killed by a weapon become friendly? Is that the name you folks give it to make yourselves feel better about dragging a man away from his wife for months at a time while she—" Irene stopped herself from going off on a tangent. She could have gone on for days with questions surrounding her husband's murder, but there would have been no point. At the end of it all, he would still be dead.

"Gentleman, thank you for stopping by. I'm sure you have other matters to tend to, so I won't keep you." That was Irene's gracious way of kicking the men out of her home.

Getting the message loud and clear, they each stood and made their way to the door.

"One last thing, ma'am," the black man offered.

From a small bag he'd brought in with him, he took

out a flag that had been folded thirteen times. With one hand on top and the other on the bottom, the man presented the flag to the widow. Placed on top was a photo of Irene and Charlie on their honeymoon, feeding birdseed to a robin.

Through teary eyes, Irene accepted the items, and with them, the reality of her existence without the love of her life.

*

Irene had been lying low for weeks. She didn't have a desire to be around anyone. Losing Charlie was a devastating blow that she had never seen coming. She felt like there would never come a day when the pain of losing him would subside. She felt the unbearable pressure to try and piece together a life for a child who was now down a parent.

Irene heard a tap at the door and ignored it. She wasn't in the mood to receive condolences from another person who'd probably just gotten wind of her husband's death. The tapping grew louder and more persistent, leaving her no choice but to see who it was. She'd never understood why there was no peephole on their door. When she and Charlie had moved into the modest home years ago, she put up a fuss about it. He kept promising he'd get around to installing one. In seventeen years, her husband had never found the chance.

Irene nearly dropped to her knees when she saw who stood on the other side of the door smiling at her. It was her brother, Robert, whom she hadn't seen in years. Robert didn't have a chance to speak any words before his sister leapt into his arms at the sight of him.

"My Lord, what are you doing here, Robert?" she asked as he squeezed her tight. The man beamed and stepped to the side, revealing yet another surprise guest. "Patricia!" Irene screamed as the two women grabbed each other. The relief of having family there with her was too much for Irene's fragile emotions. She began bawling as her guests let themselves inside.

"Oh, come on now, we didn't drive all the way down here from Michigan just to see a waterworks show," her brother chuckled. Irene smiled at her burly brother and swiped away the tears on her face. Robert was like a polar bear with a scruffy beard that scratched her face when he smooched her, but she needed every peck he had to offer.

"What are you all doing down here in Georgia? Not that I mind you being here." She gestured for them to have a seat on the sofa.

"Well, we came down here to surprise you, but it looks like you've surprised us. Either you've put on a couple pounds, which for you is impossible, or you're hiding a baby bump under all those clothes."

Irene's sister-in-law added, "I tried to get him to call you first to let you know we were coming, but you know how much he loves surprising folks." She patted her husband's hand, and he grinned sheepishly. "So it's true? You're going to have a little one?"

Irene forced a smile, and her family erupted in joy.

"Congratulations!" Patricia beamed and embraced her in-law. "How far along are you?"

"Just a few months," replied Irene with lowered eyes.

"So, where is my brother-in-law? I'm going to have to take him out and buy him some of the finest cigars that a penny candy store has to offer," Robert joked. He looked toward the back room as if the man would suddenly come walking out.

Irene couldn't fight back tears any longer. As if someone had just taken a jab at her, she jerked upright in her seat and then doubled over, howling with grief. Robert stood up from the couch and rushed to her. He was taken aback as he looked at his older sister, who he'd never seen break down.

"Sis, tell me what's going on?"

It took her several moments to compose herself. Finally, she managed to say, "He's dead, Robert. Charlie is dead."

Robert felt as if he, too, had just been jabbed. Patricia gasped. It took moments for the reality of the news to settle in.

"When did this happen?" Robert asked softly.

"A few weeks ago. Two navy officers showed up at my door and told me that Charlie had been killed. They said it was from friendly fire," the woman sniffed and welled up again.

Both Robert and Patricia embraced the widow as she wept.

"Why didn't you tell us?" Patricia asked. "You know we would have been here for you."

"I didn't feel like I could. I barely want to acknowledge it myself. I had eventually planned to say something, but I just couldn't bring myself to do it. There was no funeral or anything. I went and had him cremated. Charlie always told me that if anything ever happened to him, he didn't want a funeral and have people making a fuss and crying all over him. He wanted to be cremated and have his ashes spread at the Georgia Bay, so that's what I did. Truth is, I never thought I'd have to honor his request, because I didn't think anything would ever happen to him."

"We're here for you, Sis. Don't worry about any of it. We're here to take care of you," said Robert.

"I don't know what to do. I never thought about what life would be like without Charlie. And then having this baby really makes it all that much more difficult to deal with. Pretty soon his checks will stop coming in, and I don't know what I'll do for money. I've tried looking for jobs, but as soon as people find out I'm expecting, they turn me away. I can fend for myself and make due, but the baby...the baby doesn't deserve to be born under these circumstances."

Robert looked up at his wife whose eyes were pooling. They'd been married for years, each knowing what the other was thinking without even saying it. Robert nodded at his wife and then said, "Come back to Michigan with us. We have plenty of space up there, and there is no one to fill it but me and Patty."

She leaned her head on her brother's shoulder. Patricia squeezed her hand. "Oh, Robert," she huffed, "You know I'd never impose on anybody, including you."

"There would be no imposition. We need you there just as much as you need us. Now, I know I'm younger than you, but if it'll come down to a tussling match, I'm pretty sure I can take you," he joked.

Pondering the notion, Irene sat back and looked around at the house full of memories that would do more harm to her than good. She made the decision to leave.

*

Irene was nearly out of her eighth month, with her due date quickly approaching. The bitter chill of the Michigan winter made her miss Georgia more than expected. Other than that, she was glad she'd made the choice to move in with her brother and his wife. There were no better people to keep her company, dote on her, and help her deal with the grief that still plagued her.

Although she felt appreciative for having them to lean on, she still fought feelings of inadequacy. Her first child would arrive any day, born to a mother who couldn't support herself financially and who wouldn't get to experience the unbreakable bond of a father-daughter relationship. After privately mulling things over for months, Irene realized what she had to do.

Patricia stood at the makeshift laundry table made out of an old ironing board. She smiled softly, lifting up the onesies and other items that she'd just bought for the new baby. Irene watched a pang of sadness flash across her face. For years Robert and Patricia had tried to conceive. After suffering through several miscarriages and false hope, the couple finally gave up on the dream of ever becoming parents. Until now.

Irene walked over to her sister-in-law and clasped her hands together. Tears formed in her eyes. "Don't say anything, just listen. Now I've thought long and hard about this. I love the child that's growing inside me, and I'd do anything in this world to see to it that she's taken care of, even if I'm not the one providing the care."

Patricia tried to figure out where the conversation was going. Her brow furrowed in puzzlement. Irene squeezed her hand.

"There are no two people in this world that more deserve to be parents than the two of you. Sometimes God puts us in situations, and we don't understand them fully. We just have to obey His orders and trust that what He wants is best." Irene took a deep breath. "I want you and Robert to raise this baby as your own."

"But I—"

"Patty, I know you're prepared to give me hundreds of reasons why you shouldn't do it, but I just need you to realize that there is one good reason why you should: the baby. Her life is what's important, and I want her to have a happy and fulfilling one with the two of you as her parents. I hear you at night when you're crying yourself to sleep, Patty. I know how much you want a child and how much it pains you that women all around you have been able to conceive and you haven't. Don't look at the situation, just look at the outcome. You need this child, and this child needs you. Please accept this gift."

Patricia smoothly took a step back, placing a hand on her forehead. She turned her back to Irene who wept with her arms folded across her belly. Irene's worst fear in asking them to take on this responsibility was that they'd view her as lazy and not up for the task of motherhood. It wasn't the truth. In her heart, her act was selfless. She felt this option would be best for everyone.

Patricia finally turned back around. In spite of the tears in her eyes, her smiling face told Irene that she agreed with her decision and had accepted it. The two women embraced and cried with a mixture of joy and sadness all rolled into one. Joy for the blessing that one woman would now have, and sadness for the loss that one woman had experienced.

"You know I'll still have to speak to Robert about this," said Patricia.

"When something is destined to happen, not even my big bear of a brother could oppose it. Not that he would anyway." They embraced again, and Patricia said, "Thank you."

The baby leapt in Irene's belly. She knew she'd just given the child a shot at a better life.

*

Hutzen Hospital was quiet at 3 a.m. when Robert, Irene and Patricia arrived. The mom-to-be was in agony as her family rushed to get her checked in. The nurses at the front immediately retrieved a wheelchair and carted her off for the delivery. In an instant, Irene was upstairs preparing for labor. Patricia and Robert stood side by side with their arms locked, brimming with joy and anticipation.

A nurse slipped a pair of socks on Irene's feet and said, "Irene, the doctor is on his way in. I'm going to get you a cool towel in the meantime and some ice chips. Is there anything else we can do for you?"

"Yes," Irene responded through contractions. "You can stop calling me by my first name. It makes me feel like I'm in trouble. Everyone calls me by my middle name, Joanne."

This statement prompted the nurse to say, "Speaking of names, what have you decided to go with for your little one?"

Tucked in Joanne's hand was her favorite photo of her and Charlie on their honeymoon feeding the little red robin. She lovingly looked at the photo and replied, "My daughter's name will be Robin."

The End